PRAISE FOR *RIDGELINE*

"The characters and places Punke writes about do crackle with life."

—*Missoulian* (Editor's Pick)

"A thrilling and heartbreaking read."

—*The Saturday Evening Post*

"Punke, with his eye for detail and obsessive research, is unflinching in his portrayal of how America as we know it came to be."

—*InsideHook*

"A page-turning novelization . . . Punke skillfully weaves together the soldiers' ongoing division over the causes of the Civil War, Grummond's thirst for glory, and the Lakota's struggle for survival to create a nuanced account of the events. . . . Highly character driven as it races toward its heartbreaking, though inevitable, conclusion. Readers will come away with a knowledge not only of the battle itself, but also of everyday life in the army camp and among the Lakota. Highly recommended."

—*Historical Novel Society*

"A thrilling, gut-twisting series of sprung traps and harrowing violence— an action sequence that's very much the stuff of legend."

—*The Wall Street Journal*

"Punke is brilliant. . . . [*Ridgeline*] confirms his mastery as a writer. . . . The day of the battle is described in unflinching detail. The devastation feels real. Punke deeply respects Native American tribal history, and explains how an uneasy tribal allegiance led to battle victory. . . . *Ridgeline* transcends genre categorization—any sophisticated reader would appreciate this novel."

—*Booklist* (starred review)

"[An] engrossing account of the violence and horror of a Wyoming massacre . . . Punke makes the battle vivid, and draws deep characterizations of individuals on both sides, exploring Crazy Horse's fear of impending change, US soldiers' indifference to fighting, and a captain's lament of the breakdown of discipline and reason within the battalion's leadership. This is historical fiction at its best."

—*Publishers Weekly* (starred review)

"Richly detailed . . . fast paced . . . expansive, vivid . . . A nuanced story of conflict between Native people and whites on the nineteenth-century American frontier."

—*Kirkus*

"A foreboding sense of ruin and sadness clings to each page, and this novel transcends genre. Any reader who appreciates history will love it."

—*My Journal Courier*

"Like *The Revenant*, *Ridgeline* tackles another huge legend of the west and sets it right. With a memorable cast of characters, Punke tells the story of the Fetterman massacre, one of the final and most significant Native American victories over the US Army. A highly compelling page turner; you won't be able to put it down."

—Philipp Meyer, author of *The Son* and *American Rust*

"In his kaleidoscopic telling of a little-known battle on the sacred Lakota hunting grounds of Wyoming, Punke has created a modern classic and worthy successor to *The Revenant*. Brave, thrilling, and heartbreaking, *Ridgeline* brings the history of conquest in the American West to un-forgettable life."

—Tatjana Soli, author of *The Lotus Eaters* and *The Removes*

Ridgeline

For Traci

Also by Michael Punke

The Revenant

Fire and Brimstone

Last Stand

Ridgeline

A NOVEL

MICHAEL PUNKE

A HOLT PAPERBACK
HENRY HOLT AND COMPANY
NEW YORK

Holt Paperbacks
Henry Holt and Company
Publishers since 1866
120 Broadway
New York, New York 10271
www.henryholt.com

A Holt Paperback® and 🅗 ® are registered trademarks of Macmillan
Publishing Group, LLC.

The Library of Congress has cataloged the hardcover edition as follows:

Names: Punke, Michael, author.
Title: Ridgeline : a novel / by Michael Punke.
Description: First edition. | New York : Henry Holt and Company, [2021].
Identifiers: LCCN 2020034258 (print) | LCCN 2020034259 (ebook) | ISBN
9781250310460 (hardcover) | ISBN 9781250310477 (ebook)
Subjects: LCSH: Crazy Horse, approximately 1842–1877—Fiction. | Lakota
Indians—Fiction. | LCGFT: Novels.
Classification: LCC PS3616.U55 R53 2021 (print) | LCC PS3616.U55 (ebook)
| DDC 813/.6—dc23

LC record available at https://lccn.loc.gov/2020034258
LC ebook record available at https://lccn.loc.gov/2020034259

ISBN: 9781250310484 (trade paperback)

Our books may be purchased in bulk for promotional, educational, or business
use. Please contact your local bookseller or the Macmillan Corporate and Pre-
mium Sales Department at (800) 221-7945, extension 5442, or by e-mail at
MacmillanSpecialMarkets@macmillan.com.

Originally published in hardcover in 2021 by Henry Holt and Company

First Holt Paperbacks Edition 2022

Designed by Omar Chapa

P1

The full story of what happened in that brief hour of bloody carnage at high noon under the wintry sky of December 21, 1866, will never be known.

—DEE BROWN

KEY PLAYERS

LAKOTA
Crazy Horse: young Oglala warrior
Lone Bear: friend of Crazy Horse
Little Hawk: younger half brother of Crazy Horse
Red Cloud: Oglala chief
High Backbone: Minnicoujou chief

SOLDIERS
Colonel Henry Carrington: commanding officer at Fort Phil Kearny
Captain Tenador Ten Eyck: senior artillery officer
Captain William Fetterman: senior infantry officer
Lieutenant George Washington Grummond: junior cavalry officer
Sergeant Augustus Lang: infantryman
Adolph Metzger: bugler

CIVILIANS
Jim Bridger: scout
James Beckwourth: scout
Frances Grummond: wife of Lieutenant Grummond
Margaret Carrington: wife of Colonel Carrington
Janey White: laundress

A brief word on tribes: The Oglala and the Minnicoujou are parts of the broader Lakota family, called the "Sioux" historically by many European Americans. The Lakota allied at times with the Arapaho and the Cheyenne, broadly divided into Northern Cheyenne and Southern Cheyenne. The Lakota were traditional enemies of the Crow and the Shoshone.

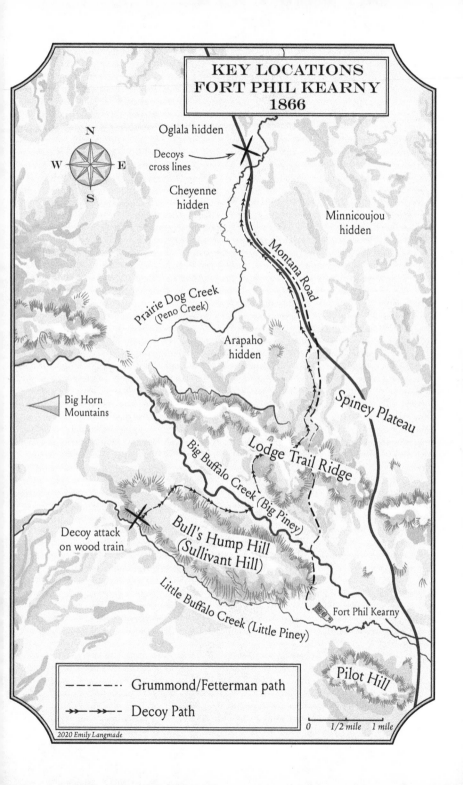

KEY LOCATIONS
FORT PHIL KEARNY
1866

N
W E
S

Oglala hidden

Decoys cross lines

Cheyenne hidden

Minnicoujou hidden

Montana Road

Prairie Dog Creek (Peno Creek)

Arapaho hidden

Big Horn Mountains

Spiney Plateau

Lodge Trail Ridge

Big Buffalo Creek (Big Piney)

Decoy attack on wood train

Bull's Hump Hill (Sullivant Hill)

Fort Phil Kearny

Little Buffalo Creek (Little Piney)

Pilot Hill

––––––– Grummond/Fetterman path

➤➤–➤➤– Decoy Path

2020 Emily Langmade

0   1/2 mile   1 mile

DECEMBER 21, 1866

Crazy Horse struggled to sort among the flood of sensations, to push away the confusion and the fear, to keep his focus on what he and the other decoys must do.

They were close enough now to see the individual clumps of sage that pushed up from the dusting of snow on the ridgeline. In the valley beyond, the great gathering of warriors lay hidden in the gullies and draws, waiting in the frigid cold for the soldiers that the decoys would lead into their trap.

He ignored the sudden sound of a cannon from the distant fort. The soldiers probably had spotted a group of scouts sent out to spy from surrounding hilltops, but the fort's big guns would play no meaningful role today. He focused instead on the scores of soldiers pursuing the decoys, regrouping now after crossing the icy creek. The horse soldiers pushed out in front of the others, spreading out to form a long line. But then, to Crazy Horse's utter dismay, they stopped.

The other decoys looked to him. Crazy Horse saw the dismay in their eyes, too, and something else that filled him with a mix of great responsibility and dread. He saw that they looked to him *for what to do*. For a while today, he had felt confident, a confidence augmented by the *winkte*'s vision. After all, as foreseen, hadn't the soldiers taken their bait, riding away from the protection of the fort in the greatest numbers ever? Hadn't the soldiers pursued the decoys to this point, a single ridgeline away from the carefully selected field of battle?

But now the soldiers halted. Did they sense the trap beyond? As his mind raced, one lesson from the past five months of fighting surged to the fore—his enemy must not be allowed to think, only to react. Raising his war club above his head and filling the valley with his war cry, Crazy Horse charged toward the soldiers' line, the other decoys instantly joining him on both flanks.

Crazy Horse looked toward his enemy as the decoys quickly closed the distance that separated the opposing sides. He had fought the soldiers enough times that he recognized some of the officers by their horses, certainly the one who rode the big white stallion. He saw the officer studying them intently before yelling out a command.

The horse soldiers fired a volley, though the decoys were still more than a hundred yards away. Crazy Horse could hear the bullets streaking around them, but he knew the decoys were beyond the soldiers' effective range. He knew that the soldiers often panicked when confronted with attack, and he knew they now would struggle to reload their clumsy, single-shot rifles in their terror of the charging warriors.

But then, only moments later, the horse soldiers fired again. Crazy Horse heard the scream of a horse and saw one of the Cheyenne tumble to the ground. Incredulous, he peered ahead, toward the horse soldiers, now no more than seventy yards in front of them. He noticed that their rifles today were different, shorter. The soldiers kept the guns to their shoulder and used one hand to operate some sort of lever on the bottom of the rifle, then instantly fired a third round. One of the Arapaho went down. As Crazy Horse watched, the soldiers continued to pour out fire, again and again, without pausing to reload, the smoke from so many rounds already thick around their line.

Crazy Horse reined his horse hard, then yelled out to the others, "Fall back!"

Sword Owner rode up beside him as they retreated. "When did they get those?" he shouted.

Crazy Horse didn't know. He had fought the soldiers led by the officer on the white horse only days earlier, and they had no such weapons then. *Now, on this day of all days!* He felt his stomach constrict, as if he had been kicked. The shots behind them continued as they retreated toward the ridgeline. When they were out of range, he stopped to look back, hoping to find the horse soldiers again in pursuit. A small group clustered around the officer on the white horse in animated discussion, but the line did not move.

He stared up at the ridgeline, achingly close. He imagined the hidden warriors on the far side, hearing the shooting and preparing their weapons in anticipation. But for what?

Have we come so close, only to fail?

Part One

JULY 12, 1866

Crazy Horse and the two other young Oglala covered the last few yards to the ridgeline on their bellies, horses hobbled for the moment below them on the hillside. They propelled themselves forward with knees and elbows, bows across their forearms, peering through the few clumps of sage and shortgrass that could grow on the dry hilltop. Crazy Horse could smell the dryness and feel the heat rising up from the earth as it breathed beneath him.

As the valley below revealed itself, his heart soared, and he forced himself to pause, scanning vigilantly from horizon to horizon, making certain he overlooked no danger. He glanced briefly to his left, at Lone Bear, and his friend smiled. Crazy Horse looked to his right at Little Hawk, his brother, still a boy of thirteen, beaming in excitement and anticipation.

Little Hawk spoke in a whisper. *"Hexaka nais tatanke?"* The elk or the buffalo?

It was good to have such a choice. Crazy Horse studied the scene and considered their options.

The Shining Mountains formed the far western horizon, their pine-covered flanks a rich green against the bleached, late summer grasses of the valley. Water, pure as the heart of the earth, bubbled up from alpine fonts and spilled off the mountains, so much that this valley, the valley of the Twin Creeks, held two streams, each cutting a serpentine path through the low ground before eventually flowing together. Thick willow stands spread outward from the water's edge. Moose often fed in such willowy valleys, and as Crazy Horse watched, a big bull lifted his head from the water at a bend in the nearer of the two creeks. Crazy Horse took it as a good sign. He remembered seeing a bull moose on the day, twelve years ago, when High Backbone, his uncle, first brought him to this valley.

They had come to hunt then, too—and for High Backbone to teach Crazy Horse how to select the best willows for making arrows. They had crawled up to this very ridge, and the scene before them on that day was as it had been on a dozen hunts since, and as it was today. There was a reason their fathers and their grandfathers had fought the Shoshone and the Crow to hunt these lands.

Crazy Horse counted the elk, stopping at fifty, the animals strung along the creek. He watched the slight, bobbing bend of the grass and felt the whisper of a breeze in his face. The nearest elk were only a couple hundred yards down the hillside, including a fat calf that was perfect for their needs. The calf, though, was three times the distance a man could shoot an arrow, and there was little cover between them. If they attempted to creep forward, it was almost certain that one of the elk would spot them and set the herd in flight.

He turned his attention to the buffalo. The small herd of twenty or so animals was more distant—a half mile to their right. The buffalo still wore their summer hides, hair mangy and mottled except where it thickened at the foreleg and shoulder. As snows approached, the hides would grow dense, the rich and heavy robes that kept lodges warm in the coldest nights of winter.

They were not hunting for robes today, nor the supply of meat that would sustain the tribe through the long months of winter. The Oglala village was two days away on the Tongue River, too far to carry meat in any quantity. Big hunting parties would return to this valley and others like it in the Moon of the Rutting Deer. Crazy Horse, of course, was gathering knowledge that would help him to guide the others when that time arrived. These buffalo, he knew, were a small part of a far greater herd. They had seen the massive swathe cut by thousands of animals moving northward, hewing to the grassy foothills and many creeks that tumbled off the eastern side of the Shining Mountains.

Crazy Horse always had found his moments of greatest peace in places such as this. Since the time he was barely older than Little Hawk, Crazy Horse had ridden away from the village, gone alone for weeks or even months at a time. His parents had worried at first, as parents always worry, but they came to understand that to be apart from the tribe was a part of their son's spirit. High Backbone advised Crazy Horse's father that such a spirit was a sign of strength. It was obvious that Crazy Horse was different, his skin and hair lighter than the others' in his tribe, but such differences should be seen as marks of distinction. When Crazy Horse rode away from the village, explained High Backbone, he was not rejecting his place within the tribe but, rather, seeking answers to questions that most people didn't know to pose.

When Crazy Horse chose not to be alone, Lone Bear was the person most likely to join him. Of Lone Bear's many attributes, the one Crazy Horse appreciated the most was his quiet steadiness. They could go for hours without talking, both perfectly comfortable, a testament to their bond. When Lone Bear did speak, he had given careful thought to his words, and Crazy Horse knew to listen.

"Will we take the elk?" Little Hawk whispered the question, staring expectantly at his brother.

Crazy Horse started to upbraid him. Unlike Lone Bear, Little Hawk spoke a lot, even accounting for his youthful enthusiasm and curiosity. His younger brother did not yet appreciate that the best way to learn was to watch, to observe patiently. Then Crazy Horse thought of High Backbone, how the old warrior answered most questions with a question of his own. "What will happen if we try?"

Crazy Horse watched Little Hawk wrestle with the question. It pleased him that his brother paused before answering, and he could see him walk through the hunt in his head.

"Probably one of the old cows will see us . . . or catch our scent before we get close."

Crazy Horse nodded, but otherwise let Little Hawk continue to think it through.

Little Hawk studied the distant buffalo. Most of the small herd grazed down in the taller grass near the creek, but two calves stood farther up the hillside, close to their mother as she wallowed in a deep bowl just below the ridge. Dust rose from the wallow as she coated herself with the dry earth, smothering the fleas that vexed her in the summer heat.

"With the buffalo, we could creep behind the ridgeline until we are close, then ride over, almost on top of them." The younger brother watched for approval in his older brother's reaction, but Crazy Horse remained impassive.

Little Hawk took a bit of dust in his fingers and threw it up in the air in front of his face. It drifted back toward him. "The wind favors us."

After staring at the buffalo for a few more moments, Crazy Horse nodded again and gave his brother a small smile of encouragement. Then, still on his belly, Crazy Horse pivoted and began to work his way back down the hillside toward the horses.

A few moments later, the three Oglala huddled, holding on horseback a short distance below the ridge, out of sight from the three buffalo near the wallow on the opposite side.

"When we go, we go fast," Crazy Horse said to his brother. "Pick the closest calf and stay on it. Wait to shoot until you're close . . . then drive the arrow deep."

Little Hawk hesitated. "How close when you loose the arrow?"

Crazy Horse studied his brother, knowing he knew well the answer. Little Hawk had never killed a buffalo, but in the days since leaving the village, the boy had asked every question imaginable about the hunt, including this one. For an instant, Crazy Horse started to show his frustration, but he paused instead and found himself thinking again about High Backbone, appreciating more and more that, among the many other things he admired about his teacher, the old warrior was patient.

Crazy Horse swung his leg over his horse's neck and dropped lightly to the ground. He called the mustang North Star for the shape of the patch that covered one eye and a part of her forehead. Crazy Horse had stolen the mare from the Shoshone three summers ago, and while there were other mounts calmer in battle, he had never ridden a horse with more skill at running buffalo. He stepped toward Little Hawk and handed North Star's braided reins to his brother.

"You ride North Star today . . . She'll show you what to do."

Crazy Horse watched the surprise and confidence that came over

Little Hawk's face, as if he had been suddenly bestowed a magical power. Every boy in the village coveted the horse, and Little Hawk barely paused before jumping eagerly to the ground, grabbing North Star's mane, and scrambling up onto the animal's back.

"Hold tight with your knees and let her run," said Crazy Horse. "Set loose your arrow when she tells you the moment has arrived."

Crazy Horse mounted Little Hawk's horse. He pulled an arrow from his quiver, quickly checking the fletching before notching it to his bowstring. Little Hawk mimicked his moves, and Lone Bear already was prepared. Without a word, Crazy Horse dug hard at his horse's flanks, and the animal charged over the ridgeline, Little Hawk and Lone Bear on either side.

Between the cover of the ridge and the favorable wind, the cow and her calves had barely an instant to react to the charging hunters. The cow, despite her size, was surprisingly agile and fleet. In a heartbeat, she took flight, the two calves on her tail. They broke to the right, giving Crazy Horse and Little Hawk the clearest line. As they clamored across the wallow, the musky scent of the cow filled Crazy Horse's nose, and he could taste the dust from the great cloud kicked up as she pounded out her retreat.

They came quickly upon a rocky outcropping, and the cow and the larger calf broke even harder to the right to avoid it. Crazy Horse watched in satisfaction as North Star, slightly ahead of him, barreled after the two animals, closing the distance but still out of range. The smaller calf stumbled at the outcropping, only slightly, but enough that a gap emerged between it and the other two. In confusion, the second calf veered away from the cow and toward the creek, where the main herd had also retreated.

Crazy Horse's pony barreled after the second calf. He could tell from the horse's sure movements that it was well trained, and he knew to trust its instincts, dropping the reins, needing both hands for the bow, relying completely on the pony to pick the path.

With dust now obscuring more of his vision, Crazy Horse focused on the sound of the pounding hooves. For short bursts, both the calf and the horse would find momentary rhythms—*bu-darump* . . . *bu-darump*—but then the uneven terrain would upset the flow, so that the pounding became irregular, more urgent somehow, building toward the moment of consummation.

The horse closed now on the second calf, and as Crazy Horse pressed his knees to hold the animal tight, he could feel its straining muscularity. Though lacking some of the skill of North Star, the horse was fleet, and Crazy Horse admired the animal's ability to place him alongside the calf. The horse devoured the gap between them and the calf, until Crazy Horse found himself beside the animal, almost close enough to touch it.

Launching an arrow from a bow was an act that Crazy Horse had repeated tens of thousands of times in his life, beginning with the tiny weapons made for small boys. He drew his breath as he pulled back on the bowstring, and as the resistance from the stout bow grew, he added strength from different parts of his body—arms then shoulders, upper chest then stomach, upper legs and then, Crazy Horse had always believed, he drew a final measure of strength from his charging horse. By the time the bow came to full draw, holding tight for a moment to aim, Crazy Horse and his horse had come together in a mass of taut muscle, poised for the arrow's launch.

The fluidity with which Crazy Horse shot a bow made the act seem wholly instinctive, yet every step had been taught, and he never aimed down the shaft of an arrow without hearing the voice of High Backbone telling him to make his target small. "Don't aim at the buffalo," he would say. "Aim at a piece of hair."

The calf's coat still carried the reddish hue of its youth, and Crazy Horse focused his gaze. The pony and the calf careened, a few feet apart, across uneven terrain at full gallop. Crazy Horse ignored everything but a tiny patch of bare hide below the buffalo's front shoulder blade. Bury the arrow in that spot, Crazy Horse knew, and it would pierce the heart.

For an instant, the whole earth became an infinitesimal target in this one time and place, poised at the tip of his arrow. It all aligned . . . perfect.

Suddenly, from his right, Crazy Horse heard a whoop and caught an auburn flash. Little Hawk had brought down his calf.

Crazy Horse sat upright and released the tension in the bow without loosing the arrow. They had no need for two calves. The horse's blood was up, though, and Crazy Horse needed a hand on the rein to pull the animal away from the buffalo. Finally, the horse turned, and Crazy Horse watched the small calf clamber free, down the hillside, bawling as it joined the retreating herd by the creek.

Breathing heavily from the exhilaration, Crazy Horse turned to look at Little Hawk, several hundred yards away on the hillside, sitting atop North Star next to the heap of the big calf dead on the floor of the prairie. *My brother's first buffalo!*

The feast Crazy Horse shared later that afternoon with Little Hawk and Lone Bear should have seen his unbridled joy continue. They completed together the ceremony of dressing the animal, taking the hide and the meat before ending by facing the head to the east so that the buffalo's spirit would always be warmed by the rising sun.

They let Little Hawk eat most of the liver in honor of his kill, but there was plenty for all of them to gorge on the sweet, tender meat. With buffalo chips, they built a small fire in the soft grass near the creek, sitting for hours, roasting meat on shaved willow sticks, enjoying the contentment of a full belly and listening to Little Hawk describe the details of a moment that he would recount for all his life. Lone Bear and Crazy Horse told the stories of their own first kills, and other stories, too, stories of hunting and war, stories of their people. They were serious at moments that demanded it, but more often, that day, they laughed together. When they were fully sated, they used the hide and fashioned a crude parfleche to carry the meat that remained, enough to feed them for days if need be.

Crazy Horse was careful to do nothing that might detract from his brother's moment, but several times he looked up to meet Lone Bear's inquisitive eyes. His friend knew him well, a fact Crazy Horse appreciated above almost all things. Crazy Horse struggled hard to keep the two rivers of his thoughts inside their own banks, to focus as he did when he aimed at the kill spot on a running buffalo. Yet, try as he might, he could not keep the streams from coming into confluence.

Yes, his purpose in this sacred valley was to hunt, to teach his little brother the ways of the tribe, to wander the land, and to harvest, as needed, its bounty. But there was another purpose . . . one that made his heart heavy with questions and fear. How could he revel fully in this day when all that it represented was at risk?

SAME DAY

Jim Bridger squinted a bit as he looked up toward the ridgeline, close now, the crest backlit by setting sun. His old mare paused a moment, tired after the long climb up the low foothill. Bridger hated to stop so close to the top, but the mare had earned a brief respite. He stroked her neck and patted her. "Good girl . . . You catch your breath."

Just ahead of Bridger was the big pine he'd been using to orient. The valley of the Powder River was still dry this far south, so trees stood out, especially one so tall. Trees like this even earned names sometimes, Lone Pine or Bent Pine or Twin Pine. This tree didn't have a name, at least not one he'd given it. But he'd seen it from a distance before and was curious now to see it up close.

He reckoned it was a hundred feet tall and probably a dozen feet around its base. Its deeply textured bark was copper brown, like the summer coat on a whitetail. The base was blackened by a long-ago prairie fire, but Bridger knew the outer skin was a full five inches thick, and a grass fire would hardly stunt it. He studied the pine's other scars, massive branches torn away by relentless winds, holes bored by beetles and birds. Bridger admired the sap that the big tree spit out to heal itself, scabbing over its wounds from within.

As Bridger craned his neck to see the top of the pine, it occurred to him that the tree was not yet tall enough to see beyond the ridge. He wondered if it would grow to crest the butte before it died, and he hoped it would. How long had the old tree been alive? he wondered. Hundreds of years, he guessed. A long time to strive for a glimpse into the next valley and whatever lay beyond.

Jim Bridger was sixty-two years old that year, at least according to the ciphering by one of Carrington's young soldiers. That seemed about right, though Bridger had never kept close track of such things. The Shoshone he had lived with for the better part of a decade kept only loose count of years, and they seemed to get along just fine without a precise tabulation. Besides, it sounded old when somebody said his age out loud. There were plenty of days when he felt it. Certainly there were enough other measurements to remind him of the passage of time. He missed the sharpness of his younger eyes, felt the cold sink deeper into his bones, wished he could still mount his horse without the pain that shot outward from his knees and shoulders and neck.

But the ledger had two sides. It was a relief not to worry any longer about puffing up his chest for the benefit of others. He found himself treasuring small glimpses of life that as a younger man he might have galloped right past. And there were still plenty of ridgelines to keep him wondering.

He pressed his heels gently against the mare's flanks and felt the same stir of excitement he always did as he approached the top of a butte. In Bridger's time on the frontier, he had crested ridgelines to discover danger—looming storms, grizzly bears, whole villages of hostile Indians spread out in the valley below. Sometimes the far side of the ridge held disappointment—fearsome mountains blocking the path ahead, a swollen river with no sign of a ford, painful emptiness at moments he'd been hopeful of eyeing the warm fire of a friend. In the grandest milestones of his life, Bridger had crested ridgelines to find pure wonder—his first glimpse of the Rockies after a boyhood knowing only plains, herds of buffalo so large that the whole earth seemed to breathe with their movements, a shimmering lake without horizon, so vast that Bridger had believed it to be the ocean. Some things he had seen before any white man in all of time.

Bridger halted the mare and dismounted just before the top, thankful for the gentle headwind that kept his scent from announcing his arrival. He moved forward slowly, keeping his profile low until he knew what lay beyond. The mare flared her nostrils, testing the breeze, and

Bridger studied her reaction. She stared back at him, unperturbed, and her big eyes made him smile.

He crested the ridge, and what he saw still took his breath away. The whites called them the Big Horns, but Bridger liked the Sioux name better: the Shining Mountains. With the setting sun now behind their peaks, they glowed amid a crazy wash of colors that had always struck Bridger as regal, or even divine—purples and pinks and blues spilling one into another, all cut through with streaking golden light, radiating outward from the sun as if it were resisting the attempt to drag it below the horizon.

As a young man, Bridger remembered gazing up at the Big Horns with an intoxicating mix of anticipation and terror. He couldn't wait to clamber across the peaks, barely looking as he went along, so excited to see what came next.

He still felt some of that excitement, though today he knew the Big Horns as intimately as he had once known the twenty acres of his father's small Missouri farm. He knew the Absorkees, too, and the Wind River Range, and the Tetons. He knew the mountains of the Three Forks—the Gallatins and the Madison Range and the Tobacco Roots. He knew the mountains in Utah, and the mountains in California. Amazingly, to Bridger, there were mountains now named for him. Bridger couldn't read, but an officer at Fort Laramie had shown him a map, printed in an actual book, showing mountains in Montana with his name written in letters across the whole range. It made him proud but also uncomfortable, and he hoped no one would ever think he was one of those people who went around scratching his own name on things.

Indeed, if there was one emotion that the mountains evoked as he grew older, it was humility. Looming peaks would always provide a welcome dash of the unknown, but more and more the mountains comforted Bridger for their timeless constancy, their steady presence, an anchor against the decades. They made him feel small, reminded him he was small, reminded some others who needed the reminding. He liked the idea that the mountains would carry on, long after the petty snarling of the day to day.

The mare snorted, and Bridger lowered his eyes from the lofty heights of the Big Horns. Three mounted Indians emerged suddenly from a coulee and rode directly toward him at a distance that Bridger guessed was no more than four hundred yards. He cursed himself for letting his guard down, philosophizing.

For an instant he considered flight, but they were too close, and the cover in this country too poor. So instead, Bridger put on the best show of confidence he could muster. He stood staring at the riders, letting them close another hundred yards, relieved that they appeared to be carrying only bows and no rifles. He made a show of pulling his Hawken from its sheath, checking instinctively to make sure the priming cap was firmly fixed. It was an old muzzle-loader, but Bridger knew how to use it and could still kill comfortably at a hundred yards.

Hawken in hand, he mounted, letting the mare walk slowly toward the approaching riders, now clearly identifiable as Sioux.

Bridger closed to a distance of thirty yards, close enough to sign, and then reined to a halt. He made sure they could see the pistol at his belt, a six-shot army Colt. They knew, of course, that they could kill him, but they would also know he'd kill one or two of them. He doubted that any of them wanted to die ingloriously at the hand of a grizzled old man, so at least he had that in his favor.

He studied the three Sioux. One was barely more than a boy, but the other two were young warriors, and unafraid in a way that suggested to Bridger that they probably had reason to be confident. Being married to a Shoshone woman, he knew the Sioux as the enemy, though he respected them for their skill as hunters and warriors. Besides, this was the heart of their land. He wondered if they recognized him, and it wasn't out of arrogance. Though the frontier was vast, the number of its inhabitants was still small. After decades out West, he was known. During the recent peace talks at Fort Laramie, he had met most of the chiefs and even translated for the Shoshone. Thick Neck, the Indians called him, for the orange-sized goiter at his collar, another of those badges of growing old.

The Sioux talked to one another in low voices, seeming to defer to the man in the middle. Bridger didn't recognize any of them from Fort Laramie, and none were old enough to be chiefs. The one in the middle stood out, lighter-skinned than the others, and with wavy hair more brown than black. There was something about him that gave Bridger particular pause—a quiet authority, a pensiveness that projected careful thought. Bridger decided not to give him too much time to form a negative impression. He reached into his saddlebag and pulled out a rope of tobacco, holding it out and nudging the mare forward. He rode directly to the light-skinned Sioux and reached out with the tobacco. The young warrior studied Bridger intently, his eyes penetrating. For a ponderous moment, Bridger wondered if one of them might move to kill him. But then the light-skinned Sioux accepted the tobacco and said something to the others. One of them dug out a buffalo tongue from a parfleche tied to the back of his pony and extended it toward Bridger. Bridger nodded and accepted it.

Bridger signed, pointing at the men and then motioning with his hand in a broad circle. *Where are you going?*

The light-skinned Sioux signed back. *Hunting.*

Bridger considered this response for a moment. It was possible, of course. Young Indian men were pretty much always hunting. More likely, though, was that these three were scouting for Red Cloud. The movement of Carrington's column was no mystery, so the Sioux would be here to learn the details. How many soldiers? How many horses and cattle? Did Carrington bring cannon?

The light-skinned Sioux signed again, pointing first to Bridger, and then making the sign for "soldier." *Are you with them?*

Bridger nodded. No sense lying. As a scout, he wore no uniform, but they knew he was with the army. To say otherwise would only hurt his credibility. In Bridger's experience, people respected you more if you told them the truth, even if they didn't like what you said.

The light-skinned Sioux emphatically pointed to the ground, then pointed to himself and the other warriors, then made the sign for "Sioux." The meaning seemed pretty clear.

Bridger just nodded in reply. He didn't have the words to debate it, even if he had wanted to do so. It wasn't about debate anymore, in any event, but he didn't know how to sign that either.

The light-skinned Sioux signed again. He pointed over the horizon, where Bridger knew Carrington's column was inching its way up the valley of the Powder. The Sioux again made the sign for "soldier," then crossed his arms at his wrists. Then he pointed to the distant east. Signing was never precise, but Bridger took the meaning. *Tell them to go back.*

Bridger stared at the Sioux, declining to react.

The Sioux leader said something to his comrades, quietly but with authority. They nudged their ponies, pivoted to the south, and rode away.

Bridger watched them for a while. They stayed below the ridgeline, keeping the foothills between them and the valley. After a few minutes, Bridger rode back up to the top of the hill, peering southward down the Powder.

In the distance he saw a rising plume of dust from Carrington's column. He calculated that the soldiers were five miles behind him, two hours or more if he waited for them to catch up, plodding along with infantry and wagons. It would be dark by then, and Bridger knew they needed an hour to pitch their tents, tend to stock, and set pickets. He decided to ride back and meet them. They were close to good water at a little spring creek he knew. Besides, they needed extra time today to talk.

In the three weeks since leaving Fort Laramie they had seen nothing more dangerous than a pack of wolves. Bridger had warned Carrington and the other officers about the rising risks as they ascended the Powder, even scolded a group of officers in front of their wives when he found them picnicking in a small canyon away from the main column, shooting off pistols for the sole purpose of hearing the canyon's echo. He knew they resented him, but he didn't care. Better to ruffle a few feathers than wait until it was too late.

SAME DAY

Colonel Henry Carrington, commander of the Second Battalion, Eighteenth US Infantry, heard the high pitch of a buffalo gnat near his ear and swatted at it. The gnat escaped and then, undeterred, resumed its attack.

Colonel Carrington sat atop a tall gray horse at the crest of a ridge in the broad valley of the Powder River, flanked on either side by a captain, also mounted. Like all his junior officers, the man to his left, Captain Tenador Ten Eyck, had a distinguished record as a fighter in the Civil War. But it was Ten Eyck's civilian career that Colonel Carrington valued most. Before the war, Ten Eyck had been both a sawyer and a surveyor, jobs that made him good with machines and gave him a keen eye for maneuvering through a landscape where obstacles seemed to pop up like prairie dogs.

Captain Ten Eyck removed his kepi and used a soiled handkerchief to wipe at the sweat that poured through the thin strands of hair pasted against his skull. "Do you think, Colonel, that the officers might take off their coats?"

The officer on the other side of Carrington, Captain William Fetterman, looked on hopefully, happy that Ten Eyck had voiced the very question he had been thinking. Fetterman, in his early thirties, was younger than Ten Eyck. Fetterman's dark sideburns dipped southward a good distance down his cheeks and then connected east and west via a thick mustache. Carrington's wife told him that the women in their party considered Fetterman attractive, and speculated that it would not be long before he married one of the ten laundresses who accompanied the Second Battalion.

Colonel Carrington pondered Ten Eyck's request, wanting to appear judicious. He had given the order permitting the enlisted men to remove their woolen jackets in the morning. The sun now was low on the horizon but still blazing hot, and he felt the sweat stream in rivulets down the small of his back. But that wasn't the point. "No, Captain," he said after a moment. "If we take off our jackets—what's to distinguish us from the enlisted men?"

Captain Ten Eyck tried not to react as he returned the kepi to his head, its narrow brim at least providing a small bit of shade for his face.

From his perch atop his horse, Colonel Carrington took a quick look forward and back, irritated once again that his column of roughly two hundred and fifty men was strung out for more than a mile along the valley floor—and that was before accounting for the cattle. All day he had urged his officers to keep the men in tighter formation, but the land, it seemed, continued to conspire against him.

For three weeks Carrington had superintended as the teamsters navigated their wagons over the endless series of *gulches* and *gullies* and *washes* and *draws*. Their scout, no less than the famous Jim Bridger, seemed to use each of these terms as if it represented a specific geographical feature. Carrington had yet to understand the distinctions, and he hadn't wanted to ask. What he did know was that they all blocked his progress.

The obstacle immediately below them at present, which Carrington guessed was something between a gully and a gulch, had a small creek in the bottom. In the worst of all worlds, as far as Carrington was concerned, the creek banks were trimmed white with alkali, which meant the water was unpotable. Fording the cattle would be difficult, because the drovers would have to drive the stupid beasts hard to prevent them from stopping to drink.

A quarter mile ahead of him, Colonel Carrington saw that the advance guard of a dozen cavalry under Lieutenant Grummond had paused on a ridgeline, Grummond apparent even at distance because of his distinctive white horse. Carrington pulled out a field glass and studied them for a moment, taking a bit of satisfaction in the fact that they were waiting, at least some small evidence of discipline.

Between the colonel and the advance guard was the bulk of his men—two companies of mounted infantry. They were called mounted infantry, though at present they lacked mounts. Horses, indeed, were among the many provisions currently in short supply. During the Second Battalion's recent, brief stay at Fort Laramie, Colonel Carrington had vented his frustration in a letter to an old Ohio friend. *We are deployed into what we're told is the most hostile Indian territory in the nation,* he had written. *And we are splendidly furnished—with everything except arms, ammunition, and horses.*

No fewer than three generals had promised him more men and supplies, including General William T. Sherman himself. When it came to arms, Carrington had hoped his men would be issued the state-of-the-art repeating rifles that had proven so effective at the end of the Civil War. Instead, the quartermaster in Nebraska had given them ancient, muzzle-loading Springfield single-shots. The Springfield was accurate but slow to load. Worse, the gun was a ridiculous weapon for cavalrymen or mounted infantry. It was too long to manage on horseback and almost impossible to reload while moving. His cavalrymen had sabers, good for close-in fighting, but only the officers and sergeants had the six-shot Colt revolvers.

When Carrington and his men arrived at Fort Laramie, the last remnant of civilization and their last hope for supply, his expectation of receiving better guns had been disappointed. Even more infuriating, not even ammunition for his antiquated arms had been forthcoming. General Sherman promised one hundred thousand rounds. The quartermaster at Fort Laramie issued a thousand, and grudgingly at that. The Second Battalion now rode through Indian country with barely four rounds per man. The situation with the cannon was little better. They had six mountain howitzers, but only a half-dozen rounds per gun.

Of his one hundred and eighty infantrymen, Carrington guessed that only about half spoke anything resembling proper English. Many were Germans, big and tough, but utterly uncomprehending of the spoken word. Of the remaining men, most were Irish, who spoke English only in theory. In practice, with their thick accents, Carrington found the Irish nearly as difficult to understand as the Germans. The sergeants' efforts to overcome these linguistic impediments by screaming louder had not, so far, resulted in marked improvements in communications.

Carrington took some solace from General Sherman's assurance that the mission of his Second Battalion was not to prosecute a military campaign against the Indians. Indeed, Sherman made clear that Carrington should seek to avoid a fight. The mission of the Second Battalion was to build a fort. By the time the army arrived in the Powder River Valley, as Sherman had foreseen correctly, a new treaty with the Indians had cleared a proper legal path for safe passage. Carrington's new fort would further signal the US Army's resolve to defend a road to the goldfields of Montana. The deterrent effect of this fort, Sherman believed, would be significant—and hopefully sufficient.

Jim Bridger, it had to be said, told the colonel the new treaty was worse than useless. Though signed by Sioux and Cheyenne chiefs, Bridger insisted that the tribes were more complicated than the negotiators at Fort Laramie found it convenient to believe. The chiefs who signed, according to Bridger, represented bands that didn't even live in the Powder River lands that had been ceded, infuriating the bands that did. The war chief Red Cloud had abandoned the Fort Laramie negotiations in outrage on the day that Colonel Carrington and his two hundred and fifty troops arrived, understanding, correctly, that the army intended to occupy the Powder River Valley regardless of the outcome of the talks with the tribes.

If Colonel Carrington's career had not prepared him as either a fighter or a diplomat, he was well suited to the task of building. As a young man, he had aspired to attend West Point, but when illness prevented it, he accepted admission at Yale. Later, he had hoped to fight in the Mexican War, but when an unexpected opportunity arose in the private sector, he pursued that instead. When the Civil War broke out, Carrington imagined a commission to lead men in battle. He had the connections for the commission, but when the military bureaucracy put him in charge of logistics, he accepted his fate. Others would win the adulation and fame. He would put them in the position to succeed by ensuring effective recruitment, ample supplies, and regular payroll. Carrington loved to read and imagined that one day he might write a novel.

As a student of literature, he valued the symbolism of the saber that he wore at his waist, but the truth, he knew, was that he had never drawn it in anger.

Nor did Carrington's physical stature inspire much in the way of confidence. Thanks to Bridger, who had seemed amused to relate the story, Carrington knew that the Sioux at Fort Laramie had called him "Little White Chief." In Carrington's vision of himself, his gray stallion, which stood at a massive eighteen hands, helped to compensate for his own small frame. Behind his back, his officers disagreed, joking about the boost from his aide-de-camp that Carrington sometimes found necessary for his boot to find the stirrup.

Colonel Carrington looked back at the trailing parts of his column. One of his officers told him that Bridger called the column "Carrington's Traveling Circus." It was another reason to be suspicious of Bridger's true thoughts about their enterprise, but as he surveyed the scene, he had to admit the label was not without acuity.

In addition to his poorly armed, horseless mounted infantry, Colonel Carrington's single company of sixty cavalrymen had yet to cohere into the dashing and fearsome dragoons of his aspirations. At least they had horses, though most of the young men riding them were new recruits with little experience or, apparently, innate equestrian skill. After deploying his advance guard, the dozen men with Lieutenant Grummond, the colonel had divided his remaining cavalry into two troops of twenty men, dispatching one group on each flank. He looked out at the flanks now, and what he saw did not please him. To his left, the twenty riders were dispersed so randomly and widely that they might have been a herd of elk. To his right, it was the opposite problem, with the riders bunched so tightly that Carrington was surprised the horses didn't collide. He made a mental note to raise his concerns, yet again, with his officers.

Near the end of the column was Carrington's twenty-piece band, marching along with both their instruments and their guns. The colonel knew there were whispers that it was frivolous to spend scarce battalion resources on a band, but he was a firm believer that the ensemble earned its full keep in the degree to which it boosted the battalion's morale. After all, was there anything more stirring to the heart of a soldier than the call of a trumpet or the beat of a drum? Did not every soldier's blood run hot when the band struck up a patriotic tune? The wives liked the band, too, none more than Margaret Carrington, and it gave all of them the comforting sense that they were not quite so far removed from the normalcy of home.

In an effort to create at least an impression of direct military utility for the band, Colonel Carrington had decided to equip them with the battalion's only repeating rifles, brand-new Spencers that were the envy of every other soldier. He had been allotted only twenty, so there weren't enough for all of the cavalry, in any event. They had the perfect number for every band member, though, and Spencers in hand, the band at least looked a bit more lethal.

Carrington's gaze wandered to the tail end of the column, where a billowing dust cloud marked his herd of more than eight hundred cattle. His officers were disdainful of the cattle, too, believing that the dusty act of herding the animals was below the dignity of fighting men. Colonel Carrington, though, had read all about Alexander and Caesar and Napoleon, not to mention Sherman, whom he himself had helped to supply. Carrington knew what every great military leader had known since the antiquities—that an army travels on its stomach. He hoped the Second Battalion would avoid the need to fight, but it could not avoid eating. And as the colonel contemplated a long winter in a desolate wilderness, he complimented himself on the foresight of traveling with his own supply of fresh beef.

Beyond the cattle, his food supplies concerned him. Some of the wagons carried barrels of salted pork and flour, along with hundreds of crates full of hardtack, but Captain Ten Eyck, who also acted as quartermaster, reported that they were Civil War surplus. The officers had been eager to organize hunting expeditions, and they had seen plentiful game most days, but Bridger warned against relying on it, especially once they had established a permanent fort. It wouldn't take long to drive the game away, particularly when they began cutting trees and operating a sawmill.

Carrington sighed deeply, something his wife said he did with growing frequency.

"Git up, you goddamn sorry bastards!" Directly below Carrington, a civilian teamster unleashed a torrent of obscenities at his mules, which responded by dragging a cargo-laden buckboard through the muck in the creek. The colonel had organized the wagons in the middle of his column, including the Conestogas that carried his wife, son, and the other officers' families. Carrington didn't like the swearing, particularly with the women and children within earshot, but the civilian contractors were difficult to control. He knew he had been lucky to hire enough teamsters in Fort Laramie, particularly with everyone running off to chase Montana gold. So he let this transgression pass. Lots of others too. He suspected, for starters, that the teamsters were the primary source of the bootleg whiskey that seemed remarkably plentiful.

Carrington could see one of the wives, Frances Grummond, the attractive young bride of the dashing Lieutenant Grummond, looking on grimly from her perch next to the teamster aboard one of the Conestogas. Carrington had been surprised that she would sit there, but his wife had told him that the confines of the wagon's canvas-covered bed made Frances feel ill.

At one level, the presence of women and children in a land so wild seemed strange, even imprudent. Again, though, Carrington appreciated the symbolic importance. The officers brought their families because they were planting the flag of the nation. The colonel knew they weren't merely bringing the military to the frontier; they brought civilization.

———————————

Evening, just before dusk, was the one time Colonel Carrington discerned a bit of beauty on the high plains. Remnants of sunlight glowed behind the distant Big Horn Mountains even at ten p.m., and there was an hour or so after dinner when the officers and their wives enjoyed the pleasure of intelligent conversation, usually, as now, with the band quietly playing appropriate music in the background. Enlisted orderlies pitched the officers' tents, big enough to stand inside and with cots for sleeping off the ground. The orderlies cooked and served the food, set up camp tables and chairs, and tended the fires.

The orderlies also brewed the coffee. Carrington knew that some commanders issued a daily dram of whiskey to senior staff, but he thought it set the wrong tone. Besides, the steaming coffee took the chill off the evenings, when the temperature dropped surprisingly fast after the blazing heat of the day.

It was all quite civilized, Carrington thought. In fact, the scene reminded him of articles he'd read in *Harper's* about the African safari adventures of British nobles. He had to remind himself, sometimes, of the danger he knew lay all around them. Bridger, who seemed always sure that disaster was about to befall them, had returned today from his latest scouting mission full of pessimism and warnings.

Carrington resolved not to fall into the trap of alarmism, and certainly with the women present he would convey nothing but complete confidence in the ability of the Second Battalion to deter any danger. It still irked the colonel that the army saw fit to pay the scout more than the commanding officer, though Carrington knew Bridger's reputation was not unearned.

Carrington cleared his throat and gave his wife a long look, a signal Margaret Carrington knew well. "Ladies," she said cheerily, then repeated her usual line: "Dawn comes early."

The women acted with a hierarchy and precision that was nearly as military as that of their husbands, and after a few minutes of polite good-nights, they retired.

Colonel Carrington and his officers sat on campaign chairs in a loose circle around the fire, its flames low but its embers seeming to breathe and pulse with heat. Bridger squatted on his haunches, Indian style, beside the blaze, poking at the embers with a stick.

"Lieutenant Grummond reports a prime site for the fort only a few miles ahead of us," said Carrington.

Lieutenant George Washington Grummond adjusted his posture to be more upright in his chair. He knew, at least at moments such as this, to compensate for a natural slouch that conveyed nonchalance or even disrespect. "As close to perfect as you'll find, sir—high ground, twin streams with good water, grass all around for the stock, and timber for building."

Carrington nodded his head. He was eager to begin the building process, and equally eager for the transportation phase of his enterprise to be complete. "Are there arguments against it?"

"It does sound like there's good timber, the most we've seen until now," said Captain Ten Eyck. "But if the timber's not close to the building site, we'll spend a lot of man-hours hauling the logs."

Colonel Carrington weighed the two arguments while the junior officers studied him, none more closely than Captain Fetterman. All day, Fetterman had listened as the colonel complained about the time they were wasting on the trail, about his fears of failing to complete the fort before winter set in. Fetterman waited a moment longer to see if anyone else would speak. When no one did, he said, "Well, I don't suppose we would want to build *too* close to timber."

Carrington looked at him sharply, and Fetterman instantly regretted speaking up.

"And why is that, Captain?"

Now everyone looked at him. There was no turning back. "Well, sir, because of the cannon."

Colonel Carrington stared blankly, afraid suddenly that he had revealed once more his lack of field experience.

Fetterman started to explain, but Grummond beat him to it. "Captain Fetterman's right, sir!" Fetterman breathed a sigh of relief as Grummond gushed, "There's a man who understands artillery! We need open field on all sides or we lose our biggest advantage against the savages."

Fetterman had known Lieutenant Grummond for only a few weeks. There had been the usual recounting of where they had served, where they had fought—but not enough time to develop a fuller sense of the man. As a captain, Fetterman outranked Grummond, yet there was something magnetic about the younger man, and Fetterman felt gratified at Grummond's praise for his views.

Colonel Carrington looked at his scout. "What do you think, Mr. Bridger?"

Bridger said nothing for a few moments, poking at the coals. "Don't ask me if you don't wanna know." Carrington remained silent, so eventually Bridger continued. "The Sioux ain't gonna attack your fort, Colonel. They know that's the one place you hold all the cards."

"So the location is good?" said Carrington.

"I didn't say that," said Bridger. "I said the Sioux ain't gonna attack your fort . . . not there, not anywhere you put it."

"So why not put it there—where it suits our purpose?"

"Because the valley the lieutenant is talking about is dead center in the middle of their hunting grounds."

Carrington bristled. "The Sioux nation signed a treaty allowing construction of a road and three forts."

"There is no Sioux nation, Colonel. I was there and I saw who signed that treaty—a couple bands that don't live within five hundred miles of this valley."

Carrington had no immediate response, allowing Bridger's words to hang in the night air for a moment like an unwelcome stench.

Captain Fetterman shifted in his chair, surprised that Bridger had spoken to the colonel with such frankness. He wished that someone would speak now, hating the long silence.

Lieutenant Grummond obliged him. "As for me, Colonel, I'm quite confident that the Second Battalion is prepared for whatever comes our way."

Fetterman and the other junior officers nodded in agreement, and their confidence seemed to steel the colonel. "Signal reveille an hour early tomorrow," he ordered. "I want us on the building site by noon. If it stands up to Lieutenant Grummond's description, that's where we build our fort."

———

Bugler Adolph Metzger dipped the corner of a rag into the small tin of polish, then rubbed it carefully along the simple but elegant curves of his bugle. The gleaming brass caught bits of light from the campfire he shared with nine other men, and it pleased Metzger, as it always did, to know that he kept his instrument pristine.

Private Schmidt was also in the band. He watched Metzger, fully reclined, with his head resting against his rolled-up army blanket. "If you gave your wife the same attention, maybe you'd be happy and snug back east instead of trudging through this bunghole piece of the world."

Metzger spent a moment trying to think of a clever rebuttal but came up with nothing. In truth, Schmidt's remark landed at a sensitive moment. Sergeant Metzger had taken to wondering lately, and one of his few firm conclusions, up until now, was that wondering led mostly to more wondering. Metzger had come to wish that he could stop all the contemplating. Yet having started, he had been unable to jump off this recent path of questioning every decision in his life that led him from the lush and cultivated hills of Bavaria to this barren and wild place.

Metzger had questioned his decision, in 1855, to leave Germany in the first place, the impetuous act of a twenty-one-year-old. For many years, he blamed his father; certainly the Bavarian schoolteacher had set expectations higher than young Adolph had been able to meet. Today Metzger was thirty-two—not old by any means—but certainly with a great deal more wisdom and experience than the young man who'd jumped a boat to America. Among his few conclusions—and this one was sobering—was that his missteps were his own.

Metzger also had taken to questioning his decision, only two months after landing in New York City, to join the United States Army. It seemed compelling at the time—an opportunity to earn board and keep while learning English. From then on, though, none of his decisions felt entirely deliberate. He had tumbled along with the army from one place to the next, landing more or less on his feet each time, but never with a sense that he might catch his breath and contemplate a bit before making his next move.

He had reenlisted in the heady month after the 1860 election of President Lincoln, a time when everyone knew that the nation was headed for civil war. When he thought about it now, he was happy to have been part of a just cause, though in truth, he had never felt the depth of passion that animated so many of his fellow soldiers. His Civil War duties took him from the nation's capital to the New Mexico Territory. He had fought in major battles, including the Battle of Gettysburg, an experience so terrifying that he had pledged, huddled on the field, that he would quit the army forever. Yet even that fear, a moment of undiluted terror when he was certain that he was about to die, had been insufficient to knock him from the track on which his life rolled along. In 1864, he reenlisted again. *What was I thinking?* His answer, as he reflected today, was this: however vivid his fear of the known, his fear of the unknown was greater.

A lick of flame from the glowing coals leapt up, briefly enveloping the end of a green willow stick on which Metzger roasted his portion of the fresh elk meat. Metzger set the bugle carefully on his blanket and tended to the meat, making sure his supper didn't tumble into the fire. He had yet to become accustomed to the prairie practice of using dried buffalo dung for fuel, though the material was everywhere and did produce steady heat.

"Hey, Metzger . . ." One of the cavalry corporals leaned forward, gesturing toward the roasting meat. There was a musical lilt to his County Cork accent that Metzger appreciated—less so the speaker behind the voice. "I'll give you half a pigtail of tobacco for your meat."

James Beckwourth, the mulatto scout, had brought in a big cow elk that evening. By the time it was divided between the three hundred people in their party, it came out to only a few ounces per man. But it was their first fresh meat since leaving Fort Laramie three weeks earlier, and even the smell of it roasting boosted morale. When on campaign, as now, the enlisted men prepared their evening meals in small squads, each group sharing a fire. Most nights the men used their mess kits to fry up a fetid rasher of salted pork, but tonight they used the willow sticks to roast the elk.

"No deal," said Metzger. After more than a decade in America, he could speak English well, though a heavy accent still belied his country of birth.

"Oh, come on," the corporal persisted. "A full share is wasted on a runt like you."

Metzger just smiled. It was true that he was one of the smaller men, far closer to five feet than to six. Nor did he display any of the physical skills that might have distinguished him as a fighting man, or even placed him in comfortable, anonymous mediocracy.

In fact, Metzger imagined, he might very well have been mustered out of the army in his first month had he not revealed, quite accidentally, that he could play the bugle. He and his fellow recruits had been sitting in their New York City barracks one night when another soldier had picked up a bugle and begun blowing it—badly, but to the great amusement of his comrades. Unable to speak English, Metzger had been desperate for some means to communicate with the other men. When the first soldier tossed the instrument aside, Metzger picked it up and began to play—a sorrowful but beautiful folk song called *"Kein schöner Land in dieser Zeit."* A few of the other Germans teared up at the familiar sound from their homeland, and all of the soldiers, German or otherwise, had been moved—Metzger's first moment of genuine connection with his new comrades and countrymen.

"Bugger off, then, you kraut-eatin' bastard," said the corporal.

"Bugger yourself," said Metzger. All the men had grown weary of the corporal. "I imagine you would if you could reach."

The men around the fire laughed.

Having discovered that Metzger could play the bugle, the army placed him in the regimental band. He could not yet speak English, but he could read music. Metzger wasn't sure whether to blame or to credit his father for the bugle, but certainly the old man was responsible. Good German professor that he was, his father believed that music opened students' minds for more serious matters such as science and math. Instead, and many were the times when Metzger considered the irony, music had opened the door for his long career in the United States Army.

A new speaker joined the conversation, and his accent too told a story—a Georgia drawl as thick as tar. "You know, Corporal . . . in Montana they say there's so much game you can eat fresh meat every night." Barely two years earlier, the Georgian had stood on the opposite side of the battle lines from some of the men at this very campfire. There were plenty of former rebels in the Second Battalion— "galvanized Yankees," they called them, Confederate prisoners of war given early release if they agreed to renounce the rebellion and enlist in the frontier army.

"We're all sick of your Montana talk," said the corporal. "If I had two bits for every time you talked about Montana gold, I wouldn't need any Montana gold."

"Do it your way, then," said the Georgian. "How much stake have you set aside on your thirteen dollars a month in army wages?"

The question seemed to stump the corporal. Bugler Metzger, though, was good at math, and his financial prospects was one of the topics he had pondered of late. The sums he arrived at using multiples of thirteen dollars worried him, especially now that he and his wife back in Brooklyn had a child. So far, anyway, it was yet another problem with no ready solution.

Sometimes it seemed like half the men in the battalion were on the verge of deserting for the goldfields of Bannock and Virginia City. Metzger was not among them, though he could appreciate the intoxicating attraction of sudden riches. Every man in the battalion had heard the stories of the miners at Fort Laramie on their way back from Montana, some of them with lumpy, sagging jackets rumored to be flush with gold dust sewn into their clothing for safekeeping. What would it be like, he wondered, to go home with thousands of dollars? He imagined his wife's pride, imagined buying a small farm or a shop to repair musical instruments. Metzger knew himself well enough to know that he would never be a miner, but neither had any other solution leapt to mind. So he added this to his list of topics that he wished he could force from his thoughts.

Metzger reached out and pulled his willow stick from the fire. At its tip, the smoldering chunk of meat spit forth tiny droplets of fat, glistening deliciously in the light of the flames. Metzger nibbled at first to avoid burning his tongue, the rich flavor overwhelming. He tried to eat slowly, to savor the moment, but he couldn't.

Later that night, as Metzger lay on the ground beneath the thin cover of his wool army blanket and white canvas tent, the vexing questions returned. Search though he might, the answers to his questions remained elusive, and despite his bone-deep fatigue, he could not sleep.

Crazy Horse, Little Hawk, and Lone Bear stood on a distant ridgeline, counting the dozens of campfires spread across the valley below. Red Cloud, of course, had known they would come. The force of soldiers, though, was larger than the great chief had expected. In the last hours before sunlight, they had counted fifty wagons, more than two hundred soldiers, sixty horses, and six of the big wagon guns, the same type that Crazy Horse had seen fired in a demonstration at Fort Laramie.

To their greatest surprise, the three Lakota had seen women and children with the soldiers. Their presence could mean only one thing. He had felt rage at the invasion of their land by the soldiers. Now, though, he felt sudden and deep fear. Everything, he knew, was about to change.

Crazy Horse was happy that the darkness masked his face. He didn't want his brother to see his thoughts. "We need to sleep now," he said after a while. "Tomorrow we go back to the village."

JULY 17, 1866

Crazy Horse, Lone Bear, and Little Hawk worked their way slowly up the last climb before the descent into the valley of the Tongue River, where the Oglala and Minnicoujou were camped.

Crazy Horse heard a haunting screech from behind him and reined his horse to look back, spotting the hawk just as it tipped a wing to catch an updraft, soaring effortlessly higher. The presence of the hawk comforted him, as it always did . . .

His father's name had been Crazy Horse before he bestowed it upon his son.

As a boy, Crazy Horse had been known among his people as Light Hair for the wavy brown locks that set him apart. He had always been on the small side compared to his peers, but High Backbone had taught him to take inspiration from the animals around him. The wolf, the cougar, and the hawk, he had explained, all were brutally effective predators—but each hunted using its own particular strength. The strength of the wolf was in the collective cunning of the pack, many animals working together to bring down prey. The cougar relied on stealth, creeping silently through tall grass, its unwitting prey, suddenly in the grasp of tooth and claw, having never been aware that death stalked so near. The hawk's vision allowed it to see for miles, then swoop down on its prey from the sky. What were Crazy Horse's strengths, and how could he marshal them in battle? Even as a boy, Light Hair had learned to rely on cunning and agility instead of brute strength.

Yet it was the vision Light Hair received at the time he became a man that most defined him in battle. He had gone forth alone in the Month of Tall Grass and searched out a high place on the plains, a great plateau whose top consisted of sandstone, carved by wind and time into mystical shapes. There he had camped and fasted for days, awaiting the vision that he hoped would guide the rest of his life.

Finally it came. Light Hair had seen a warrior, bursting from the placid surface of a high mountain lake atop a charging stallion. The rider's cheek was painted with a single lightning bolt and impressions of blue hailstones dotted his naked chest. As he galloped forward, a hawk flew behind him as if the two acted in unison.

A great storm pursued the warrior and the hawk, thunder and lightning spewing from an ominous black thunderhead whose clouds billowed up from the horizon all the way to the heavens. Somehow, the warrior outpaced the storm, but then a blizzard of arrows and bullets began to fly all around him. Miraculously, none struck him as he galloped directly ahead, undeterred.

Just when it seemed the warrior would ride on to safety, the vision took a strange twist. From behind, the warrior's own people appeared, reaching out their arms to pull him down.

Then it was over.

When Light Hair returned to his village he sought understanding of the dream from Crazy Horse, his father. His father listened solemnly as Light Hair reported every detail he could remember. After the son finished his recounting, his father sat for a while in contemplative silence. Then he offered his explanation, and it worried Light Hair that his father seemed so serious and even sad. The vision, his father said, portended great power but also danger. His father believed that his son could not die in battle, that the arrows and bullets of his enemies could never find him as their target. Yet his son would be hounded by powerful, looming danger his whole life. And while he could not be killed by his enemies, the vision foretold a more insidious danger—from his own people. Ultimately, his father told him, the true strength of the vision could not be known until it had been tested in battle.

Months later, Light Hair rode forth with High Backbone and other Lakota warriors on a raid in Shoshone country, near the Wind River.

Light Hair would charge into a storm of enemy fire—and none of the bullets or arrows would pierce his skin. He killed two of his enemies, but then, while taking the scalp from one of his vanquished foes, he heard the report of a rifle and felt a sharp pain in his leg, looking down to see blood. Soon the last of the enemies was dead. High Backbone treated the leg wound, which was not serious, and they returned to the Lakota village in celebration.

Light Hair's father heard the stories of his son's bravery in battle, riding into arrows and bullets without fear, surviving unscathed except for the injury in the midst of scalping his foe. Later they spoke quietly, father to son. His father told Light Hair that the battle had proved the vision—but with an important additional lesson. No, Light Hair could not be felled by his enemies' arrows or bullets. But the Creator had paired this great power with an obligation—he must fight not for his own aggrandizement or glory, but only for the betterment of his people. Others could lift scalps as trophies, adorn their clothing, recount their own bravery around the victory fires. Not Light Hair. He must walk the path of great humility.

His father's way was to lead by example. He was not a warrior, and so the lessons in this domain would be left to High Backbone and others in the tribe. But he could show his son the path of humility. That night, amid the stories told by High Backbone and the others about the raid in Shoshone country, Crazy Horse—the father of Light Hair—sought the right to speak at the fire. It was surprising to hear a healer speak in this setting, and the assembled tribe fell silent to listen to his words. He began by saying that he had heard the stories told by others of his son's bravery in battle. As a father, he was thankful for his son's safety. He prayed to the Creator for his son—for all the tribe's sons—to be protected in the future battles they would face in their lives.

To mark this day when his boy became a warrior and to celebrate his son's contribution to the tribe, Crazy Horse would bestow a gift upon his son. Some in the tribe wondered what Crazy Horse had to give. As a healer, he did not maintain a remuda of horses like the warriors. He didn't even own a rifle. Then Crazy Horse announced that thenceforth and forever, Light Hair would be known as Crazy Horse. He would give his son his name. And the father would take the new name of Worm.

There was a murmur in the crowd. Giving his name to his son might not be shocking, but who would give themselves a name such as Worm? Light Hair, though, understood at once. In giving him his name, Crazy Horse had bestowed his single most valuable possession—an appellation associated with his tribe's respect for a life of good work on behalf of his people. Yet Light Hair saw how his father was doing more. To show his son the path of humility through his actions, the father was taking the additional step of embracing a new name for himself that marked the earth's most lowly creature.

From that day, as a boy of fourteen, Crazy Horse had vowed to live up to his vision, to the name bestowed by his father—and to the responsibilities that came with both. He would endeavor to use his powers to be his people's greatest defender, his enemies' most relentless foe. All of this he would seek to do while walking in the footsteps of his father's humility. While others might praise him or even sing his victories, he would not. Even from his enemies, he would take no trophies.

Crazy Horse, Lone Bear, and Little Hawk paused for a moment when they first caught sight of the Oglala village below them, spread out along both banks of the Tongue River and filling the green valley below the Shining Mountains. Despite Crazy Horse's periodic need to go off on his own to explore and reflect, he always felt the pull of his people drawing him back, their embrace like the enveloping deep roots of a tree, nourishing him and connecting him to something larger than just himself.

As they rode through the village, Crazy Horse saw with happiness that the Minnicoujou had joined the Oglala camp. Sister tribe to the Oglala, the Minnicoujou were the people of Crazy Horse's mother. Before she died, she had made sure that Crazy Horse would think of the Minnicoujou as his people just as much as the Oglala. Her brother, the great Minnicoujou warrior and chief High Backbone, had taken responsibility for teaching Crazy Horse to hunt and to fight, and Crazy Horse was eager to share with him the things he had learned in recent days.

It was good to receive the greetings and warm welcome of their people as they rode into the village. They stopped briefly to exchange greetings with Rattling Blanket Woman, the mother of Little Hawk, and Worm, the father both of Little Hawk and Crazy Horse. Rattling Blanket Woman ran to bring the three young men hot meat from the cooking pot. They accepted the food gratefully, but after assuring their parents that they were in good health, they rode on to find High Backbone.

————————

Ever since learning of the soldiers' invasion a few days earlier, Crazy Horse had been reluctant to share the news. He understood, of course, the importance of what he knew, but he worried about the act of sitting with others, all eyes on him. In the hunt or on the battlefield, Crazy Horse always felt as if he were guided by an unseen hand. He trusted his instincts, trusted that he was protected by the power of the Creator. In camp, though, he felt uncertain and clumsy, as if all his fingers had been cut to stumps. When it came to talking with those he did not know well, it was as if he were attempting to push a river from its banks.

So High Backbone's presence in the camp was a gift, perhaps even a sign. With the possible exception of Lone Bear and his own father, there was no one with whom he felt more at ease.

He paused outside High Backbone's enormous lodge, so large it was said to be covered in the hides of twenty buffalo. Crazy Horse admired that High Backbone still used hides. Many tribes, and even some Lakota, now used the white trader's special cloth. As with many things made by the white man, Crazy Horse marveled at the magic of the cloth—its tiny threads woven so tightly that it shed the rain, yet light enough to carry easily. High Backbone taught his people not to depend on such supplies from the whites. Over the years, on Oglala trips to trade at Fort Laramie, Crazy Horse had seen with his own eyes where such dependency led. He had been mystified, ashamed, and ultimately angered by the bands that lived year-round near the fort. They abandoned pursuit of the buffalo in favor of handouts from the soldiers, the men slaves to the white man's liquor, the women sometimes trading their bodies to the soldiers for mirrors and shiny trinkets.

High Backbone's wife brought more food out to them, and they sat in the remnants of early evening sunshine in the deep grass along the Tongue. High Backbone sensed that his nephew had important news, but he knew to allow the young man to tell his story on his own terms. Eventually Crazy Horse worked his way through all the details, carefully describing the number of soldiers and horses, wagons, wagon guns. All of this was important, though none of it unexpected. High Backbone sensed that his nephew was holding something back, working up to something that he almost could not bring himself to say.

"They stopped in the valley of the Twin Creeks," Crazy Horse said finally.

"Big Buffalo and Little Buffalo Creek?" asked High Backbone.

Crazy Horse nodded, watching as his uncle absorbed the news, his face suddenly drawn and drained of color. The valley of the Twin Creeks was a sacred place to him, revered hunting ground.

Crazy Horse pushed on now. "They have a machine like the one at Fort Laramie," he said finally.

"Which machine?" asked High Backbone.

"The one that turns trees into boards."

High Backbone said nothing, and Crazy Horse felt as if he were telling his uncle of a death.

"There's more," said Crazy Horse. "They have women and children."

Crazy Horse watched as the sadness on High Backbone's face changed to rage. High Backbone didn't say anything. He didn't need to, because they both understood what it meant. This force did not come just to fight; they came to stay. To stay here, in the home of the Lakota.

High Backbone carried Crazy Horse's news to the three other chiefs. They sat around the fire in the lodge of Red Cloud, toward whom even the other chiefs gravitated naturally in moments such as this. In addition to High Backbone, Red Leaf was there from the Minnicoujou. For the Oglala, Old Man Afraid of His Horses held his customary place at the council fire. The crimson glow from the flicker of low flames offered the only light on their somber faces as they absorbed the information.

"This is different from any time before," said High Backbone by way of summary.

No one disagreed.

"I haven't heard yet all of the details from your time at Fort Laramie," said Old Man Afraid of His Horses. "What else did you learn there?" Old Man Afraid of His Horses had difficulty walking now and could no longer mount his horse without the assistance of his grandsons. He spoke slowly and sometimes his words slurred one into the next. His thoughts, though, remained clear, and the others respected him and listened to him carefully.

"Only bad things," said High Backbone. Both he and Red Leaf had taken part along with Red Cloud in the Fort Laramie negotiations a few weeks earlier. "The Southern Cheyenne say that thousands of gold miners have poured into the lands south of the Platte. The whites have built whole new villages—some many times bigger than Fort Laramie."

Old Man Afraid of His Horses stared intently as High Backbone continued. "The Cheyenne say the whites have brought a new type of machine to the southern plains—a giant metal wagon that rolls on rails that are staked to the ground. Instead of being pulled by horses or oxen—this metal wagon burns fire to push itself forward and belches out huge clouds of smoke. Armies of strange men with yellow skin and one dark braid are laying more of the rails, stretching them each day farther and farther toward the west. Some say they'll place such rails along their road in the valley of the Platte, and then beyond that."

"Do we think this is true?" asked Old Man Afraid of His Horses.

Red Leaf nodded his head. "My mother's people are Cheyenne," he said. "My uncle is Broken Arm, who was with Black Kettle's band, and I talked to him at Fort Laramie. He's seen these things with his own eyes—and it gets worse. Wherever the metal rails have been laid, armies of white hunters have arrived."

It pained High Backbone to watch Old Man Afraid of His Horses. He felt as if they were slapping the old man in the face—or worse, as if they had shot the horse from beneath him as he rode through the winter of his life. But there was no avoiding it. The danger before them must be discussed, confronted. Each day it became more and more clear that the survival of their people was now at stake.

"Broken Arm says these hunters shoot down whole herds of the buffalo, strip their hides, leave the rest to rot on the prairie floor," said Red Leaf. "He says that where the Southern Cheyenne had hunted for generations, the buffalo are gone. They now travel for months and see no buffalo."

High Backbone also studied Red Cloud as they spoke. The great chief listened, seeming to absorb all the words but offering no reaction. He knew this was Red Cloud's way—first to listen.

Old Man Afraid of His Horses adjusted the blanket around his shoulders. "I hear what you have learned and of course I feel the weight of it," he said. "But it's one thing to describe a problem, and another to describe what to do about it."

"Our eyes must be wide open to what this means," said High Backbone. "In fall we prepare for winter, and because we prepare, we don't freeze . . . we have food until spring."

"By prepare, do you mean fight?" asked Old Man Afraid of His Horses. "Because it's too easy to talk of fighting," he said. "When our blood is up we forget about the hard days after the fights, when fathers and mothers learn that their sons are gone forever. You mentioned Black Kettle. Remember what the whites were willing to do to him and his people? I know you are brave. But are you also ready to put your women and children in the path of such an enemy?"

No one said anything for a moment, not wanting to be disrespectful to the eldest of the chiefs. After a while, though, High Backbone said, "That's not the lesson I see from Black Kettle."

All of them knew the story of Black Kettle and his band of Southern Cheyenne. They had made peace with the whites, moved to where the whites told them to go—along Sand Creek—even flown the flag with the stripes and stars above their camp to signal their friendship.

"Black Kettle did everything the whites asked him to do and still the soldiers attacked his camp," said High Backbone. "Slaughtered his women and children . . . At Fort Laramie, the whites pretended to negotiate with us—even as Little White Chief was preparing to come into the valley of the Powder River."

A pine knot burst in the fire, sending skyward a shower of sparks that seemed to affirm the solemnity of the moment—of the decision.

Red Cloud leaned forward, and it seemed almost as if he had emerged from the fire. He was forty-four years old that year, and still strong enough to drive an arrow all the way through a buffalo. His authority, though, flowed less now from his physical prowess in battle. High Backbone had always believed that Red Cloud's unique power was his ability to express the anger of his people, but then also to give them hope, to show a path forward where moments earlier it appeared that no path existed.

"I've listened carefully as I always do around this council fire," he said. "Every man in this lodge, and every man among our people, must choose his own path."

As Red Cloud's anger rose, it reminded High Backbone of the way a drumbeat becomes steadily more insistent.

"We've listened to white lies since the time of our fathers. I was still a young man when the whites signed a paper promising to leave us alone in the land north of the Platte. Our fathers put their own names to that paper, because they believed the white man would stand by his word and they hoped to trade for peace by feeding his hunger. Now, along their Platte Road, all the game is gone . . . every water hole fouled with their waste.

"And now the whites decide the Platte Road is not enough. They find gold, and so they demand still more land . . . press at us from where the sun rises and from where the sun sets. Finally we're left with only *this* land . . ." Red Cloud paused to scoop up a handful of dirt, holding it up in front of him. "This land on which we and our families live today . . ." Red Cloud shook the fistful of earth as he spoke. "And now the white man says he wants *this land too.*"

Around the fire, every man was rapt.

"And so he sends his agents to Fort Laramie to make a new treaty, and when we who live on this land say no, he makes a treaty for this land with tribes who live far away."

Old Man Afraid of His Horses shook his head in disgust.

"And even before this treaty is signed, the white men send Little White Chief to build a fort in the middle of our home!

"My chiefs, there is no place left to go! I will retreat no more! I will fight here and I may die here . . . but I will not leave our home!"

Later that night, while the others joined around an enormous, communal fire, Crazy Horse and a few of the other young warriors sat with Red Cloud and High Backbone to learn about the chiefs' discussion earlier that day.

"We should ride against the soldiers with all of our strength before they finish their fort," said Young Man Afraid of His Horses, son of the old chief. "Now's when they are weak." Several of the other young men nodded their heads in agreement.

"Why would we fight them at the place of their choosing?" asked Red Cloud. "Even without the walls of the fort, they'll have their wagon guns."

"So how should we fight them, then?" asked Sword Owner.

Crazy Horse had seen that Red Cloud, like High Backbone, sometimes answered questions with questions. "How does a beaver take down a tree?" asked the chief.

Sword Owner looked uncertain, so Red Cloud continued. "A little bit at a time. None of his bites is large, but each one goes a little deeper than the one before."

Sword Owner nodded his head. "Eventually the tree falls."

"Let's learn how Little White Chief will fight," said Red Cloud. "While we learn, make it so that no day passes that we don't chip away at the mighty tree."

Crazy Horse had fought against the whites several times in his life— but usually scattered travelers who had wandered away from the trail along the Platte. Twice he had fought small groups of soldiers. Certainly none of them had ever confronted an army so large, and he wondered how they might be different.

"Each of you pick a few warriors you trust," said Red Cloud. "Go in small war parties into the valley of the Twin Creeks. Chip away for now, but let the soldiers know every day the cost of invading our home. Let them be afraid."

JULY 20, 1866

Crazy Horse and the dozen warriors with him heard the sounds of the soldiers long before they crested the ridge, as if a great and terrible beast marauded through the valley beyond. A hundred axes hacked at tree trunks, pines groaned as they broke and fell to the ground, sergeants shouted orders, and teamsters yelled at and whipped their stock. Loudest of all was the sawmill, whose engine pounded and whose blade screamed as it ripped into the flesh of the fresh timber.

When they moved into a concealed position on the ridgeline and could see below, Crazy Horse could scarcely believe that he was looking at the same valley of the Twin Creeks, where, only days before, Little Hawk had taken his first buffalo. Immediately beyond them, across Little Buffalo Creek, a hundred soldiers swarmed the pine forest at the base of the rounded hilltop. Scores of trees lay fallen, as soldiers used ropes and horses to drag the logs like corpses to waiting wagons.

At the far south end of the valley, all along the creek, the soldiers' enormous herd of cattle grazed and waded among the willows where, in Crazy Horse's mind's eye, ranged buffalo and elk.

Three miles up the valley, an entire village of white tents had sprung up on a small plateau that rose above Little Buffalo Creek. The soldiers had staked out the tents in perfect lines, row after row, supplanting the prairie ground completely. The start of the fort's walls had begun to take shape in the form of vertical logs sunk into the ground. Though the perimeter wall was incomplete, the soldiers already had placed the wagon guns along each of the four sides, their polished brass tubes gleaming menacingly in the unfiltered sunlight.

From one end of the valley to the other, everywhere Crazy Horse looked were soldiers—marching, riding, carrying, herding, digging, pounding, cutting . . . It reminded him of a great flock of crows swarming the carcass of a buffalo.

Crazy Horse struggled to control his emotions. Part of him felt mystified and despondent, almost unbelieving that a place he knew so intimately could be so changed in so short a period of time. Part of him felt profound anger. Inside him surged the reflex, nearly overwhelming, to fight in this moment, to gather the warriors with him and to charge into the valley.

He whispered to Lone Bear, at his side, "We could attack them there." He pointed to a small group of soldiers tending a team of horses apart from the others.

Lone Bear studied the soldiers and the valley, then slowly shook his head. "No, too many soldiers are nearby," he said. "Not here . . . Not yet."

The campfire, more than ten miles from the valley of the Twin Creeks, stood out more and more brightly as dusk slipped deeper into dark. As they rode closer, the Oglala heard the sound of boisterous voices and crazy laughter, the kind that Crazy Horse had experienced only in connection with the white man's whiskey.

No pickets guarded the camp. The dozen Oglala fanned out as they drew near, with Crazy Horse and Little Hawk in the middle. Lone Bear took a position on the far-right flank. Crazy Horse pulled his war club from his belt as he approached and the other warriors followed his lead, so that all of them had weapons in hand.

Up close, the crackling firelight confirmed Crazy Horse's suspicions about the scene he would find. Haphazardly arrayed around the campfire were two wagons and two tents owned by a trader named Cattoire. Crazy Horse knew Cattoire, a Frenchman married to a Cheyenne woman. They had tolerated him up until now. It was true, he carried whiskey into their land, and Crazy Horse loathed its influence on his people. But

Cattoire also sold lead and gunpowder, two goods that the Lakota could not obtain for themselves. The fact that Cattoire had taken a Cheyenne wife also had given him a degree of immunity.

In addition to Cattoire, eleven other men sat around the fire in various states of inebriation. Seven were miners, bound for Montana, and four, to Crazy Horse's disgust, were Southern Cheyenne. The Cheyenne seemed barely conscious.

Cattoire, a whiskey bottle in hand, peered into the darkness and turned serious when he became aware of the dozen Lakota in a half circle around his camp. "*Bonsoir, mes amis. C'est qui, la? C'est Crazy Horse?*" When Crazy Horse offered no response, Cattoire corked the whiskey bottle and set it on the ground. He stood up, swiped nervously at the corner of his mouth, and shifted to Lakota. "*Háu, mithákhola.*" Hello, friends.

One of the miners, with a thick red beard and a brace of pistols at his belt, clambered to his feet. He put a hand to the butt of one of the guns and took an unsteady step backward. "Jesus Christ, Cattoire, who the hell are they? Are they Sioux?" The other miners also stood. One, peering from beneath the brim of a shapeless hat, looked furtively to where a big scattergun lay perched against a saddle.

"Shut up, idiot!" said Cattoire. He held up his hands and said in Lakota, "Steady, my friends . . . you want whiskey? I have good whiskey— my gift to you!"

Still Crazy Horse said nothing but nudged his horse to move a few steps closer so that he towered directly over Cattoire and the miners. He looked down at the Cheyenne, one of whom rolled to his side and began to vomit.

"Shit, Cattoire!" said the miner with the beard. "They're Sioux, ain't they? They're gonna kill us!"

"Shu—" Before Cattoire could finish the word, the miner in the hat made a move for the scattergun. He managed to grab it and swing it around before Lone Bear and two other Sioux sunk arrows deep in his chest. The miner groaned at the impact, pulling the trigger as he fell backward, the roar of the big gun igniting total chaos in the camp.

Directly in front of Crazy Horse, the miner with the beard pulled his pistols, but before he could fire, Crazy Horse kicked his warhorse and the stallion leapt forward, barreling directly into the miner and knocking him to the ground. In an instant, Crazy Horse slid from his horse on top of the miner, crushing his skull with a single strike of his war club.

Crazy Horse was aware of Lone Bear dismounting and rushing forward to his right, slashing the throat of another miner who stood there for an instant, eyes wide in the horror of his own death. The miner fell forward onto his knees, and Lone Bear drove his knife deep into the man's heart. After a moment, Lone Bear pushed the miner backward to separate the dead man from the blade.

Two more of the miners died beside the fire, both too sluggish from whiskey even to fire their guns before the Oglala cut them down.

Two of the miners attempted to flee on foot, and Crazy Horse saw with satisfaction that Little Hawk was one of the warriors who rode them down. As he watched, Little Hawk lifted the scalp from one of the men, holding it skyward and crying out in elation. Crazy Horse saw that Cattoire too was dead by the fire and felt no regret. All of the white men now lay dead.

Not even the gunfire was enough to rouse two of the Cheyenne from their drunken stupor, but the two others staggered to their feet, barely able to stand, let alone resist. Lone Bear raised his knife but paused, looking questioningly toward Crazy Horse.

Crazy Horse shook his head. He stepped forward, pushing the Cheyenne back onto the ground. "Is this the character of the Cheyenne?" He began to whip at them with his quirt. "You betray your fathers . . . You bring shame on your people!" The men held up their arms in a pathetic attempt to block the quirt but made no effort to fight back. Finally, Crazy Horse's anger changed to pity, and he turned away from the Cheyenne cowering on the ground.

Some of the Oglala had climbed aboard the wagons and began to throw off the cargo: barrels of whiskey and bacon, calico cloth, mirrors, pots, tin cups . . . Crazy Horse had no need for these goods from the white man, but he was pleased to see a crate filled with pistols and several kegs of gunpowder.

Little Hawk rode up beside him, the miner's scalp held high as he shouted his war cry into the night. Little Hawk looked to his brother, and

Crazy Horse nodded at him in satisfaction, happy for his brother to join the ranks of the warriors.

The others too yelled and sang out. Crazy Horse did not join them, just as he did not take scalps. It was fine for the others to do so. Not only did he not begrudge them—he understood the combination of rage and elation that sparked their actions. But the Creator had spoken to him, explained that the path he must walk would be different from the others. Crazy Horse knew that the Creator would protect him in battle, keep him safe from the white man's bullets, but the cost of that protection was humility. Crazy Horse must not sing his own praises, must not seek out the trophies of the battlefield. Such was the balance demanded of him, and Crazy Horse accepted it as the core of who he was.

Suddenly, they heard the sound of a child's cry and a woman pleading in Cheyenne. Crazy Horse turned to see Fast Otter at the door of Cattoire's tent. Cattoire's wife spilled out, whimpering and trying desperately to shield two small children. "Please no!" she cried.

Fast Otter pushed her to the ground. "You're white now—whatever the color of your skin."

He raised his war club to strike her, but Crazy Horse called out, "No!"

Fast Otter stopped, turning to look at Crazy Horse.

"No, brother," said Crazy Horse.

All of them heard a low groan behind them and became aware of a form moving along the ground at the edge of the camp. Crazy Horse saw that it was the miner with the red beard, still alive, crawling slowly toward the wagon. Crazy Horse walked to him, the crackling firelight casting distorted shadows that rose and fell sporadically with the flames. The miner continued to crawl away, almost to the wagon when Crazy Horse reached his side.

Crazy Horse reached down and flipped the man on his back. The miner stared up in terror, blood seeping down from the matted mass of his dark hair. With one hand, Crazy Horse grabbed a thick fist of hair and dragged the man up to a seated position, so that his back rested against one of the wheels on the wagon. A piece of rope hung from the wagon box, and Crazy Horse used it to lash the man to the wheel. The miner struggled at first, but Crazy Horse tied him tightly.

Crazy Horse raised his war club to full height, arcing it downward against one of the barrels that had been tossed off the wagon. The barrel cracked open at the blow, and he struck it several more times so that its contents spilled onto the prairie floor—salted pork, greasy and slick and oozing. Crazy Horse picked up the barrel and dumped a great mass of the pork onto the miner's lap. Then Crazy Horse grabbed a smaller barrel. He broke open this barrel, too, and poured the contents, grain alcohol, on the miner, soaking him from head to foot and filling the night air with the pungent scent.

Crazy Horse turned and saw that all the Lakota now stood watching. He walked to the fire and pulled from it a flaming torch. Several times today he had forced himself to channel his anger, but not now.

He raised the torch. "With all our might, we'll fight to drive the white man from our home," said Crazy Horse. "And each time we strike, we'll make them all afraid of their fate." The Lakota raised their fists to the sky and shouted their war cries as Crazy Horse tossed the torch onto the miner. The white man screamed, first at the realization and then at the excruciating reality of the flames enveloping his body.

They left one of the tents standing, the Cheyenne woman and her children huddled beside it. Everything else they burned.

The next day, in the light, they studied the new pistols and struggled to understand their workings. They knew that the guns could fire multiple times without reloading, and before long they had deciphered the mechanism beneath the barrel that tamped down the powder and ball into the six revolving chambers. It was like a miniature version of a muzzle-loading rifle, but all six chambers could be loaded in advance.

The more his friends understood about the workings of the guns, the more elated they became. *What power!* True, Fast Otter carelessly let the hammer slip as he examined the loading mechanism and shot off the lower piece of his ear. They all laughed at that, then treated the pistols with slightly more care. Mostly, though, they imagined what being able to fire six times without reloading would do to their ability to fight at close quarters. They began shooting the guns, pleased with the accuracy compared to the cumbersome old single-shots that some of them possessed.

Only Crazy Horse seemed displeased, sitting apart from the others and continuing to study the weapon.

"What's the matter, brother?" asked Little Hawk. "Isn't it amazing?"

It is amazing. Crazy Horse had always felt wonderment at the mechanics of guns, but this represented something wholly different. Crazy Horse turned the cylinder of his new pistol and heard the tight clicks as each chamber locked in place—precisely aligned for the ball to pass through the barrel. The metal was as smooth as a stone from the riverbed, yet devoid of any irregularity. He thought of their efforts—never successful—to find perfectly straight willow branches to make arrows. And while each of their arrows was different from the others, each of these pistols was exactly the same, identical even in the smallest detail.

It's more than amazing—it's inexplicable. The enemy they faced had learned to harness forces that Crazy Horse did not understand. He had always marveled at the tools of the whites, the materials and the precision. But it was one thing to contemplate how they might have fabricated a sewing needle . . . the durability of a cooking pot . . . the perfect reflection in a mirror. This weapon put their power in a whole new light.

It was good that he and his friends now had these pistols, though Crazy Horse worried, as he always did, at how they would procure the ammunition. Another dependency. And what would it mean to face soldiers who also possessed these weapons—along with all the ammunition they needed? What if the rumors were true of rifles that could also fire many times? Crazy Horse imagined the power of an army of soldiers with such guns. While Crazy Horse appreciated the happiness of his brother and friends, he could not share in it.

JULY 21, 1866

The others were not surprised when Crazy Horse was gone from camp in the morning. His brother and friends all knew that there would be days when he simply disappeared without warning, just as there would be a day when he would return without explanation. Over the years, they had learned to carry on in his times of absence and not to worry.

Crazy Horse had already covered many miles by the time the first hint of sun appeared behind him across the eastern plain, just a glow at first, the faintest glimmer of hope that night would surrender to day. A while later, the sun would make more evident its imminent arrival, no longer a mere glow but, rather, piercing streaks of light that lit up the clouds on the horizon with colors as vivid as meadow flowers. Before long, the first birds would begin singing out to welcome the day, but before they awakened, Crazy Horse had always been amazed that a space as vast as the prairie could be so silent, as if he were the only living thing in all the world, or at least that this one moment had been set aside for him to contemplate in all-encompassing peace. Eventually the sun itself appeared, and each time, Crazy Horse would feel thankful for its seeping warmth. Even the summer nights on the plains carried a chill as a reminder of the bone-penetrating cold, never too distant.

While Crazy Horse paused to appreciate the sun, his horse drank deeply from a creek too small to have a name in the tribe. He and Lone Bear called it Fat Calf Creek, from a boyhood hunt when they first had been allowed to go away on their own. Crazy Horse had shot an elk calf, and the two boys had lived off of it for a week while they explored up the creek to its source in the Shining Mountains. The creek started small, little more than a trickle seeping from the side of a rocky face beside a green mountain meadow. They had discovered a cave on the face of the same outcropping, and had sheltered there as comfortable as a pack of wolves.

So far as Crazy Horse knew, he and Lone Bear were the only members of their tribe who knew about this place, and Lone Bear had never gone back. Crazy Horse had returned several times, and he made the cave his destination today. He was relieved, late that afternoon, to find the cave as he remembered it, the rest of the world so dissembled that he took nothing for granted. There was even firewood left in a sheltered pile from his last visit. Before dark, he shot a duck, cooking it over a small fire that soon filled the cave with the scent of roasting meat. For a moment, at least, he felt the comfort of this haven.

Crazy Horse pulled bits of the meat from the duck as it roasted and forced himself to eat them, knowing he needed the sustenance. He was never hungry at times such as this, when his whole being attempted to see a path through the thick fog of the landscape before him.

There were mysterious drawings on the wall of the cave. Crazy Horse remembered that he and Lone Bear had studied them and wondered who had left them. The colors were faded with age, smudged black from the smoke of many fires, and the style was different from any they had seen among the Lakota or any other tribe.

He added a large piece of wood to the fire, and the flames quickly swallowed the dry fuel, climbing and then reflecting off the walls of the cave in dancing, crimson light. Crazy Horse reached into his parfleche and removed the contents: a small, reddish-brown stone tied to a string; two hawk feathers; a tiny bag containing ground huckleberries, which when mixed with water formed a blueish dye. These things he arrayed precisely on a small rabbit skin that he laid out beside the fire. Then he said a quick prayer, asking the Creator for vision—for clarity and understanding.

As he lay and watched the dance of the flames, Crazy Horse thought again about the stories from the south. They had already known the horrible fate of Black Kettle's band of Southern Cheyenne, who had made the mistake two years ago of trusting the whites at their word.

This summer the Southern Cheyenne came with new stories, some so fantastic that at first, Crazy Horse had thought they could not be true. But High Backbone believed them, stories about the metal wagons that spit fire, about buffalo wiped away from the southern plains. Had Crazy Horse now not seen for himself the relentless and ruthless efficiency of the soldiers as they swarmed the valley surrounding their new fort? The weight of these thoughts pressed upon him, and he felt it as deep fatigue. For a while, Crazy Horse wondered if he was awake or asleep, but then he surrendered completely to the dream.

He stood alone on a high plateau and watched as a cloud billowed toward him, spreading outward to become larger and darker as it approached. With the cloud, there traveled sounds that seemed to emanate from thousands of places at once, yet the combined sensation was like a solid, moving wall. He became aware that he was no longer alone but, rather, in the Lakota village along the Tongue. He recognized individual faces of his people—and all of them looked up at the coming cloud, now so large that it blacked out the sun.

Suddenly, Crazy Horse felt something hit him in the face and cling to him, gripping as with tiny claws. He swiped at it, realizing it was a locust. Then other locusts began to fall from the sky, and it became apparent that the approaching cloud was a living thing, millions of locusts descending upon the village all around him. The insects began to consume the instant they touched the earth, devouring the tall grass and stripping every leaf from the cottonwoods and the willows along the creek. They covered the teepees and landed on the horses, causing the animals to panic and bolt. Dogs barked and parents cried out as the black cloud of locusts kept them from knowing the whereabouts of their children.

Crazy Horse ran toward his own family's lodge, desperate to find his parents and brother. The thick cloud obscured his vision, and he stumbled along, holding up a hand in a futile effort to block the locusts from striking him in the eyes and filling his mouth as he ran, onward and onward. Abruptly, he found himself at the top of a great hill with no sign of the village, the lodges, or his people. Indeed, all signs of the locust cloud had disappeared instantly, and Crazy Horse turned around, disoriented and bewildered, realizing that he stood on the ridgeline above the soldiers' fort. The contours of the valley, though familiar, had changed. The fort itself was a smoldering ruin, with no soldiers—no human beings—anywhere in sight.

As Crazy Horse surveyed the valley, he realized that not only the soldiers had disappeared. There remained no living thing, not a tree on a distant hillside, not a single blade of grass. A few willows still stood beside the creek, but only the brittle sticks of their stems, not even a flush of green.

He smelled smoke and found himself in the cave on Fat Calf Creek. The fire had burned down to a few crimson embers, emitting steady heat but little light in the cave. Outside, night had fallen. Crazy Horse closed his eyes, hoping he could return to the vision, hoping it would reveal not just the plague descending upon his people, but guidance on how he could fight it. Where had the whites gone? Where were his people? Was the horrible damage contained in the valley along the twin creeks, or did it extend beyond? He knew that answers to these questions were vital. Surely the Creator had not given him part of the vision only to leave the most essential aspects unrevealed.

For a long time he waited. Yet try as he might, Crazy Horse could not escape the confines of the cave, not even in his mind. Finally, the fire nearly dead, he became aware of the creeping cold. He rekindled the flames and added a fat log. In the small space, the fire should have been more than sufficient, but that night Crazy Horse could not escape the chill.

SAME DAY

Dear Journal,

Arrival a week ago at our new home, and thanks be to Providence for that! It was General Sherman himself who told us ladies to keep journals so that we could record for all posterity the history we would be living. And now it's the recommendation of my own husband that settles the location of the nation's newest outpost of civilization!

True enough that "civilization" is two tents stitched together with a canvas dogtrot in between. But the sawmill is already humming, and Colonel Carrington has promised Lt Grummond and me proper married officers' quarters before the frost sets in in earnest. With all the men at work every waking hour, who am I to doubt the Colonel's promise?

So for the time being we have a veritable city of tents, and though Mr. Bridger warns us that Red Cloud's Sioux are all about, we take comfort from the assurances of our men that no attack will come against so great a force. And of course our howitzers, gleaming brass in mid-summer sun, speak their own firm assurance!

A brief description of the valley we now call home . . . After nearly a month across the driest, most inhospitable desert, the character of the land in the days before our arrival began to change significantly. If not quite the land of Goshen, the valley selected by Lt Grummond is abundant in thick grass, timber, and good, clear water. Not one but two creeks flow off the distant Big Horn Mountains, one dubbed "Big Piney" and the other "Little Piney." Our herd of cattle finds ample feed at the far end of the valley, and to celebrate our arrival, the Colonel ordered a few slaughtered, though the bulk will be preserved of course to carry us through the long winter. The mountains themselves, perhaps ten miles to the west, are frightfully large, far more jagged and fierce than those in Tennessee, and with peaks so high as to still bear remnants of snow, despite the season.

The Colonel has placed our future fort on a gentle plateau, rising up from the valley so as to give our howitzers and riflemen full command of the field. For further vantage, a high hill to the southeast has been dubbed "Pilot Hill," atop which there's a lookout position with the vantage of a hawk, already a permanent outpost of sentinels able to scan the surrounding countryside in all directions. During the war, my husband and some of the other officers learned a system of signaling by flags that is practically an entire language to itself, and they are busy teaching this code to the others, so that soon our watchpost atop the hill will communicate with the officers below as if standing side by side.

At a distance of three miles from the fort, Big Piney splits around an island, teeming with timber, and it is from there that the wood for construction is procured. Work detachments of our soldiers chop and haul from dawn to dusk, and already the beginnings of our Gibraltar's walls stand erect, side-by-side logs sunk four feet into the ground and rising eleven feet above. Of course the protective wall is first priority, but crews of soldiers also feed a constant stream of logs to the sawmill, then stack the resulting lumber into great piles that promise a phase of the building that will soon begin to form the permanent buildings that we might more easily call "home."

I have done what little I can to make a tent seem an inviting place for Lt Grummond to return to at the end of his long days, even adding a few prairie flowers to a glass vase that has somehow managed to survive the trip unbroken. It is not surprising, of course, that the Lt barely notices such niceties. Like all the officers, he carries the heavy burden of responsibility for our safety in the midst of so dangerous a place.

I have not seen the Sioux yet myself, only the bands of friendly Cheyenne that ride in to trade bits of local information for coffee or sugar. Since arriving, though, we have all been witness to a disturbing sight—flashes of mirrors from ridge to distant ridge that Mr. Bridger tells us are the Sioux, speaking to each other in their own coded language—reporting, no doubt, our presence to Chief Red Cloud as he plots each day against us. While I know our brave men labor day and night, I can't help but yearn for the day when our wall is complete.

Signed and Attested,
Mrs. Lieutenant George W. Grummond

Frances Courtney Grummond set down her journal, a leatherbound book purchased from the Fort Laramie sutler, and turned the tiny key to lock it. Lieutenant Grummond had been angry about the price, reminding her again of the constraints of a junior officer's salary, but Frances had been firm about wanting the journal with the lock. When later she had gone back to the sutler's store alone, she had been careful to buy the second, identical journal using the secret reserve of cash given to her by her mother before she departed Tennessee. Frances tucked the first journal deep into her trunk and removed the second, unlocked it, and began to write.

Dear Friend,
I must report a terrible occurrence today. Around noontime a wagon arrived with a tarp covering its horrific cargo. A teamster pulled the tarp back to reveal the bodies of eight men, though it was not easy to tell it was men, so much had the savages done violence to them. They were naked and hacked at and riddled with arrows like pincushions. One had apparently been

burned alive, more a blackened skeleton than a corpse. For a moment I was unable to look away, my eyes repelled and yet locked on to these poor souls, so that I saw still other things had been done to these men, things so shocking and savage I cannot write of them, even here.

Mrs. Carrington says that the Colonel, while respectful of the dead, was critical of the judgment of any men traveling through this country without military protection. The Colonel, she said, comforted her by explaining that the Sioux looked for their terrible opportunities among such naïve or foolish travelers, whereas they had no choice but to respect the obvious strength of a battalion of the United States Army. I want to give full trust, of course, to the military judgment of our leader, but I must confess to a sense of foreboding that I cannot shake.

My husband too tells me to set such thoughts aside and to trust in the judgment of the men as to our safety. And yet, Friend, can I tell you that he gives me new reasons each day to question my trust in him?

It is not his drinking in and of itself that gives me such pause and concern, though I am coming to dread his late-night entry to our tent. Mrs. Carrington says that the Colonel won't touch a drop, though I know from the other wives that the Colonel is the exception rather than the rule, even among the officers. My own dear father loved his bourbon, and I remember well my mother's counsel to give some leeway to men for such things, however foolish.

What worries me most is not the Lt's drinking, in and of itself, but rather that he would lie to me about it so nakedly. Is his regard for my intelligence so low? And if he can lie so easily about something so obviously untrue, what can I trust in the other things he tells me?

Now thousands of miles from my Tennessee home, I feel keenly aware of the full gravity of my decision to marry. I will work to keep my faith in the Providence that I remain sure has led me to this place, but I must confess to a doubt that gnaws at me. All the more so now, as I am keenly aware that my responsibility is not only for myself, but also for the child that I am now certain I carry.

Sincerely Yours,
Frances

SAME DAY

Two orderlies cleared the dinner plates from the table set inside the large tent that served, until the permanent structure could be built, as the officers' mess. Colonel Carrington had assembled Jim Bridger and his three officers without the wives that night, wanting to devote the discussion to the business of the fort. For two hours he had worked his way through an extended list involving every detail of the construction, dispersing tasks for the week to follow. The two captains—Fetterman and Ten Eyck—already had received their orders, and the colonel focused the remaining tasks on Lieutenant Grummond.

"Are we clear then, Lieutenant?" asked the colonel.

"Clear, sir," replied Grummond. "My cavalrymen are responsible, again, for chopping wood."

There was petulance in the lieutenant's tone, so much so that Captains Fetterman and Ten Eyck looked up sharply, exchanged a glance, then looked to Colonel Carrington for his reaction. Fetterman could see that Grummond's tone irritated the colonel.

"Do you have something you wish to say, Lieutenant Grummond?" asked Colonel Carrington. Carrington adjusted his posture to sit more upright, presumably to project greater strength. Instead, the movement emphasized that his jacket was mis-sized, too big in the epaulet-draped shoulders, as if it was a hand-me-down that he had not yet grown to fill.

"No, sir," said Lieutenant Grummond. "Of course my men and I are ready and eager to accept any task. It's just that, well, with eight civilians massacred and desecrated only yesterday . . . within a stone's throw of our position . . . I just thought that my cavalry ought to be out running them down—making the savages pay."

Jim Bridger made no effort to stifle a dismissive snort. He had been skeptical of the officers since meeting them at Fort Laramie. While most—with the notable exception of the colonel—had experience in fighting, none of them had fought Indians.

"The Indians who killed those miners ain't within fifty miles of here anymore," said Bridger. Grummond's face reddened in anger and he started to say something, but Bridger wasn't done. "You could gallop around with your pretty cavalry for a month, Lieutenant, and you'd still never find 'em."

"Isn't that why the army pays you all that money?" said Grummond. "To use your *vast experience* to tell us where the Indians are?"

Fetterman watched Colonel Carrington struggle, recognizing that the conversation was going off track, but sputtering as he failed to synthesize his thoughts into words.

Captain Ten Eyck had no such trouble. "It's not your place, Lieutenant Grummond, to set strategy."

Colonel Carrington raised a hand, as if attempting physically to rein the conversation back under his control. "Hold on . . . our priority—not to mention our orders—is the construction of the fort. Once we have the safety of the fort as our foundation, then we can focus more on projecting our power outward."

Fetterman noticed that Colonel Carrington kept glancing toward Grummond as he spoke, almost as if he were playing to him.

"Now, of course, as commanding officer, I'm giving constant thought to our broader military position," said Carrington. "That's why I've decided"—Carrington spoke haltingly, seeming to arrive at conclusions just prior to announcing them—"to dispatch our scouts, Mr. Bridger and Mr. Beckwourth . . . on an important mission."

Bridger looked up, clearly hearing about this plan for the first time.

"Obviously we need to know the whereabouts of our enemy," said Carrington. "I need you to locate Red Cloud and his tribe and report back to me. I assume there's not that many places to hide a whole tribe of Sioux."

"Well, I doubt they're hiding," said Bridger. "But here's the rub. I know the army likes to believe the Sioux are one tribe led by one leader—like Red Cloud is the king of England or something—and I guess that would be convenient. But that ain't how the Indians work. In this part of the country, the Sioux are actually two tribes, the Oglala—that's Red Cloud—and the Minnicoujou. And Red Cloud isn't even lord of the Oglala. Each of those tribes is broken down into a whole bunch of bands made up of a dozen or so families. They might come together sometimes, if they're at war or for the big fall hunt, but otherwise they're spread all over creation, mostly doing what they please in any given season."

Bridger had their attention and seemed to be working himself up. "And that's just the Sioux. This country is also home to the Northern Cheyenne and the Arapaho. The Southern Cheyenne are coming up from the south to get away from the settlement and fighting in Colorado. Go a bit west and it's the Shoshone. Go north and it's the Crow. The Shoshone and the Crow, by the way, are enemies of the Sioux and Cheyenne. And don't assume the Southern Cheyenne will act the same way as the Northern Cheyenne."

There was silence for a moment.

Carrington rubbed persistently at the back of his neck. "Well," he said after a while. "I suppose you could put it all into some type of a . . . map."

Silence once again fell over the group, and Captain Fetterman felt it acutely. He always wondered, in such moments, if it was incumbent upon him to say something. His mind raced in an effort to conjure up an appropriate insight, or at least an intelligent question to move the discussion along. Finally, he asked, "Anything in the dispatches today about when we can expect the rifles and horses we've been promised?"

Colonel Carrington shifted uncomfortably. "No . . . to my great irritation—as you all know well."

After another brief spell of silence, Carrington finally pushed back his chair, looking at Grummond. "Well, Lieutenant Grummond, as the other married man, you'll appreciate that I still have affairs to tend to this evening on the home front."

"Yes, sir," said Grummond. "A married man has two jobs."

Colonel Carrington offered a perfunctory chortle as he gathered his hat and departed from the tent. They could hear him as he walked away across the parade grounds.

For a while, no one said anything. Eventually Captain Ten Eyck produced a pipe and began to pack the bowl. The others followed suit, and soon the sweet aroma of pipe smoke mixed with the crisp night air that circulated from the tent's open ends.

After a furtive glance in the direction where the colonel had disappeared, Lieutenant Grummond pulled a whiskey flask from the pocket of his jacket, uncorked it, and lifted it in the direction of the other men. "To the Second Battalion." Ten Eyck might not have agreed with Grummond on much, but both men liked their liquor. Ten Eyck produced his own flask, raising it before tipping back a hard slug. Grummond held out his flask to Fetterman. "Thank God for the teamsters."

Masking his irritation, Fetterman accepted the flask from Grummond and raised it. "To the Second . . ." Fetterman wasn't a heavy drinker, but neither was he a prig. He had seen the effects of liquor on many men during the war, enough to make him cautious. It wasn't the whiskey that bothered Fetterman, in any event. It was Grummond's presumptuousness. As the junior officer among two captains, he should have waited for a signal from one of his superiors before producing the liquor.

It was part of a pattern Fetterman had noticed since the end of the war—the ranks all jumbled up. Every officer in the battalion had held a higher rank during the war. Colonel Carrington had been a lieutenant general. All the captains had been lieutenant colonels. True, they were brevet ranks, an honorary designation during time of war. The US Army had been drastically reduced when the war ended, and their ranks reduced along with it. Everyone understood that, but it was always hard to go backward in matters of status. Once accustomed to being called "colonel," it felt strange to go back to answering to "captain."

Grummond had been a lieutenant colonel too. Fetterman didn't know for what reason he had been pushed down to the even lower rank of lieutenant, though there were rumors. Whatever the case, it was still the army, frontier or not. Rank still mattered, and custom. And custom was to await the signal of the superior officers in the room.

Grummond stared at Fetterman as if the captain's interior thoughts were stamped in newsprint across his forehead. Then Grummond took another long swig, almost challenging. Again he offered his flask to Fetterman. Fetterman started to refuse but then accepted. *Perhaps, on the frontier, some allowance must be made.* He took a drink and then handed the flask to Bridger.

Grummond looked at the open ends of the tent, making sure the orderlies were out of earshot, then spoke in hushed tones. "Two hours and barely an utterance on anything remotely military!"

Captain Ten Eyck tugged at his collar, his face red. "You signed up for this," he said. "We do what we're ordered."

"I signed up to be a soldier," said Grummond. "If I wanted to run a sawmill, I'd find a civilian job and make three times the money."

"Your cavalry won't have horses to ride on if we can't keep our stock inside the safety of a fort," said Fetterman. "We need a base of operation."

"I'm surprised that's what you think," said Grummond. "With your background in the war—you're a real fighting man."

Fetterman paused a moment before answering. "This isn't the same war."

"That's true," said Grummond. "Our enemy is far less worthy."

"I wasn't aware that you had fought against the Sioux," said Bridger.

"I didn't make that claim," said Grummond. "But I've done plenty of fighting. And I don't need to have fought the Sioux to know you don't win wars by hiding behind the walls of a fort."

"There'll be plenty of time to fight," said Fetterman. "We establish the fort as our base. In the spring the army will reinforce us with the numbers to take the offensive, not to mention better weapons."

Captain Ten Eyck's eagerness to play cards ultimately diverted the officers from further debate. Captain Fetterman took early leave that night. Fetterman had no more moral qualm with gambling than he did with drinking, but he was tired and felt the need to clear his head before sleeping. As he walked alone toward the barbican, he could feel the whiskey. He wasn't drunk, but his thoughts seemed to flow without the restraints he usually managed to place upon them.

Grummond's criticism of Colonel Carrington left Captain Fetterman feeling deeply conflicted. Fetterman knew, of course, that complaining about superior officers was the army's favorite leisure activity. Nothing unusual in that. And true enough, Carrington was not a fighting man. Yet Fetterman had known Carrington well during the war, had even been social friends with Carrington and his wife. It felt wrong to talk about him behind his back. Besides, not every man in the army distinguished himself in battle. There were many missions in war, and Carrington had accomplished dutifully every task ever given to him. His mission today was to build a fort. The mission of the junior officers was to support their commanding officer, not to undermine him.

Fetterman climbed the ladder to the upper platform of the barbican, and the two privates on guard duty snapped to attention, saluting.

The captain returned the salute. "At ease, men. All quiet?"

"Only wolves and coyotes, sir—feeding on the slaughterhouse scraps."

Fetterman filled his pipe and lit it. For him, night was the most beautiful time on the prairie. Never in his life had he seen such skies. Fetterman had been born and raised in Connecticut, and had fought his way across the eastern half of the country during the war. There were stars in the east, of course. But eastern horizons were hemmed close in hills and trees, the air itself screening the night sky with humid thickness. On the prairie, the vistas seemed endless, horizons broken only by distant mountains, or by nothing at all, extending until the eye could no longer perceive. And the air out west, so dry that it smelled of heat and dust during the day, was wholly different at night. Temperatures might plunge fifty degrees between dusk and dawn, the air pure and crisp, creating no filter at all between earth and sky. On nights of full moon, there was no need for lanterns, the whole world lit up in gentle glow. On nights with no moon, such as this one, the stars seemed to sense that it was their moment to command the sky without competition. Certainly they rose to the task.

Captain Fetterman wished that he might focus solely on the resplendent sky, but night was the time when other thoughts, other memories, seemed always to invade. While the night air on the plains was sweet, it carried hints of the sage that grew everywhere, and for Fetterman, the smell of sage evoked cedar.

They had dug into cedar forests at the Battle of Stones River, their orders to block the Rebel advance at all cost. The forest concealing them was so dense that it seemed impossible the Rebels could penetrate their line. Outward-facing artillery at the edge of the forest meant that the attacking Confederates had to cross a half mile of open ground in full exposure to withering case and grapeshot, like walking into the muzzles of giant shotguns. Still, they came, and in such numbers that some actually managed to breach the Union line. Into the thick forest they spilled, and Fetterman remembered the panicked and confused fighting that followed. They stood and fought despite the terror. There was no time for reloading guns, so they bludgeoned and hacked at one another with bayonets and swords and rifle butts. Fetterman could still feel the sheer desperation, the sense that he was instants away from death. Almost as powerful, though, was his memory of the men he had killed. There was no abstraction in such battle—no faceless form crumpling to the ground at long distance. At Stones River they fought face-to-face, and Fetterman had looked into the eyes of the men he killed—men who seemed suddenly, painfully human in the horror of their own deaths.

When the Battle of Stones River was over, half of Fetterman's men were dead or wounded, and the same on the Confederate side, the highest casualty rates of any battle in the Civil War. Fetterman received the first of his brevet promotions—for gallantry. His father had sent him a letter of congratulations, the only time in his life that Fetterman could remember receiving praise from the old man. Fetterman kept the letter in an old cigar box along with his Civil War medals and a daguerreotype of his mother. He took the letter out and reread it often, and one day there came a moment when, as he read the letter yet again, he experienced a sad moment of clarity—the part of him that craved such praise was stronger than the part of him that resented his need to hear it.

And so Captain Fetterman accepted the postwar reduction in rank and went off to fight Indians on the frontier. As he had in the war between the states, he would do his duty, endeavor to lend his experience to the defense of his nation and the well-being of his men. Perhaps he could distinguish himself again.

A shooting star flashed suddenly across the sky. Fetterman and the two privates watched as it flared brightly like a flaming arrow across the inky backdrop before disappearing as quickly as it had appeared.

"Crazy thing," said one of the privates, his Irish accent thick as old country fog. "They been shootin' off all night."

Crazy thing. It added to the sense of wonder that Fetterman felt about this new place where he found himself, but also to the profound feeling that this was a land that was foreign and unknown. "Don't be too distracted, Private," he said.

Captain Fetterman took the last draw of his pipe before tapping the bowl. Tobacco was one of the few luxuries he allowed himself, and the calming ritual of a pipe at night helped him to sleep. He took one last look at Ursa Major and used it to find the North Star. He knew full well where north lay, but confirmation felt comforting. In a dizzying world, it was good to be moored.

Part Two

AUGUST 14, 1866

As Colonel Carrington surveyed the perimeter of the fort, it irritated him again that they had been unable to lay it out along a perfect north-south axis. He had loved the idea of bringing full cardinal precision to their enterprise, but alas, the rise upon which they logically must build forced another concession to the land. Still, as Carrington stood with his own hand-drawn plans spread out on the field table in front of him, surrounded by frenzied work parties of soldiers and civilians, it was hard not to feel a deep sense of satisfaction.

A gust of wind suddenly blew the plans off the table, and Private Archibald Sample, Carrington's aide-de-camp, scrambled to pick them up, quickly replacing the papers and stacking them neatly. Ever resourceful, Private Sample located four fist-sized stones and placed them on the corners of the papers as a defense against more wind, which always seemed to pick up in the afternoon.

Most of the ideas for the perfect fort that Carrington had been imagining for months survived in the plans that now lay before him. Even more gratifying, of course, was the sight of the actual structure, rising up from the ground all around him in glorious, physical reality.

The entire perimeter was now complete, a defensive wall of logs rising eleven feet into the air. Its four sides created an enormous interior space of seventeen acres. Captain Ten Eyck reported that four thousand logs had been cut for the wall, and half that many again, so far, for their supply of lumber. The two barbicans already rose an additional ten feet

above the wall, one at the westernmost corner and the other at the east-
ernmost, set diagonally across the parade grounds so that between the
two of them they commanded the horizon for 360 degrees. The barbicans had been built to accommodate two howitzers each in addition to
sharpshooters.

Within the fort's walls, Carrington built the heart of his design
around a perfectly square parade grounds, reserving a place in the center
for a giant flagpole to be erected as soon as more urgent needs had been
met. The future officers' quarters would stand along one side of the
parade grounds, infantry barracks along another, with a third side occupied by the quarters for the band, the guardhouse, and a large general
store. The far end of the fort's interior space was reserved for cavalry and
teamsters, with plans for stables so that all of their horses could be kept
safe inside, away from thieving Indians.

If there was one small cloud in the otherwise blue sky of Carrington's
mood, it was the new name of the fort, the directive for which had arrived
the day before along with other dispatches from Fort Laramie. General
Sherman had decided that the nation's newest military outpost was to be
called Fort Philip Kearny, in honor of the famous officer of the Mexican and Civil wars. Carrington knew well the general's history—a one-
armed cavalryman who rode into battle with his sword in his one hand
and the reins of his horse in his teeth. Carrington was keenly aware that
Kearny was precisely the kind of officer whom the junior officers revered
and emulated, and indeed they all had been strongly approving of the
name. Carrington also knew that his own skills were far different from
those of a man like Kearny, and each utterance of the fort's name would
be a small reminder of that fact.

Well, no matter. As Carrington watched, a crew stacked a fresh pile
of lumber from the sawmill, and it filled his heart anew at the potential.
It may not be named for me—but it's my fort. Of that, who could doubt
Carrington was right?

As the colonel stood on that hot afternoon and watched his fort rise
around him, it required little imagination for him to see into the future.
This little valley in front of the Big Horns, with its gushing mountain
water, would be ideal for farms and ranches. Carrington had not yet
explored to the north, but Bridger reported many more such lush valleys

along many more mountain creeks. Surely, once the Indian threat was removed, settlers would come to this land, carrying with them their sense of ambition and their multitude improvements. Already the railroad had reached Topeka, and once the rails took the place of the Oregon Trail, even a place as remote as Fort Philip Kearny might be connected to the rest of the country.

How many great cities back east had origins as military outposts? Surely the Wyoming Territory would one day be a state. Why not Fort Phil Kearny as a state capital? If Carrington could not quite envision a great eastern city spilling off this plateau, it wasn't hard to imagine a sizeable town, with churches and schools and streets—streets laid out on perfect north-south lines! Perhaps the good townsfolk might one day name the main thoroughfare Carrington Boulevard. After all, wasn't he the founding father? For a moment, the colonel imagined himself and Mrs. Carrington returning in their old age, receiving a key to the city and delivering a well-attended speech about the wild days of taming the Indians and carving civilization from wilderness.

"Colonel! Colonel Carrington!"

It took Carrington an instant to focus back on the present day.

"Colonel Carrington!" The speaker was Private Sample, but as Carrington looked around, he also saw that Lieutenant Grummond and Captain Ten Eyck were rushing his way. "Look at Pilot Hill!" yelled Sample. "They're signaling attack!"

Carrington looked to the top of Pilot Hill, where indeed the flagman signaled wildly. *Damn it!* Carrington had yet to master the code.

Suddenly, they all heard the sound. A few scattered gunshots, yes, though the shots were barely audible against a deeper rumble from the west of Piney Creek Valley, a rumble they also could feel, vibrating upward from the earth itself.

It seemed like a wild idea when Little Hawk first suggested it. Crazy Horse and his war party had been so focused on the soldiers' cattle herd in the valley below them that they had paid little attention to the two hundred or so buffalo grazing placidly to their rear. "What if we stampede the buffalo into the cattle?"

A half-dozen civilians tended the cattle, slouched like old men on their horses in the afternoon heat, with only a couple of actual soldiers in the near vicinity. When Crazy Horse had first looked over to the hillside from which the whites took their timber, he had forced himself to push down his anger once again and to fight against the instinct to attack the main force of soldiers, who continued to hack away with their axes and teams of mules. In the time since the whites arrived, half of the distant hillside had been stripped bare of trees, ugly stumps left behind like ghostly footprints of the forest that had been.

In the distance, they could also see where the soldiers had carried the trees. An enormous log wall now rose up to encircle the village of white tents on the rise above Little Buffalo Creek.

The more Crazy Horse contemplated Little Hawk's idea, the more he began to think it might work. In fact, the more it began to seem like perfect justice. After a bit more reflection, Crazy Horse nodded his head. They crept back from the ridgeline to where two Oglala held the horses, then circled wide, half to the west of the buffalo and half to the east. Half an hour later, they had positioned themselves so that the buffalo herd stood between them and the cattle in the distant valley.

"Kill any white man who stands in your way," said Crazy Horse. "But today our quarry is the cattle. Drive them away, and we'll see how the soldiers fare with no food."

Rising up from his horse's back and raising his new Colt revolver high in the air, Crazy Horse unleashed his war cry. Then he fired a shot. The other Lakota picked up his cry and fired their new pistols as Crazy Horse dug his heels into his horse's flanks and charged toward the buffalo.

Crazy Horse knew well how to anticipate the movement of buffalo. It was always the old cows on the edges that first took notice of the charging riders. They bellowed and stamped to warn the other animals, and soon, like a great robe unfurling, the motion at the perimeter rippled toward the opposite end until the whole mass was in flight. The valley was thick with grass, yet in the dryness of the late-summer heat, the animals kicked up great quantities of dust. In a matter of instants, the mounted Oglala found themselves enveloped in the stampeding herd—and blinded by the dust.

Crazy Horse had no choice in the mayhem but to rely on his horse.

He gripped with both knees and one hand, using his free hand to hold tight to his new revolver. He'd caught a brief glimpse of Little Hawk and a few of the others in the last yards before they merged into the herd, but now, with the dust, it was impossible to tell anyone's location. He felt his pony laboring and realized that they were climbing toward the ridgeline, with the valley of the Twin Creeks on the other side. Suddenly a big bull careened in beside him, the animal's flank brushing against his horse so that Crazy Horse's leg came into full contact with the great beast. By instinct, Crazy Horse focused on the place above the bull's foreleg where he would place the kill shot, and it seemed strange not to be looking at the animals as prey. Today they found themselves in common cause, an alliance against the invaders of their home.

He still could see little beyond the terrain immediately around his horse, but Crazy Horse felt his mount crest the ridgeline, then accelerate, almost falling downward into the valley below. He could not yet see the cattle herd, but he heard scattered shots in front of him. The whites, he surmised, were firing their guns in an effort to turn the stampeding buffalo before they crashed into the cattle. But then Crazy Horse saw something that made clear the whites would not succeed: the cattle, mixed in among the buffalo. Soon there were dozens of cattle, and then what seemed like hundreds, and then a moment arrived when the cattle far outnumbered the buffalo. Whether buffalo or cattle, though, all of them were caught up in the stampede, careening to the southeast and away from the valley where they had been placidly grazing only minutes before.

Suddenly, from the billowing dust, a mounted white man emerged. He had lost his reins, gripping desperately to his horse's mane. Crazy Horse nudged his mount to come up alongside the man, a civilian, and when the white man realized that Crazy Horse was beside him, his eyes went wide in terror. Crazy Horse leveled his pistol and fired. The white man yelled out as the bullet ripped into his shoulder and caused him to lose his grip. As Crazy Horse watched, only a few yards away, the man lost his balance and tumbled to the ground. He caught a glimpse of the man's body bouncing off the ground before disappearing beneath the pounding hooves of the herd.

On and on they rode. When it appeared, on a couple of occasions, that the herd might be slowing, Crazy Horse or one of the other Oglala fired his pistol, providing fresh impetus to the stampeding animals. There were a few shots behind them at first, but those faded away, and as the raiders rode on, they finally spread out enough to see through the dust. Crazy Horse pulled his mount to a halt, looking back and around him. He caught a glimpse of Little Hawk and began to count the other warriors, breathing a sigh of relief when he could account for all of his party.

Lone Bear rode up smiling and then let loose his war cry. When he reached Crazy Horse's side, he smiled again. "Hope Little White Chief has lots of barrels of bacon."

"We have to pursue them, Colonel!" said Lieutenant Grummond. "We're losing time!"

Colonel Carrington stood with Grummond, Captain Ten Eyck, and Jim Bridger on top of the western barbican. Carrington peered through a field glass toward upper Little Piney Creek. What he could see most clearly was a great cloud of dust. What he could not see any longer was his herd of cattle.

Colonel Carrington lowered the field glass and looked at his officers. Grummond's brashness made the colonel uncomfortable, yet he did not feel a strong instinct of his own. "What do you think, Captain Ten Eyck?"

Ten Eyck pondered. "It's most of our winter food supply out there."

Grummond jumped back in. "It's not just about cows, Colonel. We need to show them we won't let them attack with no response."

Carrington looked at Bridger, who hadn't said anything the whole time. Bridger reached out for Carrington's field glass, and the colonel handed it to him. Bridger took a long time with the glass, until finally Carrington interrupted him. "Well, Mr. Bridger, what's your view?"

"Well, you won't need a bloodhound to track 'em, that's for sure. But you won't bring many of those cows back unless you send a lot of men."

"I can't afford to send a lot of men," said Carrington.

Grummond scoffed. "It's a small band of thieves! Give us a dozen cavalry and we'll bring back what's ours."

Lone Bear called out to catch Crazy Horse's attention, then pointed behind them. Crazy Horse reined his horse and pivoted to look back. A few hundred yards away were a dozen riders, their blue uniforms apparent, two ahead of the others, including one on a striking white horse. Crazy Horse studied the soldiers a moment before they dipped out of sight below a crest of the rolling hills. About half of the other warriors stopped, too, including Fast Otter and Pemmican, forming up in a loose cluster around Crazy Horse and Lone Bear. Little Hawk was the last to join them, loping up on his calico pony. The remaining warriors, farther advanced, continued to press the cattle herd, well ahead, into the open prairie beyond.

Crazy Horse pulled the revolver from his belt and tipped it to check the chambers. He had fired three times during the stampede, leaving three shots.

"Why are we stopping?" asked Lone Bear.

Crazy Horse pointed to the pursuing soldiers. "Doesn't it enrage you?" he asked. "To see them pursuing us—as if it is them chasing us from *their home*? Doesn't it enrage you to *run away from them*?"

"You know that's not how it is," said Lone Bear. "You know what Red Cloud said—that for the time being we chip away."

The two lead soldiers appeared again at the crest of a hill, now barely a hundred yards away. The rest of the soldiers—ten of them—also appeared at the hilltop. This trailing group halted, and one of them, maybe another officer, seemed to yell after the two men out in front, but they barreled ahead. As Crazy Horse watched, the soldier on the white horse drew his sword from its sheath and waved it above his head, as if throwing down a challenge.

Crazy Horse tucked his pistol into his belt, pulling out his war club. He noticed that Little Hawk stared at him intently, mimicking his move and pulling out his own war club.

"What are you doing?" asked Lone Bear. "You said yourself our task today is to destroy their supply of winter food." He pointed to the last few cattle, disappearing over a distant ridge. "We're about to succeed."

Crazy Horse looked back and forth between the cattle and the two charging soldiers. "Follow the cows if you want." He pushed his heels into the flanks of his horse and charged toward the officer on the white horse.

Captain Ten Eyck crested the ridge and saw that a cluster of the fleeing Sioux had now turned, apparently ready to confront them. Lieutenant Grummond and Private Cassidy continued to charge toward the Indians. Infuriated that Grummond and the other trooper had broken ranks with the rest of the detachment, Ten Eyck yelled after him to stop, but Grummond either couldn't hear or ignored him.

At the top of a ridge and now less than a hundred yards from the Sioux, Ten Eyck reined his horse and called out to the others to halt. "Dismount and form a skirmish line!" he yelled. "Walsh and Schmidt—hold the mounts!" Privates Walsh and Schmidt quickly gathered the reins of the other cavalrymen's horses and pulled the animals behind them. Freed of their horses, meanwhile, the eight remaining troopers fanned out into a line, a few yards between them, each dropping to a knee and aiming their rifle at the Sioux now charging toward Lieutenant Grummond and Private Cassidy.

Private Cassidy heard Ten Eyck's yell and turned his head to see the other troopers halted back on the ridge, forming into a skirmish line. He turned back to yell at Grummond, aware of the Indians now charging toward them. Before Cassidy could call out, Lieutenant Grummond heard the sound of pistol shots and saw an eruption of blood as Cassidy's forehead exploded. Grummond watched as the private tumbled to the ground.

Crazy Horse was aware of Little Hawk to his right as he charged ahead, but mostly he focused on the soldier on the white horse, his waving sword capturing the sunlight so that it almost looked like a torch. The man was so close now that Crazy Horse could see the way a wisp of hair trailed down his chin from his lower lip. Their two horses careened directly toward each other, only a few yards separating them. Crazy Horse braced for the impact, but the white horse veered at the last moment as the soldier swung his sword.

Crazy Horse raised his war club to block the sword and felt the jar of direct impact as the blade struck the club, sinking into the wood. The two horses came into contact, but at an angle. Crazy Horse heard a guttural grunt from the soldier as he absorbed the force of collision, the two riders' momentum carrying them past each other. Both struggled to rein their mounts and turn them back around. Crazy Horse smelled the dust they kicked up and saw a sudden eruption of shots from the ridgeline. He heard Little Hawk cry out and turned to see his brother fall from his horse, violently striking the ground and then lying still. Little Hawk's horse galloped off.

Quickly Crazy Horse scanned the field and saw that not only Little Hawk was down. The soldiers' organized volley had killed Fast Otter's horse and blunted the advance of the other Oglala. Fast Otter struggled to pick himself up, and Pemmican raced back on his horse to help him. Crazy Horse gave a quick look toward the soldiers on the ridge. The officer with them shouted commands as they reloaded their rifles. In a few moments, there would be another volley.

The soldier on the white horse, meanwhile, struggled to control the big stallion as it crow-hopped amid the chaos and dust. Crazy Horse took advantage of the moment to rush to Little Hawk, leaping to the ground beside him while holding his horse's reins in one hand, afraid when he saw blood along his brother's side. *A flesh wound—or something worse?* It was impossible to tell without more careful examination. Little Hawk grimaced and attempted to rise, and Crazy Horse helped pull him to his feet. Crazy Horse leapt onto his horse, then reached down to drag Little Hawk up behind him. Crazy Horse had just turned his horse to retreat when he realized that the soldier on the white horse had recovered, was now aiming his pistol at them from a distance of barely ten yards. He couldn't miss. For a moment, Crazy Horse had the gut-punch sensation that his brother was about to die.

From amid the swirling dust, Lone Bear and his horse suddenly appeared, barreling into the soldier, though the officer managed to duck beneath a blow from Lone Bear's war club that might have been lethal. The white horse crow-hopped again, the soldier dropping his pistol as he struggled to regain control of his mount. The next volley of shots exploded from the ridgeline, and Crazy Horse heard the bullets as they screamed all around. Quickly, he checked to make sure that Little Hawk had not been hit again, but his brother's grip on his waist remained firm. Kicking his horse, Crazy Horse raced away, relieved to see Lone Bear, too, retreating.

Lieutenant Grummond stared after them as the last of the savages, the two mounted double, disappeared over the crest of a distant hill. He heard a rider approaching and turned to see Captain Ten Eyck, though the rest of the troopers remained up on the ridge.

"They're getting away!" said Grummond. "Why aren't we mounting up to pursue?"

Ten Eyck said nothing as he reined his horse beside Private Cassidy's body and dismounted. He adjusted the dead man's legs so that the body was no longer contorted, then looked up at Grummond, furious. "What were you thinking?!"

"We have orders to pursue the thieves!" said Grummond.

"And you have orders to keep our formation tight!" said Ten Eyck. "Orders from me!"

Grummond started to reply, his blood up, but managed to control himself.

"This goes on your report, Lieutenant," said Ten Eyck. "Take two men and see if you can catch Private Cassidy's horse. Otherwise you can carry him on yours."

AUGUST 16, 1866

Dear Journal,

Barely a month since our arrival, and from the wild prairie
has sprouted a fort! Colonel Carrington, my condition no
longer able to be secret, has broken the custom of rank and
deemed that Lt Grummond and I are the lucky first recipients
of a home with solid walls and a proper roof. It has been one
week now since we decamped from a canvas tent to a snug but
comfortable cabin, its front to the parade grounds and its back
to the fort's wall.

Our four walls contain but a single room, and wooden
floors won't come until later, but I can hardly complain when
most everyone else still sleeps in a tent. Our soldier-carpenters
have even constructed a table and bed (complete with straw-
filled tick), and with a proper cooking stove I am the envy of
every other wife. I'm not unhappy to say that we are beginning
to exhaust the local supply of buffalo chips, and with our timber crews now producing wood in such great quantities, the
scrap from the mill provides for more civilized fuel.

Our days have begun to assume the comforting structure
of routine: reveille sounds at 5:30 a.m., though Lt Grummond,
ever restless, is often up and gone before the bugle sounds.
Wood and building crews dispatch after breakfast. As its name
indicates, "Piney Island," three miles from the fort, is the place

from which we harvest our timber. Though within sight of our lookouts on top of Pilot Hill, Piney Island is invisible from the fort itself. The constant danger of Indian attack means that some of our soldiers must stand guard while the others toil away. And even with guards, the deterrent was not sufficient to prevent Sioux bandits from stampeding the majority of our cattle herd. (More later on that sad incident.) By the time the wood crews return from their work site in late afternoon, little time remains for their military drilling and training. I know Lieutenant Grummond worries that many of his men are young and inexperienced—and many don't even speak English! He knows he needs time to turn them into the type of fighting force that wore the cavalry's yellow trim during the war, and he is beyond impatient for the business of building the fort to be complete.

Now that we're at a permanent fort, married officers take breakfasts and dinners with their families, eating meals prepared by the wives. I must confess this has been a challenge for me, and that I have much to learn about making a house a true home. With kind advice from Mrs. Carrington and others, though, I am better prepared each day. In the meantime, Lt Grummond and I are taking some of our dinners in the unmarried officers' quarters.

In addition to everything else, Mrs. Carrington deserves great credit for my favorite part of the day, indeed the favorite of all members of our little frontier community. Each night after dinner, our wonderful band assembles on the parade grounds to serenade us for an hour against the background of the setting sun. For a few moments, we might just as easily be sitting in the town square of a fine eastern city.

At 10 p.m. sharp, a single bugle plays taps, but with our men exhausted after a long day's labor under hot sun, there is little need to remind them of the need for sleep.

While the bugle calls might be aimed at our soldiers, the women at Fort Philip Kearny have nearly as much regimen to our lives, and Mrs. Carrington is every bit as serious as her husband in making sure that we contribute our share. There is a committee for everything, and I am the chair of two—one assisting Dr. Rutt in organizing and equipping our nearly completed hospital building, and another of my own invention—creating a lending library so that all of us can share books with the enlisted men.

There are ten laundresses whose quarters are near the cavalry yard. I have no reason to doubt that most of these women do their share and more toward the good of Fort Phil Kearny, though the presence of this small colony of young women among so many men creates some measure of temptation. Upon hearing one of these young women speak, whose name is Janey White, I recognized at once the accent of my own Tennessee home. When I introduced myself, it turns out that she hails not just from my home state—but from my own Franklin County! As far as we have traveled, it is true that the world is still small.

I cannot close today's entry without proper tribute to two of our brave boys, now dead in the service of their country. Two days ago Sioux bandits stampeded a herd of buffalo into our cattle, and we ended up losing most of our beef stock. Worse yet, we suffered the loss of William Covington, a civilian contractor hired to tend the herd, and Private James Cassidy. Mr. Covington was trampled by the stampeding herd but also found with a Sioux bullet in his shoulder. Though my husband could barely bring himself to speak of the event, Private Cassidy died in his arms after together they gave chase to the thieves. We buried these two brave men at the base of Pilot Hill alongside the miners killed earlier.

I refuse to end on so somber a note, so I will say that, despite the setbacks of the week, all remain confident in the ability of the Second Battalion to complete the mission it has been assigned. Colonel Carrington has decided that we must learn more about the location of our enemy, and dispatched our two scouts—Mr. Bridger and Mr. Beckwourth—to ride north and determine with greater precision their whereabouts.

And indeed each day, as this fort that is a veritable town rises up around us, who cannot feel confident and proud despite the challenges and perils along our path?

Signed and Attested,
Mrs. Lieutenant George W. Grummond

Frances Grummond turned the key to lock the journal before standing up from the crude table and walking to check outside. A few soldiers stood guard along the parapets and at the barbican, but the parade grounds were mostly empty. Indeed, it was unlikely the wood crews would be back for hours. Confident of her time alone, Frances opened her small trunk, placing the first journal inside and pulling out the second from beneath a stack of clothing.

She fumbled with the lock, so eager was she to begin writing.

Dear Friend,
How I appreciate this place where I can reveal to you my questions and doubts!

It is nearly two weeks now since Colonel Carrington issued the order that women and children are forbidden from leaving the confines of the fort. Only two weeks, and already Fort Phil Kearny feels like a prison to me.

I know that it was Mrs. Carrington who insisted to her husband that the Lt and I should have the first of the married officers' quarters, and of course I am grateful for her kind intervention. And so I find myself all the more guilty in resenting the quarters as my cell within the prison, stifling hot during the day and with a dirt floor that in this dry country kicks up a cloud of fine dust at every step. Window glass is yet another of those items rumored to be arriving on the next wagon train from Fort Laramie, and in the meantime our two small window openings are covered with canvas. If closed, they admit no light, and the dark interior seems to darken my mood. If open, they offer admittance to scores of flies, which swarm by the thousands in the nearby cavalry yard. I rush around with a flyswatter, unable to keep up with the invaders and stirring up the dust in the process!

It is true that our days are filled with activities and that Mrs. Carrington has no intention of allowing the evils that come with overabundance of idle time. By most outward appearances, she has been nothing but kind to me, and yet I sense in her a sort of constant disapproval. I have seen her disapproval on naked display with others, especially the laundresses. It is well known that some of them ply a trade in addition to laundry. (At Mrs. Carrington's advice, I have forbidden Lt Grummond from wandering anywhere near their tents.) Janey White, the laundress from Franklin County, showed up at one of our meetings and volunteered to serve on my library committee. She is my age and seems very sweet, and I was eager to accept her offer. I know her station is different from mine, but it was comforting to hear her familiar accent and I'm sure there is much that we have in common. I was about to sign her up when Mrs. Carrington stepped in and, before I could say a word, said, "That committee is fully subscribed." When I started to say that we still needed volunteers, Mrs. Carrington looked at me and subtly (actually, not so subtly) shook her head. Janey seemed to get the message and left, and I must admit that I felt sorry for her. Mrs. Carrington later told me that Janey is one of "those" laundresses. "There's a few at every post."

With me and the other officers' wives, Mrs. Carrington's disapproval usually comes in the form of a question. "Well, now, you don't want to reflect badly on the officers' wives, do you?" Or, "Do you want your husband to think you can't pull your home together?"

Do you want to hear something funny? The other day I heard Mrs. Bisbee refer to Mrs. Carrington as the "K.O.W." When I asked, "What does that stand for?" she said, "Commanding Officer's Wife." And I said, "But 'Commanding' doesn't start with a 'K.'" Mrs. Bisbee looked at me and said, "Well, you can be the first to call her the C.O.W." I thought about that one for a moment before we both burst into laughter!

Work on the committees has provided some welcome distraction, especially my little library. The enlisted men all treat me with great gentleness and respect, all the more so now that all know I am pregnant. They come from all walks of life and all corners of the states—north and south—and many from the old country too. Of course a few are more than a little rough around the edges, but it is gratifying to see their excitement at the loan of a book. I am thinking about whether the library, particularly during the long winter months to come, might expand its ambition to teach the illiterate to read, or English to the many who barely speak it.

While on the subject of "routines," I am sad to report that nearly every day now we hear alarm shots from Pilot Hill and all look up in fear to watch for the coded signal flags, which all of us have now learned to translate. Even more insidious is the Indians' own secret code. We are allowed, during the day, to climb up on the ramparts and at least to gaze out at the great landscape beyond the walls. It is common now each day to see Indians on the distant ridgeline. Mr. Bridger says that the Sioux are watching us, learning our routines and our ways. For what pernicious plan? At night, sometimes, they even camp on the distant ridges, dancing around their fires in complete defiance of our presence.

I can say here, and perhaps only here, that I find myself in a strange time of adjustment with my husband. During our long journey to Fort Phil Kearny, we had few moments alone, and now, for the first time since our courtship, we find ourselves spending significant time alone together. I am coming to feel that the company of others was a crutch to us, and now, without it, we limp unnaturally in conversation. I have seen very little of the charming officer I met in Tennessee, and more of a dour and sometimes angry man, constantly complaining about Colonel Carrington's readiness to command in the field.

The Lt asks very little about how I am feeling, even on

those days when I have obviously been ill. Once he remarked dismissively that "You'll feel better after the first three months." And I wonder, how would he know? Do the officers really talk of such things?

Sincerely Yours,
Frances

SAME DAY

Crazy Horse's war party had broken into smaller groups after driving off the cattle herd, uncertain whether the soldiers might continue their pursuit. Crazy Horse and Lone Bear retreated with Little Hawk, seeking out the nearby foothills of the Shining Mountains. They found a timbered vale and built a crude wickiup to keep the evening chill off the boy.

Crazy Horse found it difficult to think of anything but Little Hawk, and kept checking to see the rise and fall of his chest so he could reassure himself that his brother continued to breathe. It was always hard to know for certain with wounds like this, but it appeared that the soldier's bullet had bounced off Little Hawk's short rib and passed out of his body without hitting any organs. Crazy Horse and Lone Bear prepared hot poultices of sage, changing them every few hours. In a best case, the boy would be sore for a couple weeks, but if he could continue to avoid a fever, he might heal with nothing more lingering than a scar.

For a while after the sun set, Crazy Horse and Lone Bear sat outside next to a low fire, roasting fresh venison. As the black of the night sky deepened, the cloudy white splash of the Trail of Spirits grew more distinct, and Crazy Horse fought back a sense of foreboding. He wished that he could share his fears with Lone Bear. It had been uncomfortable with his friend since the fight with the soldiers, and Crazy Horse knew that Lone Bear was leaving many of his thoughts unspoken. Normally Crazy

Horse did not mind periods of silence between them. Indeed, one of Lone Bear's attributes Crazy Horse most appreciated was that his friend didn't feel the need to fill up every moment with idle chatter. This silence was different, though, like a festering sore. Crazy Horse knew that Lone Bear would speak directly to him when the moment arose, but it was not his friend's way to force a conversation. Crazy Horse would need to lance the wound himself, spark the confrontation that Lone Bear had been seeking to avoid.

Finally, Crazy Horse asked, "Do you think I was wrong to attack the soldier on the white horse?"

Lone Bear looked up from the rib he gnawed. "Yes."

"Weren't you angry too?"

"Yes."

"Then why was I wrong?"

Lone Bear stared at him for a long moment. "When you rode out to accept the soldier's challenge, did you do it for the good of the tribe—or to satisfy your own pride?"

Crazy Horse said nothing, but of course, Lone Bear had hit the precise source of the guilt with which he had been grappling since Little Hawk was shot.

"I didn't ask anyone to follow me."

"But you knew they would—including Little Hawk."

Crazy Horse started to say something, to push back—but he couldn't. He knew Lone Bear was right. It was painful to know that his brother lay wounded because of his own mistake, and even more painful to confront a mistake founded on the one sin he knew it was his solemn duty to avoid.

"I know you believe the Creator protects you in battle, and I hope it's always true," said Lone Bear. "Our people admire you—and usually they're right to follow you."

Crazy Horse said nothing, though he listened carefully.

"And I believe in the strength of your vision. But you know, too, that not everyone has the same protection as you. You know you have to think about everyone."

Crazy Horse thought about that for a while and, as was usually the case, saw the wisdom in Lone Bear's words. Crazy Horse sighed deeply, and felt the bit of relief that came from confronting his mistake directly with his friend. "What do you think we should do next?"

"Red Cloud said to learn how they fight," said Lone Bear. "Beaver away at them while we learn."

"It was good what we did with the cattle," said Crazy Horse.

Lone Bear nodded. "And we learned that they'll ride away from the fort to chase us."

"And they're strongest when they stay together. They were smart— the ones that formed the line at the top of the hill . . ."

"You saw how a few of the soldiers held the horses for the ones who fought."

"When Little Hawk is stronger, we'll go back," said Crazy Horse. "The valley of the Twin Creeks gives us lots of places to watch from high ground . . . learn more . . . attack again."

AUGUST 28, 1866

"Well, that is a hundred-dollar name if ever I heard one," said Jim Bridger, so surprised that he reined his horse to look at his companion, seeing him suddenly anew, though he had known the man for more than forty years.

James Pierson Beckwourth reined his horse too. It wasn't yet noon, but the two scouts had traveled nearly thirty miles already that day. Beckwourth liked spirited horses, and his horse, though spirited, could use the rest. Besides, he sensed he had an audience, and Beckwourth was never one to squander an audience.

"That's just my father," said Beckwourth. "My father's father was Sir Marmaduke Wainscot Beckwourth. And he's descended from no less than Sir Hugh de Malebisse"—Beckwourth pronounced it with a flawless French accent, so that Bridger could scarcely tell where the first name ended and the last name began—"hero of the Battle of Hastings, Year of Our Lord 1066."

Bridger had never heard of the Battle of Hastings, and as far as he was concerned, 1066 was part of a blurry period that included the Bible and a lot of things that happened in the land of the Israelites, wherever that was. Still, he marveled at the surprises uncovered when you dug a little deeper on people's stories.

"Now, as for my mother—they didn't even allow her the dignity of a family name, and I don't know a single thing about her lineage."

Beckwourth took a swig from his canteen, sunlight dancing on multiple earrings in each ear. Among the things that Bridger liked about Beckwourth was his dress, which made Bridger nostalgic for the heyday of the fur trade, when trappers draped themselves with gaudy adornments and made a general spectacle of themselves. Bridger himself had pursued such fashions as a young man, though over the years he had come to appreciate the attributes of store-bought clothes. Except in extreme cold, when nothing was warmer than a big buffalo coat, Bridger wore a thick canvas jacket that did a fair job of shedding water and had a thick collar that he could turn up against the wind. Bridger also was fond of a broad-brimmed beaver hat that came from St. Louis and cost him ten dollars. After many years of service, it was faded and salt-stained at the brow and the brim had begun to droop, but it still offered plentiful shade.

Beckwourth had commented that no self-respecting Indian would be seen in any of Bridger's clothing, and asked at one point if Bridger had chosen his attire as part of some clever strategy to present a less enticing target. Certainly Beckwourth pursued no such strategy—decorated from the tassel at the top of his rabbit-fur hat to the intricate rosettes of porcupine quills at the toes of his moccasins. Beckwourth claimed to be a Crow chief. Bridger was still unsure whether he believed that or not, but there was no doubt he looked the part.

Bridger didn't remember the year he first met Beckwourth—a rendezvous somewhere in the old days of the Rocky Mountain Fur Company. He remembered the novelty of talking to a free black man, the first he'd ever met. It had changed the way he thought about the Negroes, made them seem no different from regular people.

Beckwourth still wore the same silver dollar around his neck that Bridger remembered from back then. He had explained that the dollar was coined in 1798, the year of his birth, which he said made it lucky. It seemed to have worked pretty well, Bridger reckoned. Here was Beckwourth, after all, four decades later, after a life spent on the knife's edge of frontier survival. Bridger doubted that luck was enough—eventually it ran out. But skill alone wasn't enough either. He knew plenty of skillful men over the years who took a wrong step one day and ended up dead. Bridger knew better than to rely on luck, but he certainly would take it in whatever measure it came his way.

"'Spose we ought to settle on a plan," said Beckwourth. "You given it some thought?"

Bridger looked out. To the west were the Big Horns, their timbered foothills rolling downhill until surrendering eventually to the dry and flat terrain of the plains. "Well, I'd bet a month's pay they're camped on one of the big creeks coming off the Big Horns," he said. "But I'm not too keen on stumbling around blind, especially in open country like this."

"Me either," said Beckwourth. "Bound to be dozens of hunting parties and war parties prowling around."

"We could go up in the mountains . . . stay in the timber."

"Eventually we'd spot 'em," said Beckwourth. "But that'll be a tough haul."

Bridger took off his hat and scratched his forehead. After a bit he said, "Is it true about your being a Crow chief?"

"On my mother's grave," said Beckwourth. "God rest her sad soul."

Bridger chewed on that a minute, long enough that Beckwourth, who didn't like gaps in the conversation to linger, resumed talking. "Of course, in the interest of full disclosure, chief-making with the Crows is a rather informal arrangement, same as the other tribes."

Bridger nodded.

"So they never exactly pinned a feather on my topknot," said Beckwourth. "But over time they included me in the councils, followed me into battle the times I wanted to lead, allowed me to marry in with them."

"You have a family with the Crow?"

"And then some," said Beckwourth. "I have three Crow wives."

"You still on good terms?"

"Well, I'll admit I've been gone awhile . . . but otherwise, all good so far as I know. You thinking we ought to pay a visit on the Crow?"

Bridger nodded.

"Truth be told, I've been wanting to go back," said Beckwourth. "And one thing's for sure. The Crow spend a lot of time worrying about the Sioux. They'll know a lot about the whereabouts of the Sioux and the Cheyenne and any other tribe in this country."

"Then we come back with some idea of where we're goin'," said Bridger. "I like the idea of knowing what we're aiming at."

Bridger patted his old mare on the neck and, satisfied she was rested, nudged her in the flanks with his moccasined heels. They rode for a while in silence, but then Bridger said, "Three wives? I don't think I have the energy."

"Well, I'll admit it's not without its complications," said Beckwourth. "That's a good problem, in my book. But I remember you always had a practical streak."

They set their camp early, forgoing an inviting site with easy water along a small creek and instead riding up into the thicker cover of the foothill pines. At least in the trees they could build a small fire with less fear of signaling their position. Beckwourth offered to roast choice cuts of a small deer he had shot, while Bridger scouted from a bald spot on the mountainside that afforded a view north, up the Powder River Valley.

The view from the mountainside proved disappointing, or at least there had been no sign of the Indian camp that they knew must lay somewhere along the base of the Big Horns.

By the time Bridger rode back into camp, the sun was gone and smoke had drifted in from a late-summer fire, the haze casting a strange, orangish hue to the rising moon. One thing Bridger noticed as he got older—he didn't have enough words for colors. "Green" didn't begin to cover the range of hues in the Rockies. The pregnant new green of tamarack in spring was far different from the dark green of pine needles, different even from the green of the same tamarack tree by mid-summer. "Yellow" failed to capture any distinction between the shimmering aspen leaves of a crisp October day compared to the dry grasses of the same season. The blue waters of a mountain lake were far different from the inky hues of the evening sky before true night; indeed, the sky alone sported an enormous range of blues throughout the day. And "gray" was pretty much the only word Bridger knew for an infinite variety of cloudy skies— from barely dark all the way to the last shade before total blackness.

It would be a good thing to ask Beckwourth about. He knew a lot of words.

Nor were colors the only part of his life Bridger found more complicated than the words he had to describe them. More and more, these complexities vexed him and caused him angst, all the more so because he couldn't explain it properly to anybody. Maybe it was a sign that such things weren't meant for conversation. He wasn't sure that was right either, and certainly he wished he could saddle up a way to talk about it. He wondered again if a smart man like Beckwourth had any insights, and vowed to take advantage of this time together to find out.

SEPTEMBER 2, 1866

In an unruly and disordered world, Captain Tenador Ten Eyck had always found comfort in the perfection of numbers. Ten Eyck's life experience had taught him that many topics were subject to debate—but not mathematics. He loved that questions in math had an answer—a single answer, precise to the decimal point. So it was that, during the Civil War, Captain Ten Eyck had discovered a love of artillery.

A week before, Ten Eyck had handpicked a crew of ten and spent an entire day measuring distances from the two barbicans. They started at 250 yards, painting white stones in a short pile, clearly visible from the fort, and working outward from there, a new pile every 250 yards. The last pile they placed at a range of 1,250 yards—the top of a distant ridgeline, with Fort Phil Kearny more than half a mile behind them.

Tonight, a moment arrived that Ten Eyck had anticipated with a hunter's patience. As they had done before on numerous occasions since the establishment of the fort, a dozen Sioux had ensconced themselves on the ridgeline, watching the fort in defiance and flashing mirrors in the last fragments of setting sun. They surrounded the pile of white-painted stones demarking 1,250 yards; in fact, two of the warriors busied themselves dismantling the pile, tossing the stones down the hillside.

Captain Ten Eyck and Colonel Carrington stood atop the eastern barbican, watching the Indians through field glasses. After a while,

Carrington lowered his glasses. "Shall we undertake a little test, Captain Ten Eyck?"

Ten Eyck could scarcely have been more enthusiastic. "Yes, sir!"

"Fire when ready."

Captain Ten Eyck looked back at his crew, arrayed around the howitzer. "Private Edwards!"

Edwards was one of two privates standing away from the cannon, near a metal trunk. "Yes, sir!"

"Bring a round of spherical case!"

Private Edwards reached into the trunk, pulled a round of case shot, and ran forward, handing it to Ten Eyck. The case round was comprised of three parts. At the rear was a cloth bag containing the charge—sixteen ounces of black powder. At the front was what looked like a normal cannonball, though with a hole at the forward end. In the middle was a spherical section of wood, securing metal straps that held all three parts together. The cannonball, instead of being solid, was hollow, and filled with a deadly mixture of additional gunpowder and dozens of tiny musket balls. A fuse protruded from the hole at the front of the cannonball, marked at increments.

Captain Ten Eyck could barely contain himself. Their ammunition supply was too small to have allowed for live practice, so his crews had drilled endlessly without actually firing the howitzers. Ten Eyck, though, had fired thousands of rounds during the war, and now repeated the steps as naturally as if he were tying his shoes.

He pulled a tool like a pair of snub-nosed scissors from his pocket and focused on the fuse. "You see this, Private?" Private Edwards studied the fuse, which was coiled at the front end of the round, marked at one-hundred-yard increments.

"We adjust the elevation at the rear of the gun," said Ten Eyck, "then cut the fuse for twelve hundred yards." The private nodded, and Colonel Carrington looked on as well, not wanting to appear the neophyte, though he had never seen the operation of artillery up close. Captain Ten Eyck traced the fuse to a point marked *1,200*, cutting it at that juncture and discarding the small remnant that remained.

Colonel Carrington was glad when Ten Eyck explained the operation of the round to the private. "When the cannon ignites, the explosion lights the fuse"—Ten Eyck used his hand to imitate the fire from the blast reaching the front of the round to the fuse—"and as the ball flies downfield, the fuse burns down and into the rou—"

"Igniting in the air at the appointed range," said Carrington, with authority that made it seem as if he had known before.

"Yes!" said Captain Ten Eyck, excitedly. *Mathematics. Beautiful mathematics.* He handed the charge back to Private Edwards. "Cannoneers to your posts!" he ordered. The four men of his crew moved quickly into their designated positions—one on either side of the howitzer's muzzle and two back with the chest of ammunition, kept at a distance from the gun to prevent accidental ignitions. "Commence firing . . . Load!"

A big man with a drooping mustache dipped the sponge end of a ram staff into a bucket of water, twirled it to remove the excess liquid, then rammed it all the way to the breech of the gun before withdrawing it. He stood back, flipping the ram staff so that its solid end was ready.

Captain Ten Eyck, meanwhile, used a special leather patch to cover the vent—a small hole at the howitzer's breech. When the tube was swabbed, he nodded to Private Edwards, who placed the round, powder sack first, into the muzzle of the howitzer, pushing it until the ball disappeared. Ten Eyck continued to cover the vent hole while the big man with the ram staff pushed the charge home. At that point, the powder sack was seated precisely beneath the vent. Ten Eyck pulled what looked like a long nail with a handle from his pocket and inserted it into the vent, poking downward to pierce the bag of gunpowder inside the cannon's tube, exposing the powder for easy ignition.

Captain Ten Eyck nodded to another artilleryman, who wore a small leather box on the front of his belt. This man reached into the box and pulled out a brass ignition device called a friction primer, inserted it into the vent hole, and then attached a lanyard with a handle at the end to a ring on the primer. The captain loved the science of the friction primer, like a tiny combination of a match and a firecracker and filled with fulminated mercury. He was old enough to remember the old ignition system—goose quills filled with gunpowder. The new system, perfected during the war, was weatherproof and state-of-the-art.

The man with the lanyard assumed a ready position, his face away from the cannon, pulling the lanyard just enough to take up the slack.

Ten Eyck watched it all, relatively pleased with his crew. He sighted one final time down the tube, making a last adjustment to the elevation, then stood back.

"Ready!"

Colonel Carrington covered his ears.

Ten Eyck paused an instant, then yelled, "Fire!"

Crazy Horse held a small trading mirror in his hand, tipping it to catch the sun's rays. His war party occupied the ridgeline to the north of the new fort, with clear views of the entire valley of the Twin Creeks. It was an optimal vantage point, and Crazy Horse and his fellow warriors had been occupying similar positions for several days. From this height, not only could they see the valley—they actually could see down into the fort. They had begun to learn the soldiers' routines—built around sizable work parties going out each morning to cut timber, while other crews used the wood to construct the buildings in the large interior of the compound.

Crazy Horse also liked the ridgeline position because it commanded the high ground, far beyond effective rifle range, and they would know instantly if any mounted force rode out to confront them.

Lone Bear stood next to Crazy Horse, both of them studying the activity below.

Little Hawk and Comes Again stood about twenty yards downhill— beside a strange stack of rocks painted white. Watching his brother, Crazy Horse again felt the twin sensations of happiness and relief at the speed of his recovery. The boy still felt pain when he drew his bow, but had insisted on riding out with the new war party.

"What is this?" yelled Little Hawk from his position beside the white stones. "Is this a place where they pray?"

"I don't know," said Crazy Horse. "It's not the cross sign they use for worship."

Little Hawk grabbed the top rock on the pile and cast it down the hill. Comes Again began to help him, and quickly they erased all appearance of the stacked stones.

Looking again at the fort, Crazy Horse found the rate of the soldiers' progress frightening. Inside the walls, many of the tents had been replaced by wooden structures built with boards from the big machine by the creek. A week ago, they had stolen a dozen of the whites' horses during a night raid. Now, though, the soldiers had extended the fort's walls to encircle a large new area dedicated to the horses, and the soldiers brought all of their mounts inside before dark.

A few moments earlier, the fort's big gate had swung open, and a dozen cavalrymen rode out. At first they thought the horse soldiers might ride up to challenge them, but instead they turned west—toward the hillside where the soldiers cut their wood.

Crazy Horse flashed his mirror again. He knew there were other war parties in the area, though he didn't know their precise whereabouts. They had not developed a complex code, but a flashing mirror was intended to convey that soldiers were moving out of the fort.

As Crazy Horse and Lone Bear continued to watch the fort, they saw an enormous eruption of smoke from one of the towers, followed a moment later by a great blast. They realized instantly that it was a wagon gun, even before they heard the high-pitched scream of the projectile flying toward them. Then, almost directly above their heads, there was a second explosion.

Crazy Horse heard the streaking sounds of what seemed like a hundred bullets flying all around them. He heard the horses scream and saw Comes Again fall to the ground. One of the horses went down, and the others—all hobbled just behind the ridgeline—whinnied and struggled against their hobbles.

"Get behind the ridge!" yelled Crazy Horse. Lone Bear ran toward the horses while Crazy Horse sprinted toward Little Hawk, who knelt beside Comes Again. Comes Again lay facedown on the ground with a wound in his upper back and another in the back of his head. Crazy Horse rolled him over, but he knew that he was dead. Even in the immediate horror of the moment, Crazy Horse marveled at the power that allowed the wagon gun to inflict such precise carnage at so great a distance.

Together with Little Hawk, he grabbed Comes Again, dragging his body toward cover behind the ridgeline. Crazy Horse saw Little Hawk wince at the pain from the effort, but his brother pushed through it. They had just cleared the ridge when they heard the sound of another blast from the wagon gun, then the whining scream of the shell, propelling toward them.

"Lay flat!" yelled Crazy Horse, and they dropped to the ground. Again the shell exploded in the air above their heads, and once again they heard the piercing metal rain. This time, though, the ridge had sheltered them from the full destructive force of the shrapnel. Crazy Horse raised his head, surveying the damage. Another of the horses was hit, but it appeared that no more of the warriors were injured.

As Crazy Horse helped Little Hawk to his feet, Lone Bear appeared beside them with the horses. Crazy Horse and Little Hawk helped Pemmican to pull the body of Comes Again across the front of his horse. Then they threw themselves atop their own horses, galloping away, safely behind the cover of the ridgeline by the time the soldiers took one last shot with the howitzer.

"How can that be possible?" asked Lone Bear as they rode.

Crazy Horse had the same question but no answer. The whites possessed powers that could not be explained. Even more than before, it filled him with profound disquiet, as if suddenly every star had been jumbled, the landmarks against which he had always measured his path ahead disappeared.

SEPTEMBER 7, 1866

Jim Bridger listened to the crickets, in the last hour before darkness, trilling with an urgency that made it seem as if they could anticipate the deadly change of season that soon would be upon them. Bridger stretched out his legs toward the fire, appreciating the warmth conveyed even by the sound of its crackle and spit. The flames bobbed and flared in a *whoosh* of wind that passed through the tops of the cottonwoods along the creek bottom, almost as if the trees had voice.

The rain from a late-afternoon storm clung to the tall grass, weighting it so that the long stems bowed to the ground. At its mid-summer strength, Bridger had noticed, the green grass sprang back quickly, shaking off the burden. The golden grass of fall, though, was slower to recover, and in fact never seemed to return to its fulsome form. Eventually, weakened, the fall grass would confront the snows that would push it to the ground and pin it there during the long winter months. And that was it. Of course, in spring it began again for the generation of grass that followed, green shoots pushing their way up from the matted, dead grass, drawing sustenance from what had come before.

"You still hungry?" asked Beckwourth. He turned a green willow branch heavy with the fat hindquarter of a rabbit.

"No, sir," said Bridger. "It's all yours."

Bridger reckoned that they were now a hundred miles north of Sioux and Cheyenne country, deep into the territory of the Crow. They could afford a bigger fire and the convenience of sleeping near water. They had followed the lower Tongue downstream for the past two days, the Big Horns far enough behind them that they felt relatively safe. Beckwourth said he was sure they would find Goes Ahead's band well before they hit the confluence with the Yellowstone. There was buffalo sign everywhere, and Goes Ahead's people would be near the herd.

"Do you remember how Hugh Glass used to gut a rabbit?" asked Beckwourth.

Bridger looked up at the mention of the name. "I remember he was good with a knife . . ." He was sad when he spoke. "I remember he could strip the pelt off a beaver in about two shakes."

"I was there on the day the Arikara finally killed old Glass," said Beckwourth, looking hard at Bridger and speaking carefully. "You were with him on the Grand, I heard, when he got mauled."

Bridger nodded. "Yes, I was, and I did him wrong. He forgave me for my youth . . . not sure I deserved it."

Beckwourth produced a flask from his saddlebag, uncorked it, and passed it to Bridger. "I always figured forgiveness is a bit like luck," said Beckwourth. "You take all you can get, and you don't ask too many questions."

Bridger thought about that one for a moment. It was an interesting perspective. "What happened to Glass, exactly?"

"His luck finally ran dry . . . late winter in 1833. I had brought in my band of forty or so Crow, including women and children, to trade at Fort Cass. You knew it then?"

"Sure," said Bridger. "Where the Big Horn joins the Yellowstone."

"Well, anyway, when we arrived, Fort Cass was low on supplies, it being the end of winter. But they had a partner named Gardner who had put up a post about twenty miles downriver. They sent out three men to alert Gardner, Glass being one of them, so Gardner could come up with more goods to trade."

"I had heard he fell into a Ree ambush," said Bridger.

"Bad luck. A Ree war party, two hundred miles from Ree territory. But Glass and the others got caught out in the open, barely out of Fort Cass, crossing the frozen Yellowstone."

Bridger drew a deep slug from Beckwourth's flask and continued to listen, solemn.

"The Crow hate the Ree almost as much as the Sioux, so my warriors and I rode out to take revenge on behalf of old Hugh."

"Did you find them?"

"We picked up what was left of Glass and the other two. The Ree had driven poles into the snow next to the bodies—flew bits of their scalps at the top." Beckwourth stopped and took his own shot from the flask of whiskey. "I hadn't seen that particular insult before, though of course they added all the usual depredations.

"We followed the war party's trail all the way to Gardner's camp. The Ree got there first and had run off with most of Gardner's horses, but Gardner's men captured two of the thieving bastards. Gardner had the idea of trading the prisoners for the horses, but the Ree weren't interested." Beckwourth took another swig of whiskey, then handed the flask back to Bridger. "So we got in a little revenge for old Hugh."

Bridger pondered that for a long time. After a while he raised the flask. "To Hugh Glass," he said. He felt the burn of the whiskey the whole way down his throat. He handed the flask back to Beckwourth.

"To justice," said Beckwourth, and then drank.

"Do you ever think about whether what we're doing is right or wrong?" asked Bridger.

"What do you mean?" replied Beckwourth.

"I don't know exactly," said Bridger. "But I've been thinking some lately, wondering about things."

"Things such as what?"

"Well, I'll tell you one . . . When I was eighteen years old, I rode on to the Great Salt Lake—the first white man to ever see it, so far as I know."

"Pretty country."

"Pretty for sure, and wild—but that's part of my point. Have you been there lately?"

"Not for a long time."

"Well, it's practically as big as St. Louis. Half the buildings are brick, and the Mormons are even putting up a temple."

"You sound like you're complaining," said Beckwourth. "Didn't all those Mormons stop off at your fort to buy flour and repair their wagons? I heard you made a killing."

"I did okay. And I'm not complaining, exactly—just wondering . . ."

"Wondering what?"

"Well, I don't know . . . wondering if it's a good thing or a bad thing, I guess."

"What's the point of thinking about that?" asked Beckwourth.

"I guess I liked the Great Salt Lake a lot better the first time I saw it than the last time I saw it," said Bridger.

"And you think you're responsible?" said Beckwourth. "You don't think anybody else would've stumbled across Salt Lake if it weren't for you?"

"But it was me," said Bridger.

Beckwourth didn't say anything for a long time, but Bridger could tell he was chewing on it. Finally, Beckwourth said, "I do see a bit of your point, I suppose. I first went to California in 1844—five years before the rush. I can't say I liked it better after all the miners came in.

"But I'm not sure I see the merit in getting all twisted in knots over thoughts like that," said Beckwourth when Bridger was quiet for a while. "You can't change that now, anyway. That much is for sure."

"Well, I thought about that too," said Bridger. "And no, I can't change the past."

"Well, then, what's the use of all the cogitating?"

"I guess," said Bridger, "I'm wondering if you and me are doing the right thing now, scouting for the army."

"That's not a hard one for me," said Beckwourth. "The Sioux are the enemy of my people, and they always have been."

Bridger seemed confused. "Why are the Sioux the enemy of the Negroes?"

"I'm not talking about the Negroes," said Beckwourth. "I haven't talked to five Negroes since I was a boy. I'm talking about the Crow."

Maybe it was true about Beckwourth being a Crow chief, thought Bridger.

"They took me in, welcomed me, even," said Beckwourth. "They're my people now, if I have a people."

"Well, the Sioux are the enemy of my people, too, if you want to measure it like that," said Bridger. He had children by a Shoshone wife and had lived with the tribe for years.

"Then what are you all vexed about?"

Bridger didn't say anything for a while. Then he just shook his head. "Can't put my finger on it, exactly," he said finally. "Maybe I'm just getting old."

"So's your horse," said Beckwourth. "Man of your means ought to be able to buy a decent mount."

"Some things I like 'cause I'm used to 'em."

"Even if they're no good anymore—like that broken-down fleabag of a nag you're riding?"

At this, Bridger turned a notch colder. He loved his horse and hadn't invited the commentary. "She gets me where I want to go—and as fast as I need to get there."

"Just barely," said Beckwourth. "What if you need to move faster than a slow walk at some point?"

"Then I'm in a world of hurt. But I ain't that likely to outrun a Sioux war party in any event."

"Same with that old grandpa rifle?"

"I ain't that likely to win a big shoot-out neither."

"You're putting a lot of stock in quick thinking."

"It's what I got."

Beckwourth chuckled at that and then mulled a moment. "Well, you've made it this far. But I suppose men our age ought to be thinking about the next life too. Do you consider yourself religious?" he asked.

Like many things from Beckwourth, the question took Bridger by surprise. For one thing, it didn't seem to Bridger like it was the type of thing that was anyone else's business, though something about Beckwourth led Bridger to cut the man additional slack. He chewed on the question for a while before responding. "How do you mean?"

"Oh, you know . . ." said Beckwourth. "Father, Son, Holy Ghost . . . God. Do you believe in God?"

It was clear that Beckwourth had his teeth in the topic, and Bridger doubted he would let go. Truth be told, Bridger had given the subject some thought of late. That didn't mean he had been hankering to talk about it, but since Beckwourth had raised it, he was curious about the conclusions his friend might have drawn.

"Well, I was raised Christian, of course."

"Yes. As was I. By my mother, the slave. Christianity made a hell of a lot of sense for her, as I've thought about it over the years."

"Why do you say that?" asked Bridger.

"For starters, her life here on earth was about as dismal as it could get. If your earthly life is dismal, imagining there's a glorious afterlife, once you get around to dying, is a pretty compelling thing. I'm happy for her that she had that to hold on to."

"Your life doesn't strike me as dismal," said Bridger. "Does that mean you're not a Christian?"

"I doubt I am. Oh, I'm baptized and all that . . . so I guess you can't scrub that away. But I can't say I feel it."

Bridger had known many men who had strayed from the path of Christianity, but he hadn't ever met a man who confessed it so nakedly. "What do you believe, then?" he asked.

"One time, when I was wintering with the Crow, there was a missionary that came into the camp. He had a lot of trinkets that he passed out . . . That helped him build a pretty good crowd, and it was winter, so my Crow friends had some time on their hands and were patient with his stories."

"Did he convert anybody?"

"It was the funniest thing I ever saw," said Beckwourth, becoming even more animated than usual as he related the story. "Here's the Crow, with a perfectly good explanation for their lives *as they live them*, a code for good and evil, explanations for things that come from the world around them *where they live*. And then this white man shows up and tells them that some fellow named Jesus . . . in some place called Israel . . . a *couple thousand* years ago . . . got sentenced to death by a *Roman* . . . died on a cross, then *rose up from the dead*—all to forgive them of their horrible sins. *Which they didn't know they had committed*."

"So were they converted?"

"What do you think? Of course they weren't converted! Not a single goddamn one. But that missionary was the luckiest man that I ever met. He didn't know the Crow words for the insults he bestowed on them—and I didn't translate them—so they let him leave the village with his scalp."

Bridger had to chuckle. He hadn't thought about it that way before. "Do you believe in the Indian explanation for things?" he asked.

"Maybe," said Beckwourth. "Makes a lot more sense out here where I've lived my life. Maybe there's more than one explanation for something as big as the hereafter. What about you, Bridger? Do you believe in the afterlife?"

"I don't know," said Bridger. "I hope for it . . . But I'm not sure I believe in it the way I did when I was younger . . . you know, with your spirit floating up to the Pearly Gates on angel's wings."

"So what's it look like to you now?"

"You want to know the truth?" said Bridger. "I've been looking a lot lately at trees . . . including the old ones . . . and the dead ones."

"And?"

"And it's comforting, I guess," said Bridger. "I've noticed that those big old dead pines stay useful for a long time, even after the last needle drops off. The bugs keep on eating away. The bears scrape off the bark to get the bugs. The birds bore holes and nest in the trunk. Those old stumps are teeming with living things, just as much as when they were alive."

Beckwourth gave a small, pensive smile. "So you think we're like those trees—that we'll continue to be useful after we're gone?"

"Like I said—I hope for it."

"It kind of sounds like something an Indian would say."

"Well, maybe," said Bridger. "I don't mind that. I guess I've come around to their way of thinking on a lot of things."

Beckwourth stared at Bridger a long time, then nodded his head. "I hear you on that," he said. "I don't mind that either." Beckwourth held up the flask. "Here's to cogitating." He took another swig of whiskey and handed the flask back to Bridger.

Bridger took a small sip out of courtesy. He already had a pleasant sensation from the earlier swigs. Any more would just mean a headache in the morning. After a while, he said, "Funny how you haven't thought about something for a long time—then you do and it seems like it was barely a few days before that it happened. Then you think a little bit more and you realize it happened half a life ago, and now all the sudden that's half a lifetime gone."

"Some things I like to keep remembering," said Beckwourth. "Some things I'm fine leaving in the past. One thing about being out here, we're free to do whatever the hell we want whenever the hell we want to do it, and that's what we've been doing our whole lives."

"Maybe," said Bridger. "Maybe for you. Maybe even for me a lot of the time. But maybe it's just that the land out here is big enough that we can keep wandering around without ever bumping into our mistakes from the past."

"You got something you're trying to avoid?" asked Beckwourth.

"Thing or two," said Bridger. "As long as we're confessing our sins, I've got a daughter in St. Louis who I barely know. Old enough to have a family of her own, and I barely know her . . . I send her money, but I can't honestly say if I'm providing for her or trying to pay my way out of feeling guilty."

They were quiet for a while, listening to the fire and staring up into the sky in the fading light.

Bridger noticed suddenly a cottonwood seed, caught on an updraft and then drifting slowly to earth. It soared up and down a couple of times before settling on rocky terrain about thirty feet away. Bridger sat up, felt the stiffness from his knees to his neck, but pulled himself to his feet. He walked over to the barren ground and found the seed, surrounded by its cottony wings, and stooped to pick it up. He walked to the top of a cutbank, where grasses grew in rich soil along a downed tree that offered shelter from the wind. He set the seed down there, careful to find a place where it touched a bit of bare earth.

He checked the old mare one last time, comfortable that she had access to sufficient grass and that her hobble was secure. He gave her a quick scratch behind the ear and she leaned into it, as if accustomed. Then Bridger returned to the fire, stretching out to sleep.

He was surprised to find Beckwourth staring at him.

"You're a curious man, Jim Bridger."

SEPTEMBER 10, 1866

Dear Journal,

Mornings and evenings begin to grow colder, at least as perceived by a Tennessee girl such as myself. The snow on the highest peaks of the Big Horns has never disappeared, and now, already, the valley rains fall as snow on the higher slopes of the nearby mountains.

My idea of using our post "library" (in actuality, Company C's mess hall) as a place to teach reading has taken root! I go there each day after dinner plates are cleared and spend an hour or so prior to the nightly concerts by our band. Mrs. Carrington, Mrs. Bisbee (who also teaches school by day to the children), and I all teach reading to a mix of infantry and cavalrymen and even a couple of the laundresses.

I am impressed at the pluck of our students! There is no little bit of courage in sticking out one's neck in an effort at self-betterment, and with such motivation, it's not surprising our students are making rapid progress. Some arrive with rudimentary skill, but with others we must begin with the alphabet and move forward from there. The army has provided two full sets of McGuffey's primers, and after only a month we already have our best students moving into the more advanced volumes. It is heartwarming to see their pride as they graduate from one level to the next, and I have no doubt we'll have dozens more dedicated readers before the snows harness us all to indoor activities. (The prohibition for women to wander outside the walls of the fort appears permanent.)

Sunday afternoon the whole fort was spared from war surplus salt pork. Recognizing, I think, that the women and children already feel the constraints of life inside the walls of the fort, Colonel Carrington ordered a picnic along the grassy banks of Little Piney Creek. In truth, we were barely a hundred yards from the fort, but we all talked about how good it felt to "escape." Mr. Kinney, the new post sutler, made a donation of canned goods to the cause, and the officers and their families dined like royalty on cove oysters and salmon for the first course. Other canned delicacies included tomatoes, peas, pickles, and even pineapples! I had almost forgotten the taste of any fruit unless one counts dried apples. We all savored the flavors all the more, recognizing that the next such feast might be far off in the future. In the meantime, I keep thinking of the refrain from the soldiers' song, "Forty miles a day, on beans and hay, in the Regular Army, oh!"

Signed and Attested,
Mrs. Lieutenant George W. Grummond

Dear Friend,
While I can't begin to explain how good it felt to be outside the walls of the fort, I must admit that I agree with my husband about the food we all ate. It felt strange, with most of our cattle herd gone, to be dining so lavishly. Apparently all the officers were grumbling about that, and wondering about the colonel's ability to catch the attention of the army's "powers that be" in accelerating the delivery of our sorely needed supplies.

Lt Grummond is especially concerned about feed for

the horses. He says that our horses are accustomed to grain, and unlike the Indian ponies, can't sustain themselves on the prairie grasses. I have always loved horses, and as a girl my father taught me to ride. As part of my daily walk around the parade grounds I like to stroll through the cavalry yard and past the stables, petting the horses and feeding them handfuls of grass. It is sad to see how much our stock has diminished in only two months since leaving Fort Laramie. Many have bones poking at their haunches, and they all hang their heads listlessly, the veritable opposite of the spirited animals with which I associate our corps.

I, meanwhile, have taken a stand against Mrs. Carrington and I worry about the consequences. A week ago, Janey White, the laundress from Franklin County, came into the library and asked whether she might receive instruction in reading. Mrs. Carrington had not yet arrived, and I promptly answered, "Of course you can! The library is open to everyone at the fort." I began to teach her myself, and of all the students, there is none more eager to better herself.

When Mrs. Carrington arrived and saw me tutoring Janey, she made her disapproval instantly apparent. When the students had left, Mrs. Carrington pulled me aside and said that Janey is "not the type of person that should be welcomed in polite society." I will admit that I surprised myself when I pushed back, saying that I had engaged Janey in several conversations and always found her to be polite and hardworking. Mrs. Carrington seemed even more surprised than I—that a junior officer's wife would not fall meekly into line. She said, icily, "You and I must have quite different notions of 'polite society.'" Then she said something about how "we form our reputations in the company that we keep," and stormed out.

Janey has returned each night since, and every night I have welcomed her. Because of our growing familiarity, we also have engaged in longer conversations when I drop off and pick up our laundry. I learned that she married just before the war to a husband who left immediately to fight for the Confederacy. Eight months later she received a letter with the tragic news that her husband had died of dysentery. She lived with a sister during the rest of the war, her only kin.

The Union Army recaptured Franklin County near the end of the war. This was when I began a courtship with Lt Grummond and ultimately married. Janey's fortune was to take employment with the Second Battalion as one of the dozens of laundresses, and like so many other "camp followers," she has followed them since, now finding herself so far away from her native land. Of course, she has no husband, and must care for herself with her hard work and her wits. When we met I reached out my hand to shake hers, and I could tell she was embarrassed by the way her skin is savaged by long days elbow-deep in lye. And why should she be embarrassed, and not I, for the relative privilege I receive from my station, even here on the frontier? I have pondered that question all day, and not, I might add, with any answer that I feel very good about. I don't know if the rumors about Janey spread by Mrs. Carrington are true, but I try to remember to "judge not, lest ye be judged." Who are we to judge? I have not known Janey long, but I sense in her true decency.

As for my relationship with Mrs. Carrington, meanwhile, she continues to give me the cold shoulder. I worry that she will speak ill of me to the other wives, or to her husband. So far, the other wives seem not to have taken their cue from her, but I fear they might. As for Col Carrington, what if he reflected his wife's ill will toward me to my husband? True enough, Lt Grummond is filled with bile toward the Col, but I doubt he would accord me the same leeway of thought when it comes to my relationship with Mrs. Carrington. And if my husband were to be angry with me, could I blame him? All the wives know well that our role is to grease the skids of our husbands' careers, not to throw obstacles in their paths by squabbling with the wife of the commanding officer. Still, taking all of this into consideration, I find it difficult to cast aside Janey, whom life has dealt a difficult hand and who seeks so earnestly to improve herself. Can I ignore her plight and call myself a Christian?

Sincerely,
Frances

SEPTEMBER 13, 1866

"Why do we place our dead up on scaffolding?" asked Little Hawk, his face made to seem all the more somber by the unsteady light of their nighttime fire.

Crazy Horse and Lone Bear exchanged a brief glance. They had noticed how Little Hawk seemed different after his injury. Not his physical strength—he had recovered quickly and seemed little fazed in that regard. Nor had he changed his tendency, unusual for their people, to ask so many questions. Rather, it was as if being shot had impressed upon him the seriousness of adult life, all the more so at this moment of conflict and peril for their people.

"We're helping to lift them up to the Creator," said Crazy Horse. "Helping them on their way to the next life."

"And that's why we sacrifice their best horse?" asked Little Hawk. "And lay out their weapons beside them?"

Crazy Horse nodded, watching as his brother seemed to absorb this for a few moments.

There was a part of Crazy Horse that made him sad to see his brother lose any bit of the youthful enthusiasm and hopefulness that had so characterized him up until now. Yet this was the world in which they lived, and it was his responsibility to help his brother be prepared. He appreciated that Little Hawk asked important questions and seemed to reflect more than before on the answers he heard.

"Then it's good—it's *right* that we desecrate the bodies of the whites we kill," said Little Hawk. "We deny them the use of their bodies in the next life."

"That's right," said Lone Bear, and Crazy Horse could hear the anger in his voice. "What have they done with their hands in this life? How have they used their eyes? Are their hearts pure? Won't the product of their seed be more bred to be like them?"

Little Hawk reflected on this as Lone Bear continued. "It's not enough only to kill men such as this in this world. Such men deserve to suffer in the next world too."

"And why do the whites bury their dead beneath the ground?" asked Little Hawk. "Because their hearts are so dark? Their eyes so blind?"

Crazy Horse and Lone Bear both waited, each hoping the other could explain.

"Maybe," said Lone Bear, when it became clear Crazy Horse would not speak, "they see themselves returning their dead to Mother Earth?"

Crazy Horse shook his head. "When I see what they've done in the valley of the Twin Creeks, I don't see how this could be a people who revere the earth as their mother."

"Do you think it's true," asked Little Hawk, "what they say about the buffalo in the south?"

The topic was like a heavy weight pressing against their chests.

"I don't doubt that the whites would kill buffalo for the hides alone," said Lone Bear. "But I don't believe that all of the buffalo in the south are gone. Not even the whites could do that."

Little Hawk nodded, turning to Crazy Horse. Crazy Horse felt his brother's expectant gaze and knew that he sought additional assurance. He so wanted to give it. More than that, he wanted for it to be true. For an instant, he saw a flash of his dream about the locusts, how they swarmed the land and picked it clean. *Is this part of its meaning?* He thought of the power of the wagon guns, the precision of the revolvers. Finally, he said, "It's true, I think, that the whites are different from any of our other enemies."

"Red Cloud was wise to send us out to watch them, to learn how they fight," said Lone Bear.

"Do you think that we can defeat them?" asked Little Hawk. Again Crazy Horse heard in his brother's voice the need for comfort.

Crazy Horse thought hard about what he should say in reply, noticing that Lone Bear too awaited his answer. After a while Crazy Horse said, "We're lucky to have a leader such as Red Cloud. He's defeated our enemies his whole life."

This seemed enough for Little Hawk, who nodded vigorously before turning his back to the fire and pulling a buffalo robe around his shoulders. In a few minutes he was asleep.

Lone Bear was quiet for a long time, but then he asked, "Do you believe what you told him?"

"I want to believe it," said Crazy Horse. "I hope it."

SEPTEMBER 14, 1866

To the great joy of every soldier at Fort Phil Kearny, they had discovered among their ranks a man who could bake bread. He was a Frenchman named Philippe de Rouen, and his forefathers had been bakers as far back as they could account for their lineage. At most army fortifications, the baking duty rotated haphazardly among the enlisted men, with results to match. Colonel Carrington considered the discovery of de Rouen to be one of his great leadership coups. De Rouen's only request had been for two assistants, to be selected by him, and the colonel had happily accommodated.

The bakery—with its massive, brick-lined oven—took longer to complete than most of the buildings but had been ready for firing a week earlier. Morale had spiked, at least temporarily, the first day the smell of de Rouen's freshly baked bread began to waft across the parade grounds. The recipe for the bread came to the US Army via the army of Napoleon Bonaparte and contained only four ingredients: flour, water, salt, and yeast. In de Rouen's kneading hands, the simple components came together to produce much more than the sum of the parts, emerging from the wood-burning oven with a golden-brown crust that he quickly dabbed with a thin glaze of lard. The result, by frontier standards, was near miraculous, all the more so considering de Rouen's assistants spent hours sifting the flour before baking to rid it of mold, mice droppings, and in some instances, the mice themselves.

In truth, though skilled at the task, de Rouen had no particular love of baking bread. He did have an entrepreneurial streak, and in the baker's job he smelled the ingredients of a first-class opportunity. He picked his assistants carefully—two Bavarians he could trust. De Rouen knew that the baker would be given access to one of Fort Phil Kearny's most closely guarded commodities—yeast. As every army veteran knew well, the fermentation of yeast could be used to make bread; it could also be used to make alcohol. To protect this coveted commodity, the yeast barrels all bore locks to which only the baker held the keys.

Aside from the actual baking of bread, one of the baker's primary responsibilities was to ensure that the fires that heated the oven bricks never went out. It was the steady heat of the bricks, not the flames, that actually baked the bread. For the bricks to perform their function, they needed to be kept hot twenty-four hours a day, with the fire removed from the interior of the oven only for the hour or so the bread actually baked. The baker slept in a small room adjoining the bakery, rising throughout the night to add fuel to the fire.

De Rouen and his Bavarians set up their still on the first day of the bakery's operation. Ever mindful of design, Colonel Carrington had thoughtfully dug a deep cellar beneath the bakery so that supplies could be stored on the premises. There was a trapdoor and a system of pulleys to hoist up the barrels from the cellar. In the cellar, de Rouen directed the Bavarians to build a wall of flour barrels that preserved sufficient space to hide the still, and then they quickly set about to begin the production of a crude but effective brew. Based on preliminary soundings, it seemed certain that even a modest rate of production would result in the three men more than quadrupling their army salaries.

That calculus changed significantly on the third day of the bakery's operation. Or more precisely, the third night. De Rouen was asleep when he heard the door open and then the sound of boots crossing the wooden floor. He was surprised and then afraid to discover Lieutenant Grummond looming over him. He jumped up, pulling on his pants.

"Lieutenant?"

Two other men walked in behind Grummond, civilians that de Rouen recognized as James Wheatley and Isaac Fisher. Wheatley had a pretty wife, and the two of them ran a civilian boardinghouse from a building they had constructed just outside the walls of the fort. Fisher had a contract helping the quartermaster to process and warehouse incoming freight.

For a while Grummond said nothing, lighting a match and then a candle. Candle in hand, he began walking around the bakery, as if inspecting. Wheatley and Fisher both cut a slice of bread from a loaf on the worktable and stood eating.

"It's Private *de Rouen*, yes?" said Grummond. "Am I saying your name correctly?"

Grummond's pronunciation was not even close, but de Rouen nodded his head anyway. Grummond had a bad reputation among the enlisted men, and the officer's presence in the bakery in the middle of the night could bode only ill. Nor could de Rouen imagine any legitimate purpose for Wheatley and Fisher to be tagging along with the lieutenant.

"You know, Private Rouen, that I am deputy quartermaster on this post?"

De Rouen shook his head.

"Oh, yes, Private—and a serious responsibility it is." Lieutenant Grummond walked a bit as he talked, moving the candle so as to cast its light in various corners of the bakery.

"Do you know what is one of the deputy quartermaster's primary duties?"

Again de Rouen shook his head.

"To prevent stealing, Private. You see, it turns out that there are soldiers that devise clever schemes to defraud the US Army of its property." Grummond walked toward the padlocked yeast barrel by the wall, stopping in front of it.

"I think you might have a scheme right here in the bakery, Private . . ."

De Rouen didn't say anything.

"The penalties for defrauding the United States government can be quite severe. A man could be thrown into prison for five, even ten years . . ."

The candle illuminated only half of Grummond's face and cast a flickering shadow on the bakery wall. The effect, as de Rouen perceived it, was to make Grummond seem even more menacing. Grummond allowed de Rouen some time to contemplate. Wheatley and Fisher stood behind Grummond with serious faces as they gnawed, adding intimidation.

Only after a long pause did Grummond continue. "Of course, if you ask me my opinion . . . soldiers on the frontier, making a little hooch . . . not hurting anybody . . . in fact, probably making a god-awful duty station just a little more tolerable. Mr. Wheatley . . . Mr. Fisher, you were both distinguished officers during the war. Would you agree?"

They nodded. "Absolutely," said Wheatley.

"You could almost say it's patriotic," said Fisher.

Their angle became clear to de Rouen. "We can cut you in, gentlemen."

Grummond laughed. "Yes. I know. Seventy percent—paid weekly."

De Rouen scoffed. "Seventy percent! That hardly leaves enough for the rest of us to take the risk!"

"That's for you to decide. I suspect that doubling your army pay is worth the risk. Besides, Mr. Wheatley can help your volume by distributing via his boardinghouse . . . And Mr. Fisher will quash any competing product coming in from the teamsters."

De Rouen said nothing. In truth, Grummond was right. Thirty percent would still be significant. Having an officer to cover their flank would reduce the risk dramatically. Certainly he knew of no other options to enhance his meager army pay.

"Then we have a deal," said Grummond. "If I find you're cheating me, I'll see that you spend the next decade rotting in a jail cell. And by the way, if it comes down to your word against mine, I can assure you the officer will win that contest every time."

Grummond and the two civilians didn't wait for further discussion before departing into the night.

The fermentation of the first batch took a couple weeks, but soon they faced only the problem of producing in sufficient quantities to meet the overwhelming demand for alcohol on the United States Army's most distant post from civilization.

SEPTEMBER 21, 1866

Dear Journal,

A wagon train—twenty wagons—of supplies came in from Fort Laramie yesterday. There was great excitement at its arrival, but considerably less after the goods were unpacked. There is some grain for the horses, which makes my husband and the cavalrymen happy. He fears, though, that the quantity is adequate for no more than a couple weeks, and that the horses already are in such poor shape that this temporary improvement won't carry them far.

As for food for the rest of us, there is a good quantity of flour, so with our wonderful baker, we won't starve. The teamsters drove no cattle, however, and the only meats are of the salted variety. I have learned, at least, that soaking these salted "delicacies" for a full 24 hours before cooking takes away a bit of the briny bite. There also arrived great quantities of dried apples, the one fruit the army seems capable of delivering. Dr. Rutt says that they are good for me, but I swear I would trade a month's supply for a single bite of fresh peach!

Dr. Rutt was pleased at the arrival of some medicines, including opium and quinine. Here, though, there is a rumor that the quantities did not align with what had been commissioned. Colonel Carrington and the quartermaster are con-

ducting a rigorous audit of the teamsters to ensure that some
portion has not been pilfered.

Apologies, dear Journal, if my tone seems too complaining. Perhaps I should have begun by talking about the
enormous excitement at the inclusion of a month's worth of
newspapers from St. Louis! It is true that the most recent edition is three months old, but we all gobbled up the pages,
starved for news as we are. The pages were so tattered and thin
by the time they made the rounds that you could almost see
through them. Even then, we took them into the library to use
as fresh practice materials with our ever-diligent students.

Signed and Attested,
Mrs. Lieutenant George W. Grummond

Dear Friend,
There was mail with the supply train today for those lucky
enough to receive it. I, sadly, was not one of those recipients,
and I cannot conceal here my bitter disappointment. It has
been three months since last I heard from my family, and then
in a letter dated three months before that. I know the loyalty
of my mother and sister, and cannot imagine they have not
written diligently, as I have written them. And so I blame the
army, which seems no better at delivering the mail than at
delivering supplies. I ache with worry for my aged mother, for
my pregnant sister.

She has had a child by now, God willing, a child whose
name I don't even know. Has she received my letters to know
that I am with child, or the perils of the journey we endured
to reach this place? Today I couldn't help but feel even farther
away from home.

It made the sound of Janey's sweet Franklin County
accent all the more welcoming, and I lingered beside her wash-
basin for almost an hour today while she worked. I had gone

to deliver to her a few pages from the newspapers, and you would have thought I handed her a hundred dollars! She set down her work for a minute, dried her hands on her apron, and read me the headline, "Tennessee First Confederate State Readmitted to the Union." I'm not sure if she was more proud or I was!

Perhaps it was this bit of shared excitement that led her to confide in me, but she told me that Sgt Lang has been "paying her some attention." He serves in the infantry under Capt Fetterman. I have seen him, of course, a large man with sideburns and a mustache, but I don't know him. It was sweet to hear how she talks about him, and I hope he is kind to her. He has a distinguished war history, and Janey said that he served in the same company as my husband during General Sherman's southern campaign. With so few women on the post, the laundresses are paid all sorts of attention by the soldiers. Among the soldiers, as in any such large group, there is a mix of characters, and I hope for Janey that Sgt Lang is among the good ones that I know are present on this post.

Of course there are plenty of the less scrupulous, and the inventory of the supply train drove that point home. The wagons arrived with less than a third of the opium expected by Dr. Rutt. The teamsters had the usual story about broken bottles on the rough trail, but it is widely believed that there is a black market where such goods are sold at enormous profit. On such a small post, one would think that our officers will quickly ferret out the conspirators. Few things can stay secret for long.

Sincerely yours,
Frances

SEPTEMBER 26, 1866

Most nights, Bugler Adolph Metzger volunteered to play taps. The band's other bugle players avoided the late-night duty, but Metzger considered it his favorite part of the day. He stood now beside Captain Fetterman, the duty officer, near the flagpole in the center of the parade grounds. Fetterman consulted his pocket watch, and at ten p.m. sharp he nodded to Metzger.

Metzger put his lips to the bugle's mouthpiece, shaping his mouth so that no air could escape on the sides and holding his cheeks tight. Then he began to play.

Metzger loved the simple, slow elegance of taps. For most of the fort's inhabitants, he knew that his performance was less about music and more about the demarcation of time. So the perfection he sought as he played the notes was for himself, his effort to master this one song, to play its simple notes with purity and strength. As he worked his way through the well-trodden path of the melody, he felt a small but perceptible hitch as he attempted to glide with utter fluidity from one note to the next. No one else would hear it, but it bothered him.

"Beautiful, Bugler Metzger," said Captain Fetterman when he finished.

Metzger started to correct him, to point out the flaw, but then he wondered, what was the point? If the captain had enjoyed it, and he seemed sincere, then why intrude upon his experience?

Instead, Metzger said, "Thank you, Captain." Still, he knew.

A mile away, on top of Sullivant Hill, Crazy Horse heard again the horn the soldiers blew at the end of each day, recognizing well by now the particular song. He liked the song, though something about it made him sad. It was different from the other songs they played on the horn. The others were crisp and urgent, like a man talking fast. This song was slow and mournful.

One day, they had watched from a distance as the whites performed their death ceremony and placed a dead soldier in the ground. Crazy Horse had noticed that they played the same song then. It seemed an appropriate song to attach to a death ceremony, but did the whites also mourn the loss of each day, of every setting sun? In the rest of their lives, they seemed to hurry so much, heedless of consequences as they rapidly occupied a home that was not theirs, threw up a fortress in the midst of another people's sacred place. *Is this how they mourn? Is this how they ask forgiveness? Are the whites capable of such thought, of such reflection upon their actions?*

SAME DAY

"I don't know where you're getting it," said Captain Ten Eyck, raising Grummond's flask. "But here's to your procurement." He tipped the flask and then passed it to Captain Fetterman, the three junior officers huddled around the stove that filled the officers' quarters with such comforting warmth. Apart from Grummond, the other married officers—Colonel Carrington and Captains Powell and Bisbee—were at their own quarters in the company of their wives.

Fetterman already felt the pleasant fuzziness of his earlier sips of this new concoction. At first he had been conflicted. He took rules and discipline seriously, and it always felt wrong to break them. Half the post knew the bakery was the newest source of alcohol, and there were rumors, which Fetterman considered highly credible, that Grummond himself was behind the enterprise. Fetterman couldn't imagine leading a scheme that flew so directly in the face of the fort's discipline. It was a different matter, though, to contemplate leading the opposition to the schemers. Fetterman had been to war and was not naïve about armies and alcohol. He understood that, like the boiler on a steam engine, the men of an army needed an outlet, lest the pressure grow so great that the whole thing blew apart. It was all in the calibration.

Fetterman tipped back the flask and felt the sharp burn of the crude liquid, then the not-unpleasant sensation as the accumulating effect muddled his head. They were on the frontier, after all. They were in a war here, too, though so different from the war back east. It wasn't just the liquor and the stove that contributed to Fetterman's warm feeling; he valued the affiliation he felt with the other officers in these moments.

There was an additional reason that kept Fetterman from confronting what he knew to be wrong. He knew well how the enlisted men viewed those officers who made no exception for the breaking of rules. The men understood and accepted that public transgressions would be punished. A soldier foolish enough to display his drunkenness in public deserved what he got. But surreptitious drinking was more or less the unofficial army sport. Officers who understood this less official line won from their men greater respect, even affection. Fetterman had always attempted to navigate this ambiguous territory. He wanted his men to respect him, but he wanted them to like him too.

Captain Fetterman watched as the flask passed back to Grummond and admired again that the most junior of the officers had such confidence. Not even public reprimand seemed to faze him. After the stampede of the cattle herd and Lieutenant Grummond's role in the death of Private Cassidy, Captain Ten Eyck had made good on his promise to report fully the incident. Colonel Carrington had punished the lieutenant by attaching a written note to his record—and by docking a month's pay. Grummond hardly even blinked. Fetterman knew that Grummond had propagated his own version of the incident, probably enhancing his reputation as a fighter. For a week or two, Grummond had given Captain Ten Eyck the cold shoulder. Even that had passed quickly. Grummond had that ability. He just barreled ahead.

"What do you think, Fetterman?"

Fetterman looked up from his own thoughts to find the other two officers staring at him. He looked back blankly.

Grummond repeated, "What do you think, Captain, about the ability of the savages to stand up in a *real fight* with the US Army?"

Fetterman tried to clarify his thoughts, which seemed to jumble. He felt gratification that Grummond would solicit his opinion and that his fellow officers would want to hear his views. He thought of his conversations with Bridger. In his mind, he briefly struggled to construct a sophisticated and nuanced articulation. He looked again at the expectant faces of his peers.

"I'll tell you what I think," said Fetterman. "Give me eighty of our men and I could ride through the whole goddamn Sioux nation!"

Grummond burst into a broad smile and raised the flask. "Hell yes!" Ten Eyck uttered his own affirmation, reaching eagerly for his turn to drink along in approval. Fetterman watched them, basking in the fraternity. When the flask came again to him, he drained the contents, handing the empty vessel to Grummond.

"Why you wily bastard, Fetterman! I told them there was some pepper in you!"

For the briefest instant, Fetterman felt a pang that seemed to question the rightness of this approval. He pushed it down. It felt good in this moment, and that was enough for now.

They passed a flask in the enlisted men's quarters too. One man sat by the door, responsible for alerting the others to the sound of any approaching footsteps. The rest could relax—a ragtag mix of a dozen infantry, cavalry, and even a few members of the band. Metzger took his turn with the flask, pleasantly surprised that the concoction was not as vile as he might have expected. *Must be true the Bavarians are in on it.*

"He can pitch, but he can't hit worth shit," said Sergeant Lang, taking his turn on the flask. Sergeant Lang might be a stickler on some matters—keeping brass polished ranked high on his list. But he liked his liquor and couldn't be happier with the baker's new side business. The sergeant had also acquired a passion for baseball during the war, thrilled that the massive space inside the fort's walls easily accommodated a diamond. Six of the fort's companies fielded teams that now competed in a league.

"C Company ain't got nobody that can hit," said Private Thorey, who happened to be the best batter on the post.

"Well, no one's getting a hit tomorrow," said Corporal Dule. "Lieutenant Grummond announced extra drilling."

"You gotta be kidding me!" said Thorey. "Leave it to Grummond to spoil the one good thing on this post!"

"It's worse than that," said Sergeant Flanagan. Flanagan was Second

Cavalry and reported directly to Grummond. "We're doing extra drills all week. The lieutenant says it's to make up for all the time chopping wood."

Sergeant Lang took another swig—a deep one—then addressed himself to Flanagan. "You watch out for Grummond," he said. "I knew him in the war."

"I heard he was court-martialed," said Sergeant Flanagan. "And that's why he's stuck at lieutenant instead of being a captain."

"That's a true fact," said Sergeant Lang. "He pistol-whipped his own NCO . . . and shot an unarmed civilian. But that isn't even the worst of it . . ."

The other men leaned in, more than curious. There were always rumors on an army post, especially in an army filled with so many veterans. The war, of course, had been sprawling. Millions of men across half a continent. Yet it was always surprising how easy it was to make connections, to find someone who knew someone.

"I was there at Kennesaw Mountain, early summer of 1864," said Lang. "Sherman's March to the Sea. We were rolling along until we hit Kennesaw, so close to Atlanta we could almost taste it. But Johnson's men were dug in on the mountain."

Metzger listened closely. Something about Grummond had bothered him from the beginning. It was frightening, if you thought about it, the degree to which enlisted men depended on the judgment and skill of their officers. In his years in the army, he had seen many officers of poor judgment and poor skill, and he had seen the consequences.

"Grummond liked to drink then too," said Sergeant Lang. "And not just at night when he could sleep it off. One afternoon, Grummond decided to take the initiative, make a surprise attack on the Kennesaw heights."

"What happened?" asked Sergeant Baker.

"There was a corporal named Patrick Walsh—a friend of mine. He saw how drunk Grummond was, knew it was suicide to charge up that hill. He sent five men out in front of Grummond—had them pelt him with rocks. Grummond was so drunk that Walsh convinced him it was bullets, got him to call retreat."

"Come on!" said Baker. "Did that really happen?"

"On my witness and my mother's grave," said Lang. The men took this attestation seriously. Lang had his vices, and might even have stretched the edges of a tale or two. But no one questioned his family fidelity.

"Grummond's got a couple other little secrets." It was a new voice. From the shadows, just beyond the circle of light illuminated by the lamp, they saw Corporal Quinn, half reclined on his bunk. Quinn did not imbibe and rarely spoke, so they were all surprised and curious to hear him.

"I served with the son of a bitch Grummond at the end of the war—in Tennessee. Not a lot of fighting, so Grummond had time for other things . . . like cavorting with the local ladies."

"Mrs. Grummond?" said Lang. Like the other men, he liked Grummond's young wife. Unlike her husband, she seemed to have a genuine affection for the enlisted men.

Quinn nodded. "Only problem was—he already had a wife . . . and two kids."

The barracks fell silent as the men absorbed that bit of news.

"He told my captain that the lawyers could sort it out someday, but he wasn't waiting around to let someone else scoop her up."

"I'll be damned," said Sergeant Flanagan. "A polygamist on top of everything else."

"Too bad," said Sergeant Lang. "Mrs. Grummond deserves better than the likes of him."

The startling news seemed to take some of the steam out of the evening, and perhaps more critically, the flask of bakery hooch had run dry.

"This crowd's turning too serious," said Sergeant Flanagan. "And all this talk of polygamy has got my blood up . . . I may take a little stroll by the laundress tents."

Some of the men laughed, though Sergeant Lang was not among them.

"I hear the one named Janey will unbutton more than just the flap on her tent," said Flanagan.

There were more laughs.

"Watch your manners," said Sergeant Lang. A couple men laughed at that, too, thinking Lang must be joking. He stood up, though, taking full advantage of the fact that he was one of the biggest men at the fort. From his face, it was clear that Lang was serious.

Most of the men would have backed off. Sergeant Flanagan, though, considered Lang something of a rival, not least because of the usual tensions between infantry and cavalry. Flanagan felt the eyes of his cavalrymen upon him, and saw no easy way to back down. "Jesus, Lang," said Flanagan. "When did you turn so pious? Everyone on the post knows she's whoring on the si—"

For the large man that he was, Lang moved quickly, and he had leveled Flanagan with a punch in the face before the other man could finish his sentence.

The men in the barracks jumped in to pull Lang back. Others helped Flanagan to his feet, as he craned his neck and touched his bleeding mouth with his fingers. "Goddamn you, Lang! You broke my tooth!"

The cavalrymen hustled their bleeding sergeant from the barracks, and Sergeant Lang stormed off a few moments later, muttering something about "poor manners."

Metzger stayed back with a few of the others, for whom the evening's events had provided, certainly by frontier standards, a wealth of fodder for further discussion. Metzger filled a pipe and drew from it slowly, the tobacco seeming to sustain the not-unpleasant buzzing in his head from the liquor. As was his way, Bugler Metzger liked to observe a lot but say very little. Anyway, others were usually happy to carry the conversation.

Metzger knew, of course, that some of the laundresses plied their illicit trade, but he took his status as a married man seriously, so he was not among the soldiers with firsthand experience. Not that he hadn't felt tempted, lonely like all of the men and so far away from home. He knew, though, that there would come a day when he would leave his army life behind. He wasn't sure yet when or how that day would arrive, but when it came, he wanted to preserve the sanctity in which it existed in his mind. How many times had he imagined himself returning to Brooklyn to the welcoming arms of his wife and daughter? He had thought through the words he would use to share the good news of the stake he had scrambled together for their future, along with the details of how their new life would unfold. The particulars, of course, remained ever elusive. In the meantime, the power of the destination, however vague, was enough. The idea of the temporary pleasure of a quick roll with a laundress did not compare, and so Metzger felt the temptation but pushed it aside.

The oil lantern inside Janey White's tent created shadows on the walls like a scrim in one of those traveling theater productions. When she stood up and walked, her shadow seemed to float across the canvas.

Sergeant Lang stood outside, next to a large barrel of soapy water. The wool pants and shirts of a dozen uniforms hung on Janey's laundry line, swaying gently in the night breeze. He felt guilty for watching without announcing himself, yet he wanted to be sure she was alone. He had come one other time and found Janey in the company of another man, and it had rankled him for days. Lang knew that he was not the only soldier to visit Janey, but he saw no reason to flail himself with the uncomfortable fact.

He reached again into his coat pocket, feeling the assurance of the soft bit of silk. He looked around. He saw a distant sentry on the rampart and heard the sound of the other laundresses inside their own tents. Otherwise, he was alone. "Janey," he whispered, and when there was no response, he whispered the name again. "Janey."

"Who's out there?" came the suspicious reply.

Lang watched the shadow inside the tent move toward the flap.

"Who's out there?"

"Janey—it's me . . . Augustus Lang."

"Gus?"

Lang took encouragement at her use of his nickname. She opened the flap and poked her head into the night. Even in the dim light, he admired the way her auburn hair framed the pale white skin of her face.

"What're you doing?" she asked. Her tone did not seem unfriendly.

Sergeant Lang stepped forward into the penumbra of light that spilled from the tent flap.

"I wanted to see you," he said. "I brought you something." He reached into his pocket and pulled out a long length of green silk ribbon. Janey smiled. Encouraged, Lang stepped forward to hand her the ribbon.

"You brought this for me?"

Lang nodded. "The sutler's wife said she thought the green would look most pretty on red hair."

Janey's smile grew larger, and she held the ribbon against her hair. "Well, what do you think?"

"It looks beautiful," said Lang. He took another big breath before blurting, "You look beautiful."

"Thank you, Gus. It's a thoughtful gift . . . Green's always been my favorite color." She studied him a bit longer, then gave her own furtive glance around the parade grounds. "Do you . . . do you want to come inside?"

SEPTEMBER 28, 1866

Barking dogs, what seemed like hundreds of them, set off waves of greetings as Bridger and Beckwourth rode into sight of the Crow village of Goes Ahead. The dogs drew the attention of the dozens of boys who guarded the most impressive horse herd that Bridger had ever seen. Half of the boys jumped on ponies and galloped bareback into the camp. Minutes later, a delegation of young warriors charged forth, and Bridger might have been concerned if not for Beckwourth's utter calm.

Beckwourth's popularity in the camp was evident from the instant they stood face-to-face with the young warriors, who greeted the scout with obvious recognition and affection. Beckwourth enhanced the effect by reaching into his saddlebag and commencing immediately to pass out ropes of tobacco.

Two women approached as he and Beckwourth came to the edge of the village, and Beckwourth dismounted to embrace them. Bridger listened as Beckwourth spoke the Crow language with obvious fluency, though he turned suddenly solemn. One of his wives had died, he explained to Bridger. Bridger noticed that the two wives present both had stumps in place of several fingers, which Beckwourth later explained was the Crow ritual for mourning the death of family members.

Beckwourth set off another mad scramble by reaching into his saddlebag to produce red ribbon and shiny metal beads. These he presented to his two wives, but they quickly began a secondary distribution to a large group of other women. Beckwourth greeted children in a range of ages, expressing surprise at their size.

Eventually, they arrived at the largest teepee in the village. Like most of the village's lodges, it was made of canvas, not buffalo hides. The Crow had been closely aligned with the whites for as long as Bridger could remember, and one benefit of this alliance was trade. Unlike the Sioux and Cheyenne, Bridger noticed that many of the Crow men carried rifles, including a few with the new Henrys and Spencers. They were better armed, he noted, than most of the soldiers at Fort Phil Kearny.

Bridger assumed that the big teepee must belong to Goes Ahead. Several stunning horses stood picketed outside the lodge, horses worthy of a chief. Bridger also noticed the large pole rising upward from the teepee's vent, higher than the poles supporting the canvas. From the top of this pole, a dozen scalps fluttered in the light breeze.

The flap opened and Goes Ahead emerged. He, too, greeted Beckwourth warmly, and Bridger by association, inviting them inside the lodge. They sat around the glowing coals of a cooking fire over which hung a steaming iron pot on a metal tripod. They had barely sat down before Goes Ahead's two wives had put meat in front of them. They wore similar dresses, adorned with so many elk teeth that there was a clicking sound as they moved.

The canvas of the teepee admitted more light than hides, Bridger noticed, and he studied Goes Ahead. He had never been good at guessing the age of Indians, but the chief was old. His hair was silver and extended unadorned down the length of his back. His face was wrinkled like pine bark, and a massive scar extended diagonally from his forehead to his cheek. He smiled often, and when he did, a full set of teeth, surprising for his age, gleamed white.

They spoke for a long time in Crow, catching up, Beckwourth translating only the broad strokes. Bridger understood little Crow, but was content to sit beside a fire and eat the tasty buffalo prepared by Goes Ahead's wives.

Eventually, Goes Ahead produced his pipe, and they all smoked the tobacco gifted by Beckwourth. Bridger could tell they were talking about the Sioux from the change in Goes Ahead's tone. Beckwourth began to translate more.

"I asked him where they're camped," said Beckwourth. "He says he thinks they're on the Tongue, near the mountains."

"Have they scouted it?" asked Bridger.

"Not in the last month," said Beckwourth. "He says there's more Sioux war parties about than usual with all the whites on the Montana Road. And now more Cheyenne coming north with the fighting to the south. The Crow are staying up north—hoping to stay out of the fray."

Then Goes Ahead said something new. Bridger could see Beckwourth cock his head, listening intently. Beckwourth asked Goes Ahead a question, and the chief nodded his head insistently—and said something with seeming conviction.

Beckwourth looked at Bridger.

Goes Ahead said something else to Beckwourth. Once again, Beckwourth appeared to push back. Again the chief appeared to repeat himself solemnly.

"Goes Ahead says that Red Cloud sent emissaries into Crow country, called for the Crow to join with the Sioux in their fight against the whites."

Bridger could scarcely believe it. "Are you sure?"

"I asked him three times," said Beckwourth. "Red Cloud apparently sent a message saying that times had changed and they needed to change their ways of thinking. The Crow refused, but . . ."

Bridger nodded. In a half century on the frontier, the enmity of the Sioux and the Crow had been as certain as night following day. For the Crow, Red Cloud's call for new thinking and alliance had gone too far. It said something profound about Red Cloud's thinking that for the Oglala chief, it had not.

"I'm not sure the US Army understands what they're up against," said Beckwourth.

Bridger thought of his various conversations with Colonel Carrington and his officers. "I'm pretty sure they don't."

OCTOBER 1, 1866

Crazy Horse left the village unannounced and alone. The tribe needed to know the whereabouts of the buffalo herd, and he needed the time apart to reflect. It felt reassuring somehow to be engaged in a ritual so central to the rhythm of his people's lives, as if somehow nothing was changed. No activity was more crucial than the fall hunt, the success of which was essential to their survival during the unforgiving winter to come.

Yet even in this ritual he found no refuge. Instead, he discovered yet another tributary that flooded into the swift and growing current of his fears.

It took three days for Crazy Horse to find the first sign of the herd. In the past, the nearby presence of the herd was a constant. Perhaps there would be short periods of time when a wildfire or approaching storm caused the herd to drift in an unanticipated way. For the most part, though, experienced hunters like High Backbone always would have a clear sense of where the animals were.

Crazy Horse had rightly foreseen that the buffalo would hew closer to the mountains, avoiding their usual places on the plains, now heavily traveled by the soldiers and other whites. There had been no sign, though, in the first two valleys where Crazy Horse had expected to find them.

It was with profound relief that Crazy Horse encountered the first fresh tracks and scat, telling him he must be close. Within a short time, cresting a small swell, he came across the unmistakable markings of the full herd. In the wide vale below him, a great swath had been cut through waist-high prairie grass. Scat was everywhere, along with crescent-shaped tracks in dozens of sizes, from those of the small calves to the massive bulls. Spread across the landscape were dozens of the buffalo-sized depressions where the animals wallowed in the dust, desperate to relieve themselves of vexing fleas. The wind shifted, and his horse reacted; then Crazy Horse too caught the musky, dusty scent of thousands of animals. He looked in the direction of the wind and knew that the herd must be no more distant than the next valley. He nudged his horse to speed it forward.

When only a ridgeline separated him from the herd, he hobbled his horse and proceeded the last few yards on his belly. The herd was smaller than he'd hoped—hundreds, not thousands, of animals. He guessed that the shrinking spaces in the Powder River Valley forced the animals into smaller groupings than in past years. Still, for a time he had begun to fear that he would find no buffalo at all, or only at a great distance. Certainly this herd was more than sufficient for their needs through the winter. He pushed aside, for the moment, thoughts beyond the current season.

He settled in between clumps of sage, breathing it all in, watching the prairie world unfold around him. *Always watch and always learn.* Crazy Horse could hear the voice of High Backbone in his head as he remembered again the words.

For a while that day he watched the wolves that always trailed the herd. He had noticed the many ways they could seem like the lazy, playful dogs in his village. But they were different, a few of the animals always alert, waiting for their moment. When it arrived—some small separation between a few of the buffalo and the greater herd—the wolves would pounce, and in an instant the playful dogs became a ruthlessly coherent unit, working together through lethal instinct to pick off the young and the weak.

As the day stretched into evening, it was a clever fox that caught Crazy Horse's eye, the bushy-tailed animal tracking some scent as it darted from clump of sage to clump of sage. The fox kept lowering and raising its head—down to the sage, then up to test the slight evening breeze.

Suddenly Crazy Horse saw the fox's quarry. Fifty feet from the fox, a female running bird ran into open ground. Her coloring was unmistakable, streaks of rusty brown like war paint on a white body, and she propelled herself with sporadic, furious bursts on long, skinny legs. Crazy Horse knew that the running bird nested on the ground, and he suspected that the fox would prefer the contents of the nest—it must be nearby—to a bird that might take flight at any moment.

Then he noticed that the bird held one wing in an unnatural position, dragging it clumsily behind her as she ran. The fox seemed to realize the opportunity. It ducked low and began to pursue, hugging the ground and moving serpentine through the brush.

For a distance of almost a hundred yards the running bird attempted to flee, dragging her broken wing as she scurried through the brush, the fox closer and closer until it was only a few yards away, closing in for the kill—when abruptly the bird took flight.

The fox actually took a step back as if startled, resting on its haunches as it watched the running bird fly away. Crazy Horse tracked the bird as it flew a wide circle, ultimately returning almost exactly to her starting point, no doubt nearby to where her nest lay.

Far away now, the fox took a look around and then set off in a new direction, leaving the running bird and her nest behind.

Crazy Horse smiled.

OCTOBER 3, 1866

Dear Journal,

There are eleven children on the post, five girls and six boys, ages ranging from eight months to fourteen years. Colonel Carrington plans to build a school for them in the spring, but for the time being they use the chapel. They are prohibited from going outside, of course, and you can imagine how quickly the interior spaces of the fort cease to contain their energy. Mrs. Bisbee serves as the post teacher and does her best to prevent idle time. Still, there is a gaggle of boys that I see emerging from all corners of the fort, and I can imagine the stories they will one day tell of their years on the frontier. The other day I saw them tumbling one after another down the haystack in the cavalry yard, and they seemed to be having such fun that I was half tempted to join in.

Speaking of children, I play the game often of thinking about the name of our baby. This may seem silly, but I even keep a list, putting them down to see how they look in writing! Saying them out loud while alone in my quarters to hear the sound! If a girl, my current favorite is Octavia, for my sister, though I have always loved the name Faith. If a boy, I have always liked the name Nathaniel, but the Lt is intent that his son will carry his name. In any event, it's an amusing game and makes me all the more excited for the day, approaching so rapidly, when my little baby will be here.

Signed and Attested,
Mrs. Lieutenant George Washington Grummond

Dear Friend,

Can I confess to you that I live in utter terror of being a mother? Of course there are many moments that I feel great excitement, and the other women are kind and encouraging, Mrs. Jones in particular, wife of Sergeant Elias Jones and mother of the post's only other infant, a ten-month-old girl named Katherine. I spend as much time with Mrs. Jones as I can, just to watch and ask questions, and she manages the whole affair so effortlessly. Kate is her first child, so she began with no more experience than I.

Yet I feel no more prepared to be a mother than I have been to be a wife, and frankly seem to have no more inclination in the one domain than the other. When Mrs. Jones hands me little Kate to hold, the child seems most often to burst into tears. While her mother—and all of the other women—seem to know how to soothe her with just the right little bit of rocking, my efforts seem only to produce more tears. Honestly it has made me worried and sometimes blue. In my darkest moments, I must confess that I am angry that I am to be a mother right now.

Of course I have always wanted to have a family, but somehow I didn't imagine it all would happen so quickly. There are times when I am sitting here alone in my dark, tiny quarters, the wind flapping at the canvas that serves as windows, gritty dust everywhere, and I wonder how I got here. After we married, the Lt and I first were posted to New York City. I loved the excitement of that place, and it seemed so far removed from the South, so ravaged by war and so mired in the aftermath of horrible defeat.

But then, there came a day when the Lt received word that he—we—would be transferred to the frontier, to build a fort in a place, the Powder River Valley, that I had never heard of before. Now here I am, and in a few months I'll have a baby, too, with no knowledge or skill for caring for it. I find myself wondering, how did this happen, and how did it all happen so fast? I confess here that I imagine myself running away, joining a wagon train back to Fort Laramie, and making my way as quickly as I can back to my mother and sister in Tennessee, back to the place and the people I know. Of course, these moments pass quickly, not least because it's so far away. Distance is my harshest prison, and I'm wise enough at least to know there is no returning to the past. But each time my mind begins to wander down this path, I can't help but think there is something seriously wrong with me. And the thoughts are so strange and dark that I can't imagine sharing them with anyone, certainly not the officers' wives. What would they think of me?

Many times I almost feel more akin to Janey and the laundresses. Did any of them truly wish to come to this place? Can I say here that I honestly understand how a woman might resort to desperate means to provide for herself? Today Dr. Rutt instructed the officers' wives in "triage," the term used for sorting the wounded should, God forbid, our men ever suffer an attack that resulted in large numbers of casualties. Triage is a horrific process in which life-and-death decisions are made—giving priority to serious wounds, but also sorting out those poor souls who cannot survive and making a godlike decision to cast them aside. It made me think about the moral quandary of our laundresses. Don't they face a type of triage every day? When I look at their situations, I can understand where considerations of morality might seem quite secondary to the necessity of making a living, to the desperate desire to pull themselves up from the bottom rung. Is it fair for anyone who doesn't face the same brutal choices to judge?

I recognize in hindsight the privilege from which I was the

beneficiary growing up. Of course I never would say it openly now, but my family kept slaves before the war, and even after we set them free—when the Union Army first occupied Williamson County—we had Negroes for field hands and house servants. I never saw my mother cook and of course I never did. Now I watch the wives like Mrs. Bisbee who seem to juggle their many tasks effortlessly, and I wonder how they do it.

I am wise enough already to know that my view of the world from Franklin County was narrow and protected, even during war. It is true that we suffered hardship and deprivation, even nursing wounded soldiers in our parlor after the Battle of Franklin. Even then, though, I was surrounded by servants who protected us from many of the most difficult aspects of life during war. Our loyalty to the Union also meant that during occupation there was respect for our property, provision of food, and of course, once I began my courtship with the Lt, entrée to the top social rung of life after the war.

In my short conversations with Janey I know that she and others suffered in much greater measure. I am not saying that dire circumstances justify any means. I can imagine, though, in some small way, her desperation. I feel on many days that I have no control of my own life, and that I am swept along by circumstance to a place where I now am literally imprisoned in a strange new life. What must it feel like to Janey, who strives to climb each day from a starting place so much further down the ladder?

Sincerely Yours,
Frances

OCTOBER 4, 1866

It was intimidating to see them all. Even Red Cloud was present, mounted on his best buffalo runner beside High Backbone and the other chiefs. He looked to Crazy Horse expectantly, as did all the warriors. There must have been more than two hundred men between the bands of Red Cloud and High Backbone, all now assembled to hunt the herd that Crazy Horse had scouted a few days earlier.

The buffalo had moved, of course, in the days since Crazy Horse discovered the herd. But they had moved in the direction that he had foreseen, continuing to hug the Shining Mountains, now blanketing the valley along a tiny creek almost to where the Greasy Grass flowed out onto the prairie. It was not far from territory the Crow called their home, and normally the Lakota might have avoided it. This year, they had no choice.

Crazy Horse and Lone Bear, who had been given the honor of riding head when the signs turned fresh, returned now to report. Red Cloud looked to the two young warriors.

"How many?" asked Red Cloud.

Crazy Horse and Lone Bear looked to each other, both seeming to hope the other would speak first. Finally, Crazy Horse replied, "More than five hundred."

There was an excited murmur. Of course, they all had seen far larger herds, but not this season, and all of them had worried. If they handled this hunt skillfully, they might be secure for the winter. They all felt relief for the opportunity.

"How would you hunt them?" asked Red Cloud.

Crazy Horse felt the churn of his stomach as he always did in moments of public display. He took a breath to calm himself. *You know how to hunt them. This is your opportunity to share with your people.* He had given it careful thought as he and Lone Bear studied the herd's position in the valley, considered how they might attack it. He had confidence his plan made sense.

"The valley has steep hills on the north and south, and the mountains to the west. East is the only way out."

"Is it narrow enough to the east for us to block it?" asked High Backbone.

Crazy Horse shook his head, and for a moment he doubted his plan. He pictured the terrain in his mind, could see it as if he were there. "No, we should hit them from all four sides. But the first move should come from the east—so they'll run to the west, then be slowed by the hills and the mountains."

"How do we signal each other we're in position?" asked Red Cloud. He was curious about Crazy Horse, and this hunt was a good opportunity to test him. He had seen him grow up and had been hearing good things—that the young warrior had a unique mix of his father's wisdom and his uncle's skill in battle. This was Red Cloud's first chance to see the young man in a position of such responsibility.

"When we're in place, each of the four groups will signal with a mirror," said Crazy Horse. "When everyone has signaled, the group to the east will charge the herd. Once the herd stampedes to the west, the others all join in."

High Backbone nodded. He rode out and turned to face them all, raising his voice to be sure he was heard. "The Creator has given us this chance to feed our families through the winter. None of us must put himself before the tribe—wait for the moment we've planned. Only then show us your bravery and your skill."

Crazy Horse could not help but notice the seriousness on every man's face. They understood.

"Divide into four groups," said Red Cloud. "Crazy Horse—you will lead the group to the east."

For a moment, Crazy Horse felt surprise and even apprehension that Red Cloud had bestowed upon him this honor. It occurred to him, though, that the tasking made perfect sense. He and Lone Bear, after all, were the ones who knew best the position of the herd. It was his responsibility to the tribe to play this role. As for Lone Bear and Little Hawk, Crazy Horse could feel their smiles even before he turned to see them.

Crazy Horse's plan for the hunt succeeded. The group he led—from the east—charged forward first, so the herd stampeded as hoped toward the remaining hunters. Not a single man broke formation early, so that when the full attack came—simultaneously from north, south, and west—there were few places for the buffalo to run, and all of them forced the animals uphill. The landscape gave the hunters and their swift horses the advantage, and they used it with lethal effect.

For two days, practically without sleep, the whole tribe had worked to reap the full benefits of the hunt. Gutting the buffalo, staking out the hides, butchering and drying the meat as quickly as possible to avoid spoilage . . . it was filthy, backbreaking work. Tonight, though, finally they could celebrate. They danced and ate, far beyond the point where they were sated, reveling in the luxury of eating with no thought but the pleasure of the moment.

Crazy Horse looked at Little Hawk, sitting beside Lone Bear with a rib in his hand, the corners of his mouth glistening with delicious grease in the warm light of the fire.

"You're happy, brother?" asked Little Hawk.

Crazy Horse saw that his brother asked the question with great seriousness, and it warmed his heart to be the focus of his brother's concern. "I am happy," said Crazy Horse, even forcing a bit of a smile, because he sensed that Little Hawk watched attentively for such affirmation. In his way, for the moment, Crazy Horse was happy. True, they'd had to travel much farther than usual to find the herd this year. Crazy Horse could not stop himself from thinking about what this might mean in the grander scheme of the world in which they now lived. Still, they had found buffalo, and in sufficient numbers to meet their needs for this season. Crazy Horse had reveled in hunting with his brother, with his friends, and with his tribe. Usually, if the tribe had worked hard and planned well, the Moon of the Rutting Deer should be one of the happiest times of the year, a brief moment to appreciate the satisfaction of preparation before hunkering in for the onset of true winter.

Crazy Horse leaned forward over the fire, using a horn spoon to scoop a steaming mouthful from the big skull that had roasted for hours in the coals.

Lone Bear watched him, shaking his head. "How can you eat brain? Today we can choose from the whole animal—and you choose brain?"

Crazy Horse dipped his spoon again and offered this bite to Lone Bear, who screwed up his face and turned away in disgust. "It's you who's missing out," said Crazy Horse, then offered the spoon to Little Hawk.

Little Hawk hesitated, but then leaned in to take the bite. He worked his mouth up and down for a while, his face studied.

"So—how do you like it?" asked Lone Bear.

Little Hawk spit his mouthful of buffalo brain into the fire, then spit a couple more times. "It's terrible!"

Lone Bear and Crazy Horse both laughed.

"You see," said Lone Bear, "I told you that your brother doesn't know everything!"

Crazy Horse laughed at that too.

They stayed by the fire a long time that evening, talking and laughing. When the dusk finally gave way completely to night, the scores of Lakota campfires seemed to reflect back the light from the blazing stars. As much as he might appreciate his time apart, there were many moments when Crazy Horse felt great satisfaction to be in the presence of his people. Certainly during a moment like this. How good it was to bask in the glory of a successful hunt, to eat until full and then eat more, to be ready for winter, to laugh with friends, to be a part of a powerful tribe—a tribe that, left alone, could survive in this place for all time.

A dog barked, and suddenly in the light of their fire a boy appeared whom Crazy Horse recognized as one of Red Cloud's young sons. "My father wants to speak to you."

For a moment, Crazy Horse didn't know how to react, having never been asked to speak with Red Cloud. So he just sat there, slightly stunned, chewing buffalo brain.

Finally, Lone Bear hit him on the shoulder. "Hey!"

Little Hawk hit him on the other shoulder. "Go!"

Crazy Horse was surprised to find Red Cloud alone inside his lodge. The great chief sat on a plush buffalo robe in front of the glowing embers of a small cooking fire, turning willow skewers heavy with chunks of fresh meat. Tiny flames leapt up when the fat dripped down, hissing as if to punctuate the conversation.

"I want to talk to you about the whites," said Red Cloud. "I'm trying to understand them."

Crazy Horse nodded, though at first he was so surprised he didn't know what to say. He had expected perhaps to be given the task of raising a new war party. Instead, Red Cloud was asking him, a young man, for his opinion. The chief's humility made an instant impression, and Crazy Horse was struck by the wisdom of being open to learning from others, even someone so much younger and less experienced. At the same time, having been asked such an important question, Crazy Horse grappled with how to shape his thoughts, jumbled in his head like a giant knot. He struggled with how to untangle it so that his views would be helpful.

Red Cloud seemed to sense the young warrior's difficulty. "Do you hunt a buffalo differently than you hunt a deer?" asked the chief.

"Yes," said Crazy Horse.

"Why?" asked Red Cloud.

"Because the two behave differently."

"Yes. I want to know how the whites behave. I want to know how they think."

Crazy Horse reflected a moment. This was something he had considered at length. Still, he struggled to bring the contradictions into confluence. Finally, he said, "I look at some of the things they make—like their weapons—and I think, sometimes, they have great intelligence . . . in ways that frighten me."

Red Cloud nodded. "And other times?"

"And other times they behave so foolishly that I can't imagine the same men make those amazing things."

"What have they done that makes you think they're foolish?" asked Red Cloud. "In what ways are they weak?"

"Well," said Crazy Horse. "Every day they do the exact same thing, so that it's easy to know their patterns and to attack them. When we do attack, they do the same thing each time in response."

"Maybe," said Red Cloud, "they are very intelligent about some things—but foolish about *us.*"

Crazy Horse cocked his head questioningly.

"I've talked with many white soldier chiefs at Fort Laramie," said Red Cloud. "I notice they all speak to us as if we're children—or feeble-minded.

"Who is easier to fight?" asked Red Cloud. "An enemy who knows you very well, understands all of your power, respects you—or one who holds you in contempt, who maybe is even blinded by his own regard for himself?"

Crazy Horse nodded.

"We should not make the mistake about the whites that they make about us," said Red Cloud. "We need to respect their strengths, fight them when and where they can't bring those strengths to bear. But let their arrogance be their weakness. Let their belief in our weakness—be our strength.

"We must also make our numbers a strength," said Red Cloud. "I've sent couriers to invite the Cheyenne and the Arapaho to join us—a single great village."

Red Cloud paused a bit before continuing. "You showed yourself to be a leader in the hunt, and I've heard of your bravery in fights with the soldiers. I want you to take a war party back to the fort—bigger than usual."

"How big?" asked Crazy Horse.

"Fifty warriors, but not just Oglala and Minnicoujou. I want us to begin fighting alongside the other tribes. I want us to learn to work together . . . see if we can come to trust each other."

"I understand," said Crazy Horse, and he saw instantly that there could be great strength in the combination of the tribes.

"Do you know a young Cheyenne warrior named Big Nose?" asked Red Cloud.

Crazy Horse shook his head. "I've heard his name—but I don't know him."

"I met him during the talks with the whites at Fort Laramie," said Red Cloud. "He speaks some Lakota and I'm told he has the respect of his people. The Cheyenne should be here in a day or two . . . Talk to him . . . get to know him . . . and the two of you make a plan together. Use your knowledge of what the whites have done in the past. But don't make their mistake—each time you fight them, do something they don't expect."

The teepee flap opened and Red Cloud's wife, Pretty Owl, entered, carrying a flat piece of wood on top of which were several pieces of buffalo. At first, in the dim light, Crazy Horse could not make out the particular cut. Red Cloud, though, lit up—offering the food to Crazy Horse before eagerly taking some himself.

Holding it in his hand, Crazy Horse could see that it was a gristly piece of a buffalo's nose. Red Cloud popped his piece of nose gristle into his mouth, seeming to savor it, urging Crazy Horse to eat his portion.

Not wanting to seem impolite, Crazy Horse bit off a small piece and began to chew it. Of all the parts of the buffalo, the nose was the one he disliked the most. He did his best to chew it, struggling to grind the stubborn cartilage between his teeth, despite its active resistance. He didn't realize it at first, but it occurred to him that his face, between the reaction to the horrible taste and the sheer effort of chewing, must be wildly contorted.

Crazy Horse looked up and was surprised when Red Cloud burst into laughter. "It's okay to spit it out," he said. Crazy Horse saw that Pretty Owl also was laughing. "She hates it too," said Red Cloud.

Crazy Horse could not sleep that night, finally leaving his lodge and walking for a while on the edge of the village. There was no moon, which gave the sky to the stars without rival. He found comfort, as he always did, in the milky Trail of the Spirits, arrayed across the sky like a misty night cloud.

In his mind, Crazy Horse kept returning to his conversation with Red Cloud. Try as he might, he could not push away the fears and doubts that seemed to have fixed their grip like ticks. Still, Crazy Horse felt a spark of hope, and he fanned it as if building a fire in the face of an approaching storm. *If such a great and wise chief, who has seen so much, can be hopeful—shouldn't I?*

OCTOBER 11, 1866

Jim Bridger had not been surprised when Beckwourth announced that he would not return to Fort Phil Kearny. Beckwourth said that being back with the Crow had reminded him of the things he loved about his life with his people. It was clear that the Crow felt the same way about Beckwourth, so why wouldn't he stay?

So now Bridger rode back to Fort Phil Kearny on his own, keenly aware of his mission to determine the whereabouts of the tribes. True, he felt strangely ambiguous about where exactly he fit in between the army and the tribes. While he thought of the Sioux as the enemy, he felt increasingly ill at ease with his own countrymen. He reminded himself that nobody had held a gun to his head when he signed on as an army scout, and having signed on, he felt obliged to do what was expected of him. Beckwourth's conversation with Goes Ahead caused Bridger deep unease, like that first hint of changing wind that portends a coming storm.

He found himself missing Beckwourth. He had been skeptical of the man at times, especially in his younger days, finding him a bit of a blowhard. Of course, no man was without his faults. As for his attributes, Beckwourth had an interesting point of view on life. And anyways, it was nice to talk to someone with experiences similar to Bridger's—there weren't that many left. Beckwourth also asked questions. Bridger had always been surprised at how few people actually took the time to ask questions—real questions, not just the ritual courtesies of small talk.

When Beckwourth asked a question, he actually listened to the reply. No wonder he was smart. Ask a lot of questions and listen to the answers and you could learn a lot in life.

The old mare encountered a downed tree and stopped. It was small enough that Bridger was sure she could step over it, but she did not seem so inclined. He gave her a gentle nudge in the ribs, and instead of stepping ahead, she turned to look back at him with those creamy brown eyes that had always melted his heart. *Speaking of listening.* The poor old gal was tired. Fair enough. It was a good time to make camp, in any event.

Bridger had plotted a return course that took him high into the Big Horns. Traveling alone now made him all the more conscious of his exposure on the plains. As Beckwourth had reminded him, he wasn't likely to win a shoot-out. So instead of following the Tongue back upstream, Bridger had cut due west from the Crow camp, crossed the Rosebud, then followed the Little Bighorn into the mountains. From there, he bushwacked his way southeast toward the upper waters of the Tongue. It was rugged country—timbered where it wasn't rocky—and steep. It was unlikely, though, that the Sioux and the Cheyenne would go far into the mountains. If he was unlucky enough to stumble across some hunting party, at least the timber would give him cover to escape.

From the high-country end of the Tongue, Bridger hoped to get his own view of Red Cloud's village.

Bridger had always considered it amusing the way most folks thought about tracking. They often believed a scout had some ability to see a footprint on a rock or smell some scent left behind a week earlier. Maybe that's how some Indians did it, though not any of the ones that he had known. And of course, actual tracks were a part of tracking: hoofprints in dirt or mud, a blood trail from a bleeding elk, the imprint of a moccasin. And sometimes there were convenient signs: rocks recently flipped over, branches broken by the passage of a large animal, scat. These signs, when available, made tracking easy.

But tracking was less about such signs and more about thinking like the thing you were tracking. Sometimes actual tracks provided a starting point, but usually not much more. Every animal Bridger had ever tracked cared about two things: getting food and not being food. They tended to head for where there was food, water, and cover. They tended to take the easiest path, following well-established game trails when available, preferring to walk downhill instead of climbing. In windy and cold weather, most game sought the shelter of timber, and if that was not available, the shelter of a coulee or a draw. It wasn't so complicated if you thought about it, but it did require knowledge of the thing you pursued.

Bridger was now tracking a tribe of Indians, and there were not that many places to plunk down a tribe of Indians. If he were Red Cloud, he would want a sheltered valley with good water and ample grass for hundreds of horses. There would need to be game in sufficient numbers to feed his whole tribe—and to prepare food for the coming winter. Only buffalo could provide meat in that quantity. Red Cloud would want to avoid the daily worry of being established too close to the travel corridor of the Montana Road—or too close to traditional enemies like the Crow.

Bridger set up camp at the base of an enormous boulder beside a tiny rivulet, deciding against a fire despite the cover. He guessed he was no more than a ridge or two away from the valley of the Tongue, one likely place for Red Cloud, and he wasn't taking any chances. He hobbled the mare in tall grass near the water and ate pemmican supplied by the Crow. He studied a ridge to his south as he ate, topped by a rock formation that felt familiar. It was too steep for the mare and she needed the rest, so he decided to climb up on foot and have a look.

He was sweating and breathing heavily by the time he approached the ridgeline, despite the chill in the evening air. It took him longer than he'd expected—another reminder that he had lost a step or two—and he worried a bit about getting down in the fast-approaching darkness.

Bridger caught the strong smell of smoke before reaching the top. His cautiousness heightened, and he crept forward, careful to move slowly and to keep behind the cover of the pines. When he crested the ridge and looked down onto the winding ribbon of the Tongue, there were so many sources of flames, his first impression was that a massive grassfire enveloped the entire valley. As he peered more closely, though, he realized that the fires came not from one large blaze but, rather, from hundreds of smaller ones—cooking fires. He had found the camp, and its enormity stunned him. He had never seen so many teepees—not dozens or scores, but hundreds and hundreds.

Bridger estimated that the closest fires and lodges, the near end of the village, were probably three miles below him. What was remarkable was that the camp extended as far eastward as he could see, the whole prairie below him filled with glowing light.

Nor was the number of fires and lodges the only indication of the camp's enormous size. At the top of the valley, extending up into the foothills below him, Bridger looked down upon the largest herd of horses that he had ever seen—thousands of ponies, as sprawling as a herd of buffalo.

Bridger searched his mind for some point of comparison. He thought of the rendezvous at Pierre's Hole in 1832. They said four hundred white men attended that encampment along with a thousand Nez Perce and Flatheads. He remembered his awe at the size of that encampment, and yet he was sure that this one was many times bigger. *Three times . . . four times as big?* There was no way that this village was comprised of a single tribe, and Bridger thought of the news from Goes Ahead in the Crow camp. Red Cloud might have failed to recruit the Crow, but from the size of this village, it was clear that the Sioux had been joined by the Northern Cheyenne—and maybe the Arapaho too.

Again Bridger marveled that he and Beckwourth had been lucky enough not to encounter Indians on their way north. Now, clearly, he would need to stay in the high country, pick his way south until he was well clear of the camp. It would take a lot longer, but he might keep his scalp.

He realized how close it was to dark and knew he could no longer delay his return to his camp. There was a half-moon, so at least there was some light as he made his way down through the timber and scree. He thought as he walked about the purpose of such a large camp, and he wondered about the reaction of Colonel Carrington and the other officers. New information didn't cause most people to change their view of the world, in his experience. Usually they just found some way to cram it in to fit with the notions they already had.

OCTOBER 12, 1866

Dear Journal,

The arrival with the last supply train of the newspaper with the headline about Tennessee being the first state to win readmittance to the Union filled my heart with happiness. Thinking back to the terrible division before and during the war, it is no doubt a great milestone that we are weaving back together what war pulled apart. And how happy I am that my own state is leading the way.

Our troops here include not only soldiers who served in the Union but also many who served in the Confederacy. What a wonderful source of hope that men who might well have stood across from each other on the battlefield now stand shoulder to shoulder in a united effort to defend the reunited nation in its expansion to the frontier.

Signed and Attested,
Mrs. Lieutenant George Washington Grummond

Dear Friend,

I have noticed that most people here are very careful in how they talk about the war. This doesn't surprise me, and reminds me of the way it was in my own home of Franklin as the town

passed frequently back and forth during the war between
Union and Confederate, along with the fortunes of those who
supported one or the other.

Many of the men here, and all of the officers, served the
Union. But there is a large group of enlisted men that they call
"galvanized Yankees." I asked my husband about these men,
and they are Confederates who avoided imprisonment during
the war after capture by agreeing to volunteer to serve in the
Union Army on the frontier, the Union being so desperate for
men. My husband despises these men and says all of them are
merely awaiting their chance to desert for the Montana goldfields. I have one of them as a student at the library and I must
say he seems earnest and hardworking, though of course we
don't talk about the war. As with Janey, his accent on the one
hand is like a warm blanket to me but at the same time makes
me homesick.

I know about these sensitivities from my own state and
indeed my own family. My father died two years before the war
began, but he always referred to himself as a "Virginian," and
I have no doubt that he would have stayed loyal to the state of
his birth. My brother William fought for the Confederacy, and
my sister Jennie married a Rebel officer. My mother, along with
my sister Octie and brother John, stayed loyal to the Union. It
is painful even now to think of the arguments at our dinner
table in the months leading up to those enlistments and mar-
riages. I give thanks to God that all of my family survived the
war. When we were together afterward, no one talked about
it, as if, were we silent, the thing might fade more quickly from
memory. Of course the topic always lurked just beneath the
surface, like a low malarial fever that might suddenly flare.

Here on the frontier, the rough edges are more exposed,
and the conflict of recent years seems quite close to the surface.
My husband tells me that the galvanized Yankees usually keep
to themselves, and that in the barracks they divide themselves
into their own clique, sitting apart at meals and even organizing their bunks by geography. Last week, though—on a

Sunday of all the days—a fistfight broke out in the middle of the parade grounds as the Lt and I walked to church. I didn't hear the argument that led to the conflict, but the antagonists were a Massachusetts man and one of the galvanized Yankees. I did hear the stream of profanities and then witnessed the sharp violence.

Colonel Carrington was horrified and then furious that such an altercation would take place in the presence of women and children, reflecting so poorly on the discipline of his men. To send a harsh message, the colonel had the brawlers spread-eagled in the middle of the parade grounds for 48 hours, stripped from the waist up, literally burning in the daytime and freezing at night. I tried to avert my eyes when I walked past them, but could not avoid looking. Flies swarmed around their swollen faces and on the second day the skin began to peel off the tops of their sunburned shoulders. Lt Grummond says that if he were commanding officer they would have been whipped, but I could not help but feel sorry for them. When I made some comment about this, the Lt scoffed and said that women know little about the maintenance of discipline in a frontier army, and that without a strong message, "the whole fabric would unravel." I started to argue about the effect on morale of seeing brother soldiers tied up like farm animals but thought it better to hold my tongue. At least the two men now have been taken from their exposed position on the parade grounds, though they're now wearing ball and chain for a month, in the guardhouse on bread and water.

Of course it is no small thing to pull a nation back together after the horror of civil war. I know now that the end of the fighting on the battlefield is only the first step in healing the nation's wounds, and the scars in the hearts of our citizens will take much longer to heal. If our little community here at Fort Phil Kearny is any indication, we face a long journey indeed.

Sincerely Yours,
Frances

OCTOBER 15, 1866

The cowboy, Nelson Story, looked a lot like the mustang he rode, muscular and squat. The twenty-odd men he led up the Powder River Valley had their individual variations, but they were almost military in the uniformity of their clothing and accoutrements. They all wore broad-brimmed beaver hats, a bandana at the neck, a thick canvas coat, and leather chaps over pointy-toed boots. Each man was his own arsenal—a six-shooter and a Bowie knife at the belt and a repeating rifle in a scabbard on the side of his saddle. Their saddles bore fancy tooling that made them appear Mexican, and each saddle had tied to it a lariat, a rubber poncho, and a bedroll.

Story reined his horse to a halt, glancing at Bill Strong, his trail boss, who rode beside him. Story adjusted the brim of his hat to shade the sun that spilled across the valley. "You see 'em?"

"Yup," said Strong.

"Your eyes are better than mine," said Story. "Army, though, right?"

"Yup . . . Looks like a recon detachment . . . about a dozen."

Strong looked behind him, where a thousand Texas longhorns spread out for a mile in either direction, hemmed in on the edges by Strong's men.

"Well," said Story, sighing deeply, "let's get this over." He spurred his horse toward the cavalrymen, and Bill Strong quickly followed.

It had been only two years earlier that an epiphany had visited itself upon then twenty-six-year-old Nelson Story. He was mining a muddy claim along the banks of Grasshopper Creek, near the instant town of Alder Gulch in Montana Territory. The claim was productive, and with two partners, the young man ended up with a share equal to fifty thousand dollars—a sizable stake. His partners were intent on doubling down on new claims, but Story had a different idea. The shortage of basic foodstuffs in mining towns had made a strong impression on Story, along with the exorbitant prices for anything that happened to be available. Vendors able to transport tins of beef or crates of dried cod sold them for enormous profits. Barrels of salt pork labeled *US Army* showed up in the mining camps after unscrupulous quartermasters stole them to sell on the black market. And all of that food was of atrocious quality. Hunters arriving in mining camps with fresh meat earned a king's ransom for choice cuts.

As Story watched all this unfold, he began to calculate the value of a herd of fat beef cattle delivered to a place like Virginia City or Alder Gulch. Among his young wanderings, Story had dabbled in merchandising and freighting, even brought the first wagonload of dry goods to the goldfields of Breckenridge. He knew enough to suspect that the real fortune to be made in mining wasn't in the mines, but the miners. The advantage of cattle, as Story came to envision it, was that they transported themselves. All you had to do was herd them—and have the moxie to pull the trigger.

So Story stitched his Montana gold dust profits into the lining of his overcoat and rode to Texas. No matter that he knew nothing about driving cattle and had never in his life been south of Colorado. He heard that in Texas you could buy cheap cattle or even gather up semiferal animals from the plains. Already men were driving Texas herds up to Kansas railroad towns—so why not drive them farther, all the way to Montana? No matter that Fort Worth to Bozeman was two thousand miles of wilderness. No matter that hostile tribes occupied most of the territory to be crossed. No matter that no one had done it before. Story had a vision and set about making it real.

In Fort Worth, he put up his stake to fund his cattle venture, buying or otherwise acquiring a herd of a thousand Texas longhorns, famous for their ability to survive on the thin cover of shortgrass plains. He hired twenty-five cowboys, most of them ex–Confederate soldiers and a few of them with experience driving cattle up the Chisholm Trail. At Fort Leavenworth, the commanding officer told Story the Powder River Valley was aflame with hostile Sioux and Cheyenne—who would stampede their cattle at best and massacre Story and his men at worst. Story responded by visiting the post sutler, who had just taken shipment of several crates of the new Remington repeating rifles. Story bought a Remington for every one of his men, along with ammunition stocks worthy of an army.

Since leaving Fort Laramie, they had indeed been attacked by the Sioux, with two of his men gravely wounded and half their herd run off. Story organized a party to track the bandits, surprising the thieves at night, killing most of them, and recovering their stolen stock.

Now, by his estimation, after five months of arduous trekking and travail, he was less than a month from his destination of Virginia City. But he was not there yet. While his steers might fetch two hundred dollars a head in Montana, they weren't worth a penny if they died ran off in the Powder River Valley. The weather had started to turn, and beyond the Indians, Story's greatest apprehension was that a winter storm would slow or halt their progress. This was no country to be stranded in. He had heard stories of whole herds freezing in their tracks in high plains blizzards. He was too close to let that happen.

———————

Captain Fetterman and a reconnaissance patrol of a dozen cavalrymen crested a ridgeline along the Montana Road, five miles south of the fort. They stopped at the top to look into the valley below, perplexed and then amazed by what they saw in the valley of the Powder River.

For an instant they all thought it was a herd of buffalo, and certainly the way the many hundreds of animals spilled across the prairie resembled the great wild herds. As they stared a bit longer, though, they saw that the massive horns on the animals stretched out like lethal wings, and it became slowly apparent they were Texas longhorns. Leading the herd and surrounding it were around twenty white men. In the dusty wake of the herd, a team of oxen pulled a large prairie schooner. And a remuda of several dozen horses added to the remarkable procession.

"What the hell, sir?" said Sergeant Lang.

Fetterman just shook his head. He'd heard of so-called cowboys down in Kansas, driving up herds from Texas and delivering them to the new railheads. But this was the first he'd ever seen himself. Certainly he had not expected to see twenty civilians and a herd of a thousand cattle pop up in the middle of Sioux country. He was amazed they had made it this far.

As they continued to watch, two riders at the front of the herd loped up the hill toward them. Fetterman felt himself instantly attracted to the casual confidence the cowboys seemed to exude.

"Howdy, Captain," said the apparent leader of the men. "I'm Nelson Story, and we're the men of the Story Cattle Company." He didn't wait for a reply before asking, "How far to the fort?"

———

"We're pleased to welcome you to civilization's newest outpost on the frontier," said Colonel Carrington. "But I'm afraid I cannot give you permission to travel north."

Captain Fetterman watched Nelson Story absorb the news, and it reminded him of the moment when a tea kettle begins to hiss, just prior to boiling.

"I ain't asking for your permission. In fact, I ain't seeking a goddamn thing from you except to stand out of my way."

Now Fetterman watched the colonel, sharing Carrington's discomfort at someone challenging the commanding officer's authority so directly.

"My responsibility, Mr. Story—and my authority—is to ensure the safety of civilians traveling in this department. That's the reason for Directive 15-29, issued just last week."

"What the hell is Directive 15-29?" asked Story.

"Directive 15-29 provides that no party shall travel north with less than forty armed and able men. Your party, as you yourself have described it, numbers twenty-three."

"My twenty-three men have been doing just fine for four months and two thousand miles from Texas."

"I doubt you'll have to wait long," said Carrington. "It would be unusual for less than twenty miners to travel up this road any given week. They can join your forces, and you'll be fully compliant with my directive."

"My twenty-three men and their repeaters are worth a hundred of your men—or a hundred damn miners with a pickaxes!" Story began to stab his finger into the air as he spoke, as if he might physically poke the words into Carrington's head. "Besides—this late in the season, who's to say there's any more men coming up that road? We could wait all winter! And my cattle can't wait!"

Captain Fetterman found himself at once horrified and strangely admiring of the young cowboy's tone. When Fetterman had reported the presence of Story and his herd to Colonel Carrington, Carrington had mentioned the "golden opportunity" Story presented. It made Fetterman uncomfortable, though he had refrained from saying so.

Now, as Fetterman watched, Colonel Carrington made his play. "Well, I can understand your concern about your stock. And as luck would have it, the US Army is prepared to offer you the market rate— ten dollars a head—for your whole herd. You can collect your money and return home without the extra trouble and risk of travel to Montana."

"Ten dollars a head!" Little bits of spittle flew from Story's mouth. "I wouldn't sell you goddamn chickens for ten dollars a head! My herd will fetch twenty times that much in Virginia City!"

"You know, Mr. Story, I'm fully within my rights to requisition the whole herd on the spot in the name of the national interest."

"You better bring all your soldiers on the day you try that!"

Private Sample looked as if he had been stricken, and Colonel Carrington did his best to puff up his chest. "You're lucky I don't throw you in the guardhouse! There's a line you best not step over."

Captain Fetterman struggled to compose some sort of compromise, anything to deflate the tension, but no obvious solution appeared to him. A further moment of uncomfortable silence followed, before Colonel Carrington said, "You are directed to make your camp to the north—on Peno Creek—and await the arrival of more travelers from the south. I'd allow you to stay closer to our protection, but we need the local forage for our own horses. There's ample water and forage in the Peno Valley."

"Protection? How'd you do at protecting your own herd, Colonel?"

Nelson Story did not wait for an answer before slamming his hat on his head and pivoting toward the door. Carrington had recently installed a wooden floor in his quarters, the first at the fort and yet another proud step toward civilization. Story's boots pounded the wooden slats like pistol shots as he stormed toward the door, and to Carrington's great irritation, each step left a smear of gumbo mud.

OCTOBER 16, 1866

Fort Phil Kearny already was abuzz with the recent arrival of the cowboys on the day Jim Bridger rode back from his long expedition, and
the scout's return added another layer to the excitement. Bridger knew
it was urgent to talk to Colonel Carrington and the other officers, but
most of them were either drilling or on wood duty. Besides, once Bridger
learned about a pack of cowboys and a herd of one thousand Texas long-
horn cattle, camped only a few miles away near Peno Creek, he had to
go and see them for himself.

When he met the plucky leader of the cowboys, Nelson Story,
Bridger instantly liked him. For his part, Story knew Bridger by reputation and seemed pleased for the opportunity to talk to him. Upon
learning that Bridger had just returned from the north, he peppered the
frontiersman with dozens of questions about the differences between the
tribes, their locations, the terrain, and water along various paths north.
Not only did Story ask lots of questions. Bridger noticed that he listened
hard to the answers. He liked that.

Bridger explained his worry that Story's giant herd was at risk of
riding directly into Red Cloud's giant village, and offered his best suggestion for how to navigate around it to the east. Story produced a piece
of paper and a pencil and asked Bridger to draw a map. By Bridger's
reckoning, his alternate course might well add a week or even ten days
to their journey—dicey with winter approaching. But he calculated they
would still have far better odds of making it to the Montana goldfields

alive and with their herd intact. Bridger even told Story about a protected valley on the upper Yellowstone where he might keep part of his herd through the winter, given the cowboy's intention to sell some stock for immediate profit while keeping some for breeding.

It was pretty obvious from all of Story's questions that he didn't plan to stick around very long, and Bridger admired the sheer gumption of anyone who thought they could drive a thousand cattle from Texas to Montana. One of the soldiers had told Bridger that Story was under strict orders from Colonel Carrington not to leave until more travelers had collected, so their party could be larger. As for whether Story was about to break Carrington's order, Bridger considered it a matter between Story and the colonel. Bridger agreed that Colonel Carrington's rules for the size of traveling parties made no sense for these men and their private arsenal of Remington rifles.

It was only the growing darkness that reminded Bridger he ought to head back to the fort. He felt disappointed, not only because he found himself genuinely enjoying the conversation with Story, but also because he suspected that the reception for his information would be far different inside the walls of the fort.

Bridger found all of the officers sharing dinner in the unmarried officers' quarters, an event that Colonel Carrington had organized for the express purpose of hearing Bridger's report. To Bridger's frustration, they spent a preliminary period with Carrington and a number of the officers obsessing over Beckwourth's failure to return, the officers acting for a while as if it was a veritable act of desertion. Hardly short of treason, to hear Lieutenant Grummond. Bridger reminded them that Beckwourth was a civilian and had forgone his final payment. They might not like to hear it, but as an old mountain man, Beckwourth felt pretty much entitled to go wherever the hell he might want—or not.

Finally, Bridger was able to get to the nub of it, that the largest encampment of Indians he had ever seen was no more than a two-day ride away. After observing from the nearby mountains for a full day, he had been surprised to discover that the Sioux, Northern Cheyenne, and Arapaho were camped together. He also conveyed what they had learned from

Goes Ahead—that Red Cloud had gone so far as to attempt to recruit the Crow, the historic enemy of his people, to fight with him against the whites.

Bridger watched them as he related the news. What he was telling them was important, perhaps even vital, and he expected it to be received with appropriate seriousness. He was irritated that Colonel Carrington kept looking toward his junior officers, as if gauging their reaction instead of formulating his own. Grummond, meanwhile, removed his pocket watch and seemed to make a show of idly winding it.

No one said anything for a while after Bridger finished his report. Finally, Grummond returned his watch to his pocket and looked up. "You said thousands of Indians . . ." he said. "Did you count them?"

Bridger had learned patience over the years, and prided himself on being able to ignore preening from the likes of Grummond.

"No," said Bridger. "I counted lodges. More than a thousand—strung out for five miles down along the Tongue."

"Wouldn't it be somewhat common for the tribes to convene like that?" asked Carrington. "For trade, I assume?"

"It's just a big powwow for their fall hunt," said Lieutenant Grummond.

Bridger marveled at Grummond's confidence, if nothing else. "If anything, a village like that makes their hunting a lot harder," said Bridger. "That's a lot of mouths to feed, especially with buffalo being harder to find."

Captain Fetterman appeared to Bridger to be waiting until the others had finished with their questions, which took surprisingly little time. "What do you think it means?" Fetterman finally asked.

At least Fetterman showed signs of concern. "It's hard to know for sure," said Bridger. "The part about Red Cloud talking to the Crow surprised me the most. That's a hard one to explain any other way."

"Any other way but what?" asked Captain Ten Eyck.

"Any other way but they're planning on a big attack," said Bridger.

"Oh, yes," said Grummond. "The *great* Red Cloud . . . *brilliant* war chief . . . leading the world's *greatest light cavalry* . . ."

Bridger noticed how Grummond addressed himself directly to Colonel Carrington and how Carrington seemed to listen. There had been

some sort of shift since he went away. Bridger could not fathom why—
but somehow, it seemed, Grummond's influence had increased.

"We've been hearing all this talk about Red Cloud and the Sioux
ever since we came out here," Grummond continued. "And so far their
biggest victory is to steal our cows."

Bridger had begun to lose patience. "You must not be very obser-
vant, Lieutenant. He's stolen your winter food supply . . . put half your
cavalry on foot . . . forced you to pair every woodchopper you send out
with a man standing guard . . . and by my count, filled up that cemetery
he made you build with crosses equal to about ten percent of your gar-
rison. So far."

Five of Nelson Story's cowboys rode perimeter that night, tending the
herd, but the rest huddled around a large fire beside the chuck wagon.
They had finished their usual supper of beans, beef, and biscuits hours
earlier, their purpose now to decide the course of action for the Story
Cattle Company.

"If a big storm hits, we could be stuck for a week," said one of the
cowboys who had spent time in Montana.

"Or a lot longer than that," said trail boss Bill Strong. "This time of
year, you can't bank on breaks between weather. Once winter's here, it's
here. And that's what Carrington wants . . . if we're marooned, we won't
have any choice but to sell."

"I'll run off the herd to the Sioux before I sell to that bastard," said
Story.

The group was quiet for a while, sipping on mugs of coffee or clean-
ing their guns.

Story looked at one of the older men in the group, the only one, in
any event, with any gray in his hair. "You ain't said nothing all night,
Eddy. This the first time you ain't got an opinion?"

Eddy, it was true, had lots of opinions. He liked his bacon burnt and
his coffee cold. He was the only one in the crew who found reasons to
complain about the new Remington rifles, which he claimed weren't
sighted properly. He was one of the few Union men in the crew, and he

talked too much about his political views, to the great irritation of a group comprised mainly of veterans of the Confederacy. Still, Eddy pulled his weight and even a little more sometimes, so mostly they tolerated him.

"Well, truth be told . . ." said Eddy. "It just don't feel right to me to ignore the law."

"Oh, Jesus!" said Strong. "That paper-collar bastard lording over his little fort! We're the ones out here actually doing something—actually taking the risk!"

"Hold on," said Story. "Eddy's got the same right as all of us to state his opinion."

Eddy took a long swig of coffee, holding the lip of the tin cup against his face even after he had swallowed. It was a tick of his when he needed time to think of what to say. Finally, he moved the cup. "All I'm saying is, I got respect for the law. I served in the army and I got respect for the law."

There was the sound of a voice from the south. Instinctively, the men reached for weapons.

"Hold on, boys," said Story. "It's just Cooper coming in."

A few minutes later, a lone cowboy rode into the perimeter of the campfire's light. He dismounted and immediately tended to his horse, pulling the heavy saddle from the mare's back. The cook heaped food onto a tin plate and brought it forward. Cooper, his horse hobbled, squatted next to the fire and shoveled food into his mouth. Story gave him a minute to eat, but after a bit he asked, "Anybody coming?"

Cooper continued to inhale the food on his plate as he shook his head. Between bites he said, "Nobody."

"How far south did you go?" asked Story.

"Thirty miles," said Cooper. "All the way back to the Crazy Woman Creek."

"Jesus Christ!" said Strong. "We'll be sitting here until goddamn springtime!"

"Not if it's up to me," said Story, rising to his feet. He had heard enough. "Listen up, men. By how I reckon it, we got no choice but to take our leave. I know it's a big choice, so same as in Kansas, we'll take a vote. All those with me, raise your hand."

Strong's hand shot into the air with many others. A few of the cowboys were more reluctant, seeming to do a quick tabulation before join-ing the others in raising their hands. Finally, only Eddy was left, both hands around the rim of his tin cup, sipping at the coffee they all knew was cold.

Story stared hard at Eddy. "Eddy—it's your right to vote how you want. But are you sure?"

For once, Eddy didn't say anything, just nodded his head as he sipped at the coffee.

"Suit yourself," said Story. He nodded to Strong, who immediately pulled his pistol, cocking it before training the gun on Eddy's head.

"Oh, for Christ's sake! You don't need to go pulling a gun on me! It ain't like I'm going to go off and fight you boys over this!"

"Sorry, Eddy," said Story. "But we can't take any chances on tipping our hand. Tie him up."

"Christ's sake!" said Eddy again, as if a second invocation might produce a different result.

"You can ride in the chuck wagon for a day. We'll cut you loose after that. Rest of you—we ride north in ten minutes."

In the morning, Captain Fetterman led a squad of a dozen cavalrymen up the steep hill to Lodge Trail Ridge, pausing at the top to look down into Peno Creek Valley. Fetterman expected to see the cowboys and their herd of Texas longhorns. Instead, the broad valley was empty, though the tracks of a thousand cattle cut a deep swathe along either side of the Montana Road as it wound its way northward.

"Well, I'll be damned," said Sergeant Lang. He looked over at Cap-tain Fetterman and was surprised to see him laughing.

Story and his men stopped a few times to rest the cattle, an hour or two at a time, and it wasn't for forty-eight hours until they got around to Eddy. Story counted out his wages and told him he could pick one extra mount from the remuda.

Eddy accepted the cash without emotion, but when Story conveyed that he might also pick out an extra horse, Eddy wiped a tear from the corner of his eye. "That's awful decent of you, Nelson." He sniffed a bit and wiped his nose with the sleeve of his coat.

In truth, Story didn't mind Eddy. He talked too much, but he did his work. "Well, it's what you earned."

Eddy shuffled his feet and stared at the money. "I've been thinking . . ." he said. "I wish I'd voted different."

"You want back in?" asked Story.

Eddy nodded. "Do you think . . . do you think the boys will hold it against me?"

Story shrugged. "I don't know," he said. "I don't think they really liked you that much before."

Eddy weighed the news a bit glumly, though he did not seem surprised. "But no worse?"

"I don't know," said Story. "Probably not . . . Seems like a hard thing to calculate."

Eddy nodded. "Well, I guess I don't mind that." Suddenly, he thrust the wad of cash back at Story.

"All right, then," said Story. "You're on picket."

Eddy hated picket, but for once he didn't say a word.

NOVEMBER 1, 1866

Dear Journal,

Sad news since last I wrote. A drummer in the band named Robert Curry died after developing a bad fever. He was popular with his fellow members of the band, who marched with muffled drums in accompanying his casket to the graveyard near the base of Pilot Hill. The graveyard seems already far too big for a post as newly established as ours, and doesn't even include the many travelers whose comrades have no choice but to bury them in lonely graves along the Montana Road. A couple of the officers' wives asked the colonel for permission to go outside the walls of the fort to tend the graves and of course it was granted, though even that short trip requires a military escort.

Civilians arrive almost daily at the fort on their passage to the goldfields, most of them with stories of attack by the Sioux and Cheyenne. Yesterday it was a bedraggled train of ten wagons that suffered fifteen men killed at the hands of the Sioux from the time they left Fort Laramie. Colonel Carrington now requires civilians to gather in a large group before moving northward and he even ordered a detachment of ten cavalrymen to accompany this group. Still, with so many travelers and the needs of the army to defend the fort, such accompaniment will be the exception. And yet, there seems to be no shortage of men willing to take the risk. They call it "gold fever" and I guess it's well named.

The post was visited today by a small band of five Southern Cheyenne Indians whom Colonel Carrington allowed inside the fort to trade at the sutlery. I had seen the Indians who camp near to army posts both in Nebraska and at Fort Laramie—a sad lot where the effects of alcohol seem more pronounced than any other characteristic. But these were the first wild Indians I had seen up close. I was thrilled for the opportunity, though I'll say I'm happy to have seen them on our terms inside the walls of the fort, surrounded by our soldiers, and not in the wild country where they rule the land.

Their reputation for horsemanship seems well deserved. The Lt is critical of their small mustangs but I must say their mounts were beautiful and all seemed well tended and quite healthy (more than I can say for our cavalry's horses). None of the five Cheyenne had a saddle, yet each seemed so comfortable on horseback that man and horse seemed to move almost as one. Nor did any of the warriors use a bit, only a horsehair bridle tied in a loop around the nose.

As for their dress, all of them were a bit of a hodgepodge of white and Indian clothing. On the white side, two of them wore the same cotton shirts worn by most of the miners and other civilians. All of them had bangles or beads that they had obviously obtained through trade. One of the warriors wore a beaver hat. I was most interested in their native attire, and it was amazing to see up close the intricate designs in moccasins and leggings that Mr. Bridger told me are made from porcupine quills. I used to think that my mother set the standard for patience with her needlepoint, but I can scarcely imagine the time and skill necessary to fabricate such patterns using hides and other bits of wild animals!

As for demeanor, the Cheyenne were all quite polite, albeit under the constant supervision of a dozen armed troopers. They brought with them three ponies laden with furs—mostly ermine and fox—and traded for tobacco, sugar, knives, and a range of beads and trinkets. They wanted gunpowder and lead but the Colonel would not go this far in his diplomacy. In any event, after an hour's worth of haggling with the sutler, they packed up their newly purchased goods and were on their way.

A few hours later I had a lucky encounter with Mr. Bridger walking across the parade grounds and asked him about the tribes, my curiosity piqued! There is much more to learn than I had understood. The two Cheyennes—Southern and Northern—share a language but not always the same political views. There has been recent fighting, of course, with the Southern Cheyenne in Kansas and Colorado. Some parts of that tribe now seek peace, while others have been hardened further in their enmity toward us. Mr. Bridger says that with the Southern Cheyenne, you never know. Not so their Northern Cheyenne cousins, who all remain in implacable opposition to our presence in this country, which they consider to be theirs, and where they find common cause with the Sioux.

Like the Northern Cheyenne and the Arapaho, the Sioux are implacable against us. The Sioux designation is even more complex than the Cheyenne, and this tribe includes a number of subtribes and clans, making it all quite confusing, though the Sioux families in this part of the country share the same Lakota language. Mr. Bridger says the most common Sioux tribes in the Powder River Valley are the Oglala and the Minnicoujou.

Between my encounter with wild Indians and the tutoring by Mr. Bridger, an interesting day! Setting aside the military challenge faced by our soldiers, it is apparent how complex is the diplomacy that one hopes one day will come to prevail in our relations with the tribes.

Signed and Attested,
Mrs. Lieutenant George Washington Grummond

Dear Friend,

When some of the other officers' wives asked for permission to leave the confines of the fort in order to tend the graves at our little graveyard, I must confess that I too thought of volunteering—not out of any Christian sentiment, if I am honest, but for the sole purpose of escaping the confines of this awful prison that is our fort. Ultimately, the other wives told me that I should not be a part of the group in my condition and so I stayed back, locked behind the gates.

Death is not the only cause to diminish our ranks. Each week also sees an increase in deserters, some of whom find the lure of gold impossible to resist. My husband led a detachment in pursuit of five soldiers who struck out two nights ago. He found three of them walking back to the fort after the two others had been killed by the Sioux. Those three are now in the guardhouse, too, and while I understand full well the need to punish deserters, it seems strange and even silly to have them locked up when there is so much need for work. According to the Lt, we are likely to see this problem spike as the window narrows before winter makes travel too treacherous.

Can I tell you that, alone in our quarters this afternoon, writing a letter to my sister, I burst into tears? I was recalling to her my last birthday celebration before leaving Tennessee, and it made me think of how it had been then between me and the Lt. That was less than a year ago and yet now seems so distant. I cried because I remembered how charming and kind he was, the compliments he seemed so sincerely to pay me, how easily we talked and laughed. So little time has passed and yet now it seems to me that he is a different person.

When we first arrived at the fort, of course I knew that the Lt drank, but at least the occasions were infrequent. Of late, it seems he comes home drunk more often than not. And more drunk than before. Last night Capt Ten Eyck and Capt Fetterman delivered him at our door after midnight, and he was barely able to walk. When he comes home alone, I often pretend to be sleeping, but with the other officers knocking at the door, of course I rose to open it. They were drunk, too, though at least sober enough to be apologetic. The Lt, I have learned, grows belligerent when he drinks, and all his inhibitions diminish.

Last night, he went on for ten minutes with his usual list of complaints about the poor quality of Col Carrington's leadership etc., etc. I tried to go back to sleep, but this too seemed to anger him, and once he focused on me, his complaints shifted to his dissatisfaction with me and our home. He told me how the other married officers brag about the homes kept by their wives, and how he is embarrassed because he has nothing to say. How is it, he asked, that I am so slow to learn the most basic of skills? Then he actually questioned whether I truly feel ill, saying that he had never heard of a woman who used the excuse of her pregnancy to lie around and sleep all day. It was only when I burst into tears that he finally stopped his screed. He then turned away from me with a scoff, without the smallest pretense of apology, and was passed out from his drunkenness in a matter of minutes.

I was so upset that I could not sleep for hours. I wanted to storm out, be away from him. But to go where? Wander inside the walls of the fort like some crazy woman? I have confided in no one, nor could I, so there was no sanctuary with an officer's wife, and obviously not with Janey. So instead I was forced to lie in bed beside him and contemplate how much he is different from the man I thought I had married.

What am I to do now? Can I hope that this is merely a phase? I try, if only to be hopeful, to look at the Lt's circumstances in the most favorable possible light. It is true, of course, that the pressure on all of our men is intense amid the daily dangers they face. And while I admire many aspects of Col Carrington's character, it is true that he has no experience with fighting, and I can imagine this must be frustrating for the junior officers, all of whom, like my husband, fought with distinction in the war. Surely the army will understand soon the folly of failing to properly equip its most vulnerable post in the nation. Is it possible, at some point not too far distant, that a change from our current circumstances can return to me the dashing and charming young officer I met in Franklin? Or is this different man the one to whom I now am married, until death do us part?

Sincerely yours,
Frances

NOVEMBER 9, 1866

Bugler Adolph Metzger paused his work for a moment, shifting the ax to his left hand in order to examine the blister that had just burst on his right. The blister was painful, his hands unaccustomed to working with the ax. He had volunteered for the job, sort of. The band members had been given a choice between stable duty or the wood crew, part of Colonel Carrington's new push to finish the fort before winter set in.

Certainly, shoveling horse shit had been unappealing, but mostly Metzger had been eager to escape the confines of the fort. While well aware of the dangers outside the walls, inside, the cabin fever had grown unbearable. Blisters aside, he was happy for his choice. In the bright sun of a crisp fall day, the snowcapped Big Horns seemed almost to glow from within against the startlingly deep blue of the sky. Metzger also had some big thinking to do—his decision of whether to reenlist was due at the end of the year. Inside the fort, he had been unable to wrestle the decision to the ground. His one conclusion so far was that in the past, he had not been deliberate enough in his consideration. Perhaps a little distance would give him perspective.

". . . and if . . . you ask . . . her, why the heck she wore it . . ." Private Patrick Smith had been singing all morning. "She wore it for her lover, who was far, far, away . . ." Metzger judged the tonal quality of Smith's voice to be middling at best, but the man's enthusiasm was infectious. While no epiphany regarding his future had come to him, between the sunshine and the jolly tone set by Smith, the bugler found much to like about this day.

"Far awaaay . . ." Smith continued with the song. "Far awaaay . . ." Metzger wasn't surprised that Smith sang while he worked. Smith was irrepressibly upbeat, and as a result was probably the most popular man at the fort. He was missing the middle three fingers on his left hand from an artillery mishap during the war, but with his thumb and pinky intact, he could still manage a decent grip. He did just fine with the ax he swung as he continued to sing. "She wore it for her lover who was far, far away . . ."

Smith buried his ax, hacking out a fleshy chunk of the soft pine along a two-foot gash on one side of the tree. Metzger, meanwhile, took a big swing at the opposite side.

Metzger and Smith occupied a spot about three hundred yards up the slope of Piney Island. Fifty feet away, two other men, an infantry-man named Seamounts and a trombone player from the band they called Lips, worked to fell another big pine. Aside from the four axmen, most of the wood party worked at the base of the hill. There, in a wasteland of stumps left behind by the thousands of pines already cut, twenty soldiers trimmed the branches from downed trees and then loaded them onto wagons for transport to the mill. In addition to those twenty men, another twenty stood guard, a few on lookout but most sitting with their backs to the log wall of a crude stockade, built at Bridger's suggestion after the attacks became regular. The stockade was like a small cabin without a roof or door, the walls short enough to jump over but tall enough to provide cover for the men inside, ducking behind and shooting out. Colonel Carrington initially had been opposed to wasting their timber on a structure so far away from his fort, but ultimately conceded the need in light of the constant attacks on the wood crews.

"Hey, watch out!" yelled Seamounts. "This one's tipping your way!"

"Well, we do appreciate the warning," said Smith, pausing his singing. "Nothing will ruin your morning faster than a pine tree dropped on your head."

Metzger and Smith walked uphill several yards to a position safely out of range. After a few more whacks by Seamounts, they heard the deep groaning from within the pine as its few remaining sinews strained painfully to keep the weight of the timber upright. Then suddenly there was a snapping sound, not the sharp snap of a small twig but a thunderous crack like a thick bone of a massive beast breaking under strain. The tree began to fall, accelerating toward the ground and then crashing against it, bouncing once before dying in a great cloud of dust.

Half a mile away toward the Shining Mountains, lying at the crest of a ridgeline, Crazy Horse and Little Hawk watched the great tree fall. As Crazy Horse stared down at the scarred landscape below, it horrified him anew the speed with which the whites had transformed this sacred hunting ground, how every time he came back it had been degraded dramatically more.

The deep ruts of a road now cut through the heart of the valley, from the fort to the place where the soldiers stripped the hillside of timber. Thousands of stumps stood in place of the trees that once covered the low mountain, the cool shade of their broad branches now replaced by harsh sunlight that scorched the earth. Strewn haphazardly among the stumps were great piles of slash, piles of the branches that had been hacked off and thrown aside, the dead needles turned from lush green to brittle orange. Crazy Horse had not imagined that such a thing could be possible, but it was as if the soldiers had somehow managed to kill a mountain.

Every time he came to this valley, Crazy Horse felt a great wave of rage. It coursed through every vein in his body and animated every muscle with a singular desire to kill this enemy who not only invaded this sacred place but then destroyed it.

"Do you see it?" whispered Little Hawk.

Crazy Horse nodded. "Lone Bear," he said. From the southeast, there came another flash of light. Lone Bear was signaling with a mirror that he and his war party were ready to attack the sentries on the top of the hill near the fort. An instant later there was another flash of light from due south. "And Big Nose . . ." Big Nose and his Northern Cheyenne warriors would attack the last vestige of the soldiers' cattle, a small herd of about fifty animals usually guarded by a detachment of a dozen soldiers.

Little Hawk smiled at Crazy Horse. "All of us are ready."

Throughout the fall, Crazy Horse had studied the pattern of his enemy, learned the meaning of the flag signals from the sentries at the top of the tall hill, understood the predictability with which every attack was met by the soldiers—sometimes the wagon guns if they lingered within range—but always the dispatch of horse soldiers from the fort, riding out in an effort to run down the raiders.

Knowing now, as Crazy Horse did, the actions to anticipate from his enemy, he took seriously Red Cloud's admonition against allowing the Lakota attacks to fall into their own predictable pattern. Since the arrival of the soldiers, they had made a number of raids on the hilltop lookouts, the cattle herd, and the woodcutters. What they had not done before today was attack them all at once.

They first saw the puffs of smoke from the rifles of the soldiers' hilltop sentries, the sounds of the gunshots requiring several moments to catch up as they crossed the valley. Suddenly the wood crew's axes fell quiet, the soldiers halting their work to listen and to peer toward the sound.

The cattle herd grazed in a position out of Crazy Horse's vantage, but soon they heard shots from the south that they knew must come from the soldiers attempting to repulse the attack of Big Nose and the Cheyenne.

Little Hawk practically twitched with excitement. "Do we attack now too?" he whispered. Behind them, out of sight from the soldiers' wood crew, fifty Lakota warriors and their ponies awaited the signal from Crazy Horse to storm down into the valley along the creek.

Crazy Horse shook his head. "Not yet," he said. "Let the fort react to the others."

Sure as thunder after lightning, the gates of the fort swung open a few minutes later and twenty horse soldiers galloped forth. Half of them broke toward the high ground of the hill with the lookouts; half of them broke toward the cattle. Crazy Horse gave them a few more minutes to commit fully to their course, then he nodded to Little Hawk.

The four axmen—Metzger, Smith, Seamounts, and Lips—stood together, ears cocked and eyes peering in the direction of the distant

gunshots. Each of them still held his ax, but they had taken the precau-
tion of recovering their rifles, previously set aside while they worked.

"Well, it ain't no surprise there's shootin'," said Seamounts. He
adjusted his kepi to block more of the piercing sun. "They been raiding
on us all fall."

"I thought they said all of them were supposed to be off on their fall
hunt," said Lips. "It's been quiet for a couple weeks."

"Too good to last," said Seamounts.

"Well, at least it ain't us they're after today," said Smith. "They don't
seem worried down below."

At the bottom of the hill, the four axmen could see the rest of wood
crew. After a brief pause when the shots first began, the twenty men had
resumed their work trimming trunks, with no apparent concerns. The
soldiers on guard duty had gone back to sitting down, reclined against
the stockade.

"Well," said Smith, "I 'spose we ought to go back to wo—"

He was cut off by a terrifying wall of sound. Fifty Sioux warriors
stormed over the ridge, perhaps two hundred yards from the main body
of the wood crew.

"Shit!" yelled Lips. "Goddamn!"

Now the men below reacted like an ant pile that's been kicked. Both
the guards and the trimming crew grabbed rifles, firing a haphazard
volley into the charging Sioux. While a couple of the warriors tumbled
from their mounts, the vast majority charged ahead, undeterred. Having
fired their one shot, the soldiers now broke en masse for the stockade.

While most of the Indians focused on the men scrambling for the
fortification, a smaller group turned suddenly toward the four axmen on
the hillside.

"Shit, goddamn!" said Lips. "They see us!"

One of the Indians pointed at them as he urged his pony up the hill
through the maze of stumps, a half-dozen other riders trailing closely
behind.

Metzger scanned the hillside around them. There was timber above
them, but not sufficiently thick to provide cover. If they attempted to flee
in that direction, they would certainly be ridden down and killed. Nor
was there any way to run down the hill in the most direct line to the

stockade. The charging Sioux already blocked the way. As Metzger considered the options, only one path seemed possible. Beside the stockade ran a creek, and along the creek were thick willows. If they could make it to the creek, they might be able to find enough cover to reach the stockade under the covering fire of their comrades.

"The creek!" yelled Metzger. Rifles in hand, they began to run down the hillside, dodging the stumps and leaping the dead branches of their earlier harvest. The Sioux, meanwhile, were close enough, less than a hundred yards, that they heard the terrifying *whoosh* as the first arrows flew past them. Metzger had been shot at during the war on a dozen occasions, but something about the semi-silent flight of the arrows made them uniquely horrific.

Metzger heard a cry and saw Smith fall. He paused, relieved that the man had not been shot but had only tripped. Smith recovered his feet, abandoning his rifle as he dashed ahead. The fastest of the Indians was now no more than fifty yards away. It occurred to Metzger briefly that he looked like no more than a boy and yet somehow projected a predatory air in his attack that made him utterly terrifying. Metzger paused to raise his rifle, caught a brief glimpse of his bouncing target behind his sights, and fired. He could tell immediately that he had missed. Smith rushed past him, and Metzger, too, threw his rifle aside and ran. There was no time to reload; his only salvation now lay in reaching the stockade.

Below him, he saw that Lips and Seamounts had nearly made the willows. Two warriors barreled toward them, and Seamounts managed to shoot one from his horse at close range.

Several Sioux were on top of them. Smith cried out and fell, and this time Metzger could see that an arrow protruded from his side. A warrior beside Metzger—the boy—drew his bow, so close it seemed impossible for him to miss. Metzger dove to the ground, the arrow sinking into a tree stump inches above him. He jumped back up to his feet, the horse now directly in front of him, the Sioux fumbling to notch another arrow in his bow. Not knowing what else to do, Metzger slapped the horse with all his might across the animal's big snout. The horse reared and then began to crow-hop, its rider struggling to stay mounted. Metzger caught a brief glimpse of several warriors now gathered around Smith.

Metzger broke again for the willows, zigging and zagging as he ran, hopeful of making himself a more difficult target. He was close to the creek now. Seamounts and Lips had disappeared. Behind him, he heard an agonizing scream.

Metzger dove into the willows, crawling on his hands and knees in an effort to penetrate into the thickest part of the brush. He emerged from the willows at the creek and turned to his right—toward the stockade. At a break in the willows he looked back to see the Sioux, still around Smith, dismounted now. One of the warriors held aloft Smith's scalp, yelling his war cry as the others joined in. Then they pointed toward the creek, toward him, and remounted.

Metzger rose from a crawl into a stooped run, attempting to keep the willows as cover as he stumbled along in the shallow water at the creek's edge. Suddenly a large log blocked his path and he scrambled over it, startled to encounter Lips on the other side, huddled in a fetal position beside the log. "They'll find you here, Lips! They're coming!"

"If we stick our heads up we're dead!" said Lips.

Metzger didn't wait to debate the matter, continuing his hunched run. Behind him he could hear the Sioux, their horses crashing through the willows. They made a terrible, predatory sound as they hunted, and Metzger had never in his life felt a more primal fear.

He became aware of intense shooting in front of him—close by— and the stockade appeared suddenly through the willows. The soldiers now managed to lay down steady, organized fire, popping up from behind the chest-high log wall to shoot their rifles. Only fifty yards separated his position from the stockade, but mounted Sioux dashed back and forth between him and his comrades. Lips slid suddenly in beside him. "Shit, goddamn . . . Shit, goddamn . . ."

"We've got to break for the stockade," said Metzger. He saw no other way.

"How we gonna get across that?" Lips pointed at the open ground. "Our own men'll likely shoot us if the Indians don't!"

Two warriors galloped along the stockade, lying low across the top of their mounts as they each shot several arrows. A couple soldiers fired at them but missed. The second they had passed, Metzger took a deep breath and dashed for the stockade.

Behind him, he heard the war cries of the Sioux from the willows and heard the crashing of their horses' hooves, closing on him with remarkable speed. Twenty-five yards from the log wall, he saw two soldiers pop up suddenly, rifles trained at him. He threw his hands up and started to shout, "No!" but before he could, both men fired. A horse screamed, practically on top of him, and Metzger turned to see the massive animal collapse into a cloud of dust on the ground. Its rider—the boy—rolled several times but managed somehow to come up on his feet, a tomahawk in his hand, standing beside Metzger. He shoved the boy before he could recover fully, knocking him to the ground.

Two more soldiers popped up from behind the stockade, rifles trained on the boy. Before they could shoot, a rider seemed to appear from nowhere, firing a revolver at the soldiers. Metzger watched as a bullet struck one of the men in the temple and he slumped from sight. More soldiers fired from close range, but incredibly, none hit their target. For an instant Metzger caught an image of the mounted warrior's face, his hair more brown than black and a yellow lightning bolt painted on his cheek. He thought the man would shoot him down, but at that moment the boy leapt onto the back of his horse and the light-haired warrior turned to help him scramble up behind him.

Metzger lurched toward the stockade and threw his body across the top when he reached it, collapsing in a heap on the other side. More rifles fired, and Lips landed suddenly in a heap beside him.

For a moment, Metzger took panicked inventory, patting his chest and upper legs with his hands, certain that he would find an arrow protruding. He did not, exhaling in the greatest relief of his life. He saw Lips making the same assessment. "Shit, goddamn . . . Shit, goddamn . . ." Lips kept saying it, over and over.

"Hey, Sergeant!" yelled one of the infantrymen, peering over the log wall. "Oh my God, Sergeant—I think it's Smitty!"

Metzger heard the name, exchanging a quick look with Lips before joining most of the other men in peering over the stockade. At the bottom of the hill, fifty yards away, they saw a terrible sight. Private Smith crawled toward them. They knew it was Smith only through process of elimination; otherwise the soldier was unrecognizable. He had been scalped, the top of his head sliced away. He bled so profusely that his entire head appeared to have been dipped in vermillion paint, only the whites of his eyes standing out from the red glaze.

A dozen arrows protruded from Smith's back and legs. As he struggled to scoot-pull himself along the ground, they realized that his progress was impeded by several of the arrows that had penetrated all the way through from his back, poking out his chest and catching on the ground. They watched in horror as he stopped, rolling heavily to his side and then reaching slowly down to snap off one of the arrows at the point where it protruded from his chest. He winced a bit as he broke the arrow, but otherwise seemed devoid of expression, almost as if he were no longer human.

"Mother of God, we gotta help him," said one of the men.

The Sioux continued to swirl outside the stockade, firing arrows from longer range, with the occasional rider dashing closer. They left Smith alone, perhaps considering him effectively dead, or hoping that his presence might entice some of the soldiers from the haven of the stockade.

Sergeant Lang took off his kepi and rubbed hard at the top of his bald, sweaty head, as if he might push out a clear thought that otherwise was impeded. "Anyone who's not loaded, get loaded quick," he said. "I want half of you on the wall in a front line—fire on my order. Metzger doesn't have a gun, so he and I will run out and get Smitty. The rest of you that haven't fired, be ready on the wall to cover us." Lang motioned behind him. "Couple keep an eye on the back and the flanks." Lang looked around. "Everyone got it?"

The men nodded their heads. Metzger swallowed hard. It seemed unthinkable that he would go back outside the stockade, and yet how could he fail to go to the aid of Smith?

"Metzger?" said Lang. "You ready?"

Metzger nodded.

Lang pulled his revolver and quickly checked his remaining rounds. Fifteen or so men lined the wall, rifles at the ready. "Ready!" yelled Lang. And then, "Fire!" The shooters rose up and fired. Lang leapt over the wall with Metzger beside him. They hit the ground on the opposite side, and for an instant, the smoke of the volley obscured their view. When the smoke cleared, Metzger saw several dead horses in the foreground along with a number of mounted Sioux. Incredibly, Smith continued his slow crawl amid it all, now no more than thirty yards away.

The concerted volley seemed to have some effect, with at least some of the Sioux retreating. One warrior charged them, and Lang shot him with the pistol, the man tumbling dead at Metzger's feet. They sprinted toward Smith. More riders charged forward, but the second line of shooters now appeared and fired, slowing the assault.

They reached Smith, and for an instant, Metzger was unsure where to grab the man, afraid of disturbing one of the arrows that seemed to protrude from everywhere. Finally, they just grabbed him beneath the arms and dragged him to the stockade. There, many arms reached out toward their wounded comrade, hoisting him up and then behind the wall.

Metzger and Sergeant Lang tumbled over the log wall, and Metzger again did the quick check to assure himself he had not been shot. He felt wetness on his brow but realized that it was not his blood but his sweat. Eventually, he felt his breath coming more normally, felt his heart stop pounding at his jugular and brow.

He looked over at Private Smith, surrounded by a cluster of his fellow soldiers. Metzger couldn't tell if the poor man was dead or merely unconscious, but he no longer moved. They had him balanced on his side, and Lang had cut away Smith's shirt in order to inspect the arrows. All of the arrows had entered from the back and three had penetrated all the way through his body. Smith had broken off the tips to allow himself to crawl, but the shafts still protruded. Four other arrows hadn't gone all the way through, but to Metzger, it seemed certain that one or more of them must have hit something vital.

The soldiers looked to Sergeant Lang, questioning. Finally, one of the soldiers asked, "Is he dead?"

Lang shook his head.

"We need to get him to Doc Rutt," said another one of the men.

Lang nodded.

The shooting continued from the soldiers at the wall, but suddenly one of the men yelled out, "They're leavin'!"

From horseback, Crazy Horse watched the tornado of fighting amid the gun smoke and dust surrounding the log stockade, two hundred yards below him. Two of his warriors lay dead in the clearing—an unacceptable price for the limited damage they had inflicted on the whites. The soldiers had succeeded in recovering their wounded man and now seemed securely entrenched behind the log walls. From there, they could safely reload their rifles and continue to fire from a fortified position. It had been one thing to attack the wood crew when the men were exposed in the open, but fighting against soldiers behind walls was precisely the type of fight that Crazy Horse wanted to avoid.

He saw three flashes of light from near the hilltop where Lone Bear was fighting, the signal that more soldiers had emerged from the fort. The moment had arrived for their retreat.

Most of Crazy Horse's warriors had withdrawn to the same ridgeline from which he now watched the skirmish. He saw Pemmican and Fast Fox, though, and it was apparent they were steeling themselves to charge down again at the stockade. He called out to get their attention. They looked at him, and he shook his head vigorously and pointed away from the fight. Pemmican nodded, but Fast Fox ignored him, kicking his horse and screaming his war cry as he charged.

A dozen soldiers appeared from behind the crude log wall, leveling their rifles. Crazy Horse was surprised that they held their fire. Often the whites took quick shots in a fight, but this time a big soldier yelled at them, and they seemed to wait, taking their time. At fifty yards, Fast Fox turned his pony so that it ran parallel to the stockade wall. He leaned to the side of his horse, his body away from the soldiers, somewhat more protected as he fired fast shots from his bow.

A volley erupted from the rifles, a dozen guns firing in unison. Fast Fox's horse screamed and went down, and they watched as Fast Fox landed in an ungainly heap. He attempted to rise, but one of his legs seemed unable to support his weight. The soldiers who had fired their guns now ducked down below the log wall, and a dozen other soldiers popped up in their place, rifles trained on Fast Fox. He turned to run, but again his leg gave out beneath him. He fell, looking back at the stockade just as the big man yelled to fire. The soldiers' guns erupted again, and Fast Fox's body collapsed to the ground.

Little Hawk sat beside Crazy Horse on the pony of Fast Otter, one of the warriors who had been killed. He turned to his brother. "Shouldn't we ride down and help him?"

Crazy Horse turned his pony away from the stockade. "We can't help him anymore . . ." He dug his heels into his pony and rode north, toward the Shining Mountains and the place they had agreed to meet after the day's fighting. A few shots followed them from the stockade, but they were soon far from the soldiers' effective range.

They rode in silence for a couple of miles, Little Hawk beside his brother, glancing at him occasionally. After a while he asked, "Are you angry with me?"

"Yes, I'm angry at you," said Crazy Horse.

"I thought you would be proud. I wanted to show you today that I'm not afraid, worthy of fighting with you."

Crazy Horse turned to look at his brother, who in his plaintiveness seemed every bit the boy that a part of him still was. "I am proud of you, brother. And I know that you're not afraid . . . But I want you to show me that you're not foolish."

They again rode for a while in silence.

"The whites are different from any of our enemies before . . ." said Crazy Horse. "They fight only for the purpose of killing. If we fight them the way we've always fought, they'll destroy us."

***

Big Nose, leader of the war party of Northern Cheyenne, saw the three flashes of light from Lone Bear's position at the top of the hill the soldiers used for their sentinels. *Horse soldiers on the way.* It was time to break off their attack.

He looked down into the valley, pleased with the chaos they had seeded below. Two soldiers lay dead and mutilated beside a burning wagon, their bodies riddled with dozens of arrows and their limbs hacked off with axes. The remaining soldiers had quickly retreated for the fort, giving Big Nose and his Cheyenne the opportunity to drive off the fifty cattle that the soldiers had been guarding. Crazy Horse had emphasized the importance of driving off the herd, the last remnant of the soldiers' cattle and an important component of their ability to survive the winter.

Big Nose was surprised at how quickly the horse soldiers now appeared, a group that looked to number twenty or thirty. At a distance of two miles, they were visible in part by the cloud of dust they threw up as their horses pounded the dry ground. Big Nose considered holding his position. The soldiers would have to ride up a hill to reach him and would be vulnerable as they did so. He quickly dismissed the idea, though, agreeing with Crazy Horse that they needed to remain disciplined in fighting the whites. They had accomplished their objective for the day—driving off the herd. If the soldiers were stupid enough to follow the Cheyenne into the foothills—string out their forces and exhaust their horses—perhaps they would turn and fight. For now, though, they would retreat.

Big Nose called out to his warriors, many of whom were angry that they would not stand their ground. After a moment, though, all of the Cheyenne followed him toward the mountains.

They had barely ridden a mile when Big Nose saw an unexpected sight. Ahead of him, coming his way, was a large group of Indians. It was not a war party, but a small band including a couple of dozen men, women, and children. As he drew closer, he realized that they were Cheyenne—though Southern Cheyenne, not his own tribe of Northern Cheyenne. They looked ragged, as if they had been traveling a long distance. An old man rode in the front, a chief Big Nose recognized named Two Suns, whom he had met once at Fort Laramie.

"There are soldiers chasing us," warned Big Nose. "We just fought them, and your people are in danger."

Two Suns shook his head, pulling a folded piece of paper from a medicine bag he wore around his neck. "I have a paper from their Little White Chief," he said. "We're not part of your fight."

Big Nose could not disguise his disdain. He knew that the Southern Cheyenne had suffered outrages at the hands of white soldiers—wasn't that all the more reason to fight now?

"You can ride with us," said Big Nose. "If your people aren't strong enough to ride fast, we'll turn and fight the whites together."

"My people don't want to fight anymore," said Two Suns. "We have a paper."

Big Nose turned to check on the progress of the horse soldiers, now less than a mile behind them. "No one can tell you what to do," he said. Then the Northern Cheyenne rode away.

Captain Fetterman and Lieutenant Grummond halted briefly with their detachment of twenty troopers, using Fetterman's field glass to study the retreating Indians.

"What're they doing?" asked Grummond.

"I don't know," said Fetterman, peering through the glass. "But the group headed our way isn't part of the war party—they've got a bunch of women and children."

Grummond was skeptical. "How do we know they haven't all been camped together? Indians always move with their families."

"That wouldn't make any sense," said Fetterman. "They wouldn't camp this close to a fight. Besides, you can tell they're coming in."

"We'll see when we get there," said Grummond. "Let's go before we lose the lot of them."

They galloped forward again and watched as the group of warriors continued their retreat, while the haggard, mixed group continued to advance slowly toward them. As they drew closer, they saw that an old man at the front of the group held out a piece of paper, flapping in the stiff afternoon breeze.

"What the hell has he got?" asked Grummond, drawing his Colt and aiming at the old man as the soldiers advanced slowly over the last few yards. Among the men in the Indian group, there appeared to be almost none of fighting age. An older boy near the Indian holding the paper said something urgently and made a sudden move. Grummond cocked the Colt and swung it to cover the boy, and several of the soldiers readied their rifles, training them on targets now only a few yards away.

The old man with the paper kept repeating something with increasing urgency, holding forward the paper and nodding his head insistently.

"Hold your fire!" yelled Captain Fetterman, pushing his horse forward. "Lieutenant Grummond! Hold your fire!"

Grummond kept his pistol trained on the Indian boy. "I am holding my fire."

A child in the group began to cry, her mother pulling her close.

Fetterman reached out to take the piece of paper from the old man, studying the assortment of children, women, and other old men as he did so.

"Do you recognize this man?" asked Fetterman. "Isn't he the Cheyenne chief we met on the trail coming north last summer?"

"I can't tell them apart," said Grummond.

Fetterman read the letter, nodding. "This is Two Suns of the Southern Cheyenne—and this letter is the one Colonel Carrington gave him, attesting to his character and giving him right of passage."

Finally, Grummond uncocked and lowered his pistol. "If his character is so good, why's he consorting with the savages that just butchered our men?"

"You saw how it happened," said Fetterman. "They crossed trails. The colonel gave him this letter last summer because he gave us useful information about the strength of Red Cloud's forces."

"You believe what you want, Captain," said Grummond, turning his horse to give the enlisted men a better view of his speech. "I'll never believe they aren't all part of one big tribe. And I guarantee there's none of them wants to bury the hatchet anyplace except the back of our skulls."

Captain Fetterman felt his anger rising and fought back the temptation to reprimand Grummond on the spot. "Return to formation, Lieutenant." Fetterman managed to keep his tone controlled. Then he turned to the enlisted men. "Sergeant Jones, accompany these Indians to the fort."

"Yes, sir," said the sergeant.

Grummond was incredulous. "And let the others go?"

"The others are long gone, and we won't catch them with these horses," said Fetterman, seeing from the corner of his eye how the enlisted men stared at the spectacle of their two officers arguing. "Now get back in the *goddamn* formation."

Grummond too saw how the enlisted men watched. He sputtered for a moment. Eventually, cursing under his breath, he kicked his horse and fell back into the line.

SAME DAY

Back inside the confines of the fort's walls, Lieutenant George Washington Grummond led his horse toward the stable, watching as a private ran up to take the reins. Grummond's company was small enough for him to know all of his men's names. Aside from the sergeants, though, there were few with whom he had ever conducted an extended conversation.

He recognized the private who took his horse as Charles Toole, a man who previously had not stood out in any particular way, favorably or otherwise. Toole had been a part of the detachment today, just returned from the encounter with the Southern Cheyenne. He was covered with dust and also held the reins of his own mount.

Grummond noticed that Toole seemed to be lingering. "Do you have something to say, Private?"

Toole shuffled his feet. "Permission to speak freely, Lieutenant?"

Grummond nodded.

"Well, sir, I thought it was shameful what Captain Fetterman did today."

Normally, Grummond didn't think it was appropriate for officers to fraternize with the enlisted men. Today, though, he was eager to vent. "Well, I'm glad someone else sees the gall of it," said Grummond. "Can you imagine? Getting played by savages! It's shocking how far this army has fallen."

Toole nodded in vigorous agreement. "The redskins are loyal first to their race—and none of that *this tribe* and *that tribe* stuff makes a bit of difference when it comes to how they look at us. Birds of a feather . . . that's what I say."

"Colonel Carrington is letting them camp right there!" Grummond pointed to the bend in Little Piney Creek past the water gate, not more than a hundred yards from the fort's southern wall. The Cheyenne had thrown up their camp in a matter of minutes, five canvas teepees alongside half a dozen cooking fires.

"At least Carrington has ignorance to blame. Fetterman knows better," said Grummond. He saw Toole nodding vigorously, and the like-minded audience encouraged him. "That's the worst of it!" Grummond spit out the words. "Taking sides with a pack of savages over his brothers in arms!"

"Just so you know, Lieutenant, among the men—there's more than just me that agrees with how you see things."

Grummond stopped, looking hard at Toole and then briefly looking around the hay yard. It bustled with activity, but no one was close enough to hear their conversation. For a long time, Lieutenant Grummond didn't say anything, composing his thoughts. When he finally spoke, he spoke slowly, as if carefully measuring his words. "It's nice to know there's still some of us that can be trusted," he said. "And if it's only a few of us that understand the order of things, then maybe those are the ones that need to take the reins in our own hands."

Private Toole stared hard at Lieutenant Grummond.

The lieutenant stared directly back. "Group of men like that would be patriots, the way I look at it," said Grummond. "You understand what I'm saying, Private Toole?"

Private Toole nodded his head. "Yes, sir. Yes, sir, I believe I do."

"Patriots," said Grummond again. Then he turned and walked away.

Metzger had always thought the two oil lanterns in the enlisted men's barracks cast a warm glow, creating a comforting sense of shelter and haven against the darkness. Tonight, though, their light seemed too weak to penetrate far, and the faces of the men who spoke remained more shadow than light.

"I'm sick of it!" said Private Silas Porter. "They keep picking us off, a few at a time, and we keep riding out each day and practically ask them to do it again!"

Many heads nodded in vigorous agreement.

Each barrack held about twenty-five soldiers. Most nights, the men had scattered to their individual bunks by this time, taps already having been blown and the next day starting early. This night, most of the soldiers clustered around the stove in a single conversation. Most had been a part of the wood crew that day, and the experience, for all of them, remained vivid and visceral.

"Why haven't they put a cannon at the stockade?" asked another man. "We know they're scared of artillery. We're fighting with our strongest arm behind our back."

"They've been saying they were going to do that for months . . . It ain't like it's a surprise they attack the wood crews."

Metzger had wondered about the cannon today too. Ultimately, the crude stockade had saved them, but anyone who served in the war knew the value of grapeshot at close range. One shot and surely the Sioux would have fled the field.

"It ain't just where they place the cannon," said Private Charles Toole.

Metzger was a bit surprised to hear Toole speak up. He wasn't shy, exactly. He would talk if you sat down next to him at mess, but he wasn't the type of person who usually offered his opinions in larger groups.

"Think about the weapons they give us," said Toole. "Why are we still carrying single-shots when the civilians all have repeaters?"

Almost every man nodded in agreement with this comment.

"And half our single-shots aren't serviceable," said another soldier.

"Or if your rifle does work, they send you out with three cartridges."

"Two of which is wet!"

"I can't get the image of Smitty out of my head," said Private Porter. Porter and Smith both came from the same part of New York State, and everyone knew they were close friends.

Most of the men grew silent, one of those moments when it was hard to know what to say. After a while it was Metzger who spoke up. "Not many men could do what he did," he said. "To cover the ground he covered with his wounds . . ."

"What kind of savage does what they did to him?" The voice came again from the darkness outside the circle illuminated by the lamp—Toole.

"They're butchers!" said one of the other men.

"Heathens!" said another.

"You know," said Toole, "there's two dozen of those heathen savages camped not more than a stone's throw from this fort."

"Hold on a minute," said Metzger. "I heard those are Southern Cheyenne."

"And I saw the group that attacked the cattle herd and killed two of our men stop to parley with them while they were running off," said Toole. "I heard they were camped together before the attack."

"How do we know they're not plotting now to lift our scalps just like they lifted Smitty's?" said Porter. "Are we waiting for them to come outta the darkness with their knives first before we wise up?"

"But it's not—" Metzger was cut off before he could finish by the door swinging open. Reverend Woodward stood in front of them, his expression severe. "I'm afraid I have bad news . . . I've been with Private Smith . . ." The reverend paused, but the men all knew the rest. "I'm sorry, boys . . . but he's passed on to glory."

The barracks fell silent, the only sound from the wood burning in the stove. The fire inside of it seemed almost to pulsate, heat pouring off the cast-iron encasement, the flames barely contained within.

———

". . . because we're too goddamn timid to go on the attack!"

Captain Fetterman stared in disbelief as Lieutenant Grummond continued to spew. It was one thing to vent among the other junior officers, but Fetterman had never in his career seen a junior officer behave with such disregard in the presence of his commander. All of the officers and Jim Bridger sat around the crude mess table in the unmarried officers' quarters.

For his part, Colonel Carrington said little, staring, thought Fetterman, as if he had been suddenly stricken with palsy. "Well, I . . . I'm looking for counsel from all of you. But you know our orders are to avoid major engagements."

"And the US Army has not equipped us to go on the offensive," said Captain Ten Eyck. "Our horses are shot from lack of proper feed . . . We don't even have decent rifles—some of the men don't have *working* rifles."

"We've got everything we need," said Lieutenant Grummond. "We aren't fighting Robert E. Lee. The problem is we've let the savages get away with murder. We've given them every reason to keep coming back—to keep attacking us."

Captain Fetterman listened to the exchange, increasingly angry at Grummond. Of course he was as frustrated as anyone else. He also felt the instinctive desire to strike out, to strike back. But while he saw no excuse for not provisioning the fort appropriately, he understood the army's broader strategy. The first objective was to establish the fort. In the spring, they had been told, they would receive the additional troops that would allow them to take the offensive. Carrington and Ten Eyck agreed with him, and he knew that with the officers divided, he should speak up. He decided he would say something as soon as the opportunity arose.

"What would you have us do?" asked Captain Ten Eyck.

"Ride the bandits down!" said Grummond.

"Our horses can't do it," said Ten Eyck.

"That's what quirts are for," said Grummond. "We haven't tried. And I'm tired of hearing about how amazing *their horses* are. Have you seen them? If I mounted one, my boots would drag on the ground."

Captain Fetterman looked at Colonel Carrington, who looked around the room, it seemed to Fetterman, as if searching for the door. Fetterman cleared his throat, but Carrington spoke first. "What do you think, Mr. Bridger? You know this country and these tribes."

Bridger sat on a short stool near the stove, leaning into the heat that seeped out. He had spent a lot of nights in his life being cold and appreciated the luxury of warmth. He had listened to the conversation and others like it among the officers, and he was skeptical that his views would have any impact. "Well, I can tell you what they're thinkin', if that's what you want to know."

Colonel Carrington nodded. "Of course . . . know your enemy . . . That's the first rule of warfare." Carrington adjusted his posture, sitting a bit more upright, as if he suddenly had found a bit of traction. "That's what I always say."

"For starters," said Bridger, "they're afraid of your cannon. It ain't their style to ride into a fortified position, and your fort is the strongest position they've ever seen."

Carrington puffed up a bit further.

"What they would love for you to do," said Bridger, "is follow them away from the fort, out on the prairie. That's where they rule."

"Oh, for Christ's sake," said Grummond. "We rule where we go."

Bridger paused a moment and looked hard at Grummond. "Lieutenant, I've been listening to you all night. I'm sure it would be convenient if the world was as black and white as you want to believe," said Bridger. "But you don't know a thing about this country—or the people in it."

"I know what I saw today," said Grummond. "I saw four of our men hacked to bits. And another one all but skinned alive! And now we're letting half a tribe set up camp—practically inside our perimeter!"

Fetterman struggled to formulate a sentence. He wanted desperately to say what he thought—that Bridger was right, but the army had a plan. He sympathized with the instinct to strike out, but they had to play it smart. "Maybe we ought—"

"What would you have us do?" asked Ten Eyck. "Ride our cavalry over the top of two dozen women and children?"

"They aren't all women and children," said Grummond. "I'd start by putting every buck over the age of ten in the guardhouse."

"They're Southern Cheyenne, you fool!" said Bridger. "They're trying *not* to fight you. And by the way, there's a bunch of other Southern Cheyenne out there, waiting to see what you do with Two Suns. If you want to stir them up—buy yourself a bunch of new enemies—see what happens when you throw a bunch of old men and boys in the guardhouse!"

"I'm sure it's complicated for you, Bridger," said Grummond. "It's not the old days anymore. Besides, everybody knows you're married in. You even know who you are anymore?"

Bridger seethed. "I know who you are," he said. "I seen your type ever since I came to this country—thinks his pants is a little too tight between the pockets. Usually your type ends up with his dick cut off, crammed inside his mouth."

Grummond lunged toward Bridger. Fetterman and Carrington grabbed him and pulled him back, holding him as he struggled, when suddenly the door burst open.

It was Reverent Woodward, breathing hard. "There's some of the enlisted men," he said. "I think they might be about to attack the Cheyenne camp!"

Private Charles Toole led ten other men, rifles in hand, hewing tightly to the deep shadows along the wall near the southern end of the fort.

"How do we get out?" whispered one of the men nearest to him.

"There's a gap in the wall near the water gate," said Toole. "Enough space to squeeze through." As Toole looked back at the men following him, he felt a sudden swell of vindication as it occurred to him that he was finally where he was supposed to be, where he sometimes had imagined himself. He stood at the front of other men, men who listened when he offered his opinion, men who *followed him.*

Toole looked toward the south barbican, fifty yards away. He couldn't see the guards, and hoped that Higgins had completed his task—alerting them. The men on watch were members of Company C, and Toole knew they would be sympathetic. *How galling must it be to stare down at the Cheyenne camp?*

Toole reached the water gate and squeezed through the narrow space between the wall and Little Piney Creek. He felt the cold rush of the water into his brogans but didn't care. In front of him, now barely a hundred yards away, the fires of the Cheyenne encampment flickered against the dark night. He paused a moment for the others to pass through the wall, looking up to the barbican. He saw the guard looking down, not more than a few feet away. Toole couldn't discern the guard's face in the darkness, though it was clear that he stared at them. *What will he do?* As Toole watched, the second guard appeared, shoulder to shoulder with the first as the two of them spoke. Toole held his breath. Then the first guard reached to grab the rim of his kepi, tipping it. The second guard mimicked the gesture, even adding a truncated salute, and then they both disappeared.

Toole allowed himself a small smile. *Now, revenge . . .*

The last of the men cleared the gate, checking the caps on their rifles and fixing bayonets in the dim light as they gathered behind Toole. No one expected this fight to last long—one shot and then they would rely on the bayonets.

Toole noticed that they all now looked to him. Awaiting his command.

"What do we do with the women and children?" asked one of the men.

Toole stared back, suddenly uncertain. He hadn't thought about that. "Well," he said, "I guess . . . spare the squaws if you can." The men continued to stare at him, and to Toole it seemed as if they could sense his equivocation.

"And the children?"

Toole swallowed. "Every buck dies." A couple of the men chuckled. Encouraged, Toole added, "Nits breed lice."

"Jesus, Toole . . ." said one of the men. "You're hard to the core." It felt to Toole like he said it admiringly.

"Finally!" said another of the men. "Finally some payback."

And then, "This one's for Smitty!"

Toole turned and began to pick his way toward the camp. The light from the fires was unsteady, but they could see clearly enough now the forms around them. *Where are the bucks?* Then he saw two men walking between lodges. One was old and stooped—possibly Two Suns. Beside him walked a boy of perhaps ten. They were close now, less than fifty yards, easily within range of the rifles. Suddenly, a dog caught their scent and began to bark. Toole saw several of the Cheyenne pause to look in their direction. *It has to be now.* He raised his rifle and took aim at the old man, when without warning a pistol shot erupted from the far end of the camp.

"You men!" called a strong voice. "Halt where you are!"

"Shit!" said a man behind Toole. "It's Captain Ten Eyck!"

"Get out of here!" hissed another.

Almost instantly they began to scatter, splashing along the edge of the creek and tripping over one another in their pell-mell dash toward the water gate. One man dropped his rifle and made no effort to pick it up.

Toole looked back toward the Cheyenne camp. Inside the perimeter of the fires' light it was chaos—women screaming and running to gather children, men producing weapons and looking outward, fearful but ready to fight.

Ten Eyck fired his pistol again into the air. "You there! You're ordered to stop!"

Toole realized quickly that he now stood alone. Ducking his head, he turned and ran after the others.

"It's mutiny!"

Captain Fetterman had never seen Colonel Carrington so angry. He stood behind his desk with his officers and Jim Bridger arrayed on the other side.

"You weren't able to apprehend any of them?"

"No, sir," said Captain Ten Eyck. "They ran through the water gate and back into the fort."

"And the guards on the south barbican?"

"Couldn't make out the faces in the dark . . ."

"We'll conduct an investigation," said Carrington. "Ferret out every one of them. I'll see them hanged!"

"It won't be hard to find them," said Captain Ten Eyck. "Secrets are hard to keep in a place like this."

For a while it was quiet, the gravity of the moment seeming to sink in. Captain Fetterman stared accusingly at Lieutenant Grummond, certain of his involvement. He had no evidence, but nor did he have doubts. Grummond returned Fetterman's stare, unblinking.

"If I may, sir . . ." said Lieutenant Grummond.

Carrington nodded.

"Of course, there's no excuse for what those men did—but we should remember what's happened earlier this day. Some of those men watched their friends die . . . I know Private Smith was popular with the men. I wasn't part of the wood detail, but I'm told that it was a horrible thing to see what those savages did to him . . . I know what I saw for myself with the men guarding the cattle."

Part of Fetterman felt grudging respect for Grummond's ability to guide and manipulate a conversation. It's not that the lieutenant was particularly smart, but he did have this uncanny ability to read people, sense the mood, adapt himself to the moment and to his maximum self-interest. *Say something!* Fettermen struggled to compose a coherent rebuttal.

"Don't mix up two things that don't belong beside each other!" said Ten Eyck.

That's right! thought Fetterman.

Ten Eyck's face was beet red, always the case, Fetterman had noticed, when he was genuinely angry. "The Sioux and Cheyenne being savages doesn't change the duty of soldiers to obey orders—our orders!"

"It's the frontier!" said Grummond. "The goddamn wilderness . . . not to mention war!"

"Don't lecture me about war, Grummond," said Ten Eyck. "I've been to war too . . . There's a line, even in war. We're not a mob—we're an army. Or maybe you don't know the difference."

Fetterman wished he had the ability to marshal his thoughts as quickly and forcefully as Ten Eyck. Fetterman watched Colonel Carrington, squirming under the weight of decision—the horrible responsibility of owning the power to decide. Then, suddenly, Carrington fixed his gaze on him. "What do you think, Captain Fetterman?"

Now Fetterman felt all eyes turn to him. He knew what his heart told him to say. *Ten Eyck is spot on. The mutineers must be found and punished.* "Well, sir . . . obviously we need to . . ." He felt the gaze of Grummond in particular. "We need to balance both sides. I guess I would be worried about morale if we crack down *too* hard."

Fetterman heard Ten Eyck scoff. It wasn't hard to read Bridger.

Carrington turned to Bridger. "What do you think, Mr. Bridger?"

"I don't know anything about running an army, but I do know those Southern Cheyenne had no more intention to hurt you than your Ladies Auxiliary club. Killing them would have been murder, plain and simple."

They all left after it was decided. Ten Eyck stormed off without saying a word, while Grummond paused to bask a bit, his argument for forbearance having prevailed.

Fetterman walked by himself across the empty parade grounds, then perched against one of the howitzers that flanked the flagpole. It was too cold to be outside for long, but he felt like being alone. He thought about smoking his pipe, ultimately deciding not to squander his evening ritual in such an uncomfortable setting. He wondered why Colonel Carrington had given into Grummond, though in fact he understood it well. Carrington was afraid of the lieutenant, afraid of what he might do if his tantrum went unappeased, how he might sway the enlisted men.

Fetterman kept thinking about the argument among the officers, feeling regretful and even ashamed of his failure to take a stronger stand. He started to blame Carrington for his weakness. *Am I much better?* And while part of him admired Captain Ten Eyck's conviction, he resented the fact that Ten Eyck took easy refuge in a world of purity and absolutes. Yes, Grummond was wrong to excuse—and even, through his example, to encourage—the behavior of the renegades who would have attacked an innocent tribe. But Grummond was right to fear the impact on the men if Carrington had clamped down too hard. Fort Phil Kearny was a small community—and closely confined. Anger and dissention would spread like cholera—and Grummond, Fetterman knew, would use his influence to fan the disease.

Yes, Grummond had to be checked. Ten Eyck's approach, though, was too blunt. Frontal attack was not the only strategy. Prevailing in debate was not the only way to wield influence. Fetterman had seen men like Grummond before, their vanity far larger than their intellect. Such men could be controlled—channeled. Feed their ego just enough, but all the while keep control behind the scenes. That was the trick.

For a while he just sat there. The flagpole swayed in the wind, the timber creaking and the ropes rapping against the wood as they strained against their ties. Eventually Fetterman's eyes followed the towering flagpole up to its top, searching, but the massive banner had long since been lowered for the day. He searched the sky above, usually ablaze with a million stars. Tonight, though, low clouds held the darkness in tight.

NOVEMBER 25, 1866

Jim Bridger had an aversion to doctors that had lasted more than thirty years, and it was not without cause. The last time he visited one had been the rendezvous of 1835, a doctor named Whitley whose primary line of business was the sale of a liquid called Doctor Whitley's Elixir. The liquid may have been dubious in its healing properties, but he sold out quickly because it caused a near instantaneous state of drunkenness.

Bridger's purpose for the visit in 1835 was removal of an arrowhead from his back—a three-year-old wound at the time. Dr. Whitley had performed the operation in the open air with Bridger slumped forward over a tree stump covered with a buffalo robe. Half a bottle of the elixir had numbed Bridger up, though not sufficiently. In the long interval between the day a Blackfoot warrior shot the arrow into his back and the day of the surgery, cartilage had grown around it, necessitating a good deal of hacking and tugging for removal. By the time the surgery was completed—more than an hour after it began—a crowd of almost fifty onlookers had gathered to watch. A fair amount of gambling ensued on the outcome, with Bridger himself intervening to wager the sum of his possessions. "Easiest bet I ever made," he had told Beckwourth one night. "If I lost, I wasn't going to care."

So it was perhaps not surprising that Bridger had walked up slowly to visiting Doc Rutt, succumbing to the decision only after satisfying himself over a period of months that he liked and trusted the man.

"You're still feeling poorly?" asked Doc Rutt. Rutt shriveled up his face when he talked, which distorted his features, and he viewed the world through spectacles as thick as a beefsteak, which distorted his eyes.

"Mostly in the morning," said Bridger. "My legs get so stiff I can barely make 'em bend."

"That's rheumatism, I'm afraid . . . No doubt all that standing in cold water those years when you were trapping," said Doc Rutt. "Well, that—and getting old."

"Anything to do about it?" asked Bridger. "Other than dyin'?"

Doc Rutt allowed himself a small smile. It was nice to have some other people around who were closer to his age. "Not particularly," he said. "And I expect this is one where the cure is worse than the disease." He reached to Bridger's neck and poked at the goiter. "This bother you much?"

"Not since I gave up being vain."

"The vanity is easier to cure than the goiter," said Rutt. "At least for some."

"Out here the vanity usually cures itself," said Bridger. "One way or the other."

Doc Rutt handed Bridger a bottle with a brown liquid. "Take a swig or two of this at night," he said. "It won't make the rheumatism or the goiter go away, but it may help you sleep better."

DECEMBER 2, 1866

Edmund Johnson, private secretary to President Andrew Johnson, stared down at the paragraph that vexed him. All of the president's military officers agreed that his speech, to be delivered the next day, must address the "Indian question." Beyond that, they had been singularly unhelpful in suggesting the language with which to summarize the situation out west.

Certainly they all felt the political pressure. All during the fall, the newspapers had screamed headlines about Sioux atrocities in a place called the Powder River Valley. Almost every day, it seemed, there was some lurid new story about the latest attack on some hapless Argonaut or, worse yet, some helpless emigrant family. True, a few of the abolitionist Quakers had picked up the cause of the Indians, but hardly enough to matter against the din on the other side.

The president, all of his advisors agreed, could not deliver a message to Congress on the state of the union without providing some statement of reassurance about the West. Johnson flipped again through his notes, underscoring a couple of pertinent facts, and began to write . . .

> The army has been paid promptly, carefully provided with medical treatment, is well sheltered and subsisted, and is to be furnished with breech-loading small arms. Treaties have been concluded with the Indians who have unconditionally submitted to our authority and manifested an earnest desire for a renewal of friendly relations.

Johnson read through the paragraph with a general feeling of discomfort, so much that he looked again at his notes, confirming each statement against what the generals and the secretary of war had reported. He prided himself on taking careful notes, and he was certain that he had accurately captured the language from the cabinet meeting.

True, the statement did not align with popular conceptions of the situation on the frontier. But weren't conceptions sometimes—misconceptions? Wasn't it true that the newspapers sought first and foremost to sell newspapers and would often twist their facts to suit a narrative that achieved their goal? Surely the president's generals must have the best information about this faraway and wild place. Johnson allowed his mind to wander for a moment, imagining what it must look like out there in the Powder River Valley, wild savages all around . . .

The clock on the mantel chimed, reminding Johnson of his deadline. He gave his paragraph on the Far West one final read, then turned to drafting a passage welcoming the pending establishment of a new Canadian parliament in Ottawa.

SAME DAY

Crazy Horse rode beside Red Cloud as they picked their way through the massive village along the Tongue, and he could not help but be impressed at the collective heft of the tribes. The Cheyenne and the Arapaho now camped together with the Oglala and the Minnicoujou in the largest gathering that Crazy Horse had seen in his life. It felt like they could ride from sunrise to sunset without ever leaving the village.

Today, for the first time, the chiefs of all the tribes would convene in council. Red Cloud had asked Crazy Horse to accompany him to the council, and of course Crazy Horse accepted the great honor of sitting with the chiefs.

As they rode along, Crazy Horse was surprised at first that the conversation was not more serious. Red Cloud talked about the weather, and then about a minor irritation with his wife, and then about a toothache that made it uncomfortable for him to chew jerky. Crazy Horse had expected that the only discussion would involve great matters of strategy, questions of how they would fight the whites. Eventually those questions did come.

"You say you believe the soldiers will follow you from the fort?" asked Red Cloud.

"They have every time," said Crazy Horse.

"What was your biggest war party," asked Red Cloud, "up until now?"

"The three groups of twenty."

"The three attacked in different places at the same time?"

"Yes," said Crazy Horse.

"This time, take a hundred of our warriors—but hold them together. Find a spot away from the reach of the wagon guns to set your ambush . . . And it's important that we continue to fight alongside the Cheyenne—and the Arapaho, too, if we have a good council today."

"We could ask the Cheyenne to lead the decoys," said Crazy Horse. "Big Nose understands the patterns of the soldiers—and I trust him."

"Good," said Red Cloud.

Crazy Horse almost found himself wishing that Red Cloud would push back more, not sure he was ready to accept the responsibility of his opinion helping to decide such important matters. The young warrior still had many questions of his own but felt intimidated to pose them. "They won't expect such a large force, but . . ." He left his thought incomplete.

"But what?" asked Red Cloud. "I need for you to tell me all of your thoughts—not just the ones you think I want to hear."

Crazy Horse looked at the chief and said, "I worry about our discipline."

"Our ability to hold to a plan?" asked Red Cloud.

Crazy Horse nodded. "Many want to fight the old way."

"For their own glory? For the coup they'll count and the story they'll tell around the fire?"

Crazy Horse nodded again.

Red Cloud creased his face in worry. They rode along for a while longer before the chief said anything more. "I know your father well, and I've always respected his wisdom and vision. I see your father in you—and also High Backbone's ability to fight and lead. It's a rare thing to have both of these gifts. Since the summer, there's no one in our tribe who's done more to fight against the soldiers, learn their ways.

"Our old ways of doing things run deep . . ." the chief continued. "So deep that they're a part of who we are. Asking people to change such things is like asking them to hack off a piece of themselves. But it's our responsibility to our people to persuade them. We have to succeed, because there's no other way."

Crazy Horse agreed, though Red Cloud's words only reminded him of all the reasons he was worried. He hesitated at first to ask the question at the heart of it all, wondering if it was somehow a sign of weakness to share his doubts and fears. Finally, though, he just asked, "Do you think we can defeat them . . . not in a battle, but in a war?"

Red Cloud reined his horse to a halt and looked directly at Crazy Horse when he spoke, seeing the mixture of fear and hope in the intense eyes staring back at him.

"I know we can't ride up to their fort—burn it down. Even a great force would be cut down by their wagon guns, by rifles shooting from a distance behind the protection of their walls."

Crazy Horse waited and listened, knowing there must be more.

"We talked before about the weakness of the whites," said Red Cloud. "Their belief that we're inferior to them, incapable of complex thoughts . . ."

Crazy Horse nodded, beginning to see the chief's vision.

"It's their beliefs about us that give us our opening," said Red Cloud. "Imagine the shock of defeat, if you've never imagined such a thing could be possible."

"Do you think they would abandon the fort?" asked Crazy Horse.

"Perhaps," said Red Cloud. "Perhaps they would decide there are places other than the valley of the Powder, easier places where they can live without the constant fear . . ."

"Fear of us," said Crazy Horse, and he wanted to believe it, embrace it as a true and certain path. For a fleeting moment, he wondered if he should ask Red Cloud about his vision of the locusts, but then he pushed back the thought, not wanting to trample on his own hope.

DECEMBER 6, 1866

The high vantage reminded Red Cloud of the plateau he had climbed as a young man, when he sought his vision. It was more of a bench than a summit. Behind him, to the west, the Shining Mountains rose much higher. But below Red Cloud's position—to the east, north, and south—he had the best view possible of the valley around the tiny headwaters of Prairie Dog Creek.

Red Cloud had learned the virtue of patience over the years—or at least resigned himself to the need for it. As he waited, he found it particularly difficult to apply in practice. Others—like Crazy Horse and High Backbone and Big Nose—would do the fighting. His responsibility was different, and it was difficult to adjust to this new role. His responsibility today was not to fight, but to watch . . . to observe and to think.

If all the warriors held to their plan, they had an opportunity to strike a significant blow. Yet from his position on the high ground, Red Cloud reflected on the enormity of their challenge. Crazy Horse, the young warrior with the old soul, had described it well. They fought not only the whites and all their frightening powers. They fought also against their own instincts and traditions, old ways of doing things that gave order and honor in the world in which they had always lived, but which was changing now with dizzying speed. In a strange thought, it occurred to Red Cloud that in their fight to preserve their old ways, it was necessary now for them to change their old ways. He hoped, of course, that they would prevail in this war, and then they would go back. But a part of him wondered, *Can we ever go back to the place we were before?*

To Red Cloud's southeast, Bull's Hump Hill separated his position from the fort and hid it from view. A flash of light flickered from another hilltop to the south, the mirror signal that the Cheyenne's attack on the wood train had begun. Almost immediately, Red Cloud heard a smattering of gunfire, likely just the crackle of the few small arms carried by the wood crew itself. If Crazy Horse was correct, a significant force of soldiers now would dispatch from the fort in pursuit of the raiders.

The task of the Cheyenne would be to lure them into the Peno Creek Valley. Once down in the valley, Oglala and Minnicoujou forces led by Crazy Horse and High Backbone would surround them. More than a hundred warriors would ambush the whites, far from the protection of their fort and wagon guns. It was a good plan, carefully constructed together with the other big chiefs. Now, as Red Cloud watched, the first Cheyenne decoys rounded the end of Bull's Hump Hill.

Crazy Horse stood neck to neck with his warhorse, stroking the mustang's sleek hide and whispering to calm the animal. She was nervous this morning, flaring her big nostrils and stamping with every shift in the breeze. Little Hawk struggled with his mount, too, mimicking Crazy Horse's efforts to calm him. Among his many worries, Crazy Horse wondered how all of them would keep their horses under control until the trap was sprung. Lone Bear flashed a small smile. They teased him because his horse was notoriously slow. He smiled now, Crazy Horse knew, because the mare was also unnaturally calm. Not even gunfire rattled her.

At least their position was well concealed. At first glance, the terrain in the upper valley of Prairie Dog Creek appeared to be open. This was illusion, though. Dive into it, and the valley was a massive tangle of deep draws, willow-cloaked creek beds, and coulees carved by time into hillsides. There were hundreds of places to hide, now filled with a hundred Minnicoujou, Oglala, and even a few Arapaho.

The gunfire behind Bull's Hump Hill was closer now. At first, there had been only the scattered shots of the wood crew. By now, Crazy Horse was certain, the horse soldiers were in close pursuit, firing at the Cheyenne as they chased.

Then Big Nose came into view, his big black horse distinctive as was the lance that he carried in battle. Little Hawk turned to look at his older brother, and Crazy Horse gave a small nod of reassurance. His horse stamped, and Crazy Horse whispered to her.

He watched as Big Nose pivoted his mount to look back at his small band of Cheyenne warriors and the horse soldiers that pursued them. At first, Crazy Horse had been skeptical about the value of fighting together with the Cheyenne. He didn't exactly distrust them, but it was difficult to communicate, and he wondered why both tribes weren't better off fighting on their own. Red Cloud had been insistent, reminding Crazy Horse that it was he who had argued that the tribes must fight differently than in the past. One advantage of the tribes was numbers, but only if they worked together. They had to learn, to change.

As Crazy Horse watched now, he saw the skill with which Big Nose managed to lead his warriors even as he conveyed the impression of haphazard, fearful retreat to the soldiers.

More of the Cheyenne came into view, and then, for the first time, Crazy Horse could see—from the southwest—the horse soldiers that pursued them. He estimated twenty riders. They held a tight formation, disciplined even in chase. In the past, this would have been a bad sign. In the past, they normally aimed to spread out the pursuers and then pick off the front or the back of the weakened force. Today, though, the valley concealed the greatest force that they had ever assembled—and they hoped to entice the largest force possible into the trap.

Lone Bear caught his eye—pointing to the southeast, the far end of Bull's Hump Hill. There were flashes of light, and Crazy Horse realized that it was the sun, reflecting off the brass buttons of a second group of horse soldiers about the same size as the first. Unlike the other group, though, this one was spread out. Two riders in particular rushed ahead, one on a big white horse. *The officer from the fight over the cattle herd?*

Lone Bear and Crazy Horse exchanged glances, shaking their heads in frustration as they silently shared the same apprehension.

Big Nose and the Cheyenne descended into the valley. Farther back, the first group of soldiers had paused, sitting back at a distance of several hundred yards. The main body of the second group also had paused. But the two soldiers in front of that group charged ahead, along with a trailing gaggle of a few other riders.

The Cheyenne rode directly past Crazy Horse's position, close enough that he could smell the dust raised by their horses as they passed. By now the handful of leading soldiers had closed to within a hundred yards of the decoys, ineffectively firing pistols as they pursued them. If the soldiers had looked carefully they might have seen the concealed Lakota, but it was apparent to Crazy Horse that their blood was up. They were intent on the decoys and blind to anything else.

Crazy Horse turned to the dozen or so Lakota that he could see, concealed in positions behind him. He held up both hands in front of his chest to signal *stay put.* Behind the lead group of charging soldiers, the bigger groups had now started to move cautiously toward the valley. *It's working. . . . Here they come . . . A bit more . . .* Lone Bear looked at Crazy Horse and nodded.

The two lead soldiers rode directly past Crazy Horse's position. He admired the muscularity of the big white horse and took note that the officer riding it—clearly the one he had seen before—carried a sword in addition to the pistol, but no rifle. Crazy Horse's mare stamped and started to whiny, but he reached up to pinch her nose—a last resort to keep her quiet.

Big Nose and the Cheyenne continued their flight, the two white riders now deep in the valley and a handful of the trailing group also within the trap. The riders had thrown up dust as they charged past, and Crazy Horse struggled to see the position of the two bigger groups—the true quarry. Then, peering through, he could see they were still advancing—now barely two hundred yards from where they would descend into the valley. *A few more moments and they will all be inside the trap . . .*

The thought had barely crossed his mind when he heard a piercing war cry from across the valley. He looked over to see a Lakota—he couldn't tell whom—break from cover and charge after the soldiers. Crazy Horse watched in dismay as the closest whites reined their horses, leveling their pistols to fire at the lone warrior. After that, events seemed to accelerate, like water tumbling over a series of rapids. Several other warriors broke cover, yelling at the top of their lungs as they charged toward the whites in the valley. Crazy Horse saw the two lead riders skid to a stop, twisting in their saddles to look behind them. Beyond the valley, meanwhile, the two big groups of soldiers stopped dead in their tracks. By then, it seemed that every warrior in Prairie Dog Valley was charging toward the handful of whites in their midst.

From Crazy Horse's perspective, it was a disaster. Instead of trapping the mass of soldiers, they had sprung the trap when all but a few were safely outside their circle. He looked at Lone Bear in dismay, then both leapt onto their horses.

The few soldiers who had ridden into the trap whipped at their horses in a desperate effort to flee back toward the other whites. Crazy Horse dug his heels into the mustang's flanks, and the horse leapt forward. He pointed his mount directly at a soldier firing a pistol as he rode. The soldier saw Crazy Horse, aimed the pistol at him, and pulled the trigger . . . nothing. The soldier tipped the pistol to examine it, and Crazy Horse could see his terror as he discovered it was empty. Panicked, the soldier threw the pistol to the ground and used his hand to slap furiously at his horse's flank in an effort to urge more speed.

Crazy Horse tucked his own pistol into his belt, reaching instead for his war club. He pulled alongside the soldier's horse, their two animals crashing into each other, then careened side by side. Crazy Horse let go of the reins and left the mare to find her own path. The soldier lifted his sword arm across his body, eyes wide as he stared at Crazy Horse. With his left hand, Crazy Horse grabbed the sword arm, while with his right he crashed the war club into the man's face. He could feel the satisfying crunch of the contact, the sensation of bone breaking beneath the blow. The soldier pitched backward from his horse, rolling a couple of times when he hit the ground, but then rose.

There was a flash of white, and Crazy Horse saw the soldier on the big stallion dash past, flanked by two warriors but slashing viciously with his sword. One of the warriors tumbled from his horse.

Suddenly, Little Hawk appeared, crashing his own horse into the dismounted soldier, the impact throwing him backward. Little Hawk slid fluidly from his horse and was on him, hacking again and again with a knife as the soldier went limp.

Looking around, Crazy Horse saw a couple of other soldiers pulled from their horses by swarming Lakota and Minnicoujou and cut to bits.

Crazy Horse looked uphill toward the two big groups of horse soldiers. Instead of descending into the valley, they had wisely joined their forces on high ground. They were dismounting, forming into organized lines while some of the soldiers moved the horses to the back. Instead of coaxing all the whites into a trap in the valley, they now faced an organized force of soldiers holding high ground. Crazy Horse could scarcely contain his rage.

The rider on the white horse, still swinging his sword wildly, appeared close to escape. Crazy Horse watched, incredulous, as two warriors approached him, using their bows—not to shoot the soldier but, rather, attempting to loop the horse's head.

Crazy Horse watched as the soldier's sword cleaved the skull of one pursuer, who tumbled lifelessly to the ground. The soldier swung and missed at the other, who pulled back. The soldier kicked hard to urge his horse forward—galloping toward the big group of soldiers on the high ground.

A couple of Minnicoujou gave chase, and in his rage, Crazy Horse considered joining them. He realized, though, the folly of riding toward the soldiers entrenched in their hilltop position, and knew that others, including his brother, would follow him up the hill into the waiting rifles. Even the Minnicoujou retreated when half of the soldiers on the skirmish line fired a volley with their long guns.

Crazy Horse became aware of his heavy breathing and pounding heart as he watched the officer on the white horse approach the other soldiers. Lone Bear and Little Hawk appeared beside him, and Crazy Horse felt a moment of relief at their safety. Mostly, though, he felt rage, and not at his enemies, but at his own people. Today they had failed.

From his hawk's vantage, high on the bench, Red Cloud watched it all unfold. How he wished he could reach down today, hold his warriors back when necessary, then push them forward when the moment was propitious. Or at least fight himself, release his anger and frustration in the cathartic act of combat.

He could see clearly how close they had been to executing a strike that might have killed forty whites. Instead, as nearly as he could tell, they might have killed four. Worse, half a dozen of their own men were dead.

As Crazy Horse had feared, they had lacked the discipline to execute the complex plan, instead falling victim to the temptation of their individual stakes in the fight. He had watched, incredulous, as a few warriors tried to capture a horse! As if such a thing mattered in the world they inhabited today.

And yet, as much as Red Cloud felt frustration and anger, there was something else too. Yes, they had failed today. But like that day as a young man, so many years before, Red Cloud, high on the plateau, saw a vision.

Lieutenant George Washington Grummond could hear the pounding of hooves behind him from the closest Sioux, peering back again at the five savages still in pursuit. He heard the terrifying hiss of another arrow as it passed within inches of his head, and prayed they wouldn't take aim at the easier target of his horse. He had seen Bingham go down and watched the savages rip apart his body like a pack of wolves. Grummond had dropped his quirt, smacking repeatedly at the white stallion's rear haunch with the flat of his bloody sword, desperate to goad more speed from the big animal.

He was still two hundred yards from the safety of the twin line of soldiers at the top of the rise, close enough to see Colonel Carrington and Captain Fetterman, mounted and staring down at him. He could see, too, the faces of the men on the twin skirmish line, half kneeling in front and half standing behind, all of them with their rifles trained at his pursuers. *Shoot, goddamn it!* Leave it to Carrington and Fetterman to count bullets in the middle of a battle.

At a hundred yards, Grummond heard Fetterman yell, "Fire!" and the front line of rifles erupted with a great cloud of smoke. Grummond heard one of the Indian horses scream and looked back to see the animal go down, throwing its rider to the ground. The back line of riflemen stepped forward, taking aim on Fetterman's command as the others reloaded. The second line fired, and Grummond saw another pursuer pitch from his horse. The rest of the savages pulled up, paused a few moments to survey the field, and retreated.

Grummond reached Colonel Carrington's line, visceral and unbridled in his ire, directing his words at the colonel. "Are you a fool or a coward for letting them cut us to pieces out there without offering help!"

Carrington seemed to recede further into his too-large uniform, stammering as he searched for a response.

It occurred to Fetterman that this was normally the moment when he could count on Ten Eyck to jump in, but he wasn't here today. Fetterman had no choice but to step up. "You're way out of line, Lieutenant!" he said.

"Am I?" yelled Grummond. "Where were you ten minutes ago?"

"Where were you?" demanded Fetterman. "I'll tell you where . . . out of formation! Blowing a hole in our tactical cohesion!"

"Tactical cohesion?" Grummond scoffed. "What is that? Some chapter in the field manual?"

Fetterman fought back his rage, assuming that Colonel Carrington would jump in as commanding officer and end it. Carrington, though, appeared almost disoriented, looking around uncomfortably and gripping tightly his still-smoking pistol. It occurred to Fetterman that this was the first time that the colonel had ever fired a gun in battle.

"This is not the time or place to debate our views of army tactics, Lieutenant," said Fetterman, struggling, once again, to keep his voice controlled, to avoid another scene in front of the enlisted men. "Now fall in line."

DECEMBER 7, 1866

It was a long day's ride from the soldiers' fort to their camp on the Tongue, and mostly they rode in silence. The Sioux and the Cheyenne had split apart, and even among the Lakota, the Minnicoujou rode apart from the Oglala.

It was not exactly that there had been anger between the tribes, though angry words had been exchanged. All of the big chiefs had agreed that there had been ample blame, that many had failed to exercise restraint in springing the trap—robbing all of them of what might have been a big victory. As for Crazy Horse, he had directed his greatest venom at Kicking Bird, not only a member of his tribe but a cousin. After the fight, he had learned that it was Kicking Bird who first broke cover. Lone Bear had never seen his friend express such anger.

A few miles from the village, Crazy Horse was surprised when Red Cloud rode up beside him. It had grown cold, winter clearly upon them, and the big chief was draped in a thick buffalo robe to fend off a chill that permeated even in sunlight.

"You think yesterday was a defeat?" asked Red Cloud.

"Yes," said Crazy Horse. "To sacrifice a victory because of stupidity is a defeat."

Red Cloud nodded. "That's true," he said. "But don't assume that victory always occurs in one blow, or a straight line. All of us are learning new ways . . . Some learn faster than others . . ." He gave a tight smile. "I've been thinking about how we convince our brothers of the importance of discipline in our war with the whites."

Crazy Horse looked at Red Cloud.

"When we hunt the buffalo, the whole tribe works together to make a success from a plan with many pieces. In our last hunt, you saw how every man held his position until the trap was sprung?"

Crazy Horse thought about this as they continued along.

"We need to bring the discipline of our hunt to our warfare. In the hunt, no one would put their own glory before the tribe. We hunt to secure the survival of our people, not to count coup or steal horses."

Crazy Horse nodded. They were fully capable of discipline when they wanted to be.

"You were right about how the whites would fight," said Red Cloud. "Do you think they'll fight that way again?"

Crazy Horse nodded. "Yesterday they sent the most soldiers ever. I think the greater their numbers, the less they fear us. They all would have ridden into the trap if we had held our positions."

"Yes. And I think it's even more than that," said Red Cloud. "I think the greater their numbers, the more they hold us in disdain."

"What do you think we should do next?" asked Crazy Horse.

"What would it take to get them to send even more soldiers from the fort?" asked Red Cloud.

Crazy Horse pondered for a moment, then said, "A fatter target . . . more decoys . . . and maybe we could make the trap twice as big—allow greater space for them to ride in?"

"No," said Red Cloud.

Crazy Horse looked at him, confused.

"Truly different," said Red Cloud. "We won't make the trap twice as big—we'll make it ten times as big . . . twenty times as big."

Crazy Horse stared at Red Cloud as he thought about it.

"We have one more chance to fight together before we scatter for winter," said Red Cloud. "I want the whites to confront something not only that they have never faced. I want them to confront something they have never even imagined . . . especially from us."

Suddenly, Crazy Horse, too, saw Red Cloud's vision. "All of us."

DECEMBER 15, 1866

Captain Fetterman stepped inside Colonel Carrington's office to find the colonel behind his desk, reading a letter, the junior officers and Private Sample all standing in front of him. Fetterman noticed that Private Sample, who tended to mirror the mood of the colonel, seemed particularly tense. He kept digging into the back of his neck, as if vexed by an itch he could not quite reach. His eyes, meanwhile, darted from officer to officer, hoping, it seemed, that one of them might say something to calm the tension in the room.

It was instantly evident to Fetterman that the officers had been arguing, even from how they had arrayed themselves. Lieutenant Grummond stood to one side, his arms crossed and his hands stuffed beneath his armpits, as if making some physical attempt to contain a further outburst. At the other end of the desk, Captain Ten Eyck's plump face shone red and his temple vein stood out in stark relief, practically pulsing.

"You don't have to read between the lines to see that Cooke is covering his own fat ass," said Captain Ten Eyck. Ten Eyck respected chain of command, certainly to include his own commanding officer. But he also hated army bureaucracy, and this letter from General Cooke struck Ten Eyck as army bureaucracy at its worst—second-guessing from afar to appease politics from even further afar.

Colonel Carrington contorted his face again, looked up from reading, then ripped off his glasses—waving an official-looking piece of paper as he spoke. "Of course there's not a word in here about any of my requests for men and supplies and horses!" Carrington handed the letter to Fetterman. "Captain Fetterman, see if there's something we've missed."

The masthead on the letter showed the seal of the United States Army in the upper left-hand corner, and in the right, with a star beside the name, General Philip St. George Cooke, along with his title, "Commander, Department of the Platte." Fetterman read quickly through the text:

> Colonel: You are hereby instructed that so soon as the troops and stores are covered from the weather, to turn your earnest attention to the possibility of striking the hostile band of Indians by surprise in their winter camps.
>
> An extraordinary effort in winter, when the Indian horses are unserviceable, it is believed, should be followed by more success than can be accomplished by very large expeditions in the summer, when the Indians can so easily scatter into deserts and mountain hiding places almost beyond pursuit.
>
> You have a large arrear of murderous and insulting attacks by the savages upon emigrant trains and troops to settle, and you are ordered, if there prove to be any promise of success, to conduct or to send under another officer such an expedition.

Fetterman saw them waiting expectantly for his reaction. The tension among the officers had grown untenable over the past weeks, like steam in a boiler, and he had wrestled with how to release it. This time, though, he had come in with a plan, and he was determined to speak up. His strongest instincts, of course, aligned with Captain Ten Eyck. The army by its nature was lumbering and conventional, but Fetterman remained confident that its underlying institutional virtues would land on the correct course of action over time. Wasn't that how they won the war? Prevailed against the radicals and rebels? Which wasn't to say he didn't sympathize with Lieutenant Grummond. Fetterman, too, bristled at the army's complete subservience to conventional thinking, at the glacial pace of decision-making. *How to navigate between the poles?*

"Well, that's rich," said Fetterman, waving the letter. "Advising us about the health of Indian horses when we're lucky if we can field thirty mounts."

"Yes!" said Carrington.

"And it's not just the horses!" said Ten Eyck. "Where are the new carbines we've been promised for the cavalry?"

"You're all so focused on the logistics that you're missing what's important!" said Grummond. He grabbed the letter from Fetterman, reading from it, punching words as he went along. "'You have a *large arrear* of murderous and *insulting attacks* by the *savages* upon emigrant trains and troops *to settle* . . .' Aren't you listening? It's plain as day! There's a score to be settled, and we have the commanding general of the Department of the Platte *ordering* us to do it!"

"That's bold talk," said Ten Eyck. "And I hope it feels good to vent your spleen and say it . . . but how do we settle this score without horses and guns? You plan to run up to Red Cloud and throw a rock at him? At least they've got bows and arrows—and they know how to use them."

"We go on the offense," said Grummond. "Just like General Cooke says. We haven't tried that one single time in four months of sitting here."

Fetterman worked to formulate his thoughts. "Perhaps, Colonel . . ." Fetterman felt the discomfort of their stares, but today he pushed forward. "There's discretion built into these orders . . ." Fetterman took the letter back from Grummond, reading from it. "It says the '*possibility* of striking' and '*if there prove* to be any promise of success . . .'"

"Oh, for Christ's sake!" said Grummond.

"Hold on," said Fetterman. "I'm not finished. We reply to the general with a factual accounting of our readiness—put it on the record—requesting the appropriate level of horses and equipment for the winter campaign he seeks."

Grummond started to interject again, but Fetterman raised his hand and continued. "We also take an immediate step, which you report to the general."

Colonel Carrington listened intently. "What immediate step?"

Fetterman looked at Grummond as he spoke. "Like Lieutenant Grummond says, we're all angry about our inability to respond to attacks."

Grummond stared back, seeming a bit surprised.

"What if you announced a new policy, Colonel? What if we kept every serviceable mount saddled and ready—and their riders too—so that we can respond instantly to any attack?"

"What about weapons?" asked Ten Eyck.

"Well," said Fetterman, "I've thought about that. Why don't we concentrate what we have. It doesn't make any sense for the marching band to carry the Spencers. We could give those to Grummond's cavalry."

Colonel Carrington felt a bit of discomfort at this. In their whole battalion, they had only twenty of the Spencers—the modern repeating rifles that were the envy of every soldier on the fort. It had been his decision to give the Spencers to the band, in part because there hadn't been enough to issue them to all of the cavalrymen. But more so, if he was truthful, because he was sensitive at the appearance of deploying a band to the frontier. In Carrington's mind, having the band members carry Spencers at least gave them the appearance of fighting men.

"That's still only twenty rifles," said Ten Eyck.

"But at least we'd have them in the best hands," said Fetterman.

Grummond started to nod. "You give twenty of my men repeating rifles, and there's no pack of savages that can stand in our way."

Colonel Carrington watched the conversation unfold, nodding his head periodically. "I like this," he said after a while. "A new policy . . . that's what we need . . . Private Sample, we'll draft it up." His enthusiasm seemed to grow as he talked himself through it. "I could even announce it to an assembly of the men."

Private Sample scratched notes furiously on a pad with a pencil. "Yes, sir. I'll get a draft ready for your signature."

"And don't forget the letter back to General Cooke," said Colonel Carrington. "There's a detachment traveling back to Fort Laramie tomorrow, and I want my letter to the general to go with them."

Captain Fetterman placed two dollars on the counter in the sutlery, his last cash until payday. The sutler accepted the coins and pushed the bag of Old Virginia pipe tobacco across the counter. The southern brands had disappeared during the war, of course. And even now some former Union soldiers refused to smoke them. As for Fetterman, though, he viewed the ability to procure Virginia tobacco as another reason to celebrate the end of the war. Hadn't Lincoln said "with malice towards none"? Well, this was part of Fetterman's effort to forgive.

He turned to walk out of the sutlery and found Captain Ten Eyck standing in the doorway. "I think you and I need to clear the air," said Ten Eyck.

Fetterman sighed, wishing that it was late enough to avail himself of the new tobacco. "All right."

They stepped outside onto the mostly empty parade grounds, the only sound the occasional stiff snap of the massive flag.

"I'm having a difficult time getting a bead on where you stand," said Captain Ten Eyck.

"Oh," said Fetterman. "In what sense?"

"I know you're too smart for all the Grummond rah-rah," said Ten Eyck. "Why'd you stand up for that blowhard this morning?"

"Can we speak candidly, Captain?"

"You can agree with me or not," said Ten Eyck. "But I think I've always been clear on where I stand."

"Listen, we both know we're walking a knife's edge here. You've seen how the colonel is easily"—Fetterman searched for a word—"persuaded . . . And give Grummond credit—the man knows how to persuade."

"So your solution is to let Grummond have his way?"

"Not all of it . . . not always . . . but we throw an occasional bone. Let him chew on that for a while. A guy like Grummond—you can channel him. Maybe he doesn't do things the way you would, but he's a fighter. We're in a dangerous place, and it'll get even more dangerous when we go on the offensive in the spring. If we can channel him, he'll be useful to us."

Captain Ten Eyck mulled this awhile. "I don't know . . . I just don't trust him."

"Of course not," said Fetterman. "I didn't say we should trust him. What I'm saying is we should steer him. The colonel can't do it, so we do it—behind the scenes."

"You really think we can do that?"

"Look," said Fetterman. "Let Grummond claim victory—get a little bit of what he wants. In a month, it's the dead of winter. I don't see the army coming through with horses and arms before then, which means—"

"Which means there won't be a winter campaign," said Ten Eyck.

Fetterman nodded. "So the colonel announces a new policy. Maybe we ride out and run off a couple bands of raiders. Remember, the tribes'll be hunkering down soon too."

"And in the spring?"

"In the spring we hope the army comes through with what they've promised."

As if on cue, it began to snow.

DECEMBER 17, 1866

Captain Fetterman was surprised to find Jim Bridger on the western barbican, watching intently as Lieutenant Grummond drilled twenty cavalrymen in the open valley below. The two men exchanged polite greetings before both resumed watching the drills. Even at the distance of several hundred yards, Grummond's angry shouts carried to the fort. Grummond attempted to form his men into a skirmish line and then to move the line forward in order. Even at a slow trot, however, the formation quickly degenerated, ragged at best, the semblance of a line quickly disappearing.

Grummond ordered the line to halt, then called for the cavalrymen to pull their rifles from saddle scabbards. He then called out "*ready,*" "*aim,*" and "*fire!*" On the command of "*fire,*" there was no actual firing, merely the pantomiming of the action. The soldiers appeared clumsy with their weapons, treating them like the novel objects that they were.

"I guess Carrington gave them the repeaters?" said Bridger.

Fetterman nodded. "Yes, the colonel finally decided to take them away from the band."

"Have they fired them yet?" asked Bridger.

"Two rounds each," said Fetterman somewhat sheepishly. "It's all the ammunition that can be spared."

Bridger didn't say anything.

"I know you find much to fault in our strategy," said Fetterman. "But you understand we're doing the best we can in the circumstances . . ." It wasn't clear if he was talking to Bridger, or speaking aloud some debate he was conducting with himself.

Bridger remained silent, and Fetterman had learned that it often was necessary to be quite direct with the old scout. "I wish you would speak more in our discussions with the officers, Mr. Bridger. We value your experience."

Bridger looked at Fetterman directly. After a while he said, "I've said my piece plenty of times and it's doesn't seem to be getting any traction. And I don't recall you chiming in."

Fetterman bristled. "You don't see everything. Besides, frontal assault's not the only way to attack." He took a deep breath. "Look, I know I'll never beat Grummond in a debate—but there's more subtle ways of influencing things."

"You seem like a smart man," said Bridger. "I heard your men respect you and I heard you earned that the hard way in the war. Remember, they look to you for judgment—for your judgment."

"I'm working things in my own way," said Fetterman. "Grummond's a fool, but I understand his kind. It's true he's hoodwinked the colonel, but I have a plan. Grummond is the type of man who can be nudged in the right direction—pushed along without even knowing you're there."

Bridger listened and seemed to reflect on what Fetterman had said. After a while he said, "The Shoshone set grass fires sometimes in the late summer. All that burnt grass makes it grow in thicker and greener the next season. If you do it right, the buffalo practically fall over themselves to graze on it."

"What's your point?" asked Fetterman.

"A few years back, some of the younger warriors in the tribe I lived with set a fire in a dry year. The fall rains came later than usual, so there was nothing to check the flames. It ended up burning for more than a month—thousands of square miles . . . not only prairie, but up into the timber in the mountains. Drove away the game. Our tribe ended up having to move close to Sioux lands, ended up in a couple fights, lots of Shoshone killed."

"So what's your point?" asked Fetterman again.

"My point is—it's not easy, playing with fire . . . A little wind comes up, and all of the sudden you got something you weren't expecting."

They continued to watch the drilling below. Lieutenant Grummond yelled commands for reloading the rifles, and many of the cavalrymen struggled to hold their horses stationary while they manipulated their new weapons. Several of the horses pivoted so that they faced the opposite direction of the others. Two men jumped from their horses and appeared to search for something on the ground—apparently dropped cartridges or the spring-loaded tube that pushed forward new rounds into the rifle's chamber. Grummond rode forward to the men on the ground, screaming now as the soldiers struggled to regain their saddles.

Fetterman struggled again to formulate his thoughts, let alone his words.

"Biggest mistakes I made in my life were when I let others push me into things when I knew they were wrong," said Bridger. "Walk your own road. I know that's easier said than done . . . especially in a place like this."

Before Fetterman could say anything, Bridger touched the rim of his floppy hat, which he somehow managed to wear without seeming foolish. "Good day, Captain."

DECEMBER 18, 1866

The porch of the Bale of Hay Saloon in Virginia City, Montana Territory, wasn't much as a place to sit, especially in the cold. The man sitting there, Millard Dupont, had only gone outside because he was fairly certain that two drunken miners inside the saloon were likely to begin shooting at each other in a minute or two. Only a few days earlier, Dupont had struck pay dirt, and the last thing he wanted was to go and get shot after finally finding a bit of gold.

At least there was a sunny spot, the planks of the saloon porch catching the last few rays of afternoon sun. Still, Dupont pulled his collar up in a futile effort to keep a cold wind at bay. He counted twenty-two horses tied up to the hitching posts between the Bale of Hay and Gilbert Brewery, the second-most popular drinking establishment this end of town. He marveled again at the growth of the town in the six months he had been there. According to the *Montana Post*, the new newspaper, the population had quadrupled in 1866 to four thousand souls, give or take a couple dozen Chinese. Between Virginia City's exploding population and the difficulty of bringing in supplies, one consequence had been outrageous prices, and Dupont was relieved for the bit of respite afforded by turning up color in the sluice he ran with two partners.

When Dupont first heard the sound, he thought that a whole tribe of wild Indians was swooping in to attack the town. There had never been such an attack on Virginia City, but speculating about the possibility was such a frequent topic of conversation among the miners that

Dupont had come to have a quite vivid scenario in his head for just what such an event might look like.

Certainly the sound he heard was as he had imagined—the pounding hooves of hundreds of animals. There was yelling, too, though this was not the high-pitched war cries of savages but, rather, white men yelling "*Git up!*" and "*Go cow!*"

Looking down Wallace Street toward the ruckus, Dupont was shocked at what he saw: a herd of strange, long-horned cattle that must number many hundred. For Virginia City, Montana Territory, the beasts were as foreign as if they had been catapulted across the ocean from China. There were men surrounding the herd, and while white men, they too were strange, working their horses so effortlessly that man and beast moved as one.

The man who rode up front had obvious stature that gave a sense of martial order to the group. He peeled off the point position directly in front of the Bale of Hay, watching from horseback as the whole herd passed by him and continued through town. One of the other men rode abreast as he passed. "Where do we put 'em?" he asked.

"Get outside of town a mile or so," answered the lead man. "Set pickets and shoot any man that thinks they get our Texas beef for free."

Dupont was standing by now and realized that he had been joined by every Bale of Hay patron, including the two combatants, who seemed to have forgotten completely their quarrel. The patrons of Gilbert Brewery had disgorged into the street as well, along with every other person in every other building on Wallace Street. It felt like a Fourth of July parade.

"Texas?" asked Henry Gilbert, owner of Gilbert Brewery and often self-appointed spokesman for everyone else. "Who the hell are you?"

The man on the horse ignored the question for a while, watching the cattle make their way farther down the street as people continued to emerge from buildings to watch and point excitedly. They could see his kit up close now, and studied it. He had a big Mexican saddle with silver medallions, a lariat looped over the horn, and a mangy wool blanket tied behind the cantle. He wore a six-shooter at his right hip, and on his left side a repeating rifle protruded from a sheath, butt forward.

Eventually the man turned to the assembled crowd, removing his hat in a broad gesture.

"Ladies and gentlemen, I'm Nelson Story," he said. "My men and I just drove this herd of cattle two thousand miles from Fort Worth, Texas. We fought wild Indians three times and white scoundrels twice. We buried two of our brave friends on the trail. Tonight we aim to eat a hot meal and soak in a hot bath . . . and tomorrow we aim to sell the good people of Virginia City some fresh beef."

A great cheer went up from the crowd.

DECEMBER 19, 1866

Dear Journal,
One faces challenges in life, and in such moments one must

Frances Grummond sat for a long moment, staring at the partial sentence
and wondering what to write next. Eventually the ink at the tip of her
quill dripped, punctuating the mostly blank page with an unsightly blot.
She set down the quill and ripped the page from her journal, wadding
it and tossing it aside, where it came to rest beside a pile of other such
wads of paper. Then she locked the journal and returned it to her trunk,
removing her other journal and fumbling with the lock in her eagerness
to open it.

Dear Friend,
I have no place to turn but to you, no one but you with whom
I can share the terrible news revealed to me today. There is no
way to dress it up. Already I have wrestled with it for hours,
searching not so much for a silver lining as for some vision of a
path leading forward. I see no path but I know I cannot write
about what has happened in any form except the harsh, brutal
truth. Perhaps writing down what has happened in the black
and white of ink on paper will help me to see what so far has
remained elusive.

I am heartbroken beyond any depth I might previously

have imagined possible, but even more so, I am angry at my own self for the willful ignorance by which I allowed myself to be led to this place.

Here is what happened, unadorned—

At noon today I gathered the laundry as I do each week and walked across the parade grounds to the laundresses' tents. I left our clothing with Janey, and as I always do, lingered to engage her in a bit of small talk about the affairs of the fort and its inhabitants. It was apparent at once that something was wrong. While normally cheerful despite her station, Janey today seemed distant and quite sad. I asked her what was wrong, and at first she demurred with some excuse about "feeling under the weather."

After I left Janey, I thought about it all day, so much so that I decided to go back to see her again. This time, when I asked her if something was wrong, she burst suddenly and inexplicably into tears. "Oh, Mrs. Grummond," she said, "I learned something horrible."

I felt my head spin, and I braced myself for what I long had feared—that Lt Grummond had succumbed to the temptation of one of the laundresses. While such infidelity would have been crushing (and for all I know may well be true along with everything else), it pales by comparison to the actual story that Janey proceeded to tell.

"You know I am friends with Sergeant Lang," she said, "who served under your husband in the war. He told me some things about the lieutenant. At first, I vowed not to pass them on, but then I put myself in your place. You've been so kind to me, and I know if it were me, I would want to know."

My mind continued to race as I tried to imagine what secret might possibly be revealed. Even in my imagination I did not come close to the truth. In the words that followed, Janey revealed to me that I am not the first wife of my husband. Nor will my child be my husband's firstborn. Indeed, he is the father of two children who live with the first wife in Detroit. If this were not enough, Sergeant Lang also told Janey that my husband had not yet completed his divorce of his first wife when he married me, making me an unwitting part of a polygamous union. And of course the shock of all of this comes on top of the hard punch in the stomach that is the collection of stone-cold lies upon which the whole of my relationship with my husband is built. And it is on this aspect that I have been most fixated in the hours since learning this news. Not just the dozens of conversations in which he lied with his words, but the infinite instances in which he lied in his silence.

And then comes my anger at myself. Even in the beginning, my intuition told me to be cautious of this man. Instead of asking questions, though, I saw in him what I wanted to see, or at least what I hoped he would become. As I have thought back over the recent months, it all seems so clear, the warning signs so obvious. But by consequence of my willful ignorance, I now find myself deep in his web, married to him, carrying his child, and thousands of miles from my family. I want to reveal him for the charlatan that he is, but how can I do so without turning my own life to even greater chaos?

Sincerely yours,
Frances

DECEMBER 20, 1866

Bugler Adolph Metzger stood shivering beside the flagpole along with Lieutenant George Washington Grummond. The clouds that night clung tight so that the stars and moon provided no light, the lieutenant's oil lantern the only illumination on the parade grounds. Grummond breathed out a cloud of condensation, stamped his feet, and rubbed the sides of his arms in a futile attempt to stay warm.

Metzger held his bugle so that the mouthpiece nestled in his armpit, trying to keep it from freezing. He had, despite the frigid temperature, once again volunteered to play taps.

Lieutenant Grummond gave a perfunctory glance at his pocket watch. "Close enough," he said. "Let's go."

Metzger resented the sloppiness, though coming from Grummond, it didn't surprise him. Keeping time was one of the few ties to civilization on a frontier post. The people of the fort regulated their day with the bugle calls, and Metzger's mission was to help them to do so accurately. Metzger deliberately took his time, breathing on the mouthpiece to warm it, moving his mouth and cheeks to loosen them for playing.

"Holy Christ, Metzger! Blow your goddamn horn and be done with it!"

After a few more moments, Metzger began to play.

He was surprised, given the cold, that the notes rolled out so smoothly. And something about the hemmed-in clouds seemed to hold the sound within the bubble of the fort, making it more intimate and pure. Halfway through, it occurred to Metzger that he had played it perfectly to that point, and he focused every ounce of his being on the half unplayed. Though he had blown taps a thousand times, he appreciated anew how much he loved the simple and haunting notes of the song, how each bled into the next in a seamless progression toward the end. Lieutenant Grummond shuffled impatiently, but at this point, Metzger didn't even notice. He had merged completely with his instrument, and through his instrument with the song. Before the last run, he breathed in, then breathed out into the trumpet, and let the final note tail out and fade, morphing into the dark night in perfect decrescendo until it was no more.

He had done it.

"Could you have made it last any longer? I'm freezing my ass off!" Lieutenant Grummond spun around and stormed off.

Bugler Adolph Metzger didn't care.

Part Three

DECEMBER 20, 1866

The big chiefs sat on their warhorses near the place where a tiny rivulet found confluence with Prairie Dog Creek. The tribes, too, were flowing together, and it gave Crazy Horse a stirring sense of hope and strength to see the chiefs assembled. The presence of Red Cloud showed the importance of the battle that would take place the following day—not a fight or a skirmish, but a battle. It was especially good to see High Backbone, here to represent the Minnicoujou.

Crazy Horse also recognized Box Elder, a war chief of the Northern Cheyenne, and Black Coal of the Arapaho. Behind them, the white man's road trailed down from the distant ridgeline before eventually dipping into the creek. Thin sheets of ice formed along the banks in the quiet water, but mostly it flowed too rapidly to freeze. Crazy Horse, Lone Bear, and a dozen of the other young warriors were also nearby.

"Why do you think they'll come down the road?" asked High Backbone. "Everything fails if they don't."

The question was for Crazy Horse, because it was he who had suggested this place for the trap. "We watched the soldiers all through the fall, and they follow a pattern in response to every attack. We'll have to be skillful to lead them here, but their road will draw them too."

"This is a good place to fight," said Box Elder, who spoke some Lakota. "There are many good places for us to hide . . . and the soldiers can't see this place from the fort."

"But why would they come so far from their walls and wagon guns?" asked Black Coal.

"It won't be easy," said Crazy Horse. "But they're hungry for glory and blood—and they underestimate what we might do against them."

Crazy Horse studied Red Cloud as they spoke. He knew that the great chief's opinion would matter most, and yet his face was difficult to read. Then they all heard the approach of a horse from the north and turned to see a solitary rider. Red Cloud nodded in approval and said, "Let's hear what Moon has to tell us."

Crazy Horse had first noticed Moon when both of them were young. Even at the age of six or seven, it was clear that Moon was different from the other boys. Like Crazy Horse, Moon had asked to seek his vision at an early age.

A number of things became more clear when Moon returned from his quest to explain the vision he'd received from the Creator. He was *winkte*—two-souled. In his vision, he learned that though he was physically a man, it was his destiny to live his life as a woman both in actions and in dress. His family felt great happiness to have their hopes confirmed. Before, Moon's actions often had seemed confusing. But if the Creator had given him the wisdom of both men and women, no wonder that he would see the world in a different way. And to hold such wisdom in one body was known by all the Lakota to be a special gift, though also a burden that the *winkte* carried on behalf of the tribe. The people of the tribe sought out Moon's counsel in all variety of matters, from insights into love and family relationships to prophecy about the hunt and war.

Crazy Horse knew that the Lakota would never undertake a battle as momentous as the one that loomed tomorrow without first consulting Moon. It was reassuring to watch his friend riding toward them on his sorrel pony. He wore a dress adorned with elk teeth and bells at the sleeves that made the whole thing jangle as he moved. On his head Moon wore a black cloth, wrapped and twisted around his flowing black hair.

Moon cocked his head as he approached, reining his horse in front of them. He studied the assembly of chiefs, understanding its implication, then turned his horse so that he could look at the broad valley surrounding the two creeks.

"This is the ground you've chosen for the fight?"

Red Cloud shrugged. "Perhaps."

Moon reached into a small leather satchel that he wore around his neck, first removing a small braid of sweetgrass. He sniffed at the grass before grinding some of the dry leaves in the palm of his hand. Then he blew into his palm and watched as the tiny particles dispersed on the light prairie breeze. Next Moon took a whistle carved from the bone of an eagle and blew it, the eerie treble filling the valley and ascending the hills. He seemed to follow the sound with his eyes, then nudged gently at the sorrel's flanks with his heels. They all watched as he rode across the creek and up the white man's road to the hilltop.

For a long time he zigzagged along the hilltop, moving erratically, forward and back, left and right, with no pattern discernable except to him. Occasionally Moon stopped, looking in one direction or another and blowing the whistle. Several times he dismounted from the sorrel to examine some detail on the ground. Once, he put his ear to the earth and lay there for several moments, listening. Finally, he turned and rode back toward them, splashing across Prairie Dog Creek before reining to a stop in front of the chiefs, breathing heavily and holding up his hands, each cupped as if containing water.

"I have found ten of our enemies," said Moon. "Five in each of my hands. Do you want them?"

The chiefs were silent for a moment, but then Red Cloud spoke. "No," he said. "We do not want those men. It is not worthwhile." He pointed at the other chiefs. "Look at the tribes represented here today. Ten is not enough for all of us."

Moon nodded. "I will go and see if there are more." Then off he went again, scouring farther up the ridgeline along the white man's road. When he came back the second time, his hands, he said, were filled with twenty soldiers, but again Red Cloud shook his head. Moon came back a third time, with twenty soldiers in one hand and thirty in the other. Yet again Red Cloud said that the number was not sufficient for such a great force of tribes.

On Moon's fourth attempt—the sacred fourth—he rode his sorrel far beyond where the men below could see him, though they could hear the high wail of his whistle drifting down from above them in the hills.

On this fourth trip, Moon went all the way to the top of the far ridge-line, to where he could see the soldiers' fort in the distance. Only then did he ride back into the valley of Prairie Dog Creek, scooping up soldiers from every dip and gulley along the way, from behind every rock.

As he approached the chiefs this time, Moon swayed from side to side on his horse, struggling to balance some great, unseen weight. He labored to cross the creek, just managing to arrive in front of the chiefs before falling from the sorrel to the ground. Looking up at the chiefs he said, "Answer me quickly . . . I have a hundred or more!"

At this Red Cloud raised his lance to the sky and let out his war cry, and then all the others joined in. Crazy Horse and the young men leapt from their horses, pounding the earth beside Moon to slay this future foe, and then lifting the *winkte* from the ground and embracing him for the strength of his vision.

A hundred! Crazy Horse considered the number and thought of Red Cloud's strategy of delivering not just a defeat to the whites—but a jolting shot. It was almost hard to imagine killing a hundred soldiers in one fight. Again, though, he let himself draw hope from the power represented by the great assembly of tribes.

Before they returned to camp, Red Cloud and the other chiefs came to their final decisions, with Red Cloud speaking for all of them. "This place where Moon touched the ground has his strong powers," said Red Cloud. "Tonight we will pick ten decoys representing all the tribes. And if they can do it, they will lead the soldiers to this spot." Red Cloud drew his arm back and thrust his spear with full force into the packed and frozen ground of the road. Crazy Horse and the others stared at the place, just beyond where the whites' road crossed the creek.

"If the decoys can make it here," continued Red Cloud, "they'll form two lines with their horses, and then cross the lines where my spear stands. That will be the signal to begin the attack. Any warrior who attacks before this moment will have betrayed his people, no less than if they had ruined the fall hunt. All of us chiefs must make this clear above all else." Red Cloud pointed with his arm in a wide arc around the valley. "We'll be hidden all around, in greater numbers than the whites would ever imagine . . . and in the center of our circle, Moon's hundred soldiers will meet their fate."

The chiefs had agreed that the enormous encampment of warriors would build no fires that night despite the frigid air. They camped now less than a half day's ride from the fort, and nothing must jeopardize the element of surprise. The glow from so many fires would have been visible for miles and the scent as if a whole forest was ablaze.

Crazy Horse, Lone Bear, and Little Hawk huddled close to each other for warmth as they tried to force down a bit of jerky. Only Little Hawk succeeded in swallowing more than a few bites. Not even the tension of looming battle killed the boy's appetite.

"How many of us do you think there are?" asked Little Hawk.

Lone Bear looked up from sharpening his knife. "I heard that with the Cheyenne and Arapaho, we may be two thousand."

"How many is that?" asked Little Hawk.

"Like twenty of our winter camps," said Lone Bear. "Only all warriors."

Little Hawk cocked his head, wrapping his mind around a force so great.

It had been dark when they arrived back at the warriors' camp from the scouting mission to the valley of Prairie Dog Creek, so they had not been able to see the assembled warriors in daylight. Crazy Horse, too, grappled for a time with the number. For him, the comparison was to the soldiers at the fort, whom they had counted at various junctures as the soldier forces built up over the course of the fall. He remembered his awe at the three hundred soldiers who lined up during the day they first raised their giant flag with their perfect lines and synchronized firing and cannon. Such force had seemed omnipotent, and Crazy Horse still worried at the power of the white man's weapons. Yet having studied the soldiers, he had seen the cracks in the foundation of their strength. And he felt pride that Red Cloud had been so successful in marshaling such a force in the face of the invaders. Now if the tribes could just fight together.

They did their best to prepare their weapons by the light of a waning quarter moon, sharpening arrowheads with whetstones and filling quivers. The Lakota who possessed rifles—most did not—insisted on carrying them, more as symbols of status than as effective weapons. Crazy Horse, though, had left his rifle back in the winter camp. Part of his decision was practical. The single shot might be acceptable for some hunts, but not for fighting. In his rawhide quiver, Crazy Horse carried twenty arrows. His range with the bow might be shorter than with the rifle, but he could fire at ten times the rate. Crazy Horse's choice of weapon was also philosophical. For him, the rifle was not a symbol of power but, rather, dependence, dependence on the white man for powder and shot. How could you win a war if you relied on your enemy for the very weapons you used against him?

He made a small concession in carrying his new pistol. At least it could be fired multiple times before reloading. For truly close fighting, though, Crazy Horse relied most on his savagely lethal war club. Here, Crazy Horse departed from some of the older men who still carried coup sticks, meant not to kill an enemy, but to touch him in the face of death. Crazy Horse's experience had taught him that there was no counting coup on the whites. Such noble acts of bravery were part of a form of warfare now dead. The whites fought for one purpose only—to kill. To fight against them with any other objective was a weakness for them to exploit.

Against the deep silence of the frozen night, they heard the whinny of horses and then the soft plodding of horses' hooves, slowly approaching their position. The three friends stood, the moonlight now illuminating the forms of a dozen or more riders. To his surprise, Crazy Horse recognized Red Cloud and High Backbone at the front of the group, along with the Cheyenne chief, Box Elder, and the Arapaho chief, Black Coal. Behind the chiefs rode a group of young warriors, two of whom Crazy Horse knew well—American Horse, the son of the Oglala chief Sitting Bear, and Sword Owner, Red Cloud's nephew. He recognized Big Nose, of the Northern Cheyenne. From their dress, he could see that two of the other young men were Arapaho. It was odd to have this group appear in the night, and Crazy Horse exchanged glances with Lone Bear, both of them confused.

The group reined their horses in front of the three young Lakota. Then Red Cloud spoke. "Crazy Horse," he said. "We're here tonight to bestow upon you a great honor."

Crazy Horse looked to High Backbone for some signal, but his uncle offered no hint.

"For your bravery and your knowledge, the chiefs of the four tribes have picked you to lead the decoys in tomorrow's battle." Little Hawk and Lone Bear both smiled in their happiness, but Crazy Horse offered no sign of his own emotions. Inside, he felt a deep sense of honor that was pushed away quickly by the daunting weight of responsibility.

Red Cloud gestured toward the warriors behind him. "You'll go before dawn with two Cheyenne, two Arapaho, and five other Lakota. Together you'll attack the soldiers' woodcutters. It's you who's told us what will happen next."

Crazy Horse nodded. "They'll send soldiers from the fort to defend the woodcutters."

"And your job will be to lead them to the place shown to us today by Moon," said Red Cloud. "You and the other decoys will cross Prairie Dog Creek, then cross your horses in two lines as the signal for attack."

Crazy Horse nodded again.

"The soldiers have seen us use decoys before," said High Backbone. "They won't be easy to entice . . . You'll need to be in range of their rifles."

"I understand," said Crazy Horse. He did understand, as did the others. Some of the decoys would certainly die tomorrow.

"The decoys will camp here tonight with you so that you can talk and prepare," said Red Cloud. "Ride out so that you can be in place before the sun rises. The rest of us will leave before dawn, too, so that we're in place before you lead them into the valley."

With no further ceremony, Red Cloud and all the chiefs but High Backbone rode away. High Backbone looked down at Crazy Horse from his saddle. "When we went to Prairie Dog Creek today, I thought of the times that you and I hunted there and in the other valleys nearby, years ago."

Crazy Horse nodded. The same memories had flooded over him.

"All of those times before flow together into tomorrow. It's a place of strong medicine for you," said High Backbone. "Of destiny." Then he too rode into the darkness.

Crazy Horse turned to see Lone Bear and Little Hawk beaming in the subdued evening light. Little Hawk rushed up to him, shoved him backward using both hands against his chest, then embraced him. "My brother—leader of the decoys!" Suddenly his face turned serious. "I have something for you."

Crazy Horse looked at his younger brother questioningly.

"I want you to ride Arrow tomorrow."

"But Arrow was my gift to you."

"She's the best warhorse in our family. You said so yourself. I want you to ride her for all of us."

Little Hawk's face looked suddenly so solemn that Crazy Horse scarcely recognized him. Not knowing what else to do, he nodded. "Thank you, my brother."

Lone Bear had been watching, smiling, but now he, too, turned serious. "I have something for you too," he said. His friend reached behind his neck and lifted his necklace over his head. Even in the darkness, Crazy Horse knew well what hung at the end of the leather strap. It was the four-inch claw of a grizzly bear. At only fourteen, Lone Bear had killed the grizzly with an arrow through the heart. Such was the fame of this kill that it gave the boy his name.

Crazy Horse was stunned. "I can't take that, Lone Bear . . . It's your talisman."

"You were with me when I killed this bear," said Lone Bear. "If you wear this, tomorrow I'll be with you." Seeing Crazy Horse's continued reluctance, he said, "You need it more than I do . . . And surely you won't offend me by refusing my gift." He gave a tiny hint of a smile, and placed the necklace around Crazy Horse's neck.

Crazy Horse touched the massive claw, and it was as if he could feel the strength of the great animal flowing into his heart. Then he embraced his friend. "You're my brother too."

SAME DAY

Dear Friend,

If yesterday I thought my life could not become more chaotic, today I discovered an anger and sadness and uncertainty even greater than what I imagined before. It is 1:30 in the morning and I write this alone in my quarters, my life so upended that I cannot begin to imagine what will come next. I have no tears left to cry, and all that is left is to hope that some greater understanding might come through writing it all down.

A little after 9:00 this evening, I returned to our quarters after the usual evening session teaching reading. As I approached I was surprised to see light inside. I opened the door to find the Lt, drunk and disheveled, sitting amid the contents of my trunk, strewn about on the dirt floor. In his hands he held this journal, the lock pried open.

He began to yell at me, and I will admit that at first I felt terrified and even guilty, as if it was I that had done something wrong. He was barely coherent but he raged about how I had betrayed him and kept secrets from him and how I had broken my vows as a wife. In the shock of it all I think I stammered at first and I may even have begun to retreat behind an apology but then there came over me, like a giant wave, a righteous outrage at the reality of the situation, at the reality that he somehow had the gall to accuse me of secrecy!

I took a step toward the Lt and I pointed my finger at him and I yelled at him with no regard for how my voice might carry. I threw at him all of my knowledge of his past, demanded his explanation for the lies upon which our entire relationship is founded. At first he was so shocked that I had stood up to him that he said nothing. Then, though, I could see a look come over him of desperation and malice, like a cornered animal. He stood up and he began to stammer something before realizing that he had no words to justify his actions. What was left to him was physical violence, and he lunged toward me before I had any opportunity to flee. With one arm he grabbed my shoulder and with the other he slapped me full force across the face. I felt no pain in the shock of it, and as I reflect on it now, I see the irony that even as he attempted to exert his strength over me, he admitted how feeble he truly is. Trapped, confronted with his sins, he had no defense but to strike out. I loathe him in this moment and I can never forgive him, but I see him for the pitiable, weak man that he is. We stared at each other in that moment, each of us knowing that we had forever crossed a line from which we could not turn back. I also saw in that moment that it was he who had the greatest fear. I ordered him to leave and I told him that he could never come back. He tried to formulate some words but failed, and then he ran out the door.

I confront now the horrible question of what I will do tomorrow. If I have clarity on one thing, it is that I cannot remain married to this man, nor even countenance his presence ever again in my quarters. As I have tried to imagine what this will mean in the tiny world we occupy inside the walls of the fort, at first I felt enormous embarrassment. It seems impossible to imagine the conversations I will have, the knowledge of everyone knowing that I have been such a fool, and then being locked inside this fort that is now more than ever a prison, with him and with the derision of all, until such time as I can make my way back home.

As I write this now, though, I find myself arriving at a

different conclusion. Yes, I have made a mistake in judgment
in trusting this man, in failing to see the true nature of his
character. I must live with that mistake and its consequences,
including the embarrassment of so many people knowing
that I have been a fool. But there is a fundamental difference
between my foolishness and his evil. No brazenness or shame-
lessness by the Lt can mask that. So tomorrow, I will meet
with Col Carrington and I will tell him every bit of this story.
Far from seeking to hide the truth of my situation, I will tell it
to everyone, tell it myself. I must hope that people will hear my
story and understand it. I am afraid, of course, of how this will
all unfold. I cannot know, and I cannot control the reactions
of other people. But nor can the Lt change the truth.

Sincerely yours,
Frances

DECEMBER 21, 1866—DAWN

The ten decoys rode away from camp at the first faint glow on the eastern horizon with Crazy Horse at the lead. Arrow had a natural inclination to run, especially in the company of other horses, and the bay kept pulling her head in protest at the bridle. It was only ten miles to the place where Crazy Horse intended to attack the wood crew, but he had planned their departure to allow ample time for a slow walk the entire distance. True, he had never seen ten finer ponies in one group. Just as Little Hawk had insisted that his brother ride the best horse available, so, too, the friends and families of the other decoys. Despite the strength of their mounts, Crazy Horse knew that the horses would face a great challenge that day—running for miles from the soldiers before the battle even began. They needed to guard carefully every reserve of the ponies' strength. Besides, it wasn't as if leaving before dawn had cut short their sleep. Between the excitement of the coming battle and the bitter cold, few in the camp had slept at all.

In his last preparations before leaving the war camp on that dark, frigid morning, Crazy Horse had performed the ritual of his war paints, a ritual with origins in the vision quest of his youth. From his parfleche he removed an ermine pelt and spread it out on the frozen ground. Wrapped inside the pelt were tiny pouches, and from one he poured into the palm of his hand a small quantity of a yellow powder made from the gall of a buffalo. To the powder he added his own spit, mixing it until the paste reached the appropriate consistency. Then he took a finger, dipped it in the paint, and drew a yellow lightning bolt on his cheek.

Next he prepared black paint from another small pouch filled with finely ground charcoal. This he smeared on his hand, then used the black paint to make three handprints on each of Arrow's rear flanks, the prints symbolizing his union with his horse in the coming battle.

Finally, Crazy Horse reached into the medicine bag he wore around his neck and removed his sacred stone, the yellow-and-rust-colored rock that he first had seen in his vision, then gathered with his father upon return from his quest. This he tied tightly behind his ear. He thought of High Backbone's words a few hours before, and it occurred to him that in preparing his war paint for battle, he also fused the learnings of his past to his present, and thus to his hopes for the future and the future of his people.

In addition to the decoys, another thirty warriors rode along to join in the attack on the wood train. Crazy Horse had advised the chiefs that only if this attack was sizable would the soldiers send out a relief party of sufficient size. No force of soldiers as big as that prophesized by Moon had ever ridden forth from the fort, and for the prophecy to be realized, many pieces must come together in perfect symmetry.

Little Hawk and Lone Bear were among the additional warriors, and it heartened Crazy Horse to ride into this battle with his brother and his friend.

They spoke very little as they rode. Each understood his role, and each had the heavy company of his own thoughts in a moment that all knew was the most important of their young lives.

Crazy Horse felt a great sense of responsibility in being chosen as a member of such a group, let alone to lead it. He knew and respected the other Oglala, though they were not close friends. There was Sword Owner, a nephew of Red Cloud. As a boy, Sword Owner's name had been Skinny. He was still skinny, an attribute that helped him grow into one of the tribe's finest horsemen. There was American Horse, son of Chief Sitting Bear. Crazy Horse saw that American Horse was wearing that day a distinctive tunic usually worn by Sitting Bear, decorated with a dozen flowing white skins of ermine. They danced and shimmered with the motion of the horse in a way that made it seem as if the tunic were a living thing, a terrifying vision when paired with the point of a lance. American Horse carried the lance, too, its lethal tip at the end of an eight-foot staff wrapped in sinew to reinforce its strength.

The different languages among the Lakota, the Cheyenne, and the Arapaho decoys made communication difficult. Still, it helped that Crazy Horse and Big Nose had fought with each other before. All of them spoke smatterings of the others' tongues, but mostly they relied on sign language—and the earlier guidance from their chiefs.

It took more than an hour before they reached the valley of Prairie Dog Creek. There was ample light by then for Crazy Horse to point out the features of the field they had chosen for the battle—in the reverse order of how the fight would unfold. They arrived from the north and came first to the place where the whites' road crossed the creek and where—if all went well—they would separate and cross their horses in two lines—the signal for the attack to begin. Crazy Horse could still feel the strong presence of Moon as he told those who had not been there about the *winkte's* vision. He showed them how the whites' road stretched down along the top of the narrow bench, surrounded on both sides by the deep gullies where their fellow warriors would lie in wait. As they walked their horses up the road, they caught their first glimpse of the most critical feature of all—the distant ridgeline that they must entice the soldiers to cross.

Eventually they came near to the ridge but did not crest it, aware that they would be visible to the soldiers' lookouts who manned the hilltop to the south of the fort. Crazy Horse now knew well the flag signals that the watchmen used to communicate with the fort. In a few hours, they would rely on these watchmen to signal that the wood train was under attack. For the time being, though, the war party relied on stealth, and so they stayed below the ridgeline.

They rode due west for two miles, keeping Bull's Hump Hill as a screen between them and the fort. The snow line started about fifty yards below the top of the hill, a fact that made Crazy Horse even more cautious—the snow would make them and their horses stand out, even at a distance of many miles.

Crazy Horse kept close watch on the eastern horizon, gauging the time and the corresponding habits at the fort. A bank of steel-colored clouds cloaked the east so that the sun rose in ghostly shadow. Only when he could see the outline of the full sphere did he halt the war party, turning his horse to face the men who rode with him.

"Sword Owner and Big Nose will go with me to look from the top," said Crazy Horse. "The rest wait here."

The three scouts left their horses behind, climbing up Bull's Hump Hill on foot. The gently rounded hilltop was covered with a light crust of snow but mostly bare. They crawled the last few yards and then went flat on their bellies as they crested the hill. Neither Crazy Horse nor Sword Owner spoke Cheyenne, but little talking was needed. Crazy Horse hoped again that all of them understood the mistakes from the attack two weeks earlier, the necessity today that they work together— and above all remain patient.

Normally the icy snow beneath his belly would have chilled him to his core, but today his focus was so intent that he barely noticed it. He felt the pounding of his heart at his jugular, and his breath seemed suddenly short, as if a great rock rested on his chest. Then the fort came into view, perhaps two miles down the little valley.

Smoke rose up from dozens of chimneys inside the stockade and to Crazy Horse it made the fort seem like an animate thing, a sleeping beast exhaling into the frozen morning.

He had gazed upon the fort many times before. In fact, he had crept to this very spot to spy upon the soldiers on days that looked almost exactly like today. He had laid traps and waited for the whites to stumble into them. None of it was exactly new, and yet today, all of it was different. Every day before led to this one, but this was the day when they might strike a truly lethal blow. Today they sought not just to kill a few of the men from the fort. From Red Cloud, Crazy Horse understood that today they sought to strike such a blow that it would drive the whites away for good.

For nearly an hour they lay in place, watching the fort and the valley below. Along the stockade wall, he could see the tiny profiles of the soldiers standing guard, occasionally moving back and forth. On two occasions the big western gate swung open. The scouts held their breath in expectation, hoping that the wood crew would emerge. Instead, on the first occasion, five men walked out on foot and then trudged up the tall hill to the south where the soldiers kept their lookouts, replacing the men at the top, who then trudged down.

Another time the gate swung open and a wagon emerged, but then the gate swung quickly shut. The wagon proceeded toward one of the little buildings in the fort's constellation and stopped there, proceeding no farther.

After a while, the initial adrenaline began to fade, replaced by the seeping cold. "Where are the woodcutters?" asked Sword Owner.

"Wait," said Crazy Horse. In truth, though, he was riven with fear that today, perhaps, they would not come. The pattern had been fixed for months, with few aspects of the soldiers' routine more consistent than the daily expeditions for wood. The whites' appetite for trees seemed insatiable, and Crazy Horse could remember only one morning—the first day the soldiers raised their giant flag—that a wood crew had not been dispatched. Perhaps, though, they had changed their routine with the arrival of winter? It had been a week since Crazy Horse, Lone Bear, and Little Hawk last watched the soldiers from the hilltop. Crazy Horse began to feel sick in his stomach at the thought that two thousand warriors were moving into position barely three miles away—all awaiting a chain of events that began with a wood crew leaving the fort. All there because of his advice to the greatest men of his tribe and others, his advice to Red Cloud, to High Backbone—who had trusted his word. He imagined the shame of riding back to tell them that no soldiers were coming.

As the sun rose higher in the eastern sky, it burned through the early morning clouds, and the scouts had to shade their eyes with their hands to study the fort. After a while, though, they saw the enormous flag in the center of the fort come to life, fluttering at first and eventually flapping in a rising wind until it was almost perfectly horizontal. The wind carried new clouds, swallowing the sun and hemming in the valley. Crazy Horse wished that Moon were there to interpret the signs, but he took them as reassuring. The Creator chose today to hurl a storm at the fort.

They were stiff with cold when Big Nose nudged Crazy Horse and nodded his head in the direction of the fort. There was an increase in the number and activity of soldiers at the top of the tower on the wooden wall, tiny smudges of motion against the gray backdrop behind them. It was easier to study the fort now that the clouds blocked the sun. Another good sign.

Then the big western gate swung open again. This time, three horse soldiers rode out, followed by a large group of soldiers on foot. Crazy Horse guessed there must be thirty or even more. Eventually six wagons rolled out behind the men on foot, then another group of soldiers as large as the first behind the wagons. Crazy Horse instantly forgot the cold, and the three scouts exchanged glances, smiling. It was one of the largest wood crews that Crazy Horse had seen—and it now rolled directly toward them.

Sword Owner and Big Nose looked to Crazy Horse expectantly. He motioned with both his hands—*wait*.

To attack the wood train, Crazy Horse had chosen the place where the road to the pine forests passed closest to the top of Bull's Hump Hill. When the wood train reached this point, the raiders assembled on the backside of the hill would charge across the top, ride as close as possible, and shoot their arrows into the mass of soldiers. It was a form of harassment that the soldiers had seen many times before—and that was the point. The large number of soldiers accompanying the wood crew meant that they anticipated such an attack. If they reacted as in the past, the lookouts atop the southern hill would wave their flags—and a relief force would dispatch from the fort. Then it was up to the decoys to entice the relief force—if Moon was prescient, the largest ever—into the valley of Prairie Dog Creek.

Time seemed to slow down as the wood crew advanced the two miles from their position. Crazy Horse attempted to calculate carefully the amount of time it took the soldiers to cover the first mile. The three horsemen led the way, with two of them fanning out on the flanks. The rest of the soldiers stuck to the narrow road that cut the broad floor of Little Buffalo Valley.

When the soldiers had covered half the distance to their position, Crazy Horse nodded to Sword Owner and Big Nose. The three men stayed flat to the ground as they turned around and then crawled out of sight of the valley. When they were clear of the ridgeline, they stood up and hurried down the hill to the forty-odd warriors assembled below staring up expectantly, all huddled close to their horses for warmth.

Little Hawk was the first to speak. "They're coming?"

Crazy Horse nodded. "A big group—forty or more."

The assembled warriors smiled at one another in excitement.

"Listen," said Crazy Horse. "We'll walk our horses up the hill until we're just below where we can be seen. On my signal, we ride over the top—attack at full gallop."

"How long before we break off the attack?" asked Sword Owner.

"We need to fight them long enough for the fort to send out more soldiers," said Crazy Horse. "Once they send them, we'll act like we're running away—back over Bull's Hump Hill toward Prairie Dog Creek."

Sword Owner nodded. Crazy Horse used signs to convey the same message to Big Nose. It wasn't clear at first if he understood, but one of the Lakota spoke a bit of Cheyenne and helped to translate. Eventually Big Nose too nodded, then spoke in Cheyenne to his tribesmen.

"Everyone but the decoys goes straight to Prairie Dog Creek and finds cover," said Crazy Horse. "You saw the place this morning. The decoys will stay back with me and we'll entice them into the valley."

"Remember," said Sword Owner, "no one breaks cover until the two lines cross past Prairie Dog Creek."

"Anyone who puts his own glory before his people has betrayed us all," said Crazy Horse.

Big Nose nodded again and said something in a stern tone to the Cheyenne.

Crazy Horse looked at Little Hawk and Lone Bear, mounted now and near his side. He nodded to them, and they nodded back. Crazy Horse put his hand to the bear claw necklace, and his friend put his hand to his heart.

Then, without a word, Crazy Horse turned Arrow up the hill and gently nudged the horse's flanks with the heels of his moccasins. The horse wanted to run, and Crazy Horse had to pull the mare back to keep her at a walk. The others spread out so that all of them climbed the hill in a long line, side by side.

Twenty yards from the top, Crazy Horse stopped, raising his hand to signal the others. He cocked his head to listen, the wind at first the only sound. Then the clamor of the soldiers carried up from beyond the ridge: the creak of the wooden wheels and leather tack; the shouts of the teamsters; the marching feet of forty men. The sounds were close already, and growing closer, the moment for attack perfectly calculated.

Crazy Horse took a quick look left and right, the warriors now holding their bows along with the reins. He reached behind his back and pulled an arrow from his quiver, gripping it with his left hand against his bow. Up and down the line, the others followed his lead. Those few with rifles or pistols checked again to make sure priming caps were seated in place. With his right hand, Crazy Horse touched the pistol on the left side of his belt, the war club to his right. Then he patted Arrow's thick neck; the moment had finally arrived to let the warhorse run.

The sounds from the wood train grew louder still—clearly now close, barely across the ridge.

Crazy Horse raised his bow above his head and unleashed his war cry, as if the tension of recent hours and the rage of recent months found release in this roar. The others picked up the call, and it turned instantly into a terrible wall of sound. As for his horse, Crazy Horse didn't nudge her onward as much as release her. At the first slack in the reins, the great animal charged over the top of the hill.

It had begun.

DECEMBER 21, 1866—PREDAWN

Adolph Metzger had slept fitfully all night and awoke well before reveille on the morning of December 21, irritated that he could not fall back asleep. It wasn't the cold that had awakened him. The constant milling of wood ensured sufficient scrap so that all of the barracks could burn their stoves promiscuously. In fact, toasty barracks might be their one luxury at Fort Phil Kearny. Perhaps that was the problem. He remembered his mother, good German that she was, warning that sleeping in a warm room caused nightmares. Metzger remembered dreaming but couldn't remember the dream. He thought hard about it. For an instant, as if the dream was coming back to him, he caught flashes of gold, or maybe sunlight on metal. Before the images became clearer, though, they were gone.

He tried for a few minutes to fall back to sleep but to no avail. Finally, he rose—quietly, not wanting to wake his fellow band members, slipping on his uniform and stepping outside. It was frigid but peaceful on the parade grounds all alone, a good setting for introspection. The events of the fight at the stockade had stamped a deep imprint on Metzger, filled him with a terror that he had not known since the war. He had been sure, for several gut-churning moments, that his demise was upon him. And for what? At least in the Civil War he had felt a sense of righteous purpose, that if he died, it would have been for the great cause of maintaining the union, emancipating the Negroes. Now, though, what did he care whether the road to Montana traversed one valley or the next? He had heard Colonel Carrington and a few of his fellow enlisted men make the argument for a national manifest destiny of occupying the continent from sea to sea. But why? He thought of the resistance of the Bavarian people to generations of invasions from outsiders, and imagined that if he were Sioux or Cheyenne, he, too, would fight against the foreign forces.

So what was he doing in Dakota Territory, one of the invaders? Of all the questions he had posed to himself in recent months, this was the most important—and the one to which his answer was least sufficient. Now, though, he had resolved to change the course of his life, to take charge of his own destiny in a way that he never had before. His reenlistment decision was due in ten short days and he had decided that he would not join up again. He had drifted along with the US Army for too long, mostly because it had been easier than any alternative. As a result, he now realized, he had ceded the power of initiative in his own life, found himself in a place wholly apart from his own choosing. He didn't know exactly what he would do next, but whatever path he followed would be one that he had chosen himself.

He climbed up on the ramparts and stayed there for a long time, watching the first gleam of light on the eastern horizon. As he stood contemplating the frozen predawn, it occurred to Metzger that the new day was the twenty-first of December—winter solstice, the shortest day of the year. Yet another thing he had learned from his father, back in the day when the professor still hoped that his son would grow up to be a good German scientist. The science aspect of solstice had not inspired the young Metzger, but a more philosophical aspect of the day had made an impression. The shortest day of the year, winter solstice marked the moment from which every day thereafter for the next six months would see a tiny bit more sun. There was something fundamentally hopeful in that. A good day for resolutions.

For reasons Metzger could not quite explain, he felt suddenly the need for company. He took one last admiring glance at the rising sun, then, assuming that some of his other bandmates would be up by this time, he wandered back to the barracks.

Lieutenant George Washington Grummond shifted uncomfortably on the bunk in the unmarried officers' quarters, the place he had sought refuge after Frances kicked him out. Grummond had said nothing to Ten Eyck, the only occupant, upon his entry. A shared affection for drink was the two men's only point of convergence, but at least they had that. When Grummond needed a place to imbibe, Ten Eyck not only allowed it but usually joined in. At present, he snored loudly from the other bunk.

Grummond's head raged from the baker's brew, and he wondered if he could fall back asleep. For a moment, he thought about going back to his own quarters. *My own goddamn quarters.* As he thought of the things that Frances had written in her secret journal, he felt his anger rising anew, then turning to outrage as he considered again the number of hours that she had toiled away behind his back, scribbling out her little commentary. He could not bring himself to admit what was also true: Frances's anger was different than in the past, more visceral and fierce. He was afraid of her reaction if he returned tonight—afraid of this aspect of her that he had never realized was there, lurking beneath the demure veneer of her southern charm.

———————

As now happened most nights, Jim Bridger awoke to pain. This day, though, seemed worse. His neck was the immediate source, a sharp crick that fired outward like a lightning bolt through his right shoulder and then along the whole length of his arm all the way to his fingertips. He adjusted a rolled-up army blanket in an effort to find a position that might provide relief. It helped a bit for a moment, but just enough to allow him to become conscious of the dull aching in both knees.

He wondered whether it would be possible to fall asleep again. Some nights he managed it, but some nights he would lay there for hours, daylight eventually signaling that he might as well get up. Some nights he managed to distract himself back into sleep. One trick he liked was to imagine certain routes he had traversed in his younger days, starting at one end and then traveling forward in his mind, landmark by landmark. Sometimes with this trick he was asleep before he reached his destination. Other nights, he might wander half a continent and still not find sleep. He suspected this might be one of those nights.

From a position on the eastern barbican, Colonel Carrington noted the sun, now significantly above the horizon. To the north, dark, low-hanging clouds telegraphed the changing weather. Carrington studied them, calculating whether the wood crew could churn out sufficient work in advance of any storm. Private Sample stood beside him, waiting expectantly.

Carrington turned away from the outside world to survey the world inside the walls of Fort Phil Kearny, the world that he had created. Sure, a few refinements remained to be completed. The infirmary and a few other buildings, to the colonel's great irritation, still lacked proper shingles on their roofs. Still, he could not help but feel the pride that came with accomplishing one's mission. As for those few things undone, Carrington was intent on finishing them before the elements attacked with full vigor—and Bridger said those days were coming soon. Carrington noted that Big Piney Creek was now frozen from bank to bank, the small trickle of open water midstream having disappeared overnight under the frigid, clear skies. He squinted toward the south to glance up at Pilot Hill, its rounded top at sufficient altitude to maintain the white frosting of snow. In the low valley around the fort, though, yesterday's afternoon warmth had melted it away and left behind the somber cover of matted, dead grass.

The breeze picked up, suddenly colder. Carrington glanced toward the giant flag at the middle of the parade grounds. Earlier it had hung limp in the breezeless early morning. Now it gently waved, pushed southward by the rising northern breeze.

Finally, Private Sample spoke up. "Do we send out the wood crew, sir?"

The colonel nodded, watching the direction of the wind and clouds. "Yes—as quickly as they can rally." He adjusted his collar against the wind. "Who's leading the detachment?"

"Corporal Legrow, sir."

Carrington pondered a moment. He had observed Legrow before and considered him a steady sort. "Good. But tell the corporal I want forty men instead of twenty today."

"Forty in addition to the wood crew?"

"In addition." Carrington wasn't taking any chances. Fetterman, who seemed to have a good eye for such things, had estimated the Sioux had launched their trap on December 6 with as many as two hundred warriors. A force of forty soldiers would not match another such attack man for man, but it would be sufficient to hold a defensive position, certainly until such time as relief could be sent out from the fort. Carrington reached into his pocket and pulled out his watch—ten a.m. sharp.

"Do we allow them any horses, sir?" asked Private Sample.

"How many do we have this morning?"

"Lieutenant Grummond reports around thirty mounts field-ready."

Colonel Carrington cursed under his breath and felt anew the anger that flashed each time he was reminded of their pathetic state of arms, horses, and provisions. He started to make a caustic remark but thought it inappropriate to show his true emotions to an enlisted man. Instead he simply said, "Three horses are all we can spare."

"Yes, sir," said Private Sample. Then he saluted, climbed down the ladder, and scurried off toward the south end of the fort where the teamsters had assembled the wood crew's half-dozen wagons. Ten minutes later, the mill gate opened and the crew departed, heading northwest on the well-worn road to Piney Island. Approximately half the detachment would be responsible for the actual cutting of wood, while the other half would stand guard, ready to repulse any attack. From his position atop the east barbican, Colonel Carrington watched the wood train depart through the mill gates. Corporal Legrow and the infantrymen marched in front, with the two other mounted infantry on the flanks. The wagons trailed behind, to return later, piled high with the timber that was the sustenance of Colonel Carrington's ever improving city, a city like an island amid a wilderness sea of mountains and plains.

Pleased that he would squeeze another day of timber harvest before additional snowfall, Carrington descended from the barbican, irritated that his sword made mobility so clumsy, then made his way across the woodyard toward the mills. Private Sample had reported trouble with the machine that planed shingles, and Carrington wanted to be sure it was operating properly in advance of the arrival of new timber.

The colonel was inside one of the sawmills half an hour later when he heard the bugle sounding assembly. He hurried outside, peering upward toward Pilot Hill. There, Carrington counted as the signalman waved the big red banner in circles around his head . . . five times. The signalman paused, lowering the flag before raising it to repeat the signal. Private Sample arrived, breathless, to state the obvious. "Wood train's under attack, sir! Major attack!"

Carrington peered northwest, toward the base of Sullivant Hill. By now the sound of rifle shots echoed down the valley. Carrington could see the puffs of smoke rising from his troopers' guns along with mounted Indians on the side of the hill, but otherwise the scene was hard to discern. With Private Sample trailing a half step behind, the colonel hurried back inside the fort and toward the western barbican. As he crossed past the cavalry yard and the parade grounds, he noted with satisfaction that the men were assembling. Indeed the horses—that is the thirty-odd mounts deemed ready for action—already stood saddled, in line with his recent orders that they be ready for deployment on a moment's notice. He allowed himself a brief moment of self-congratulation at the foresight.

"Private Sample, I want the infantry assembled too—be quick!"

As Colonel Carrington and Private Sample hurried past the married officers' quarters, he noticed Mrs. Grummond on the path in front of him. She stood there, almost as if she was waiting for him. Despite his distraction, the colonel stared at her. In the distance, the shooting continued. She started to say something, but then, looking up toward the flags on Pilot Hill, she stopped.

Colonel Carrington slowed briefly as he passed her. "Mrs. Grummond?" He kept walking, but now turned back to stare at her.

She had a strange look on her face, no doubt worried by the attack. She said nothing though, instead shaking her head. Carrington turned back and hurried on.

At the barbican, Carrington climbed the ladder. Private Sample handed him his field glass, and the colonel turned westward. The field of vision through the glass was frustratingly small. Low clouds had drifted across the top of Sullivant Hill—but the colonel could catch repeated flashes of Indians, darting down on horseback from the misty ridgeline toward the train on Wood Road. Carrington felt his heart racing and took deep breaths in an effort to steady the field glass. He had never been good at looking through a glass—the bouncing, narrow field of vision making the broader scene difficult to discern. This combined with the Indians' chaotic style of attack. Mounted warriors darted suddenly into view, close to the wagons, loosed an arrow or two, then galloped away. As usual, there was no cohesiveness to their plan. He assumed, based on the signal from Pilot Hill, that the body of attackers was large, though the limitations of the field glass made it difficult to tell. Certainly there appeared to be a couple dozen warriors at least. He didn't intend to err on the side of dispatching too small a party.

The wagons, he could see, had formed into a protective corral, with the infantry inside, shooting outward. Through the scope, Carrington spotted Corporal Legrow, inside the breastworks but still mounted, directing the scattered fire.

Captain Fetterman arrived on the barbican, breathing heavily. "How many attacking, sir?" he asked.

"I'd say forty at least . . . maybe more . . . Call out the full relief force!" ordered Carrington.

"The full force, sir?" Fetterman seemed surprised. Never before had they deployed so many men. "All infantry and cavalry combined?"

Colonel Carrington hesitated, but then pushed ahead. "I'll hold Captain Ten Eyck's B and E Companies in reserve, but I want you and Lieutenant Grummond supporting the wood detail."

"Yes, sir," said Fetterman.

Something in Fetterman's tone made Carrington wonder if he was overreacting. "It's just that . . . well, the attack force looks to be sizable . . . maybe fifty or even more," said the colonel. "I don't want us outmanned." Carrington handed Fetterman the field glass. "See what you think."

Captain Fetterman peered through the glass toward the skirmish site. The shots continued, though they seemed more scattered now.

Suddenly from behind, they heard the sound of men marching, then the shouted command of "Company . . . halt!" They looked down to see Fetterman's Company A along with the remnants of other companies, perhaps fifty infantrymen all told, standing in formation on the road along the parade grounds, the flag snapping above them in the wind that now blew stiffly from the north. Moments later, Sergeant Augustus Lang scrambled up the ladder onto the barbican, stopped before Carrington and Fetterman, then saluted. "Company A reporting for duty, sir."

A few shots continued from the northwestern end of the valley of Little Piney Creek. Fetterman stepped forward formally. "My infantry's ready, sir. Grummond's cavalry can follow in short order."

"Yes, of course . . ." agreed Colonel Carrington. "They'll catch up en route."

Fetterman nodded. Carrington took a final glance through the field glass before turning back to his senior officer.

"Captain," said Colonel Carrington, effecting his most military tone. "Your orders are as follows: support the wood train . . . relieve it . . . and report to me. You understand?"

Captain Fetterman nodded resolutely. "Of course, sir."

"Do not engage or pursue the Indians at the wood train's expense— and under no circumstances cross over Lodge Trail Ridge. Are we clear, Captain?"

"Yes, sir," replied Fetterman, saluting crisply.

Carrington returned the salute, then pulled the watch from his pocket: 11:15.

Fetterman scrambled down the ladder and hurried to his horse, swinging up into the saddle. He pivoted his horse in order to survey the forty-nine infantrymen standing at parade rest along the main road beside the parade grounds. First Sergeant Lang stood at the front, off to the side, looking to Fetterman for his orders.

From the corner of his eye, Fetterman could see Colonel Carrington flanked by Private Sample. He also saw that a group of officers' wives had emerged from their quarters, bundled in their shawls, watching the events on the parade grounds. He noticed Martha Carrington and beside her Frances Grummond and some of the laundresses. For a moment, he wished that he had a wife of his own to watch proudly as he rode forth to defend the interests of the nation, a wife to whom he could return after doing battle. That thought, though, passed quickly, and he refocused his mind on the task at hand.

"First Sergeant Lang!"

"Yes, sir!"

"Where's my bugler?" asked Fetterman.

Adolph Metzger had been standing nearby, holding on to the reins of a nervous horse. "Here, sir," he said.

"Well, come forward, bugler!" said Fetterman. "You're little use if you're not beside me."

"Yes, sir," said Metzger, holding tight to his gleaming bugle as he also held on to the saddle horn, seeking clumsily to pull himself atop the mount.

"Stay close, no matter what," said Fetterman. "I need my orders relayed the instant I convey them."

"Yes, sir," said Metzger again. He had felt this before, the significance of his task. He knew well that in the midst of a battle, the sound of the trumpet could mean the difference between orderly execution of a plan—and utter chaos.

Captain Fetterman took one final look up and down the line, proud of his troops. "Sergeant," he said. "Our orders are to relieve our fellow soldiers on the wood train! Let's move out!"

"Yes, sir!" Sergeant Lang turned to face the assembled infantry, barking out his orders. "Attention!"

The men snapped to attention.

"Carry . . . arms!"

In unison, the men lifted their rifles so that they held them waist high, thumb and forefinger around the trigger guard.

"Shoulder . . . arms!"

The men lifted their rifles from waist to shoulder.

Looking down from his mounted position, Fetterman felt some pride at the improved precision in the drilling movements of his men. At the same time, he felt embarrassed and angry at their pathetic old Springfields, and regretted anew that there had been so little ammunition available to practice shooting. At least they would bring their numbers to bear. When combined with Grummond's cavalry, they would field more than eighty soldiers, the largest detachment ever dispatched from Fort Phil Kearny. He felt confident this show of massed force would be sufficient to run off whatever Indians were about today. He noticed the storm gathering. One big snowfall and he imagined that would be the last they'd see of the Indians until spring.

Sergeant Lang gave a quick look up and down the line. "Company, double time . . . forward . . . *march!*" The infantrymen moved forward in unison at a trot.

After a minute of watching the infantry march past him, Captain Fetterman gave his horse a casual kick with his heels and a gentle leftward tug on the reins. The big thoroughbred turned and moved forward. Metzger, too, gave his horse a nudge with this heels, though his mount offered no reaction. Fetterman moved quickly to the front of the column as Metzger watched, mortified at his failure to keep up. *Damn, I hate horses!* He tried a nudge with his heels again, and when it again failed to produce the desired result, he used the open face of his gloved hand to slap the animal's rump. The horse leapt forward, and soon Metzger had managed to catch up, falling in a few yards behind Captain Fetterman.

They passed beneath the gate and left the fort behind them. Metzger looked back. On the rampart, he could see Colonel Carrington, field glass in hand—looking up toward Pilot Hill. Behind Carrington and the fort's stockade, only the flagpole was sufficiently tall to be seen. Metzger turned away from the fort and looked to the north, the wind hitting him full in the face. The in-between trot of his horse was ungainly, and as he struggled to keep up with Fetterman, he nearly dropped his bugle. He realized that he had not even placed the bugle's lanyard over his head, and quickly did so. That instrument, he knew, was his larger purpose. The landscape on which he now found himself might be wholly foreign, but in the polished bugle, he had his one bit of mooring.

Through the haze of pain, Bridger at first attempted to slip back into the relative peace he found in sleep. A succession of intrusions, though, defeated him. First he heard the bugle calling assembly. He heard the shouts of the noncommissioned officers, screaming at the enlisted men to move, then to move faster. He heard men running, disorganized, then eventually the uniform stamping of the infantry, marching in formation. Later came the clomp of hooves, the snort and whinny of horses, and the creaking of leather tack as the cavalry rode toward the gates.

What ultimately pulled Bridger back from the chasm of continued slumber was the unmistakable voice of Lieutenant Grummond: "Find me

more goddamn horses or I'll see you in irons for a month!" It occurred
to Bridger that, if he stayed in bed, Lieutenant Grummond would likely
take his horse. She might be old, but she was serviceable, which was more
than could be said for most of the army's mounts. Bridger was deeply
fond of the old mare, and he did not intend to relinquish her to a lout like
Grummond.

Bridger grimaced as he swung his legs over the short bunk. Bend-
ing his knees caused excruciating pain, pain that intensified with every
pound of weight that he placed upon his rheumatic joints. He grabbed
his pants and his boots, struggling to bend his body enough to pull them
on. He stood, unsteady in the combination of pain and drowsiness. His
gun belt was looped on the bedpost and his fingers were clumsy with the
buckle as he strapped it around his waist, leaving behind his coat in his
hurry as he limped from the barracks.

When he opened the door, the outside air was cold and he was briefly
aware of the wind, stiff and from the north, but he ignored it as he limped
as quickly as he could toward the stables. He kept his horse behind the
hay yard, and as he approached it—hurrying more now—he could see
the flagman on Pilot Hill waving the signal for a large Indian attack.
He ignored that, too, suddenly indifferent to the movement of the US
Army or the Sioux or the Cheyenne. What he cared about was his horse,
and he could now see her, outside of the stable. Lieutenant Grummond
stood beside her, directing an enlisted man who threw a saddle across
her sway back. Another enlisted man stood a few paces away, holding
Grummond's big white stallion.

At ten yards Bridger stopped, Grummond suddenly aware of his
presence. He turned to face Bridger, staring at him as the enlisted man
tightened the saddle's cinch.

"We need your horse, Bridger," said Grummond.

"And I'm not obliged to lend her to you."

"We're under attack and there's not enough mounts. I'm requisition-
ing this animal in the name of the US Army." Grummond grabbed the
mare's reins and started to hand them to the enlisted man.

Bridger pulled the Colt from its holster, leveled it at the center of
Grummond's chest. "You take a single goddamn step with my horse and
you'll be dead a second later."

The enlisted man took a step back, startled.

Grummond studied Bridger hard. "I doubt you got the gumption or the aim, old man."

Bridger pulled the hammer to full cock, the *ker-click* of the action sounding surprisingly loud. "Test me if you want."

Grummond stared a bit longer at the muzzle of the Colt. "You are a crazy old bastard," he said, but he dropped the reins. "There'll be hell to pay for this when I come back."

"I ain't hard to find."

Lieutenant Grummond stormed off, the enlisted man in tow and Bridger's pistol still trained.

Bridger waited until the cavalry yard was empty before he holstered the Colt. He removed the saddle from the mare and returned her to the stable, aware again of both the cold and his pain. He stuck around a bit longer, though, feeding the mare a lump of sugar from his pocket and scratching behind her ear. Eventually he couldn't take the cold anymore, but only then did he limp back to the barracks.

Grummond, his cavalry trailing behind him, continued to hear scattered shots from the western end of the valley. He stood in his stirrups—trying in vain to see outside of the fort's walls. Nor could he see Fetterman's infantry, though he knew they had departed the north gate approximately fifteen minutes earlier. He tried to push thoughts of Frances from his head, his anger focused for the moment at Bridger.

In front of him along the parade grounds road, Lieutenant Grummond saw Colonel Carrington and Private Sample. He also saw the cluster of wives, huddled together for warmth as they watched the swirl of activities unfolding on the parade grounds. From the corner of his eye, Grummond could see that Frances stood among them, but he did his best to appear as if he was unaware of her presence.

Grummond reined to a halt in front of Colonel Carrington. "Company . . . halt!" he yelled out, and his troopers reined up behind him.

"Lieutenant Grummond," said the colonel. "Are your men and horses ready for duty?"

"Yes, sir." Grummond's reply came without hesitation.

"The new Spencers—your men are comfortable with them?"

"Comfortable enough, sir."

Colonel Carrington nodded. "We fight with the tools in our hands."

"Yes, sir."

"Your orders, Lieutenant, are to join Captain Fetterman's command, obey his orders—and never leave him. Do not cross Lodge Trail Ridge. Do you understand your orders, Lieutenant?"

"Yes, sir!" Grummond saluted and Carrington saluted back. Again from the corner of his eye, Grummond could see Frances break away from the small cluster of the women, turning her back and walking hurriedly away. He felt a flash of fury that she wouldn't stay and watch along with the other women. *Can't think about that now.* He called out the order in his most authoritative voice. "Company . . . forward . . . ho!"

Twenty-seven heavily armed cavalrymen set instantly in motion at his word, and the rush of exhilaration he always experienced at the power of commanding came to trump the anger he felt toward his wife. This was a moment for focus on the enemy, a foe that only two weeks earlier had killed his fellow soldiers and sent him fleeing for his life. Not today. Today they rode forth in true force—prepared for the enemy they would meet. He would attend to Frances later.

They were barely a hundred yards outside the gate when Sergeant Baker called out to Grummond, "Sir, hold up! Hold up, sir!" Baker pointed back to the fort, and when Grummond turned around he saw Colonel Carrington looking down and gesturing from the sentinel's walk behind the stockade.

"Jesus Christ!" muttered Grummond to the sergeant. "What the hell does the old man want now?"

"Lieutenant Grummond!" yelled Carrington.

"Yes, sir?"

"Are your orders clear?" Colonel Carrington cupped his hands to be heard from the palisade. "Join Captain Fetterman. . . . follow his orders . . . and do not cross Lodge Trail Ridge!"

"Heard you before, Colonel," shouted Grummond. "Clear as crystal." He offered a perfunctory salute, then spurred his horse and rode in the direction of Fetterman and his infantry, by now half a mile ahead.

"Goddamn parade officer . . ." said Grummond to the sergeant.

Back on the rampart, Colonel Carrington pulled his watch from his pocket and checked the time—11:35 a.m.

Sitting atop his horse in the column behind Lieutenant Grummond, Private Charles Cuddy ran his bare hand over the glass-smooth wood of the Spencer. Like the other cavalrymen, he was proud to possess the new weapon. Proud, and like the others, sure that his new gun gave him powers far beyond the limitations of his old Springfield. How could it not? For the cavalry troopers, receiving the rifles had been like a combination of Christmas morning and a medal ceremony. What gift was more important to a soldier than his primary weapon? As for the medal ceremony, to carry such a state-of-the-art piece of weaponry signified the importance of the cavalry: best troops—best guns. Cavalry always led the way. They were the best, the bravest, and of course it made sense that they would carry the finest arms.

True enough, it did bother Private Cuddy that there had not been more time for practice. They had each been allowed to fire two rounds, hardly enough to develop any feel for the weapon, let alone make adjustments. Soldiers figured some things out through experience—like where to align the tip of the front sight against the rear sight. Some of the Spencers' possibilities, of which the men still loved to brag, seemed wholly theoretical.

But such misgivings, thought Cuddy, were trifles in the scheme of things. One of his fellow troopers had seen repeating rifles used in the war, and he said the sheer number of bullets they threw out was like a curtain of steel. Enemies encountering such force melted like butter in a frying pan. Cuddy and his fellow cavalrymen had given endless speculation to the impact on savages—confronting a detachment of repeating rifles for the first time with their stone-tipped arrows made from sticks.

How long had he listened to the stories of the men who fought in the great battles of the war and wished that he had his own tales of bravery and valor to share around the campfire? Today, perhaps, his day would come.

―――――――――――

The gunshots continued steadily from the cluster of wagons on the Wood Road, along with the war cries of the Indian raiders galloping around the wagons on all sides—occasionally darting close enough to shoot an arrow. Both sides made a fair amount of noise but neither inflicted much damage on the other.

Crazy Horse had withdrawn from the skirmish early, and now paid little attention to the fight, sitting atop Arrow about a third of the way up Bull's Hump Hill and staring intently at the fort. Sword Owner and Lone Bear sat on either side of him. A few minutes earlier, the gates had opened and a large force of infantry disgorged from the interior and began to march toward them. It was difficult to count the men, but Crazy Horse was certain that it was the largest force that he had seen dispatched from the fort. Still, it wasn't enough.

"Where are the horse soldiers?" asked Lone Bear.

Crazy Horse shook his head. It was mounted soldiers who would be most likely to engage in pursuit.

A bullet thudded into the dirt about a dozen feet from their position but none of the three Lakota paid any heed.

The infantry had progressed about a half mile from the fort when the big gate opened again. Crazy Horse held his breath and squinted against the distance. Again, it was difficult to estimate the numbers, but there was no question that a large group of horsemen rode out from the fort. Together with the soldiers on foot—this was a force to match Moon's prophecy. This was a force worthy of the trap that awaited only a few miles away. Now to get them there . . .

Crazy Horse again raised his arm in the air to be seen by his fellow warriors, still on the attack, circling the wagons below. He yelled out to capture the others' attention as he rode at a cantor—back up Bull's Hump Hill heading northeast. Every fifty yards or so he made a show of stopping, looking back toward the warriors who now raced to catch up with him, but also looking and pointing worriedly toward the soldiers, barely emerged from the fort. By now, all of the warriors had broken off the attack and joined behind Crazy Horse in the retreat.

At the crest of Bull's Hump Hill, Crazy Horse paused again. A soldier at the top of the hilltop to the south of the fort waved his giant signal flag slowly up and down. The marching soldiers stopped.

Sword Owner and Big Nose rode up beside Crazy Horse, also looking back to study the flag and the soldiers.

"What's the flag mean?" asked Sword Owner.

"It means they think we're retreating," said Crazy Horse.

"They will follow us?" asked Big Nose in his broken Lakota.

"We'll see." Crazy Horse loosened Arrow's reins, and the horse bolted forward again, soon disappearing down the northern slope of Bull's Hump Hill. The other raiders quickly followed him—over the hill and away from the approaching soldiers. In a few instants, the southern face of the hill was empty, the tracks in the snow the only evidence of their passage.

SAME DAY—11:40 A.M.

Captain Ten Eyck rode into the fort from Pilot Hill, having watched the beginning of the attack on the wood train along with the sentinels. He found Colonel Carrington engaged in intense conversation with two mounted civilians—James Wheatley and Isaac Fisher. Both men held shiny new Henry rifles, and Wheatley was busy loading his, pushing cartridge after cartridge into the gun's breech from a bulging coat pocket that seemed to hold an endless supply.

"Jesus, Wheatley! How many cartridges does that thing hold?" asked Ten Eyck.

"A whole tribe's worth—long as I shoot straight," said Wheatley.

"You know what they say about the Henry . . ." said Fisher. "Load on Sunday and shoot all week."

"These gentlemen are volunteering to ride out and join in with our detachment," said Carrington to Ten Eyck. "Fetterman and Grummond are dispatched . . . I need you and your men in reserve."

Ten Eyck knew both the civilians fairly well. Wheatley and his wife ran the boardinghouse. Fisher had a civilian teamsters contract. Ten Eyck knew that both had been Union officers in the war, and both now worried that Indian troubles were undermining what might otherwise be lucrative business.

"I'm sure Captain Fetterman would appreciate these men's firepower," said Ten Eyck.

Carrington pondered the civilians' request. For a moment he considered the numbers remaining at the fort—now less than half his total command—and barely any horses save his own. He wondered vaguely where Bridger was, and remembered Doc Rutt mentioning that the scout had been ill. Still, Carrington's overwhelming concern was ensuring that Fetterman's force was adequately manned. Wheatley and Fisher were veterans and their Henrys would add a good measure of shock value if any Indians were stupid enough to ride into them.

Carrington turned to the two civilians. "All right. I'll permit it. Report to Captain Fetterman and follow his orders strictly."

"Yes, sir," said Fisher. "And thank you, sir. I aim to get the scalp of Red Cloud himself!"

"Just be sure to hold on to yours," said Ten Eyck, and they all laughed.

As he passed beneath the gate, Wheatley finally finished loading the Henry—sixteen shots with only a quick lever-action in between.

The infantry had progressed barely a half mile from the fort, just shy of the base of Sullivant Hill, when Sergeant Lang called out to Captain Fetterman, "Sir, look at Pilot Hill!"

Captain Fetterman reined his mount and turned to look back at the sentries atop the hill, their blue uniforms standing out in stark contrast against the icy snow on the hilltop. No longer did the signalman turn the flag in circles to warn of attack. Instead, he raised the banner high, then brought it straight down. After a pause of several seconds, he repeated the same signal.

Bugler Metzger looked up at Pilot Hill, too, his horse standing next to the captain's.

"They've broken off the attack," said Metzger.

"Company, halt," said Fetterman, and Sergeant Lang quickly shouted out the order. With the crunch of the infantrymen's boots suddenly stopped, there was no sound in the valley except the wind. Fetterman strained to listen.

"No more shots from the wood party," said Sergeant Lang.

Fetterman shook his head, peering along the face of Sullivant Hill. The raiding Indians now galloped at full speed away from them—northeast toward the crest of the hill. They were spread out and disjointed. A few of them pointed toward the soldiers as they rode, streaming over the crest of the hill and then disappearing beyond.

"They're retreating," said Lang.

"Yes . . ." agreed Fetterman, calculating. "We might cut them off if we circle around the opposite side of Sullivant."

"But our orders, sir?"

Fetterman paused a minute, thinking. "The wood train's safe . . . Our orders are to not cross Lodge Trail Ridge—so we'll stay on this side." Fetterman pointed toward the attack site, then up and over Sullivant in a sweeping arc to the northeast. "But we might surprise them as they come around the back side of Sullivant."

Lang nodded. "Yes, sir."

Fetterman turned from the west to the east. "Let's get across Big Piney and then make our way along the valley floor. If I'm right and they pop up in front of us—we'll hit them with a volley or two to keep them on their way."

Sergeant Lang called out the order, and the infantry was again on the move, this time pivoting to the northeast, toward Big Piney Creek and the Montana Road.

Metzger by now had gained a bit more control of his horse, and managed to stay close to Captain Fetterman's side as they made their way toward the creek. Metzger peered northward, hoping that the Indians would not appear as Fetterman had predicted. He'd had his full stomach of Indian fighting, and no further desire for fighting of any variety for that matter. He marveled, when he thought about it, that he had managed to stay alive as long as he had. No longer, though, would he leave such things to fate. It was liberating to think about a new and different life.

Colonel Carrington would spend the rest of his life reflecting on the day. In hindsight, strange things began to happen almost as soon as the two civilians rode away from the fort. First came a new signal from Pilot Hill, noticed by Private Sample.

"He's signaling the attack has stopped," reported Sample to Carrington. The two men stood with Captain Ten Eyck on the northern-most point of the stockade, watching the progression of Lieutenant

Grummond's cavalry as it rode out to link up with Captain Fetterman's infantry. Still farther back, but gaining ground quickly, were the two civilians. Carrington turned his field glass to Pilot Hill, and sure enough, the signalman repeated the up-and-down motion of the flag that signaled that the Indians had pulled back.

Turning back to check on Captain Fetterman, Carrington watched as the infantry stopped, Fetterman also looking back to interpret the signal from Pilot Hill. After a moment of consideration, Fetterman turned his infantry away from the wood train—moving to his right and marching to the northeast—toward Big Piney Creek, the Montana Road, and on the far horizon, toward Lodge Trail Ridge.

"What are they doing, sir?" asked Sample.

Carrington had the same question. But after a moment's contemplation, he said, "Not to worry. I imagine Captain Fetterman has calculated that the Indians will retreat around the back of Sullivant Hill."

"Yes," agreed Ten Eyck. "He'll give them a little surprise."

Captain Ten Eyck had borrowed the field glass and swept the horizon surrounding Fetterman's infantry, scanning first directly north—where the retreating Sioux would be most likely to emerge—then working his way east, tracking slowly along the Montana Road. Suddenly he stopped. "Cocky bastards!" he said.

Colonel Carrington turned to look.

"Due east," said Ten Eyck. "Under that scrubby tree on the ridgeline." He handed the field glass to Carrington, though when you knew where to look, the glass wasn't necessary. A half mile away—at the opposite end of the valley from the raid on the wood train—two Indians sat calmly beneath a short tree on the hilltop, one wrapped snugly in a blanket as they surveyed the fort in the valley below them.

"What the hell?" said Carrington. "What the hell are they doing?" With the field glass, Carrington, too, scanned the horizon. Eventually the field of vision arrived back on Fetterman and the infantry—but there was no other indication of Indians.

"Are those two Indians in range of your howitzers, Captain?" asked Carrington.

"Absolutely," said Ten Eyck.

"Drop a couple rounds of case shot on their heads."

"Yes, sir!" Ten Eyck scrambled off in the direction of the east bar-bican. Barely a minute later, Carrington and Private Sample heard the explosion of a howitzer, watched the barbican disappear in a billowing cloud of black powder smoke, and heard the whistling of the case round as it careened toward the two Indians on the hilltop.

Colonel Carrington put the glass to his eye just in time to see the shell burst—long, perhaps fifty yards behind the two Sioux. At the explosion, though, Carrington was surprised to see a dozen other Indi-ans rise up suddenly from concealed positions. They dashed away from the fort, toward the crest of the hill, but not before Captain Ten Eyck fired another round. This time he had honed the fuse, the shell explod-ing directly over the heads of the retreating Sioux. They had been smart enough to fall flat against the ground at the sound of the shot, but Car-rington counted two bodies that did not rise up as the others sprinted over the ridgeline.

"What do you make of it, sir?" asked Private Sample.

"Usual spies, I should think," said Carrington. He had been at the post long enough to understand the patterns of his foe, and he also knew well the importance of projecting confidence to his men. This was hardly the first time a scouting party had stationed itself in a position to observe the activities at the fort. No doubt these Sioux were ready to commu-nicate with the band of raiders that would soon emerge from behind Sullivant Hill. Their practice of using signaling mirrors, of course, was well known.

"No doubt they were ready to signal their comrades of Fetterman's approach," said Carrington to Sample. "Our artillery has foiled their plan."

"Yes, sir," agreed Sample.

With authority, Colonel Carrington snapped the telescoping field glass down into its tube and handed it to Private Sample. Once more he checked his watch: 11:50 a.m. A productive morning, all things consid-ered. Most important, the wood train had still been able to continue on its way to Piney Island. Carrington didn't look forward to the afternoon that he would spend drafting his weekly report to General Cooke, but it was part of the job. He began to descend the ladder from the barbican, happy at least for the progress on the fort that would fill his report. "I'll be in my quarters if needed."

SAME DAY—11:50 A.M.

Captain Fetterman and Bugler Metzger were the first to cross Big Piney Creek, side by side on their horses, breaking the thin ice and clearing a path for the infantry. Fetterman didn't like to make his men march in the discomfort and cold of sopping shoes, but he wanted the vantage of the higher ground along the Montana Road, and that meant crossing the creek. The freezing water was thigh-deep at its deepest point, and the smooth leather soles of the men's brogans afforded little traction against the slippery rocks of the streambed. A couple of the men slipped, dousing rifles and drenching powder charges.

As he waited for his men to cross, Fetterman removed his gloves to blow on his frozen fingers, then shook his hands, feeling the tingling pain of circulation returning. *Damn, it's cold.* With Fetterman, Metzger, and Sergeant Lang waiting on the far bank of Big Piney, Lieutenant Grummond and his cavalry caught up, their horses crashing into the water of the creek and quickly fording.

Grummond rode directly to Fetterman, pulling up his horse and saluting. "Reporting for duty, sir."

Fetterman returned the salute. "The colonel explained our orders?"

"Of course, Captain. But you saw from the signal that the wood train's already safe."

Fetterman nodded. "I'm banking the Sioux will retreat around the backside of Sullivant Hill and come out in front of us." He pointed to the northwest—where they now could see the backside of the base of

Sullivant. Then he pointed to the right. "We'll stay up on the Montana Road where we've got the high ground."

Lieutenant Grummond started to say something when he was cut off by the sound of a howitzer. Everyone looked back toward the fort and tracked the screaming path of the shot. The shell burst almost due east of the fort, about a thousand yards from the position of the relief force. Flushed out by the explosion, a dozen Indians leapt from concealed positions and ran for cover. Less than thirty seconds after the first shot, a second shot spit forth from the howitzer, this time bursting almost directly over the heads of the retreating Indians. The men of the relief party cheered as a few of the Indians fell.

"Bully for Ten Eyck!" cheered Lieutenant Grummond. "Give 'em a little taste of the white man's medicine!"

Captain Fetterman stared hard in the direction of the Sioux flushed out by the cannon shot, who now had disappeared. Their numbers weren't concerning—a dozen warriors. It was a bit odd that they had staked out the eastern side of the fort, but hardly without precedent. The soldiers had become accustomed to war parties watching their movements from various points on surrounding hills. Fetterman felt additional comfort in the size of his own force. He looked back to the west, awaiting hopefully the emergence of the raiders who attacked the wood train.

Crazy Horse could scarcely breathe as he and the others approached the mouth of the little vale that lay north and west of Bull's Hump Hill. In a matter of moments they would see whether the soldiers had taken the bait. All of them peered to their right as they rode along, straining to see and desperate to know.

Crazy Horse was not surprised when he heard the distant discharge of a cannon, then the explosion of its round—out of sight and to the southeast. Red Cloud had sent lookouts to watch the far side of the fort, and the soldiers inside must have spotted them.

Suddenly, as they rode deeper into the vale, the soldiers appeared. Crazy Horse felt a jolt stream through every vein in his body, as if he had been struck by lightning, the combination of relief and exhilaration unlike anything he had ever experienced. He saw that the foot soldiers and horse soldiers had combined, the horsemen having just crossed the creek.

The soldiers saw them too. Crazy Horse could see the mounted officers, including the one who rode the white stallion, pointing and conferring. Then the horse soldiers moved into the forward position. The raiders, too, must react—as if surprised and afraid. Crazy Horse spun his horse to face the others. "All but the decoys—break now for the far side of the ridge!"

Crazy Horse watched as Little Hawk quirted his pony and broke with the others toward Lodge Trail Ridge, a quarter mile to the north. His eyes locked briefly with Lone Bear and his friend smiled and raised his fist before galloping off. Crazy Horse raised his own fist in reply, then turned back toward the soldiers.

He had hoped they would charge forward immediately, but instead they formed into lines, the horse soldiers in front of the foot soldiers. This was the worst thing the soldiers could do. Instead of rushing forward, toward the ridgeline and the trap beyond—they now stopped in their tracks. This was exactly the type of defensive line that Crazy Horse had seen them use to great effect, marshaling the range and strength of their rifles. Never had he felt such urgency. *We have to get them moving again!*

———

"Captain, look!" Fetterman turned to see Grummond pointing toward the backside of Sullivant Hill. There, as Fetterman had anticipated, the war party that raided the wood train had just emerged—perhaps four hundred yards in front of them and to the north, moving northeast in the direction of Lodge Trail Ridge. It looked to be around forty riders, the bulk of whom immediately whipped their horses at the sight of the soldiers, galloping away in retreat, angling away from Fetterman's forces and up the hill toward the top of Lodge Trail Ridge.

"They're breaking for the Montana Road," said Grummond.

On the far side of Lodge Trail Ridge, the officers knew, out of sight from their current position, the Sioux would intersect the road. Its well-worn path would make for easier riding in the raiders' retreat.

Fetterman continued to study his quarry. Lagging behind the main group of retreating riders, ten warriors held back, facing toward Fetterman's forces and appearing to confer among themselves.

"Rear guard?" asked Grummond.

Fetterman nodded. "That's my guess too." Fetterman bit his lower lip, calculating. "Sergeant . . ." he called out.

Sergeant Lang stepped forward. "Sir?"

"Deploy the infantry as skirmishers. No firing until my order—we're still out of effective range." The sergeant yelled out the order, and the infantrymen hurried into position, spreading out from a long, deep column into a wide line.

"Lieutenant Grummond . . ."

"Yes, sir," said Grummond.

"I want your cavalry on point and out on the flanks."

"Yes, sir!" replied Grummond. He yelled out the order and the cavalry began to move into place, quickly riding in front of the infantry and forming their own line.

"Let's get within a hundred yards and then give them a volley or two," said Fetterman.

"I've been dying to give them a taste of the Spencers," said Grummond, with an eagerness that caused Fetterman again to feel unease.

"Let's be sure I'm clear . . ." said Fetterman. "Our orders—*your orders*—are not to cross Lodge Trail Ridge. And I don't want gaps between your cavalry and my infantry."

Grummond scoffed. "You sound like the old man, Captain. Except you've actually been to war. You know how long plans last before the battlefield changes them."

"I know we're going to obey our orders or suffer the consequences."

"Come on, Captain. The only consequences that matter are out there." Grummond pointed toward the Sioux, then paused a moment, giving a small smile that somehow managed to make Fetterman feel like a confidant. "Tactical adjustment . . ." Grummond nodded his head in the direction of the fort. "You sure as hell know better than *him*."

Fetterman hesitated. He hated Grummond's persuasive charisma even as he felt himself drawn to it.

Grummond seemed to sense the opening. "If I'm right, we don't even have to apologize."

Fetterman started to respond, to repeat that they were not to cross Lodge Trail Ridge. But before he could say a word, events seemed suddenly to accelerate, then to cascade out of control. He heard pounding hoofbeats behind him and turned to see two civilians whom he recognized as Wheatley and Fisher splash across the creek, then gallop up before skidding to a halt. Wheatley gave a little salute and said, "Reporting for duty, Captain. Colonel Carrington sent us." Fetterman noticed their tall horses, snorting and champing at the bit and looking significantly better-tended than the army stock. He noticed and appreciated the Henry rifles they carried. Besides, he knew both of the civilians to be seasoned war veterans. Both were critical of Carrington's policies and tended to bluster, but they could back it up. There might be a way to make use of them.

Before Fetterman had even a moment to think, he heard Grummond call out, "Here they come!" Fetterman turned back to see the ten rear-guard Indians charging toward them, whooping and yelling as they closed to a distance of perhaps two hundred yards.

Crazy Horse struggled to sort among the flood of sensations, to push away the confusion and the fear, to keep his focus on what he and the other decoys must do.

They were close enough now to see the individual clumps of sage that pushed up from the dusting of snow on the ridgeline to the north. In the valley beyond, the great gathering of warriors lay hidden in the gullies and draws, waiting in the frigid cold for the soldiers that the decoys would lead into their trap.

He ignored the sound of the cannon from the distant fort. The soldiers had probably spotted a group of scouts sent out to spy from surrounding hills, but the fort's big guns would play no meaningful role today. He focused instead on the scores of soldiers pursuing them, regrouping now after crossing the icy creek. Their horse soldiers pushed out in front of the others, spreading out to form a long line. But now, to Crazy Horse's utter dismay, they had stopped.

The other decoys looked to him. Crazy Horse saw the dismay in their eyes, too, and something else that filled him with a mix of great responsibility and dread. He saw that they looked to him *for what to do*. For a while today he had felt confident, a confidence augmented by Moon's vision.

Yet now they halted. Did they sense the trap beyond? As his mind raced, one lesson from the past five months of fighting surged to the fore—his enemy must not be allowed to think, only to react. Raising his war club above his head and filling the valley with his war cry, Crazy Horse charged toward the soldiers' line, the other decoys instantly joining him on both flanks.

Crazy Horse peered toward his enemy as the decoys quickly closed the distance that separated them. He had fought them enough times that he recognized some of the officers by their horses, certainly the one who rode the white stallion. He saw the officer studying them intently before yelling out a command.

The horse soldiers fired a volley, though the decoys were still more than a hundred yards away. Crazy Horse could hear the bullets streaking around them but he knew the decoys were beyond the soldiers' effective range. He knew that the soldiers often panicked when confronted with attack, and he knew they now would struggle to reload their clumsy, single-shot rifles, in their terror of the charging warriors.

But then suddenly, mere instants later, the horse soldiers fired again. He heard the scream of a horse and saw one of the Cheyenne tumble to the ground. Incredulous, Crazy Horse peered ahead toward the horse soldiers, now no more than seventy yards in front of them. He noticed that their rifles were different, shorter. The soldiers kept the guns to their shoulders and used one hand to operate some sort of lever on the bottom of the rifles, then instantly fired a third round. One of the Arapaho went down. As he watched, the soldiers continued to pour out fire, again and again without pausing to reload, the smoke from so many rounds already thick around their line.

Crazy Horse reined his horse hard, then yelled out to the others, "Fall back!"

Private Charles Cuddy felt a sense of elation when Grummond's command to fire finally came, so eager had he been to put the Spencer to use. He was positioned in the skirmish line—ten yards from the riders on either side of him—all of the troopers having reined their horses to a halt. Cuddy worked the lever on the Spencer and sighted down the short barrel, careful to keep the muzzle from being too close to his horse's head. They had all heard stories of fellow cavalrymen who blew their horse's brains out with careless shots.

Cuddy leveled the sights on one of the charging Sioux, attempted with little success to steady his breathing—and pulled the trigger . . . Nothing. He pulled back the Spencer to look at it and realized that he had forgotten to pull the hammer to full cock. He quickly cocked it— the Indian now noticeably closer—barely taking the time to aim before pulling the trigger again. This time the weapon fired with a robust kick. Instantly his horse bucked, spooked by the gunshot.

The smoke from the first cavalry salvo obscured the view. When it cleared an instant later, the Indians had not halted their charge, now less than a hundred yards in front of Grummond's line of horsemen, nor did it appear that any of the Indians or horses had been hit. The cavalrymen worked the levers on the Spencers, the action expelling the empty shell casing while chambering the next round. Grummond yelled "Fire!" again, and the cavalry fired a second volley.

Private Cuddy was still fighting to keep from being bucked off his horse when the command came for the second salvo. He was barely able to hold on to his saddle, let alone fire again.

The cavalry's second salvo was only slightly more successful than the first in striking their charging targets. The surprise of it, though, seemed to stop the Indians. After a ponderous moment, the savages retreated— galloping away toward Lodge Trail Ridge. They were quickly out of range, and Lieutenant Grummond yelled to cease firing. Many of the cavalrymen either didn't hear him or couldn't stop shooting with their blood up. Grummond and the sergeant eventually screamed out the order several times before finally the Spencers fell silent.

Sword Owner rode up beside Crazy Horse as they retreated. "When did they get those?" yelled out Sword Owner.

Crazy Horse didn't know. He had fought the soldiers led by the officer on the white horse only days earlier and they had no such weapons then. *Now on this day of all days!* He felt his stomach constrict, as if he had been kicked. He had seen one such gun—taken from a miner they killed in the fall. They had studied it and mused over how it worked. There had been a box with strange bullets in brass casings—the gunpowder, bullet, and primer all together in one piece. There weren't enough of the bullets to experiment with the gun and truly understand it. Black Moccasin, who had struck the fatal blow on the miner, ultimately had taken the new weapon and presented it as a gift to his soon-to-be father-in-law. Now, it appeared, the horse soldiers all had them, and Crazy Horse wondered if the foot soldiers had them too. The new guns hadn't made them better marksmen, but the rhythm of fighting he had known seemed to be changing before his eyes. The whites' old guns might have had longer range than their bows and arrows, but the bows had always given them the advantage of more rapid rate of fire.

Had Moon's vision taken all of this into account? Crazy Horse tried to push the doubt from his head. *Nothing to do now but to fight on.*

The rapid shots behind them continued as they retreated toward the ridgeline. When they were out of range, he stopped to look back, hoping to find the horse soldiers again in pursuit. A small group clustered around the officer on the white horse, but the line did not move. He turned to look back at the ridgeline, achingly close. He saw in his mind the hidden warriors on the far side, hearing the shooting and preparing their weapons in anticipation. *But for what?*

Have we come so close, only to fail?

Sword Owner and Big Nose rode up beside him, also looking back. "They're close," said Sword Owner. "Maybe we should just keep riding and they'll follow."

Crazy Horse shook his head. "We have to be more sure." He looked back down at the soldiers, still in their skirmish lines. "Listen, brothers. We'll all break for the ridge, but I'll pull up, make them think my horse has gone lame."

"We could act like we're coming come back to help you," said Sword Owner.

Crazy Horse nodded. "We need to gleam like their gold—so close that they can't help but reach for it . . . Let's go!"

They broke for the ridgeline.

Captain Fetterman struggled to see through the cloud of smoke that hung over Grummond's cavalry after the fusillade of fire from the Spencers. *What the hell is happening?* The frigid air above held the black powder haze close to the ground, and it took a long moment before Fetterman could see that the ten Indians who had charged the cavalry now galloped away, following the others who already had retreated over Lodge Trail Ridge.

Fetterman felt a small bit of relief that Grummond and the cavalry at least held their position. A few of the cavalry horses had bolted, unaccustomed to gunfire, but for the most part Grummond's cavalry line still stood arrayed in front of the infantry.

The Indians were barely a hundred yards away from being able to duck behind the cover provided by Lodge Trail Ridge when one of the raiders pulled up, leaping from his horse. Once on the ground, he lifted his horse's foreleg, examining it, all the while looking back fearfully at the cavalry behind him.

"His horse has gone lame," said Sergeant Lang, who stood next to Fetterman's horse as they both tried to survey the field before them.

Fetterman prepared to ride up to Grummond, consult on their next move, when suddenly Grummond and his cavalry charged off toward the warrior with the wounded horse. "Goddamn it!" said Fetterman, turning to Wheatley and Fisher. "You two get out there with him, tell him to hold up. I don't want a gap between his cavalry and my infantry."

"Just like the old days!" said Wheatley. "Come on, Fisher!" The two civilians spurred their horses and galloped after Grummond.

As Fetterman continued to watch, Grummond's men fired randomly from horseback as they dashed ahead. Already the cohesiveness of the cavalrymen was breaking down. Once again, Grummond raced the farthest out front, a few of his men keeping up but most falling behind. To Fetterman's outrage, the gap between the cavalry and the infantry was more than four hundred yards. Nor was the ongoing gunfire effective. Shooting from the bouncing back of a horse was a skill that few soldiers possessed, and certainly not these men with their brand-new rifles. No more Indians fell.

Giving Fetterman one small bit of reassurance, he could see

Wheatley and Fisher gaining ground as they galloped toward Grummond. "Metzger!"

The sound of his name didn't register with Metzger at first. Instead, he sat on horseback trying to sort out the various threads of the action erupting around him. He had been in battle before, of course, but he never had grown accustomed it. Each time he felt the terror anew, just as he did at this moment. He took a quick breath in an unsuccessful effort to calm himself. "Here, sir." He kicked his horse and the animal took a couple steps toward Captain Fetterman.

"Blow recall!"

Metzger put the bugle to his lips and blew recall.

As Fetterman, Metzger, and Sergeant Lang watched, Lieutenant Grummond reined his horse and looked back. Grummond's men, most of whom had been trailing him, caught up, halting their mounts in a cluster around their commanding officer. With their fast horses, Wheatley and Fisher had nearly reached the lieutenant.

Lieutenant Grummond's first sentiment was frustration at the inability of his men to shoot worth a damn. It was all well and good that they now had the Spencers, though more shots, as Fetterman had feared, did not make them better shots. A few of his men had already fired all seven of their rounds, and now struggled to remove the long magazine tube from the butt of the rifle in order to reload. Leather gloves made their fingers clumsy, so most men removed them. In the cold they fumbled with the brass cartridges, some of the shells dropping to the ground. One trooper, as Grummond watched in disgust, dropped the whole tube, dismounting to recover it. A few wasted more ammunition by continuing to fire random shots in the general direction of the Indians. The Indians had fired a couple of retreating shots from old single-shot rifles, but most of the warriors appeared only to have bows and arrows.

"Hold your fire!" yelled Grummond. "Wait till they're in better range!"

As if recognizing the brief opportunity, the warriors with the dismounted Indian charged back down from the top of Lodge Trail Ridge to assist him. Most of them clustered protectively around the downed

Indian, but one rider galloped past him—directly toward the cavalrymen, quickly closing to a hundred and fifty yards, then a hundred . . . The warrior was close enough now that the troopers could discern the vermillion stripes he had painted on his face. They could also see that he carried nothing more lethal than a crude war club.

Grummond couldn't help but admire such noble folly, a lone warrior with a stone tied to a stick—riding into a squad of Spencers. The warrior's war cry was otherworldly, sending a chill down Grummond's spine that made it seem for an instant as if it were the troopers who faced the greatest danger. Savage or not, Grummond respected the sheer moxie. However brave, though, the savages had yet to comprehend the superiority of their foes. "Fire!"

A dozen rifles went off at once, and the Indian's horse collapsed, pitching its rider headlong to the ground. Incredibly, the warrior rolled a couple times and was back on his feet. He paused for a moment to shake his war club at the troopers, still defiant, but then finally turned to retreat on foot in the direction of Lodge Trail Ridge.

Grummond heard again the sound of the bugle blowing recall. He knew that a bugle call was an order, just as much as spoken words. Sergeant Baker looked nervously back toward the infantry. They were separated now by a distance of more than a quarter mile, but certainly the distance was not so great that Baker could fail to make out Captain Fetterman—atop his horse next to his bugler, also mounted. And certainly they could hear the bugle clearly.

"Sir," said Sergeant Baker, "they're blowing recall."

"I know goddamn well what they're blowing!" said Grummond, focused again on the retreating Indian, who dodged and weaved as he ran. The troopers' shots set off little geysers of dirt all around the warrior but failed to bring him down.

Wheatley and Fisher arrived, pulling up beside Grummond. Wheatley snorted in disgust. "Jesus Christ, Grummond—your men couldn't hit water in a lake." Pivoting sideways on his horse, Wheatley leveled the Henry on the retreating Indian, then coolly squeezed the trigger. The Indian pitched forward. Wheatley worked the lever to chamber another round. "See how you do it, boys?"

Fisher, meanwhile, leveled his rifle at the more distant target—the

Indians surrounding the rider with the lame horse. Fisher fired, missing the Indians but grazing a horse. The animal reared.

As the troopers watched, they could see now the panic in the actions of the Indians near the ridgeline. The warrior with the lame horse seemed to reject an entreaty from one of his comrades to ride double. Instead, after looking back at the soldiers, he pulled his horse by the bridle, dragging the animal up toward the ridgeline. The others, still mounted, hurried along on either side of him, also taking frequent, fearful looks behind them in the direction of Grummond's cavalry.

Another warrior dashed down toward the Indian that Wheatley had shot, still alive, struggling to climb on back of the horse with the assistance of his comrade.

"The son of a bitch ain't dead yet," said Wheatley. He aimed the Henry and fired. They could see Wheatley struck the wounded Indian again as he slumped forward, the warrior in front reaching back to keep the wounded man from falling off as they struggled clumsily on horseback toward the cover of the ridge.

The echo of the second bugle had barely faded from the windy plain. "What do you aim to do, Lieutenant?" asked Wheatley.

Sergeant Baker looked to Grummond expectantly, as did Fisher. Grummond hesitated.

"They're escaping," said Fisher.

"You know what they say, Lieutenant . . ." said Wheatley. "Fortune favors the bold."

Grummond pulled at his collar, as if his shirt was choking him. As he watched the raiding party, the warrior with the lame horse paused at the ridgeline, flanked by the others. As the troopers looked on, the warrior turned back toward them, pulled his bow from his back, then an arrow from his quiver. He drew the arrow, arching his bow high before releasing the shot. He was far beyond effective range for a rifle—let alone a bow. The shot wasn't intended to kill but, rather, to insult.

"Arrogant bastard," said Grummond.

"Why wouldn't he be?" asked Wheatley. "They've been getting away with this shit for four months."

Grummond didn't look back before giving the order. "Back in the skirmish line!"

"Good instinct, Lieutenant." Wheatley and Fisher wheeled their horses to take a position to the right of Grummond. The enlisted men, too, began to fan out on their horses along the two flanks.

Sergeant Baker looked at Grummond, incredulous. "Sir?"

"Form a skirmish line, Sergeant—or ride back to the infantry and tell them you don't have the stones to do your job!"

Grummond didn't bother to call out further orders before spurring his horse and charging up toward the ridgeline. As Sergeant Baker watched, a few of the enlisted men hesitated, but in a matter of instants, all of them were in motion, barreling after Grummond and the two civilians. After a last glance back at the infantry, Baker, too, spurred his horse.

Ahead of them, the Indians disappeared over the ridgeline.

Captain Fetterman watched in impotent rage as Grummond's cavalry charged up toward Lodge Trail Ridge. Fetterman viewed holding their forces together as the lynchpin to their success, indeed, the lynchpin to avoiding the type of disaster that nearly befell them only a few weeks earlier. He cursed himself for leaving Grummond any zone of ambiguity— any space for interpretation. Still, even if they had crossed into some gray zone earlier, the bugle call colored everything from that point forward in black and white. He expected impetuousness from Grummond, but ignoring the bugle was naked insubordination.

To Fetterman's right, Bugler Metzger sat atop his horse, equally incredulous. He knew well the difficulty of maintaining order on the battlefield. Still, if there was anything he appreciated about his role, it was that he gave them all some small chance for coherence—some small bit of clarity amid inherent chaos.

Sergeant Lang, afoot on the other side of Captain Fetterman, could scarcely contain his own fury. "I've never in my career seen an officer ignore a bugle call." The service chevrons on Lang's forearms stood for his twenty years of experience in the army.

Metzger felt somehow as if he had failed in his duty. "Do you want me to blow it again, sir?"

Fetterman shook his head. "It's not that he didn't hear it," said

Fetterman. "He just won't listen." The captain pondered a minute, wishing that he could think faster, or slow down the swirling events. The Indians, even the trailing one who pulled behind him the wounded pony, had disappeared over Lodge Trail Ridge. Grummond's cavalrymen were now all in pursuit, roughly arrayed in a skirmish line but with the lieutenant and the two civilians already opening a gap up front. Captain Fetterman held out a final bit of hope that they would halt at the top of the ridge—perhaps fire a couple rounds into their fleeing foe and then stand pat.

Sergeant Lang shook his head in continuing disbelief. "He's not even looking back to see if his line's intact."

Fetterman had come to understand Grummond. His blood was up, and that was all that mattered.

"What are we going to do, Captain?" asked Lang.

Fetterman cursed again to himself, biting hard at his lip as if he might stab himself with some bit of clarity. He removed his gloves, rubbing his hands together again in an effort to warm them. "I want us double-time up to the ridgeline . . . get where we can at least see."

The sergeant studied him hard. "To the ridgeline?"

"You heard me, Sergeant . . . To—not beyond."

"Yes, sir."

"I'll form up the men myself. I want you to take the bugler's horse . . . Ride out and catch Grummond—convey that he's in violation of direct orders. Tell him that my direct order to him is to rally his men back on me immediately. Understood?"

"Yes, sir."

Metzger dismounted and handed the reins of his horse to Lang. Lang mounted, saluted, and galloped off toward Lodge Trail Ridge.

Moments later, Metzger found himself trotting on foot beside Fetterman's horse as they climbed the hillside, still a few hundred yards shy of the ridge. They continued to hear scattered shots from beyond the crest and Metzger, like all the infantrymen, struggled to interpret their meaning. The cold wind increased as they neared the top, straight at them from the north. His face felt numb and he wondered if he could articulate his mouth sufficiently to blow the bugle. It occurred to him that he was marching once again in a direction not set by himself. Beginning with Colonel Carrington's orders back at the fort, Metzger had heard clearly the discussion of the significance of Lodge Trail Ridge. Yet for him, the ridge had its own meaning. For him, he resolved, the ridgeline would be a turning point, a place and a time beyond which he would take control of his own future.

Captain Fetterman tried to keep his own analysis of the shots more professional. For the moment, he needed to set aside his anger at Grummond and focus on pulling his force back together. He continued to hear the promiscuous shooting from Grummond's troopers on the other side of Lodge Trail Ridge. Clearly the troopers lacked the discipline that the new repeating weapons would require of enlisted men, and Grummond was hardly the type of officer to instill it upon them. Still, while Fetterman was eager to gain the vantage of the ridgeline and see with his own eyes what lay beyond, the continuing shots suggested little more than the minor skirmish that had been apparent on this side of the rise. The best he could tell, Grummond's men continued a haphazard pursuit with sporadic firing.

Fetterman's intention was to gain the high ground, wait for Sergeant Lang to catch up with Grummond, and then cover the return of the cavalry to the infantry. From the top of Lodge Trail Ridge, Fetterman calculated, his fifty infantrymen would hold a strong position. Few of the Sioux were armed with rifles. With bows and arrows, their effective range was barely fifty yards, and certainly not more than seventy. Even with his troops' poor marksmen, he trusted their massed fire to create an effective shield at a hundred yards—twice the Indians' range. Fetterman calculated that they could defend the hilltop all day if they needed to do so, especially with the infantry and the cavalry rejoined. Eighty rifles on the frontier was formidable—even if the Sioux had managed to reassemble a force the size of December 6's.

As he rode up the hill at the pace of his marching men, Captain Fetterman surveyed the field before him. The infantry skirmish line spread out for a hundred yards with Fetterman in the middle. In contrast to Grummond's cavalry, Fetterman was pleased that his infantry was maintaining its discipline as it marched.

Metzger struggled to hold double time as they climbed the hill, the cold air biting as he sucked it into his lungs. His feet kept slipping and he cursed the infantry's flat-soled brogans, focusing on placing one foot in front of the next. There was little vegetation on the exposed hillside except for the knee-high sage and clumped buffalo grass. The grass, at least, provided a bit of traction. Suddenly he passed a fresh pool of blood and realized it must be from the Indian who had been shot. Metzger had needed no reminder, but the blood underscored again the stakes. He looked to the ridge, now close, and continued to trudge toward the top.

Desperate to gain the vantage of the ridgeline, Fetterman fought against the instinct to gallop ahead of his men. He would not sacrifice the sanctity of his formation. Over the ridge, the sporadic shots continued, though they sounded more distant now. Grummond's men, it seemed, were continuing their pursuit. Fetterman imagined briefly how he would reprimand Grummond when they reunited. His actions this time were unforgivable, beyond any ambiguity, and Grummond would deserve the court-martial that certainly awaited him. Fetterman cursed himself for believing a man like Grummond could be channeled.

At thirty yards from the crest of the hill, Captain Fetterman again quickly surveyed his line, pausing also to look back toward Fort Phil Kearny, visible in the distance with Pilot Hill rising behind it. He estimated that approximately forty-five minutes had passed since they departed the fort and that they were now almost three miles away from its gates—not a short distance to cover at double time over rough terrain. He knew his men on foot were tired. His line was holding up pretty well, given the circumstances—bowing a bit in a couple places where some of the men struggled up the hill but for the most part still coherent.

He pushed his horse northward across the final few yards to the ridgeline, reining to a halt at the top as he absorbed the scene in the sprawling valley below. "Company . . . halt!" The order trickled outward along both flanks and soon all the men had stopped on the top of Lodge Trail Ridge, all of them looking ahead.

Crazy Horse's heart had raced wildly at the elation of looking back to see the twenty-plus horse soldiers charging across the top of the ridge and down toward the valley formed by Prairie Dog Creek. He knew that if they could just entice the horse soldiers to clear the ridgeline, they would continue their pursuit, like water on the side of a hill that can flow only one direction. The officer on the white horse led the way and Crazy Horse felt that he had come to know him.

He marveled at the perfect placement of the white man's road—down the plateau like a spine that dipped gradually toward the crossing of the Prairie Dog Creek. Because the sides of the plateau fell away sharply, visibility on both sides was limited. Crazy Horse kept looking both to his west and east, afraid that he might see some warrior who had not taken care in hiding himself or his horse. But he saw nothing. There were draws and gullies and scrubby small trees, but nothing to indicate the two thousand warriors ready to rise up as if spawned that moment by Mother Earth Herself.

It seemed appropriate somehow that the soldiers would follow their own road into the maw of the trap. The decoys were careful to keep their distance close—always just at the edge of rifle range. But there now seemed little doubt that the horse soldiers would keep chasing. Crazy Horse looked back periodically at the officer on the white horse, charging out in front, leading his men to death. *But will the foot soldiers follow?*

Then, almost miraculously, Crazy Horse looked back and saw the profiles of foot soldiers rising on the ridgeline, the officer on his horse in the middle but then scores of his men, spread out across the ridge in a long line of cobalt shadows against the stormy gray backdrop of the winter sky. Now only one question remained. *Will the foot soldiers too descend from the ridge?*

From the ridgeline, Captain Fetterman's eye was first drawn to his cavalry—tiny mounted figures at least a half mile out front and maybe more. He cursed Grummond again and wondered if Sergeant Lang had been able to catch him.

Fetterman could see clearly the Montana Road to the north along a long, narrow plateau running perpendicular to Lodge Trail Ridge and descending eventually into a crossing of Peno Creek. On both sides of the plateau, the terrain dropped off steeply into broad valleys, veined with scores of gullies and coulees, some deep enough to contain creeks or seeps and supporting clumps of willows or even small trees. Broadly though, the vista felt wide and open—the Big Horns eventually rising up in the west but the eastern horizon unbroken.

Fetterman peered northward again toward Grummond and his men, realizing that he had forgotten his field glasses in his haste to leave the fort. Even with his naked eyes, though, he could make out the Indian raiders, still out in front of the cavalry, now descending the spine on the Montana Road—retreating toward where the road crossed Peno Creek. Grummond's twenty-seven cavalrymen and the two civilians barreled after them, spread out haphazardly along the top of the narrow plateau on both sides of the Montana Road. Fetterman could distinguish Grummond's white horse and the civilian dress of Wheatley and Fisher along with three or four cavalrymen at the front, with the rest strung out for a hundred yards back behind. It reminded Fetterman less of a military maneuver and more of magazine accounts he had read of fox hunts in the English countryside. Not only had Grummond separated his cavalry from the infantry—he had failed, once again, even to keep his own cavalry intact as a cohesive fighting unit.

Sergeant Duggan appeared from the right flank, breathing heavily. Like Sergeant Lang, Duggan was one of those steady noncommissioned officers that made up the army's foundation.

Again, Fetterman wished that he had time to think things through, to consider the options in some methodic and systematic way. He quickly scanned the vast, empty landscape on both sides of the plateau, devoid of any sign of life except to the north. The wind blew harder on the ridgeline, and Fetterman felt the penetrating cold. His horse snorted and stamped. He clenched and unclenched his fingers in an effort to restore the circulation.

"I dispatched Sergeant Lang to bring them back in," said Fetterman. It felt authoritative to say he had done something, as if he were in some way master of the situation and not merely reacting.

Sergeant Duggan shifted uncomfortably. "Can I ask, sir—do you aim for us to sit up here and wait?"

"You know our orders," said Fetterman.

"Yes, Captain, but Grummond shuffled the deck . . ." Duggan looked hard at Fetterman. "It wasn't you that rode over the ridge, sir . . .

but now that he's done it, I'm worried about leaving the cavalry hanging out there. It'll be you that gets blamed if things turn bad."

Fetterman continued to peer northward, feeling like his head was caught in a vise. Duggan wasn't wrong. *Goddamn it!*

"My aim's been to get our forces back together," said Fetterman. "Undo what Grummond's done." He pointed northward. "For all we know there's two hundred Sioux down along Peno Creek—just like two weeks ago."

Sergeant Duggan nodded.

"The Montana Road follows the high ground," said Fetterman, pointing. "We could make our way from here, stay up high along the spine . . . reel Grummond back in."

Fetterman pulled his glove back over his still-stiff fingers, used the back of the glove to wipe at his nose. He saw no better course. *What else am I supposed to do?*

Ten yards from Fetterman, standing on the ridgeline, Metzger struggled to catch his breath after the double time scramble up the hill, made more difficult by the traces of snow as they neared the crest. They had halted at the top for a few minutes where Metzger, having heard Fetterman's earlier discussions about their orders, assumed they would stand pat. Standing nearby now as Captain Fetterman talked to Sergeant Duggan, he caught snippets of their conversation. To Metzger's horror, they seemed to be seriously considering chasing after Grummond's cavalry.

As Metzger watched the cavalry continue its sporadic shooting at the retreating Indians, it occurred to him that he carried no weapon. The band members had relinquished their Spencers to the cavalry two weeks earlier. He had been issued a clunky Springfield in its place, but hadn't even remembered to grab it from the barracks when the call came for assembly. He never had been much of a marksman, but carrying a gun at least gave some feeling of security, illusory or not. As he knew well from the war, in a worst case, a big rifle at least could serve as a club.

Metzger watched the conversation between Fetterman and Duggan come to an end, with both men nodding in seeming agreement. As Metzger feared, Fetterman barked out the new command. "Double time! Forward . . . march!" The order propelled Metzger in the precise opposite direction from where he so fervently wished to go.

———————

Four miles away, on top of Pilot Hill, a sentry stood next to his comrade, studying the infantry through a field glass. He had watched as the cavalry chased a few Indian riders over the top of Lodge Trail Ridge. The infantry took longer to arrive and had halted for a while at the ridgeline, but now they moved forward. He turned to the other man on duty and handed him the glass. "They're all going over Lodge Trail Ridge." A minute later, the last infantryman disappeared from sight. Even the lookouts were blind.

———————

There was a discernable moment, on a charging horse, when the animal's stride transitioned from canter to gallop. Grummond loved that moment. At a cantor, a rider feels ungainly, jolting up and down on the giant animal's back like a wholly unnatural appendage. At the moment a horse hit full stride, though, the motion of horse and rider become liquid smooth, as if the horse had shaken its earthly harness and the rider is magically merged into a single being.

War added yet another element to this potent force of man and horse. Fill the hands of a cavalryman with a Colt and a saber, line dozens of horses side by side, and propel this force against an enemy. Grummond remembered the moment in his first cavalry charge when his complete terror transformed into an awareness of the power he wielded. He remembered the terror he saw in his enemy's eyes at the sight of him, the sensation of riding over his fleeing foes, smiting them down with saber thrusts and pistol shots that rained death as if he were a god.

When Grummond came west, he heard the talk in the barracks about the Indians as the greatest light cavalry the world had ever seen. He had scoffed then and he scoffed now as he watched the ragtag savages retreat before his mighty onslaught. Perhaps a few times before, the US Army had made the mistake of riding into unknown country with too few men, but today they deployed in full force.

Grummond glanced left and right. Wheatley and Fisher flanked him on either side. He envied them their horses—the best that money could buy, and lavishly tended with all the imported grain they could eat. He resented that they had pulled ahead of him at a couple of junctures, though now he was back in the lead. Grummond, after all, was the commander of the cavalry and it was for him to lead the charge. He admired their rifles but was not envious of them. Officers didn't carry rifles—only pistol and saber. As a commander, his job was not to snipe at long range. His job was to lead his men with boldness and panache, to inspire them through example. At close range, when it mattered most, his pistol and sword were the weapons of choice in any event.

Now Grummond looked ahead. The vanguard of the cavalrymen had closed to within a hundred yards of the rear-guard Indians, close enough for Grummond to see clearly the war paint on the rear haunches of their ponies. No longer did the savages make any pretense of fighting back. They flailed at their horses, and it occurred to Grummond that even Indian ponies—known for endurance—would be fading after the extra riding compared to the cavalry. Grummond watched the Indians looking back frequently and fearfully. *No more of their insults now!*

Grummond glanced back, irritated again that so few of his men could match his pace. Still, most were close enough that they would catch up quickly. Besides, with the civilians' Henrys, it was the fleeing Indians who were outgunned.

As Grummond charged forward, the Montana Road began to dip down from the spine-like plateau along a gentle descent toward the crossing of Peno Creek. His horse accelerated on the downhill slope and a plan occurred to him. There was no bridge across the creek and the water would slow the Indians. If Grummond and the civilians could close the gap before then—say to fifty yards—they could pull up, dismount for steady shots, and let the rifles work their magic. They might not take down all of the raiders, but Grummond was confident that they would send the survivors back with renewed respect for the consequences of attacking the United States Army.

Grummond angled his horse toward Wheatley, the nearer of the two civilians, yelling out when he had closed to within ten yards, "Pull up when the Indians hit the creek!"

"Pull up?"

"We're close enough for your rifles!"

Wheatley nodded. Fisher, on the other side, had noticed the interaction and looked to Grummond. Grummond drifted to Fisher and conveyed the order.

As Grummond had hoped, the Indian ponies seemed to be losing some ground. As the savages neared the creek, the lead pursuers had pulled so close that Grummond could see the details of the individual warriors. He noticed that several of the Indians wore the braids more characteristic of the Cheyenne than the Sioux, who in battle usually left their hair flowing and loose. Strange, he thought, that the Cheyenne would be raiding with the Sioux. A couple of the savages had hairstyles that didn't appear to be Sioux or Cheyenne—stranger still.

Peno Creek ran faster than Big Piney and had not frozen. Grummond could not help but be impressed that the Indians did not hesitate, crashing into the water at a gallop, completely confident in the sure-footedness of their ponies. Still, the creek slowed the horses.

"Now!" yelled Grummond, reining his horse hard and leaping to the ground. Wheatley and Fisher followed his lead, dropping their horses' reins and assuming a firing position with their rifles resting on one knee. All of the men began to shoot, even Grummond, who fired his Colt though he was out of range for a side arm.

Grummond gave a cursory glance behind him, happy that a couple of his better troopers were approaching. As for the rest, perhaps missing out on this last part of the fight would be sufficient lesson that next time they'd need to work a little harder to keep the pace.

Someone struck one of the Indian horses, which whinnied in pain before dumping its rider. Grummond was amazed at the speed with which the Henrys could be fired: *BANG*, crank the lever, aim again, and *BANG*. The shots spit forth from the short barrels like lightning bolts, one after another. Grummond was sure that all sixteen rounds could easily be fired in the space of thirty seconds if the shooter so wished. *Remarkable!* Another savage toppled from his horse. The smoke from the shots thickened, making it difficult for a moment to see their targets.

Crazy Horse used his knees to grip tightly at Arrow's flanks as the horse struggled briefly to climb the far bank of Prairie Dog Creek. He heard the thud of a bullet penetrating flesh, then the scream of a horse. On his right, Black Shield's horse collapsed beneath him, throwing the Cheyenne to the ground. The man struggled at first to gain his feet and gather his dropped weapons, but seemed unhurt.

More bullets splashed into the creek and the bank, and the horse soldiers were close enough now for Crazy Horse to see details of their short rifles. When the soldiers worked the lever on the bottom of the guns, the weapons seemed to spit something out to the side—and the gun somehow was instantly ready to fire again. The two civilians fired with particular speed, and Crazy Horse heard the scream of a bullet passing close to his head. He looked beyond the horse soldiers, though. His only concern—the only thing that mattered—was the scores of foot soldiers on the distant ridgeline.

Elation surged suddenly through Crazy Horse's entire body as if carried on a bolt of lightning. A half mile to the south, the entire force of foot soldiers was now descending the ridge toward the road, already deep inside the trap.

He turned back to the other decoys. There was no sign of Big Nose, and Crazy Horse assumed that the Cheyenne must have tumbled from the back of the horse on which he had been so precariously riding double. Black Shield, his horse shot from beneath him, was now on foot. Incredibly, most of them were alive—and still mounted.

"Now!" yelled Crazy Horse, pointing. "Half with me to the right—half left! Then we cross paths!"

Grummond stopped firing his Colt after three shots of his own when he saw that all of the Indians had now managed to cross Peno Creek. He watched another of the Indian horses go down, and saw one of the raiders looking worriedly back toward them. When they were all clear of the creek, they kicked at their horses and galloped off, so desperate now that they abandoned the horseless warrior behind them.

Suddenly, they split their force into two groups—one veering east off the Montana Road and the other veering west. Grummond was surprised they hadn't divided their forces before, which would force the pursuers to divide as well. It was a standard Indian tactic.

But then the two groups of savages did something strange. Instead of continuing, one toward the east and one toward the west, they turned again and began to ride directly back toward each other, each group forming into a line.

Wheatley lifted his head briefly from his rifle. "What the hell are they doing?"

A cluster of five or six troopers caught up to Grummond and the civilians, reining up. "What do we do, sir?" asked one.

"What do you mean, what do you do?" yelled Grummond. "Shoot your goddamn rifle!"

The Indians ignored the rifle fire, the two lines continuing to ride toward each other, temporarily forming an X pattern as one line crossed through the other on the Montana Road. It struck Grummond briefly that it was almost as if they were performing a maneuver in a parade.

What happened next had so many elements that, at first, the great tidal wave of sensations was almost paralyzing, so many perceptions simultaneously that none of them registered, none was comprehensible.

Grummond was aware of the movement before he was aware of the sounds. The eye is drawn instinctively to the smallest bit of motion, able to distinguish movement even at great distance or against a backdrop that otherwise might camouflage an object from view. This, though, was no small movement. Nor were the distances great. The whole, barren prairie surrounding them had come to life. Every gully and bush, every mound of dirt and clump of sage, even the thin blades of dead grass. Every element of the landscape seemed to have conspired in hiding a great and shocking secret.

The sounds, as Grummond began to perceive them, were equally horrific. The war cries came first. Grummond had heard the Sioux battle cry before, so it wasn't the terrible novelty of something unknown. What was terrifying at this moment was the sheer volume of the cries—that they came from every direction and in such numbers as to have no precedent, no antecedent to which his experience might attach.

The sounds of the horses came next. Their own cavalry mounts snorted and whinnied at the appearance of this brethren herd around them. The Indians' horses, having somehow been muzzled before, were now liberated to join the cacophony and did so with the full spectrum of their vocalizations. Then came the fierce pounding of hooves, churning at the prairie floor, so many that the plain quaked at the collective jolt.

Lieutenant Grummond heard the explosion of a full infantry volley behind him, and for the first time, it occurred to him to look back toward Fetterman and his men. Far back, so much so that the men appeared antlike, he could see the long blue line of infantry spread out in skirmish formation, well down the hill from Lodge Trail Ridge. Grummond took the smallest bit of comfort that most of his cavalry had caught up to him, but their numbers—twenty-seven plus the two civilians—seemed suddenly paltry.

The most terrifying sound was more subtle, not fully perceived by Grummond until men and horses around him cried out and began to fall. Arcing clouds of arrows descended upon them from every direction. They hissed as they flew, like some animated demon drove, and when they found flesh their metal heads made a sickening, meaty sound of heavy impact—*THWACK!*—followed by the screams and groans of their targets. Grummond's horse cried out and he saw an arrow protruding from its rear haunch.

It was all numbing at first. Nor did the conclusion, when finally it did arrive, seem remotely possible. But then Grummond put it all together, the realization inescapable. He scanned quickly in every direction. This was not dozens of savages or even hundreds. There must be a thousand at least, and maybe more. All around them. Grummond had led his men into the middle of an intricate and brilliant trap. A brilliant trap set by savages, thousands of savages working together in calculated conspiracy.

Lieutenant Grummond struggled to see a path of escape. Wheatley and Fisher had remounted and appeared beside him.

"Jesus Christ!" yelled Wheatley.

"We gotta get back to Fetterman!" said Fisher. "Wheatley and me will try and cover you from behind that rock." He pointed to a single low rock, perhaps seventy-five yards behind them, prominent as the only bit of available cover. "Slow 'em down for as long as we can."

Grummond nodded, seeing no better alternative. Already the Indians had closed to within a hundred yards on every side but one, immediately behind them on the Montana Road to the south. The small group of raiders that they had chased now rode at the front of the closest group—hundreds of riders approaching from the north, having crossed back across Peno Creek. *Swarming hordes.* All the sounds were louder now, already much closer in the space of the few seconds since the trap had been sprung. Had there been more time he might have wondered how he had managed to miss the signs of such an enormous gathering, but there was no time. Instead he yanked hard at his horse's reins to turn it, at the same time spurring viciously at the animal's flanks.

Grummond never bothered to yell retreat. There was no need. At least five of his troopers already lay dead on the ground. The rest began a desperate race to reunite with Fetterman and his infantry, far up the Montana Road.

In a deep gully directly east of the white man's road, High Backbone felt the sharp pain of inhaling frigid air. He tightened the rawhide belt at his waist, cinching more snugly a vermillion Hudson's Bay blanket with three black stripes that he had fashioned into a poncho. Normally the thick wool blanket kept him warm, but it was hard to stay warm when standing still. Adjusting the belt helped in some small measure to limit the icy air that otherwise seeped in, though not enough actually to feel comfortable. He shuffled his feet while remaining vigilant to stay hidden, noting with satisfaction the discipline of the two hundred Minnicoujou warriors that occupied with him this concealed position not far from the crest of the ridgeline that separated the valley of Prairie Dog Creek from the view of the soldiers' fort.

He thought, too, about the other times he had been in this place, including the times he had come here with his young nephew, Crazy Horse, to teach him the skills of a hunter. So different and so distant, in some ways, from today. Yet he was proud that he had helped to shape the small-framed, pensive boy into the respected young warrior who now carried such great weight on his shoulders. They were hunting today, too, all of them, with the future of their people at stake.

Nearby, one of the Minnicoujou horses snorted and stamped its feet, and High Backbone cast a stern look at its owner. The man reached up to pinch the animal's nose in an effort to quiet him. High Backbone was grateful, at least, for the direction of the wind—directly from the north. It blew their horses' scent into the whites instead of the other way around. If the wind had carried the smell of the whites to the Indian horses, the animals likely would have responded—revealing their positions. As it was, the whites' horses would smell the Indian ponies when they crested the ridge, but High Backbone doubted the ability of the soldiers to pay attention to the reactions of their mounts. Hopefully the soldiers left the old scouts, men experienced enough to know, back at the fort. High Backbone felt grateful, too, for the warmth the day before that had melted most of the snow. The tracks of two thousand Indian horses would have been apparent, even to the whites.

High Backbone heard gunshots from behind the ridge and forgot instantly about the cold, peering up through the thick willows. Up and down the Minnicoujou line he could feel the sudden ripple of tension from his tribesmen. In some ways, the Minnicoujou's position was the most crucial of all the tribes because they were closest to the ridge. For the trap to succeed, they would need to wait patiently while the entirety of the soldiers' forces paraded past them, only then breaking cover to seal off the retreat. If a single Minnicoujou jumped, put himself before the tribe, they would squander the opportunity that this great convocation of warriors presented for the first time in High Backbone's life—the opportunity to destroy a white army in its entirety, wipe them forever from the face of the Lakota home.

High Backbone held his breath when the first of the decoys galloped across the ridgeline. He counted the riders, reaching five and still not seeing his young nephew. *Have they killed him?* Two decoys came over the ridge riding together on one horse, the man in back clearly wounded, but neither had the distinctive light hair of Crazy Horse.

Finally another rider appeared, and High Backbone felt a moment of relief when he recognized not only the light hair but also the sorrel horse of his nephew. Soon though, barely a hundred yards behind the decoys, the first white horsemen crested the ridge. One was an officer on a white horse, High Backbone just close enough to discern the golden gleam on the shoulders of the man's blue coat. The other two men, though, wore civilian clothing. After a few moments, more horsemen appeared, two dozen or more. None of them paused a bit before diving into the valley behind their officer. They fired rifles as they rode, and High Backbone was surprised that the guns could fire again and again without reloading. He looked worriedly toward the decoys, who kept pausing to look back at their pursuers, keeping the distance close. The horse soldiers continued to fire rapidly, though High Backbone saw with relief that their shots failed to find their targets.

He heard a sound next to him and saw Eats Meat crawl up beside him. "Is it time?" asked Eats Meat.

High Backbone shook his head. "No," he said.

There should be many more. High Backbone had counted twenty-seven horse soldiers. Normally, they would attack such a force without hesitation. Today, though, the aspiration was far higher. They were here to fulfill the prophecy of Moon. High Backbone held great confidence in the Oglala *winkte*, and waited for the additional scores of white soldiers that he expected to arrive soon.

Several minutes later, a mounted officer was the next to crest the ridge. Unlike the earlier whites, this man halted at the top, staring intently into the valley below him. Then, appearing at first like shadows in a dream, the dark forms of the foot soldiers began to rise up from behind the hilltop, five or ten, then twenty, then fifty men at least, spread across the ridge in the line formed by the whites when they prepared to fight. All of these men halted, too, staring down toward the scattered shots that still rang out from the horse soldiers—now at least a half mile in front of the foot soldiers and maybe more.

From the far left of the soldiers' line, a soldier on foot hurried toward the officer in the center. The two men talked back and forth, pointing toward the horse soldiers. After a while, the two men fell silent, side by side and staring out before them. High Backbone held his breath, fearful that the foot soldiers would sense the trap, turn back. But then, the mounted officer yelled out an order—and the long line of soldiers began to descend into the valley of Prairie Dog Creek.

High Backbone felt his heart soar and begin to beat so rapidly that it seemed as if his chest might not contain it. What he now watched was

exactly what the *winkte* had foreseen—the largest group of soldiers ever
to ride out from the fort! Never in his life as a warrior had he known a
moment as thrilling as this one, nor a moment where so much depended
on the outcome of the fighting to follow. He looked at Eats Meat and
the other Minnicoujou near to him—all of them looking between the
soldiers and him, expectant for his signal. Now, High Backbone knew,
the only thing that could undermine the plan was if the tribes attacked
too soon—left the soldiers a line of retreat to the fort. He shook his head
sternly and used both hands to signal *Wait!*

The few minutes that followed seemed to High Backbone to be the
longest of his life, as if the movement of the sun toward the horizon had
somehow been held in suspension. The soldiers funneled from their wide
fighting line into a narrow column centered on the white man's road. At
their closest point, no more than a few hundred yards separated the soldiers from the concealed positions of the Minnicoujou. The wind picked
up and High Backbone watched the officers' horses turn their heads and
snort, no doubt picking up the scent of the hundreds of Indian ponies
hidden all around them. High Backbone and the other Minnicoujou again
used their hands to squeeze the nostrils of their horses, fearful the animals would whinny. As for the soldiers, their focus seemed to fix on
the road before them, from where the scattered shots continued. Though
he could hear the shots, High Backbone's concealed position, low in the
valley, prevented him from seeing the decoys or the horse soldiers that
pursued them. Eventually all of the foot soldiers passed farther down
the road, through a small field of boulders and then beyond. All of the
Minnicoujou held tight to their positions, waiting, High Backbone knew,
for him to signal the attack.

Then all at once it changed. From the north, the wind carried an
avalanche of sounds. There was an increase in the number and intensity
of the gunshots, it was true. The bulk of the sounds, though, came not
from guns—but from the thousands of warriors that High Backbone
knew had leapt forward from their places of hiding. He heard the war
cries and the thunder of hooves and he could sense the power of the
moment.

He leapt to the back of his horse, raising up to see down the white
man's road. The foot soldiers had stopped at the sounds of the sudden

attack, the trailing edge of their formation a few hundred yards beyond the outcropping of large boulders. High Backbone could sense their shock—see them moving uncertainly, in different directions, a few firing their guns haphazardly. He saw the officer on the horse, turning round and round to survey the field, could feel him discovering the size and power of the forces now throwing themselves against him from seemingly every direction. The officer looked to the south—back toward the fort. This, High Backbone knew, was the soldiers' only chance. It would be the Minnicoujou who would deny it to them.

"Follow me!" yelled High Backbone. "Cut off their escape!" He kicked his horse and charged up the slope toward the road. All up and down the gully, he could see his fellow warriors rising up from concealed positions, throwing themselves onto their ponies, and joining in behind him. It was as if their horses, too, had been waiting for this moment, drawn back like arrows, but then forced to hold back their power, now unleashed. In a matter of instants, they crossed the road and then moved beyond it.

High Backbone reined his horse and turned to look back to the north—toward the foot soldiers. Two hundred Minnicoujou now stood in a line below the ridgeline from where only minutes earlier the soldiers had descended. It was evident to High Backbone what now must be evident to the soldiers as well. There was no way out.

Then he heard a war cry from his right and saw Eats Meat pivot his horse and ride directly toward the foot soldiers, waving his tomahawk as he galloped, far ahead of the others. A group of the soldiers turned toward him and some began to shoot. At first they hurried their shots in fear and missed the lone Minnicoujou, and in a few instants he was among them, alone, crushing one soldier with his horse and bashing the head of another with his war club. But then, in the midst of so many soldiers, not all of them could miss. Eats Meat grabbed his chest and pitched backward from his horse.

Up and down the Minnicoujou line, Eats Meat's fellow warriors cheered at such bravery. "Come, brothers!" yelled High Backbone. "Let us all do our part!" Two hundred Minnicoujou charged forward.

Before the attack began, Captain Fetterman kept standing in his stirrups as he descended the Montana Road from Lodge Trail Ridge, desperate to see what was happening in front of him. The road ran north and perpendicular to Lodge Trail Ridge along the top of another narrow, spiny ridge. From the infantry's position, the hilltop descended eventually into the Peno Creek Valley, the road occasionally dipping sharply as it followed the natural contours. When it dipped, it created blind spots, frustrating Fetterman's efforts to see Grummond and his cavalry. Apparently, all of them had dropped behind one of the contours, far in front of the infantry.

Again, Fetterman fought the instinct to gallop ahead of his men. It seemed ironic to think about discipline in the midst of Grummond's breakdown in order, but Grummond's actions made Fetterman's steadiness all the more important. He was pleased that his infantrymen maintained their formation as they continued north at double time. He knew they were tired.

As Metzger trotted down the gentle slope not far to the left of Fetterman, he came to a rise, strewn with a dozen boulders, as if a giant hand had tossed a jumble of stones like dice onto the hilltop. He watched Captain Fetterman maneuver his horse between the rocks, some flat to the ground, some barely knee-high, a few as high as a man's waist. For some reason, Metzger noticed the golden glint of lichen on the stones as he passed through them. From somewhere far in his past, he remembered his father telling him about lichen, the life that somehow sprouted from the harsh surface of a rock. *What a strange moment to recall such a thing.*

The north wind battered directly against Metzger's face like repeated slaps. It dried out his eyes when he squinted into it, causing them to water profusely, but then it blew the tears across his cheekbones, freezing his skin and starting the same blurry pattern all over again. He kept blinking in a futile effort to clear his vision.

Once clear of the boulders, Metzger glanced to his left—toward the Big Horns. The spine of hilltop along which the Montana Road ran was mostly barren of any vegetation larger than grass and sage. From their position though, the terrain fell steeply into a valley, and Metzger noticed briefly the twisted network of draws and gullies. He couldn't see as well to his near right, in part because the hill dropped steeply on that side, too, but the landscape seemed similar. Mostly, though, Metzger kept his eyes to the front, scanning ahead.

Like every enlisted man, Metzger suffered from a limited knowledge of the big picture, of the strategy that propelled them forward. Today, through proximity to the officers, he knew more than most. From what he had heard over the course of the past hour, what mattered was pretty simple. They needed to get Grummond and his cavalry back in the fold. Only then could they go back to the fort. So like Fetterman, Metzger kept squinting into the growing north wind, hopeful that the cavalry soon would come cantering back toward them, having abandoned their reckless pursuit of the Sioux raiders. Metzger was tired and cold. The large force of soldiers today gave him some comfort, but he always felt increasing disquiet with every step from the safety of the fort. This was a foreign land and he traversed it as a foreigner, never feeling that his instincts offered protection.

They had advanced another two hundred yards beyond the boulder field when it started.

From Captain Fetterman's position atop his horse, he was the first to understand. He heard the war cries and scattered rifle shots and his eye perceived the sensation of movement everywhere, as if the barren land was erupting. Of all the thoughts that flooded over him, two resonated most clearly. Most immediately, it was the sheer numbers that shocked him. Fetterman had been in enough fights to have a good feel for estimating the strength of his foes' forces. In his time on the prairie, he had never seen an Indian gathering of more than a hundred warriors. This force reminded Fetterman of the great battles of the Civil War, when the Rebels threw thousands of soldiers onto the field of battle. *Thousands! How is this possible?*

Even as this first shock sunk in, Captain Fetterman became aware of something else, something ultimately even more terrifying than the great number of savages. Hundreds of mounted warriors *already were racing to cut them off from the south—from behind.*

Fetterman scanned the horizon in all directions, and everywhere it was the same—a screaming, demonic wave sweeping toward them. He heard the sudden spike in the firing to their north—the repeating rifles of the cavalry and the civilians in what was now an unbroken barrage of shooting. Though he still couldn't see Grummond's men, their rate of fire told him everything he needed to know. Clearly Grummond faced the same scale of attack from the one direction—north—that Fetterman could not see for himself. To the west, meanwhile, where he could see most clearly, the entire horizon seemed filled with Indians rushing up the hillside toward him. Only the steep incline leading up to their spiny plateau stood to slow their attack. The closest Indians were no more than two hundred yards away. Fetterman couldn't see as well to the east, but he saw Sergeant Duggan firing his pistol rapidly. Presumably there was no shortage of targets coming up the hillside to the east.

But most concerning was the flurry of activity behind him—to the south. It was the direction back to the fort and the only plausible direction for retreat. Already, though, Captain Fetterman estimated there must be a hundred warriors racing to spread across the slope below Lodge Trail Ridge.

Sergeant Duggan appeared suddenly at Fetterman's side. "Holy Christ!" An arrow protruded from his arm, which he plucked out with a swift tug. "You think we can break through to the fort?"

Fetterman shook his head emphatically even as he continued to survey the field. "Too many horses . . . They'll run us down." *Think!* Some of his men were firing—wasting precious shots when the Indians were still out of effective range.

"Hold your fire!" Fetterman screamed the command, with only mixed results.

Fetterman knew that his failure to control Grummond had led his men into this trap, but perhaps he could still lead them out. If they could regain some bit of high ground back among the boulders, they might hold out. Surely Carrington would hear the sounds of the battle and send reinforcements. Perhaps Sergeant Lang would bring Grummond back, allow them to put the cavalry's repeating rifles to concerted and deadly effect. *Against so many?* He didn't know, but there was no better option.

He turned to Duggan. "We'll fire one salvo at a hundred yards, reload—and then break for those boulders!"

Duggan looked dubiously toward the outcropping behind them. "Not much there . . . but I don't see anything better."

"Ready!" Fetterman called out the order. "Aim!" The nearest warriors had closed to a hundred yards and Fetterman waited until a few more of the Indians came into range. "Fire!" Every infantryman with a loaded weapon pulled his trigger and there was a great *clap* of gunfire, the results instantly veiled in smoke from the same shots.

"Reload!"

From his perch, mounted above the others, Fetterman allowed himself a small bit of hope. Fetterman estimated that fifty guns had been ready to fire, and the salvo had ripped into the leading line of Indians, many of whom tumbled from their horses. Those not hit stopped their advance to duck for cover. The instant that Fetterman could see the men closest to him had been able to reload—perhaps twenty seconds later—he yelled to the bugler. "Blow retreat!"

For several moments after the trap was sprung, Metzger absorbed the events around him as if he were somehow not a part of the scene but, rather, watching it from outside of himself. It was strangely fascinating that so many Indians could appear so suddenly, as if somehow transported by magic and then materializing out of thin air on the plains all around them.

It all became real when an arrow from an arcing shot buried itself in the chest of Nathan Foreman, a friendly man from New York City with whom Metzger often had shared his mess. Foreman groaned at the impact, the arrow penetrating through the bone of his sternum and then driving deep into his lung. Foreman went wide-eyed in shock, dropping to his knees. Metzger sprang to his side, easing him back onto the frozen prairie. Foreman, though, began to cough and when he did the blood was already at his lips. All battlefield veterans of the Civil War knew instantly which wounds were fatal, as this one certainly was. Foreman knew too. His eyes went from the arrow protruding from his chest to Metzger, terrified. Metzger knew there was nothing to say. In a manner of minutes Foreman would lose consciousness from the loss of blood, and moments after that he would be dead. Foreman reached out his hand toward Metzger, and Metzger gripped it tightly. There was nothing else to do, but at least he could do that.

"Bugler! . . . Metzger!" The sound of his name pulled him back from the intimate universe between him and Foreman, back into the swirling chaos that was everything else.

Metzger turned to see Captain Fetterman screaming down at him from the back of his horse. "Blow retreat!"

Metzger gave one final squeeze to Foreman's hand, then stood up, reaching for his bugle. He put the icy mouthpiece to his lips and blew. The first notes came out distorted and unclear. *Do your duty.* He inhaled deeply and blew again. This time the notes emerged with clarity and authority. All around him, his fellow soldiers turned at the sound, desperate and hopeful that some instruction—some higher authority— might deliver them from the horrible fate that seemed otherwise so certain.

Fetterman cast one last gaze to the north—toward Grummond. Nothing but prairie, though the sounds of fighting from that direction were intense. *Can't wait.* He caught a glimpse to the east—Sergeant Duggan, ducking on one knee as he reloaded his Colt. To the west, clos- est to him, he saw the Indian hordes—picking themselves up after the infantry salvo—charging forward again. Fetterman knew their situation would not improve.

He stood in his stirrups for his men to see him—pointing with his sword behind him, toward the boulder-strewn hilltop, two hundred yards behind them. "There!" he yelled. The bugler continued to blow retreat. The infantrymen broke into a desperate race to the rocky rise.

Suddenly, Fetterman felt a sharp pain in his side and at the same moment his horse screamed and spun halfway around. Fetterman just managed to pull his foot from the stirrup so that he wasn't pinned as the dying animal crashed heavily to the ground. He rolled clear of the horse, looking down at his side to see blood darkening the navy of his coat. Afraid, he put his hand to the wound. He felt pain at his short rib, and hoped that the bone had prevented the bullet from piercing any organ. If an organ was pierced, he was dead anyway, so further attention to the wound was of no consequence in any event. He struggled to his feet, his Colt in his left hand and his sword in his right, and ran with the others toward the boulders.

Metzger felt the brief satisfaction of knowing that he had done his duty when the moment called, provided some small bit of direction amid the chaos. The sentiment was quickly overwhelmed, though, by the sheer terror of everything else. With the other infantrymen who were able to do so, Metzger heeded Captain Fetterman's order and began to run for the little boulder-strewn hilltop, two hundred yards away.

Sergeant Lang weighed north of two hundred pounds and his galloping horse strained at the load, bathed in sweat despite the bitter cold. Lang was a hard man with a soft spot for horses, and it pained him to whip at the horse to urge it forward. An infantryman, he had no spurs. Nor a cavalryman's saber. He had passed several of Lieutenant Grummond's troopers as he sped down the Montana Road on the narrow spine of prairie hilltop, surprised at how spread out they were—at the utter lack of military comportment among the cavalry.

Sergeant Lang was still several hundred yards behind Grummond when the Sioux trap was sprung. He had not yet descended toward Peno Creek, and his higher position on the Montana Road gave him one of the best vantages from which to see the great, arcing scope of the forces now charging toward them from all directions. He reined his horse to a halt, and in a matter of instants, cavalrymen were careening back past him headed south. If it was possible, there was even less order in their retreat than there had been in their attack.

Down below him, he saw Wheatley and Fisher leap from their horses beside a couple of large rocks. Immediately they turned to the attacking Indians and began to pour down fire from their Henrys. Their shooting was cool and effective and seemed to slow the attack at first. In contrast to the promiscuous cavalrymen with their new Spencers, the two civilians did not waste their shots. Already half a dozen Indians or their horses lay dead in an arcing formation roughly fifty yards in front of the two men. The lethality of these two rifles clearly surprised the Indians, some of whom now pulled up—or turned their horses in an effort to flank the two civilians instead of riding headlong into the withering fire. To Lang's seasoned eye, though, the numbers on the other side were overwhelming, like nothing he had seen since the war. The sangfroid of the two veterans and the shock value of their firepower might slow the Indians down, but it would not stop them.

Sergeant Lang possessed a good measure of sangfroid himself, and for a moment, he was able to coolly detach himself from the scene and to evaluate it, as if his own survival did not turn on his conclusion. Clearly their only chance was retreat back to the south, back toward the infantry. If they could reunite on some defensible ground, perhaps they could hold out long enough for Colonel Carrington to send reinforcements from the fort. The first challenge, in any event, was to reunite their forces—rejoin Grummond's cavalry to Fetterman's infantry.

Order in the cavalry already had broken down completely, and Lang felt another intense flash of rage at Grummond. He watched as more horsemen dashed past him, wide-eyed and desperate—all retreating back toward Fetterman, but with none of the advantage that concerted action might have given them. Each trooper now sought only one thing—to save his own life.

Lang heard an angry hissing sound as an arrow passed within inches of his head. He turned to the west and saw how quickly the Indian masses were advancing. The closest—scores at least and maybe hundreds—were now were within range of bow and arrow, and the volume of the streaking shots spiked upward. Lang heard a loud *THWACK* and at first feared his horse had been struck, but then saw the arrow protruding from the thick leather of his saddle. *To hell with this.* Lang had just made the decision to turn his own horse back to the south when Lieutenant Grummond galloped up the hillside, reins in his left hand and saber in his right.

Grummond saw Lang but didn't slow. As he passed by, Lang yelled out. "Lieutenant! Captain Fetterman orders your men back into formation with the infantry!"

Grummond turned and yelled back. "Damn fine idea!"

A mounted warrior, face painted half in black, appeared suddenly from the mouth of a coulee not more than thirty yards away, yelling and charging toward Grummond with his coup stick raised. Grummond responded instantly to the challenge, pivoting his horse to charge directly at the warrior.

The two horses collided violently, Grummond's rearing. The Indian swung his heavy coup stick toward Grummond, but missed. Grummond in turn swung his saber, catching the Indian solidly across his upper arm. Grummond felt the satisfying *click* as the saber hit bone, and he knew at that instant that he would prevail against this foe. The Indian groaned in pain and, as Grummond anticipated, recoiled in shock at the severity of the blow. The Indian had painted the upper half of his face in a shiny mixture of black ashes and grease, so that the whites of his eyes stood out starkly. The effect might have been fierce, except that now the Indian knew he would die. Grummond had seen before the eyes of foes wide with terror in this moment. He was impressed that these eyes showed no fear but, rather, what seemed more like surprise, as if disbelieving that this moment would arrive in this way, that it would arrive so suddenly—now.

It was a fatal flaw for soldiers to hesitate at such a moment, and Lieutenant Grummond was alive because he never had. Grummond wrenched his sword back, far behind him. His horse went back down to all fours, placing him perfectly beside his enemy. Grummond used the momentum of his horse's motion and pivoted at the waist when he swung, to bring the full force of his own body into the blow. The sword struck the Indian at the middle of his neck, and Grummond marveled that it could pass entirely through with what felt like so little resistance. The Indian's head toppled from his body and fell to the ground, the blood shooting skyward from the body like a geyser before it also slumped lifeless to the ground.

Grummond felt the elation that he had always felt at such moments, the rushing sensations of fear followed by focus followed by total conquest.

Suddenly he was aware of a dull force at the back of his head and next felt the sensation of falling. He knew that his body was striking the ground but he did not feel pain. He lay there for an instant, on his side, then shook his head and rolled semi-upright. He saw now the Sioux warrior who had struck him, dismounted and looming above him, war club raised for the death blow. Grummond heard a shot from behind him and the Indian tumbled backward. Grummond turned to see Sergeant Lang, smoke rising from his pistol. The sergeant was dismounted but still clinging to his horse's bridle, not more than ten feet away.

Grummond reached to grab for his own horse. Somehow he had to regain his mount, but a mounted Sioux darted in, grabbed the animal by its bridle, and was gone. Grummond looked down the hillside, where dozens of warriors now swarmed nearby, the closest barely twenty yards away. Scores more just behind. He was aware of the intensification of hissing of arrows and then heard Lang groan, looking back to see the sergeant down on a knee, two arrows in his chest. Lang managed to raise his pistol again and fired, striking the nearest Indian. Grummond knew that Lang would not survive and stumbled toward him, desperate to take his horse. The sergeant fell from his knee to his side. Grummond reached him and ripped the reins of Lang's horse from his hand.

Lang's eyes glazed, but he seemed somehow to look beyond Grummond. Grummond managed to place his boot in a stirrup and swung himself up into the saddle. He had lost his pistol but still gripped his sword.

Sergeant Lang said something, and Grummond looked down.

"Goddamn you to hell, Grummond," said Lang. His voice was strained but fully cogent and purposeful. "You killed us all."

Grummond ignored him and had just started to dig his spurs into the horse when he heard the crack of a pistol and felt an exploding pain. The pain began in his back, but when Grummond looked down he could see blood seeping from the front of his breast. He turned to see Lang, the sergeant's smoking pistol pointed at him.

Grummond fell from his horse but was still alive when the Sioux warrior grabbed him from behind by a thick handful of his hair. He felt the knife as it sliced across his forehead, and then he felt the tearing sensation of his own flesh as the warrior ripped his scalp backward across his head. Grummond screamed. For Lieutenant George Washington Grummond, the most intense sensation was not the pain but, rather, the complete shock of being conquered.

Three Sioux reached Sergeant Lang. Lang knew he was dead, and struggled to compose some peaceful thought that might help him to maintain his honor in this final moment. An image of green ribbon flashed through his mind in the instant before a war club crushed his skull.

When the decoys crossed their horses along Peno Creek and Private Charles Cuddy watched the hundreds of warriors arise suddenly from the gullies and grass, nothing in his prior experience offered any point of comparison. He was too young to have served in the Civil War. All he knew was that it was terrifying and primal and otherworldly.

At this point, only one other trooper was anywhere near Cuddy, and both of them reined immediately to a halt. Lieutenant Grummond and the two civilians had descended all the way down the hill, where they had poured fire into the retreating decoys, but they now retreated themselves—pell-mell back up the hillside, back toward them.

Cuddy turned to the other private. "What the hell are we supposed to do?" The other man said nothing, but pivoted his horse, spurred it viciously, and galloped back toward Lodge Trail Ridge. Cuddy gave a brief glance to his Spencer and wondered how many shots he had left. *Two? Three tops.* The sergeant had told them to keep careful count while shooting, but Cuddy had lost track in all the excitement. There was no way that he was going to reload now, with hundreds of savages charging toward him. He held tight to the rifle but spurred his horse too. He passed two other troopers consumed in the same chaos, but they, too, quickly turned, and all of them whipped their mounts up the hill with every bit of strength they could muster.

If there was an identifiable zenith in the life of Crazy Horse, it occurred at the moment that he signaled the attack along with the other decoys. Not a single warrior of any tribe had foiled the plan, all staying hidden until the signal. At the agreed moment, they had emerged in a unified force the likes of which Crazy Horse had never before seen.

He immediately turned Arrow to face south—ready to charge back across Prairie Dog Creek. He took quick notice of how the tribes were arrayed. Ahead of him and to the west, he recognized the tall lance with the eagle feathers carried by Sorrel Horse, the Arapaho chief leading the charge of his tribesmen as they swarmed forward from their position along the small rivulet that ran parallel to the white man's road before flowing into Prairie Dog Creek. The Arapaho were the closest to the horse soldiers; a few were firing guns, but most were firing arrows that arced toward the whites in a blizzard of piercing death.

Crazy Horse glanced back to see his own Oglala rushing south toward him—on and beside the white's road. Up Prairie Dog Valley toward the distant ridgeline, he could see the Cheyenne, some of them already charging toward the ridge from the west to cut off the soldiers' escape to the fort. Crazy Horse couldn't distinguish High Backbone, but he saw the Minnicoujou to the southeast, racing to close the only gap in the circle of death about to envelop the whites. *No place to ru*—

Arrow screamed and pitched to the ground. For an instant, the impact of striking the earth took Crazy Horse's breath away, and for a few moments he fought to regain it. He peered up from the ground, and a bullet crashed a few inches from his head into his dead horse. He crawled quickly behind the horse, using the animal as a barrier, then peered out, up the white's road.

The two whites who were not soldiers had taken a position about one hundred and fifty yards up the hill from the creek, sheltered not only behind a large rock, but also behind the corpses of their horses, so perfectly placed for defensive purposes that Crazy Horse suspected the men had killed the animals themselves. Crazy Horse had watched with disdain the actions of the horse soldiers, firing their rifles wildly and then retreating in chaos in the face of the attack. These two men and their fast rifles were altogether different. They fired rapidly—but calmly and with deadly precision.

As Crazy Horse watched, one of the men directed his fire into the position of the oncoming Oglala. The other, perched at an angle to his comrade, fired into the onrushing Arapaho. Crazy Horse was horrified at the carnage already inflicted by these two men. The warriors, slowed in their charge by the small creeks and then the steep hillside, made fat targets. And the two civilians seemed never to miss. Every shot of these lightning-fast guns seemed to find its target, and what seemed like dozens of Lakota and Arapaho and their horses already littered the hillside below this rear guard. The horse soldiers, meanwhile, had cover in their desperate effort to rejoin forces with the foot soldiers farther up the hill. Somehow these men with the rifles had to be killed. As Crazy Horse continued to watch, two Arapaho managed to approach within range of their bows. Skilled warriors, they ducked behind the necks of their ponies and leaned out to launch their arrows. In an instant, the two civilians shot the horses, and when the two Arapaho rose up from beside their dead mounts, the fast guns barked—and the Arapaho, too, pitched to the ground.

Crazy Horse heard a rush of hooves behind him and looked back to see Lone Bear and Little Hawk, with Little Hawk leading an extra mount. Crazy Horse leapt onto the horse. "Quick," he said. "I'll distract the two with the fast rifles. You two work your way behind them."

Crazy Horse dug his heels into the pony and splashed across the creek. Lone Bear and Little Hawk crossed, too, but turned quickly to the east.

Scores of Oglala and Arapaho worked their way toward the two civilians, but more cautiously now, respectful of the effectiveness of these men and their powerful new weapons. Crazy Horse, though, kicked his pony and dashed flamboyantly forward. Almost instantly, his action had the desired effect, drawing first the attention and then the fire from the men behind the rocks and dead horses. At first he rode straight toward the men, ducking his head low and to the side of his horse and peering out from behind. Seeing the shots from the two men and hearing the near misses of their bullets, he changed his approach to make his path more erratic, himself a more difficult target. He closed to within a hundred yards before realizing that he needed to give Little Hawk and Lone Bear more time. He veered to the right, advancing another forty yards, but also exposing himself and his horse in partial broadside.

He saw the flash of the muzzle and at the same instant heard the thud of the bullet hitting his horse in the chest, just behind the front leg. The galloping animal collapsed in a cloud of dust, and Crazy Horse found himself unhorsed for the second time in the space of a few minutes. Another shot bounced beside him, and he rolled behind the horse for cover, reaching into his quiver for an arrow. He popped up and took a shot, though the position of the two shooters exposed little of their bodies. Looking back down the hill from his concealed position, Crazy Horse could see that his charge had inspired others to advance up the hill. The arc of arrows toward the two white shooters seemed almost continuous, hardly broken between one arrow and the next.

When Crazy Horse peered out again toward the two whites, he noticed that one of the men, for the first time, seemed to be struggling with his rifle. In Crazy Horse's own experience with guns, he knew that black powder could quickly cause the weapons to foul, even after a limited number of shots. At the rate these men fired, it seemed remarkable that their weapons would not eventually jam. Indeed, while one man continued to pour fire on the ever increasing number of targets, the other continued to struggle with the metal lever on his rifle, looking up worriedly to scan the battlefield, his desperation clearly rising. At one point, he half stood to gain leverage on the rifle, and Crazy Horse saw his shot.

Rising up from his own protected position behind his dead horse, Crazy Horse drew his bow, feeling the familiar connection between his own muscle and the scarcely contained power of the weapon. He held his breath as he sighted down the arrow, seeing the man's heart and raising above it slightly to compensate for the distance. Some archers held too long on their target, but High Backbone had taught Crazy Horse not to wait. The moment he was on target, he shot. Crazy Horse could see the blur of the speeding arrow in flight before seeing the white man wince, but he saw that the arrow had struck the man's arm instead of the more vital target he intended. Crazy Horse reached instantly for another arrow, but the white man ducked again so that he offered no shot. Meanwhile, the other man swung around and fired at Crazy Horse, missing but forcing him to take cover himself.

To the east, a hundred yards behind the two white men, Lone Bear and Little Hawk saw their own opportunity. They had approached cautiously until now. The shooters focused their attention and their fire at the Oglala and Arapaho swarming toward them from their positions along the creek. Lone Bear and Little Hawk knew that Crazy Horse was part of the distraction—and also that the distraction might not last. Now the man already struggling with his rifle had been struck with an arrow. The ground between them and the shooters offered no cover, but the moment for showing their own bravery had arrived.

Lone Bear turned to Little Hawk. "Let's go!" They kicked their ponies and charged forward. Their fast horses covered the distance to the two white men in a matter of instants. The white men heard the sound of pounding hooves and swung suddenly around. Little Hawk saw the expressions on the men's faces and admired that they did not show fear. One of the men pitched forward toward them, an arrow standing upright in the middle of his back. The other leveled his rifle and fired, and Little Hawk heard Lone Bear groan in pain and caught a flash of him pulling up.

Little Hawk was too close to do anything but continue forward, so he aimed his horse directly at the white man still standing. His horse leapt into the air to clear one of the boulders behind which the men had sheltered, and Little Hawk could do no more than hold on. Through his horse he felt the impact as the animal collided full force with the white man, who was thrown to his back on the tawny dead grass of the hillside.

Little Hawk's horse stumbled slightly but found its feet, and he struggled to rein it to a halt. He looked back to see the white man still on his back but raising himself on one elbow. Little Hawk leapt to the ground, rushing to the white man. The man's rifle lay ten feet away from him, but Little Hawk saw that he was reaching for a pistol at his belt. He had started to pull it when Little Hawk pummeled the man's skull with his war club, feeling the full force of his blow against the man's head and then the warm spatter of blood on his face.

He was standing over the dead white man when Crazy Horse rode up beside him on a horse that Little Hawk did not recognize. Loose horses, their riders killed, now wandered the battlefield. "Come on!" yelled Crazy Horse. "Where's Lone Bear?"

Dozens of Oglala and Arapaho swarmed the small space where the two white men had held out for so long. A few paused to plunder and desecrate the bodies, but most veered to the south—along the white man's road, in the direction of the retreating horse soldiers.

Already they heard many shots from that direction and could see the Cheyenne streaming up the western hillside from their own concealed positions in the draws and along the creek. There now were more warriors on the most distant hillside, too, the one leading up to the ridgeline across which the white foot soldiers had so recently marched. Those looking up from below knew full well the significance of these riders. The far ridge was the only escape route for the soldiers. If the tribes controlled it, the soldiers were trapped in the middle. Every warrior now hurried in the direction of the fighting, intent on joining the battle farther up the road.

"Where's Lone Bear?" repeated Crazy Horse.

"I'm not sure," said Little Hawk. "I think he was hit when we charged the white men."

"Show me where," said Crazy Horse.

The two had barely ridden a hundred yards when they saw Lone Bear's horse, partially concealed in a deep draw. As they galloped toward the horse, they saw Lone Bear sitting on the ground beside it, leaning forward on his knees. The side of his deerskin tunic was red with blood.

Crazy Horse and Little Hawk hurried to their friend's aid, surprised to see an arrow protruding from his side.

"Are you okay?" asked Little Hawk. "I thought it was the whites that shot you!"

Great clouds of arrows had been unleashed, the ground thick with them like grass in areas surrounding the entrenched position of the two white men with the rifles.

Crazy Horse examined the arrow in Lone Bear, holding it gingerly at the point where it entered his body. It seemed not to have penetrated deeply, fixed in a rib. With a swift motion, Crazy Horse yanked backward, the arrow seeming to dislodge cleanly. Lone Bear winced and took a deep breath, then blew it out in short puffs. Blood trickled from the wound, but not badly.

"Can you ride?" asked Crazy Horse.

Lone Bear nodded. "Yes."

Crazy Horse and Little Hawk helped Lone Bear to his feet. He was unsteady at first, but then seemed to find his grounding. He groaned when he mounted his horse, but pulled himself upright without assistance. "Let's go . . ." he said. "Before we miss the rest of the fight."

An instant later they were galloping up the white man's road toward the intensifying sounds of battle.

Colonel Carrington sat at a large desk in a room in his quarters that he had built as an official office. Both the desk and the office were indulgences on such a remote outpost, and he knew there had been chatter among some of the officers. This, however, was a domain where Carrington felt full confidence and where he would not compromise. He was the leader of this outpost, with critical and ongoing administrative duties. Frontier or not, he required a proper place to do his work. Just now he was midway through a long letter outlining the additional supplies that Fort Phil Kearny required to weather the long winter.

Mrs. Carrington appeared suddenly in the doorway, her face serious. "Private Sample's here. He says it's urgent."

Sample appeared in the doorway, breathing heavily, his face flush from the cold. Carrington knew instantly that something was wrong when Sample forgot to salute. "There's shooting from Lodge Trail Ridge, sir."

Carrington was aware of his wife looking on, concerned.

"Well, it's no surprise that Fetterman's men are skirmishing," said the colonel. "I imagine he's cut off the raiders as they retreated behind Sullivant Hill."

"That's what it was at first," said Sample. "But now there's a lot more firing." He paused for a moment, looking at Mrs. Carrington and shifting his feet. "None of us has heard anything like this . . . like a big fight."

Carrington grabbed his greatcoat and headed for the door. Once outside, he was instantly aware of the shooting, and Private Sample was right. The sounds coming from the direction of Lodge Trail Ridge sounded nothing like any skirmish before. There were no organized volleys; nor was this the scattered firing of ten or even twenty rifles. This was the urgent, persistent staccato of what had to be all of the cavalry and infantry firing, reloading, and firing again. It sounded unorganized . . . desperate. It didn't sound like a skirmish. It sounded like a battle.

On top of the eastern barbican, Colonel Carrington used his field glass to search desperately in the direction of Lodge Trail Ridge. He could see the ridgeline, but there was no sign of any of his troops. Clearly they had ignored his orders, passed over the ridgeline, and now, as nearly as could be perceived, the largest detachment he had ever dispatched from the fort was involved in a major engagement on the other side.

Carrington looked behind him toward Pilot Hill. "Anything from the signalmen?"

"Nothing, sir," said Private Sample.

"It would appear that they have defied my orders," said Carrington, speaking more to himself than to the private. "Defied me."

Private Sample felt supreme discomfort. He had no inkling of what one was supposed to say in such an instance.

Carrington was quiet for a while, but then he said, "Find Captain Ten Eyck. Quickly. Tell him what may be happening. Tell him to rally a relief detachment."

"How many men, sir? We don't have many left defending the fort."

It was an obvious point, and Carrington cursed himself for not thinking of it. "Tell Ten Eyck to take half of Company C and as many civilians as he can muster." Carrington had another thought. "Private Sample . . ."

"Yes, sir."

"Take my horse and accompany Captain Ten Eyck. You can act as courier if needed."

Fifteen minutes later, Captain Ten Eyck and this new relief detachment marched out of the fort at double time. Just about everyone who remained inside the fort had turned out to watch, the same piercing question etched on all of their faces. Colonel Carrington saw Margaret in the middle of a cluster of wives, standing erect, an arm around another wife on each side.

Colonel Carrington checked his watch: 12:20. The firing from over the ridgeline continued, but he couldn't see a goddamn thing.

For a while, the only thing that mattered was getting to the boulders. Sergeant Metzger had noticed the outcropping when they passed by on their way downhill, the only abutment of any note on the otherwise open passage of the Montana Road along the high rise. Taken in its totality, their situation was far too overwhelming, and so Metzger simply focused on making it to the boulders alive.

Captain Fetterman had bought them some time. The effect of fifty rifles firing in unison—even the old single-shots—was significant. Fetterman also had taken advantage of that brief moment of discipline to make the men reload. Now, each of them at least had one shot—one shot to defend himself in the two-hundred-yard dash to the rocks. Already they could see the hordes of Indians charging toward them from both sides of the Montana Road, as if they stood in front of a stampede that approached from every direction at once.

Metzger had barely started to run when a trooper he recognized as Private Cuddy dashed past him on horseback. Blood painted his horse's front and rear flanks from two arrows, still protruding. Cuddy's eyes conveyed his terror, and he used the flat of his saber to slap at his wounded horse in an effort to force some last bit of effort from the animal. Twenty feet in front of Metzger, the horse collapsed to the ground and heaved a final, heavy breath, as if relieved that it could die. Private Cuddy crashed to the ground in a tangled pile. Metzger arrived at Cuddy's side and helped the man to his feet.

"Where are we supposed to go?" asked Cuddy.

Metzger pointed. "The boulders."

Metzger could see Cuddy's mixture of disbelief and disappointment and fear. Cuddy had hoped that if he could survive to rejoin the infantry, Captain Fetterman would have some plan for salvation. Already they could see that there was a large group of mounted Indians on the far side of the outcropping, crashing down from Lodge Trail Ridge. Already they were surrounded.

Metzger made no further effort to persuade Cuddy. Seeing no alternative, he ran, pushing his bugle, still slung around his neck on its lanyard, to the small of his back. There were Indians everywhere now. A few infantrymen fired their guns but most just ran.

Cuddy heard a terrifying cry and saw three Indians on ponies at a distance of no more than forty yards charging up the hill toward him. He cocked the Spencer, aimed at one of the horses, and fired. The horse pitched to the ground but the other two riders continued to barrel toward him. He worked the lever on the Spencer, cocked it again, and pulled the trigger. This time, there was no explosion of the firing gun, but only the paltry snap of the hammer. The two riders were close now—no more than twenty yards. In desperation, Cuddy worked the lever again, hoping somehow rounds remained. *Why didn't I keep count?* He pulled the trigger and again heard the thin snap but no shot. *Too late to reload.*

The first rider barreled into Cuddy, knocking the trooper onto his back. The second rider pulled up beside him, firing an arrow that buried itself in Cuddy's side. Cuddy groaned in pain but managed to regain his feet. An Indian on foot now charged him, yelling and raising an enormous war club. Cuddy grabbed the Spencer by the barrel and swung it at the warrior's head. He felt the crack of contact, and the warrior fell, but at the same time he heard a strange sound, like a stone striking water. He felt no pain, but realized that another arrow now protruded from the center of his chest. He realized that he was lying on his back on the ground, though he felt no sensation at all. The last thing he saw was a war club, decorated with human scalps, arcing toward his face.

Like his men, Captain Fetterman ran. He tried, as they stampeded up the hill, to keep some semblance of the broader picture of the battlefield that he knew, as commander, it was his responsibility to see. All along the high spine of land he saw the blue blur of his infantry in a race against what seemed like thousands of Indians—rising up from the valleys around them.

He had seen hundreds of men die in the war, but this was different. As he ran he caught flashes of his men being run down, pulled to the ground, hacked and torn to pieces as if set upon by a pack of wild animals. He heard their screams not only of pain but of terror. He saw the fear in the eyes of his men as they ran and fought, and tried to shove down his own overwhelming sense of dread. *Think!*

Fetterman kept glancing behind him as he ran, still hoping Grummond's cavalry might show. Their combined forces might give them some chance. A cavalryman galloped past him. "Private!" He screamed at the man, who turned briefly. Multiple arrows protruded from the man's horse and his face conveyed his overriding fear. He whipped his horse and galloped ahead. Fetterman saw a handful of other cavalrymen and a few horses without riders—but mostly he saw Indians. An instant after the cavalryman rode past, he watched as the soldier was shot from his horse, tumbled backward, then was dragged by his mount across the prairie with his boot stuck in the stirrup.

As Fetterman tried to focus, he became aware that the rapid firing from the north had lessened dramatically. The fear that the handful of troopers he had seen represented the only surviving remnants of Grummond's cavalry seemed suddenly plausible.

Sergeant Duggan appeared next to him, firing his pistol before pointing to Lodge Trail Ridge. "Captain, look!"

Fetterman looked south. For an instant, he had been hopeful that a relief force had arrived. Instead, Sergeant Duggan was simply discovering what Fetterman already knew. Having occupied all of Lodge Trail Ridge, the Indians now attacked downward from the high ground. A wave of numbness washed over the captain, as if all his senses had suddenly been dulled. He blinked and shook his head and fired a random pistol shot. He realized that his sword was gone.

"What do we do, Captain?"

There was no good answer. "The boulders," he finally blurted out. "Keep going." Their only hope was that relief was on the way, nearby, perhaps just beyond the ridge. *Get to the boulders and hold out.*

Fetterman stumbled, and as the sergeant helped to pick him up he noticed the large amount of blood that now stained his left side. *Can't think about it.*

If any thought prevailed over Fetterman's fear, it was the aching realization that he had allowed himself to follow Grummond, to descend from the ridgeline chasing behind a fool.

A minute later, Fetterman had reached the outcropping. As he looked quickly around him, he guessed that less than half of his infantrymen had made it this far. The couple of surviving cavalrymen had set loose their horses and crouched behind the boulders, having realized there was no direction to ride that was not filled with charging Indians. Sitting on top of a horse only made them targets.

Not only were there so few surviving soldiers, but the boulders themselves were not the cover that Fetterman had hoped. A few were waist-high, but hardly a bastion given the force aligned against them. The men huddled behind the rocks, a few seeking desperately to reload their guns, but many merely cowering protectively. As he watched, a mounted Cheyenne warrior crashed toward them, his braids a clear mark of his tribe. An infantryman, in full panic, fired his gun without removing the ramrod, which propelled from the muzzle like a spear into the chest of the charging Cheyenne.

Cheyenne! It became obvious to Fetterman for the first time that they faced a combined force of Sioux and Cheyenne, and he felt a new wave of confusion and dread. He struggled to keep his thoughts linear, desperate to lock on to some semblance of a plan. In the midst of it all, the strangest things seemed suddenly to occupy his mind.

It struck Captain Fetterman, suddenly, that he was no longer cold.

Fetterman paused for a moment and looked down at his bloody hand. An hour before he had been frigid, his fingers numb and barely working, even inside his gloves. He had thrown the gloves aside at some point, bare fingers the only way to handle the caps when reloading the Colt. He tipped the Colt to examine the pistol's chambers, all empty but one. Smoke drifted skyward from the barrel, and the pattern, strangely, reminded him of his father's pipe.

For another brief instant he reflected on the jarring mix of sensations. Certain things seemed to slow down so that every detail jumped out as vivid in the extreme, even as everything else accelerated wildly—a vague and dizzying swirl of smoke and horses and Indians and streaking arrows.

Fetterman felt a stabbing pain and looked down to see an arrow protruding from his upper thigh.

"Captain!"

He looked up to see Sergeant Duggan, and for the first time he saw true panic in the eyes of a man he had long respected as unflappable.

"Captain—they're closing in all round!"

Now waves of sound rushed in, pummeling him with a force like punches, a hideous cacophony of guns and screams and dying horses. Fetterman shook his head, as if he might clear it that way, ignoring the arrow in his leg as he tried desperately to peer through the smoke that shrouded the plain around him.

For the briefest of instants, it felt to Captain Fetterman as if there was a concerted pause in the movement around them, as if the assembled tribes had stopped to catch their breath or, rather, to draw a great breath before pushing to the end.

Then they all came at once. Not just the circling, dashing horsemen—but now also hundreds of warriors on foot, somehow even more than before, from everywhere and all at once. What was inescapable to

Fetterman at that moment was that they could not survive, that in a matter of instants they would be overrun, hacked to pieces.

Fetterman became aware that Sergeant Duggan was standing beside him. Duggan gripped his pistol in his right hand but he held his left hand to his temple, his mouth open as if in shock but his face otherwise strangely devoid of emotion. He neither fought nor tried to protect himself in any way.

"Mother of God," he said to Fetterman, his voice more shocked than panicked. "We're done for."

Nearby they heard the crescendo of screams from the soldiers as the crashing wave of Indians washed over their remnant of a perimeter.

Captain Fetterman looked at Duggan, whose eyes formed a desperate question. They had talked about this moment, all of them, but in times of comfortable abstraction, far distant from the terrifying urgency of this instant in which they must now decide, must now act. Fetterman looked around him one final time, but it was all the same in every direction.

They stared at each other an instant longer before Fetterman gave the slightest nod of his head. He spoke the command quietly, words normally barked out with conviction and force.

"Ready . . ."

Fetterman confirmed the one remaining loaded chamber.

"Aim . . ."

Fetterman pointed his pistol at Duggan's temple, even as he stared at the barrel of Duggan's Colt now pointed toward his.

His last word was almost a whisper . . .

"Fire."

Twenty yards away, huddled beside the rocks, Bugler Adolph Metzger watched in disbelief as Fetterman and Duggan killed each other. A man beside him used the toe of his boot to work the trigger on his own rifle, its barrel tipped into his mouth. Most of the men, though, had no remaining bullet to end their own lives. Some prayed or whimpered. A man called out for his mother. A few tried futilely to run away before being cut down.

As Metzger watched the bodies of Fetterman and Duggan collapse to the ground, the sentiment that came to overwhelm him was rage. At first, briefly, rage at the officers for leading them to this place of death.

But this sentiment dissolved quickly into inescapable fury at himself. It was he who had chosen for so long to follow. He now found himself at the end of that path, and it was too late to turn back.

In blind rage, Metzger began to fight.

A warrior with an enormous, bloody war club stood over an infantryman, bashing repeatedly at a body already dead. Metzger screamed with every bit of his force and barreled into the Indian, knocking him to the ground. Metzger landed on his bugle, grabbing it as he stood up, the only weapon he had, bludgeoning the Indian on the side of the head with such force that he could feel the instrument crumple. The Indian ceased moving, but Metzger continued to strike him again and again and felt the man's blood splash into his face.

Metzger looked around him, surrounded now by a ring of Indians. He charged the nearest one, grabbing at the man's hair with his left hand and gouging at his eye with a thumb while crashing the bugle against his enemy's skull. Metzger felt searing hot pain in his back, and it occurred to him that he had been stabbed. He turned to find a warrior stabbing at him with a large knife. He screamed, a sound he did not recognize as his own, feral and crazed. He swung his bugle at the warrior with the knife, but clumsily now, and the warrior easily dodged the blow. Metzger lunged again at the warrior, who again dodged. The world around him began to spin. Metzger's focus seemed to come in and out, the distorted faces surrounding him staring back, the warriors with their horrific paint and weapons, but no one now lifting a hand against him. He raised the bugle and tried again to strike a man with a buffalo bull hat in front of him.

From the ring of warriors, High Backbone stared curiously at the soldier with the brass horn. He was a small man and didn't look like a natural fighter, though his face was spattered with blood. As High Backbone looked around, it appeared that this white man might be the last still living. All the men huddled among the rocks had been slain. There appeared to be no more horse soldiers. The few soldiers who had fled had been easily run down. They had watched as some of the soldiers took their own lives. Few had shown particular bravery—except now this man.

Though staggering, the soldier lunged at High Backbone, clumsily swinging the horn. High Backbone could see that he was mortally wounded in multiple places, and simply pushed him back onto the ground. Still, the man struggled to rise, first rolling to his stomach, then pushing up on his hands and knees, then managing somehow to balance on his knees only. Clearly he wanted to stand, but too much of his life had bled out of him. The soldier's face showed no fear, only sadness, and something about it made High Backbone sad for him.

Most of the men in the circle around the wounded soldier were Minnicoujou, and all deferred to High Backbone, watching this brave white man and awaiting the signal of their chief. It was time to end the man's suffering. High Backbone stepped forward and with a single, swift motion ended the man's pain.

Metzger slumped to the ground. In his last clear thought, he focused on the dim sparkle of golden light against his trumpet. He had always worked to keep his instrument clean, and he felt disappointment at himself that the metal was crumpled and stained by mud and blood.

In the moments before the end of the battle, Crazy Horse, Lone Bear, and Little Hawk had raced to join the Minnicoujou fighting the cluster of surviving soldiers at the outcropping of boulders. Crazy Horse spotted the bullhorn headdress of High Backbone and guided his horse toward his uncle.

"It's good that you're alive," said High Backbone. "You did a great thing today."

Crazy Horse knew that praise from his uncle was not easily won, and he felt honored by the words. He watched his uncle study the position of the soldiers, now reduced to small clutch among the field of boulders. The shots that continued were spaced widely, and the danger now seemed greater from errant arrows than from the soldiers' guns.

"Brothers!" shouted High Backbone. "Let's go finish this!"

A great cry went up from the Minnicoujou, and every warrior on the battlefield charged toward the soldiers among the boulders. Crazy Horse charged forward, too, though he made no effort now to lead. There was killing to be done, and it was necessary, but the battle was over.

Earlier he had admired the bravery and skill with which a few of the whites had fought, but as he drew closer now, he was surprised to see some of them killing themselves. He saw Little Hawk among the warriors who had begun to scalp and otherwise mutilate the bodies. As was his practice, Crazy Horse would not partake, but he understood fully the rage that animated such acts. These men who had been so blind to the beauty of the land did not deserve their eyes in the next life, or the use of their fingers or feet, or the ability to spread their seed. And so it did not shock Crazy Horse to see the orgy of violence that now surrounded him. Whatever uncertainty he felt about the future of his people, it was good, today, to be a part of a victory so complete.

In the end, only one soldier was left alive—a small white man who fought bravely with a brass horn as his war club. He fought on even after he was stabbed a dozen times. Finally, High Backbone took pity, ending the man's life out of mercy. A young warrior had started to scalp the soldier but High Backbone had stopped him, the others understanding that he would be spared mutilation in regard for the brave way that he had died. High Backbone pulled a buffalo robe from his horse and draped it across the small man's body so that all would know to leave him untouched.

There came a moment in the aftermath when the unconscious force that gripped Crazy Horse in battle, making him intensively aware of every danger around him, loosened its grip. He felt his breathing return to normal, was able to separate himself from the battle. He touched his chest as if to confirm that his heart still beat within, and it was then that he felt the bear claw of Lone Bear's necklace. His heart suddenly raced again as he scanned the battlefield for his friend.

He ran to Little Hawk, catching his brother's arm as he raised his war club to bash at the body of a soldier, naked and staring lifeless from the frozen prairie floor. "Where's Lone Bear?" His tone was urgent, almost panicked. "Have you seen Lone Bear?"

The question seemed to surprise Little Hawk, bringing him back from this frenzied place he now occupied. He looked confused at first, disoriented. Then he shook his head, suddenly worried too. "I don't know . . . He was with us"—Little Hawk pointed to the trail descending back down the long ridge, now scattered with the bodies of soldiers and Indians and horses—"as we rode up." Crazy Horse grabbed his horse's mane and pulled himself onto its back, then galloped down the road. His momentary elation at the scale of their victory was subsumed, suddenly and completely, by his fear.

After barely a minute's ride he saw Lone Bear's horse, up ahead and off the side of the road, its head drooping to the ground. Beside the horse he saw that a man lay on the prairie floor. Crazy Horse pressed his own horse to urge it forward faster, dread now gripping him so tightly that he wondered if he might lose his stomach. He leapt from his horse as he arrived at his friend, rushing to be beside him.

Lone Bear's eyes were open, but at first they seemed not to register that Crazy Horse had arrived at his side. Blood had frozen around the wound on the lower left side of Lone Bear's chest, but not before much had spilled. Crazy Horse took his friend's hand and was shocked at how cold it felt, the fingers frozen stiff and almost solid. He tried rubbing the hand and blew against it—big, rapid breaths in an effort to warm it.

He remembered Lone Bear's necklace, reaching desperately to remove it from his own neck, to place it back on Lone Bear. How vain and selfish had he been to accept his friend's talisman. *Look at what I've done!* Crazy Horse felt a new wave of anguish, certain that he had caused this injury to his friend.

Lone Bear coughed, blood appearing at the corners of his mouth, but then his eyes seemed to clear and he focused intently on Crazy Horse. "Did we win?"

Crazy Horse nodded. "Yes, brother. As Moon foresaw . . . a great victory."

"Little Hawk is okay?"

"Better than okay," said Crazy Horse. "He fought bravely and is unhurt."

"Then I feel at peace as I die."

Crazy Horse struggled to find the words to match the reeling thoughts in his head. His first instinct was to deny that Lone Bear would die, to encourage him to take strength, to fight. But he knew that his friend would die, and soon. After a while he said, "I shouldn't have taken your necklace." He felt his tears begin to stream.

A small smile crossed Lone Bear's mouth. "I wanted you to have it," he whispered. "So that we would always ride together."

As Crazy Horse watched, the light in Lone Bear's eyes seemed almost to flicker, like the fading wick in a bowl of tallow, and then it was clear that the life had gone out of him. Crazy Horse felt a low groan escape from his mouth, and he lowered himself slowly until his head came to rest on Lone Bear's chest. He sobbed then, uncontrollably, holding the body of his dead friend, wishing that it might be different.

After a while Crazy Horse heard the pound of hooves behind him, but he didn't look up.

Little Hawk climbed down slowly from his horse, staring at his brother and the body of Lone Bear. For a long time he just stood there, uncertain what to do. Finally, he walked forward and knelt beside Crazy Horse, reaching his arm across his brother's back to grab his shoulder, pulling him close. He held him like that for a moment, then said quietly, "Brother, more soldiers are coming."

Crazy Horse took a deep breath, pressing his hand one last time against Lone Bear's heart before pulling back.

Then he turned to look at Little Hawk. His brother was covered in blood from his face downward, though clearly he was uninjured. "On the ridgeline," said Little Hawk, pointing behind him.

Crazy Horse stood up, his joints suddenly stiff from the cold. He looked past the ongoing frenzy at the boulder field to the ridge beyond, wiping the tears from his eyes to see more clearly. On the ridge stood two lines of foot soldiers, one behind the other. He did a quick count—a tiny fraction of the number needed to confront the great force of the tribes. They were out of rifle range and had stopped moving—as if the ghastly scene in the valley below had rendered them paralyzed. Crazy Horse scanned the soldiers quickly to make sure they had not carried with them the wagon guns, but he saw none.

"Will they come down and fight us?" asked Little Hawk.

Crazy Horse shook his head. "No. And there's no need for us to sacrifice more of our men attacking them on the top of a hill. We fulfilled Moon's prophecy."

They watched the hilltop for a few more moments. Some of the Indians around the boulders taunted the soldiers and motioned them to come down and fight, but the soldiers did not take a single step forward.

Crazy Horse turned and reached to the back of his horse, where a blanket was tied behind the rawhide saddle. He loosened the blanket and unfolded it. "Help me with our brother."

———————————

Captain Ten Eyck panted heavily from the double-time climb to the top of Lodge Trail Ridge. At first, as he peered down, it was difficult to discern what had happened.

"Mother of God," said one of the sergeants in what seemed barely more than a whisper.

Ten Eyck had begun to imagine many forms of calamity as he climbed with the relief party up to the ridgeline, but he had not been prepared for this. Like the other officers that day, he was shocked by numbers for which there was simply no precedent. Several hundred yards below them on the Montana Road, hundreds—perhaps even thousands—of Indian warriors swarmed a rocky outcropping, spreading outward in waves from there.

Ten Eyck's immediate fear was that this great force might turn on him and his men, charge up to their hilltop position. Indeed the savages began to jeer at Ten Eyck's detachment, some waving the soldiers forward and others baring their asses in goading disrespect. Ten Eyck cursed again that he had no cannon.

"Form a skirmish line!" he yelled. "One line forward—one behind. Private Sample!"

The private appeared at his side, still leading Colonel Carrington's big horse.

"Yes, sir," said Sample.

"Ride back and report a massive force of Indians—more than a thousand, perhaps many more. Request again the dispatch of two howitzers and any men that can be spared."

"Yes, sir." Sample paused a moment, uncomfortable. "What do I say, sir, about our men?"

"I can't see any of them," said the sergeant.

Ten Eyck and his men searched for the blue uniforms of their living comrades and did not see them.

Then one of the enlisted men yelled from down the line. "There they are—they're all dead! I see them, Captain—they're all dead!"

As the captain and all the others studied the valley, they did not find the blue of army uniforms but, rather, the stark white of naked skin. They began to see bodies, often in the midst of clusters of Indians, who bludgeoned and hacked at the corpses in what seemed like demonic possession. With eyes suddenly adjusted to the horrific nature of this activity, Ten Eyck and his men now began to see bodies everywhere in the valley below.

"Heaven help us . . ." said Ten Eyck in shock. "Can they all be dead?"

From the top of a distant plateau, Red Cloud felt an elation different from any in his life. He had won many victories in his years as a warrior and a chief, but never anything like this. He marveled at the completeness of their conquest, saw that they had killed every soldier who rode into their careful trap. Along with this happiness, he felt enormous relief, acutely aware of the responsibility of sending so many men into battle.

He saw now the new group of soldiers on the ridgeline, sent out too late from the fort to make any difference. Briefly he contemplated whether they should attack these men, too, or even the fort itself. Both of these ideas, though, he pushed aside. The soldiers on the ridgeline were inconsequential in the victory they already had won.

Red Cloud's plan had never been to ride over the fort but, rather, to shock the whites into retreat. Had they achieved the necessary shock today to bring about this result? Perhaps the whites would seek an easier path to the places they dug their gold. Only time would tell. Certainly, though, the victory they achieved had given them a chance. As for the fort, even without the scores of soldiers they killed today, many remained. More important, the fort bristled with wagon guns.

Beyond these practical considerations, Red Cloud also believed in an ebb and flow in life's events. The Creator already had bestowed upon them an enormous gift in this day. He questioned the greed of pressing now for more. Already they had fought deep into the Moon of Midwinter, setting aside many of the preparations that he knew were necessary to ensure they would be safe against the brutal months ahead. They had fought this battle because they had no choice. Now, though, they needed to try to return to the rhythms that dictated their lives.

Red Cloud offered a brief prayer to the Creator, thanking him again, then turned his horse toward the outcropping of boulders to join his people, to revel together in the greatest victory they had ever known.

From the northeast barbican, Colonel Carrington was a taut jumble of nervousness and fear, anger and self-doubt. He had watched for half an hour while Captain Ten Eyck had marched his relief column toward Lodge Trail Ridge. After the creek crossing, he felt he had practically willed his men step by step up the long hill to Lodge Trail Ridge. There, he watched Ten Eyck form a double skirmish line, fearing it meant they were preparing to confront an assault.

Then he saw Private Sample galloping back toward the fort, surely with news of the fate of Fetterman and his men. It took an excruciating ten minutes for Sample to cover the distance. By that time, all of the fort's inhabitants had gathered inside the gate to await the news. The soldiers not dispatched with Fetterman or Ten Eyck, around a hundred, stood with rifles at the ready around the ramparts. Carrington saw his wife standing near Mrs. Grummond, who was arm in arm with one of the laundresses. The laundress sobbed, though Carrington could see that Mrs. Grummond, admirably, managed to keep her composure.

Carrington descended the barbican and hurried to the gate, which swung open as Sample rode in on the gray. Sample reined the horse in front of the big group, looking at Carrington.

"It's bad, sir." Sample struggled to catch his breath, and his face was ashen, looking back and forth between Carrington and the wives.

"Tell us, Private," said Carrington.

"There's a thousand Indians or more over the ridge—they're calling for Captain Ten Eyck to come down and fight. He's asking for two howitzers."

"A thousand! Are they attacking Ten Eyck's position?"

"Not when I left, sir."

Carrington paused for a moment. "And Captain Fetterman and his men?"

Sample swallowed, looking again to the wives. "Captain Ten Eyck is afraid Captain Fetterman's party is all gone up, sir."

"All gone up?" said Carrington, confused.

"Yes, sir. All gone up . . . All dead, sir."

Gasps and cries rose up from the assembled crowd.

Next to Mrs. Grummond, the laundress collapsed to her knees, rocking back and forth in silent anguish. Mrs. Grummond dropped beside her, pulling the laundress close, her own face stoic. Other women, too, began to sob, and some of the men on the ramparts.

Colonel Carrington felt as if he were suddenly stricken, his mind numb even as he searched for the right order, desperate somehow to set things back on track.

"Colonel . . ."

Carrington became aware of Private Sample's voice, as if calling across a great distance.

"Colonel . . . Captain Ten Eyck is requesting reinforcements—and two howitzers. Should we send them, sir?"

Colonel Carrington looked around him, at all the shocked and fearful faces looking back to him. "We can't . . . We can't spare the men or the cannon, and we don't have the horses to haul them, even if we wanted to." He took a deep breath. "Ride back out, Private. Tell Captain Ten Eyck to act with extreme caution. We need him back here to defend the fort."

SAME DAY—1:10 P.M.

The moment of Private Sample's return with news of the massacre was the most confusing of Frances Grummond's life, more difficult even than the conflict created within her family by the war. She felt the immediate anguish of Janey at the loss of Sergeant Lang, almost as if it transmitted directly between their two bodies as she held her friend. She felt the gravity of the moment—the deaths of so many men, many of whom she knew as friends and all of whom had shared this tiny community they had built together from the ground up over the past five months. She also understood fully the danger that the fort and its inhabitants still faced, vulnerable now against direct attack by this huge force of Indians. In all of this Frances felt grief and fear, bone-deep.

Yet Frances felt another thread of emotion, instant and equally powerful. It shocked her at first and felt wholly wrong, yet it flooded over her so completely that there was no way to deny it: she felt relief that veered almost into elation at the death of her husband.

Paralyzed for a long time by this swirl of emotions, Frances simply sat on the hard ground and held tightly to Janey. The colonel and Mrs. Carrington and others came to pat Frances on the shoulder and offer words that, though well intentioned, disappeared the instant they were spoken. After a while, Janey began to shake, not only in her anguish but also from the frigid air that seemed to settle behind the log walls of the fort. Frances gently urged Janey to her feet and led her back to the Grummonds' quarters, taking her inside and setting her down on the bed. She wrapped Janey in a shawl, then set about to stoke the fire in the stove and to boil water for tea. It felt good for those moments to be focused on Janey and occupied with tangible tasks.

Around dusk, Frances heard commotion from outside. Darkness had fallen when, an hour later, there was a knock at her door. She opened it to find Colonel Carrington. He glanced behind her at Janey, still huddled in the shawl on the bed. "I'm very sorry to disturb you," he said. "But may I come in for a minute?"

Frances nodded and the colonel entered. Then he delivered the lines that he had practiced in his head as he walked to the Grummonds' quarters.

"I'm sorry, Mrs. Grummond, that I have only grim news to share," he said. "Captain Ten Eyck has come back and confirmed our worst fears. He recovered the remains of forty-nine of our fellow soldiers. I'm afraid that thirty more of our soldiers and Mr. Wheatley and Mr. Fisher are still on the field."

Colonel Carrington was having a difficult time reading Mrs. Grummond's reaction. The eyes of the laundress, whom Carrington had learned was named Mrs. White, were bloodshot from what had obviously been hours of crying. Mrs. Carrington had told him that Mrs. White, a Confederate widow and apparently a woman of mixed repute, had nevertheless been betrothed to Sergeant Lang. It appeared that the poor woman was exhausted. Mrs. Grummond, though, was strangely composed. Perhaps, thought Carrington, she has poured all of her strength into supporting Mrs. White. *Perhaps it's her way of pushing aside the difficulty of dealing with her own feelings.*

When Frances's lack of any response become uncomfortable, Colonel Carrington continued with his lines. "I'm afraid that the remains of Lieutenant Grummond are among those still on the field." He looked behind Mrs. Grummond to the laundress. "Mrs. White, nor have we yet to recover the remains of Sergeant Lang." Colonel Carrington did his best to occupy the full space of his uniform. "I understand it must be horrible for you to know that your loved ones are not yet in our full embrace. I want both of you to know that at dawn, I will personally lead a detachment of our men, and we will not rest until we have brought all of our soldiers home from the battlefield."

Mrs. White began quietly to weep. After another uncomfortable pause, Frances finally nodded her head. "I thank you, Colonel." Colonel Carrington nodded back, stepped forward to give Mrs. Grummond a quick, awkward embrace, then departed into the night.

Janey stayed with Frances that night. They said very little to each other the next day, though each seemed to find quiet comfort in the presence of the other. Mrs. Carrington and some of the other women whose husbands had not ridden out with Captain Fetterman came by with breakfast, and then with lunch. Frances appreciated the gesture and their efforts to find meaningful words, though of course there were none. Reverend Woodward came, too, and they prayed together for strength and for the souls of the departed.

In late afternoon there came another knock at the door, and Frances again found Colonel Carrington. The frigid cold had continued through the day. Apart from bare hands, Carrington wore his full winter gear and appeared to have just returned from his gruesome mission. Frances invited him inside.

"As I promised you, we have brought back Lieutenant Grummond and Sergeant Lang," said the colonel. This time, Carrington knew not to wait for responses, instead barreling ahead. "I'm afraid the savages have committed depredations against all of the bodies. Doctor Rutt will prepare all of our men for burial, but there can be no viewings."

Frances saw now that Colonel Carrington carried two envelopes in his hand. On one was written *Lt Grummond* and on the other *Sgt Lang*. He handed the Grummond envelope to Frances and the Lang envelope to Janey. "I hope this gives you a small measure of peace . . . My prayers are with you." Carrington looked at Frances. "Please don't hesitate to ask me or Mrs. Carrington for anything," he said. Then he tipped his hat and departed.

Hands trembling, Janey opened her envelope. Inside was a lock of hair. She took a deep breath and then slowly let it out. This time, though, she did not weep. Instead, she reached to embrace Frances, holding her tightly before pulling back. "I'm grateful to you for letting me stay with you," she said. "I need to go now, and I know you need your own time too."

They embraced again; then Janey gathered her shawl and left.

After Janey was gone, Frances stared for a long time at the envelope. Finally, still standing, she opened it. Within, she recognized immediately the dark, coarse hair of her husband. Quickly, she closed the envelope, then strode rapidly to the stove. She opened its cast-iron door, the fire inside roaring with renewed life at the breath of outside air. Without hesitation, she threw the envelope inside. Then she watched as the flames leapt up to swallow the envelope and its contents, the fresh fuel so combustible that it was gone almost instantly, practically evaporating before her eyes.

Frances felt a wave of powerful emotion, the strangest sensation of her life, as if a crushing weight on top of her had abruptly been lifted away by some unseen hand. Through this strange Providence, she was free of him. For a brief moment, she posed to herself the question of whether she should feel guilty. But then she quickly pushed this sentiment down, and made a silent vow never to consider the thought again.

Another impulse occurred to her, and she hurried to her trunk, throwing open the lid. She rummaged inside to find the two journals. She unlocked one and opened it, seeing the *Dear Friend* introductions to her secret entries, and set it carefully aside. The other journal she grabbed, returned to the stove, and threw it in, the flames seeming eager to receive this fuel too.

As she watched it burn, her legs felt suddenly weak. She lowered herself to the floor, afraid that otherwise she might collapse. She sat there, holding her swollen belly and watching the journal as the flames eventually consumed it. Only then did she begin to weep.

APRIL 1, 1867

Crazy Horse sat alone atop his horse, looking down into the valley of the Twin Creeks.

It seemed strange that this was the ridgeline, indeed the precise place on the ridgeline, where he and the other decoys had led the soldiers to their deaths only a few months before. He remembered turning back to look at the pursuing soldiers, wondering if they would follow, and knowing that everything else depended on whether they did.

A band of snow clung to the ridge, winter's last grip. The snow melted away quickly as the hill swept down into the valley toward the fort. Crazy Horse tried to focus on the faint sheen of green that just managed to press up from the matted dead grasses of the season past. His eye, though, was drawn to the fort, as if swept there by the swift current of a river, its waters pressed between the narrow walls of a canyon.

It struck Crazy Horse that the fort seemed very much alive. The massive flag billowed in the stiff spring breeze and smoke rose up from dozens of chimneys. In the big open space inside the fort, soldiers marched in formation and at the far end, horses fed from a stack of hay. Beyond the fort, toward the lookout hill, he saw the place where the whites put their dead and he saw that they had now put up scores of their white crosses.

The view from the ridgeline came with a stiff wind and today it blew in from the southeast. Bright sun gave an illusion of warmth but there was no hiding from the wind's bite. When he first heard the sound of the drums he thought it came from within the fort, but then realized it came from farther beyond—from over the horizon to the south. Soon the sentinels on the lookout hill were waving their flags to signal an arrival. Now inside the fort soldiers scrambled, running to look outward from positions at their towers and along the ramparts.

It took several more minutes before the column first came into view. As Crazy Horse watched, four officers crested the hill where the Montana Road came up from Fort Laramie. Then he saw mounted scouts out on the flanks. Next came horse soldiers and then row after row of the soldiers on foot, long knives gleaming at the tips of their rifles. There were wagons too; Crazy Horse counted more than sixty. Then came a remuda of horses, and last, a new herd of cattle—hundreds, maybe a thousand. On and on they streamed over the distant hilltop, flooding into the valley of the Twin Creeks, filling it up, supplanting the land with their great and swarming mass.

Crazy Horse had seen all of this before. They looked like locusts.

APRIL 16, 1867

His sense of smell, like his vision, was not as acute as in the past. But Jim Bridger had no problem appreciating the scent of spring rain, dense and sweet as it mixed with the earth and grasses to convey the pregnant potential of the season.

It was a frivolous thing, to climb Scott's Bluff. Certainly that was the old mare's opinion. She saw no reason to veer from the flat and inviting valley of the Platte to scramble up the steep plateau. Knowing it was frivolous, and feeling for his horse, Bridger dismounted and led her, at least sparing the mare the burden of hauling him.

Still, he saw good reason to make the effort. He had seen the towering plateau on dozens of earlier voyages but never paused to climb it. Decades ago, Bridger heard a story about Scott, the formation's namesake. In the early days the man apparently had been traveling near the bluff when he had been shot by Indians. He managed to escape, eventually crawling up against the base of the plateau to die alone. Bridger didn't remember anyone knowing more of Scott's story than that, but at least the poor soul left some mark for his sufferings. Bridger wondered if Scott's family had been informed of his death, or if his descendants knew that there was now a prominent bit of land with his name on it in the valley of the Platte River. Bridger knew a fair number of places like that, places given the name of some poor bastard—the only thing known about them being that they died, usually in some fashion that was not peaceful.

If he thought about it, and lately he did, Bridger felt lucky to have left his name on a place or two without having had to die for the honor. He wondered if his children knew, and he hoped they would be proud of him.

Truth was, his time with Beckwourth had set Bridger to thinking about all sorts of things. It was as if his time with his old friend had bored a hole in a dam. For a while the dam had pooled up all sorts of his thoughts, but now they all came flooding out. It was irritating, in part. Some things he might well have been content to leave lie. Then again, there was something cowardly in that approach that didn't sit right.

One part of his conversation with Beckwourth had stuck with Bridger the most—the part about whether he and Beckwourth and the other trappers had been free to do "whatever the hell they wanted," as Beckwourth had put it. Bridger had thought about that over and over, mile after mile as he had made his way south from Fort Phil Kearny, and now east from Fort Laramie.

Certainly they had a lot more freedom than most men, and Bridger was grateful for a life that had allowed him to wander half a continent. As he had reflected, though—if he was honest with himself—it occurred to him that some part of that freedom had come at the expense of other people.

Since the Fetterman Massacre, as it had already come to be called, Bridger had been thinking a lot about the Indians. True, the Sioux and the Cheyenne had won a great victory and the United States Army had suffered a great defeat. Colonel Carrington had been relieved of his command, and it was whispered that his career was ruined. At Fort Laramie, there were rumors that the whole Montana Road might be abandoned along with the forts that guarded it. Bridger was skeptical about that. Maybe the whites would turn away for a while, but he was pretty sure that eventually they would turn back, certainly so long as there was gold in Montana.

In his almost half century on the frontier, there had been ebbs and flows, but the direction of the current always had been clear. The war between the states had distracted people back east for a while, but Bridger already had seen the swell of easterners now that the war was over, and it didn't seem likely to abate. He had trouble seeing how the Indians would fit in. One time, Colonel Carrington had mentioned a plan to turn them all into Christian farmers and Bridger had laughed out loud. Anyone who thought that would work had never spent time west of the Mississippi. The more Bridger thought about the Indians, the more he felt nostalgic or even sad. He pushed those thoughts from his mind, though. Beckwourth was right about one thing—no sense worrying too much about things that can't be changed.

He felt a bit the same way about his three wives, all of them now dead. As he reflected, he believed that he had treated them all well; certainly he hoped he had. He knew that he had endeavored to be kind. He had always assumed that they understood he was a wanderer, and that wandering off periodically was a part of the bargain. But had they understood? Had he been honest enough? And was it a fair bargain in any event? Nothing he could change now, and he had no interest in marrying again.

His children were a different matter. He had kids by all three of his wives—some still with the tribes, some he had sent back east. He had seen his children with the Shoshone a few years back, but none of the others for more years than he could account. The more he thought about that, the more it bothered him. At the Crow village, it was evident that Beckwourth had the affection of his wives and his children. And when Beckwourth told Bridger that he would stay with the Crow, he told him that part of his decision was his desire to watch them grow up.

Bridger was amid this jumble of thoughts when his first encounter with a telegraph machine at Fort Laramie caused him to make an impetuous decision. Some of the officers had taken him to see the machine, and explained how it worked, how a message could be sent across the country instantaneously. Skeptical but intrigued, Bridger had paid the sum of five dollars to send two lines to his daughter in faraway Missouri. *Hope you are well. Would like to visit.* Then he had worried and paid two dollars and fifty cents for an additional line: *If it is not an inconvenience.*

In what seemed to Bridger to be a miracle at every level, a young boy tracked him down the next day with a paper that the boy said was a return message from his daughter. He asked the boy to read it. *We are well. You are the grandfather of three fine boys and we hope you will visit soon.* The message had filled Bridger with waves of emotions he had not expected. For the first time in his life, he felt a powerful attraction away from the Rocky Mountains.

Bridger's mind had been so occupied with his thoughts that he barely had time to feel tired before he reached the top of Scott's Bluff. Now, though, at the summit, he had to marvel. Bridger had never thought of the Platte as one of the more beautiful rivers, but the sun had settled low in the Platte Valley, and it almost seemed as if the river, stretching out as far as the eye could see, was ablaze in golden light.

There were more plateaus in both directions, not as big as mountains, but, nonetheless, impressive chunks of rock jutting up abruptly from the surrounding prairie. This had been Cheyenne territory when Bridger had first come west, and Bridger could see why they liked it. Of course there were no buffalo here anymore. Even now, Bridger could see three separate clusters of emigrant wagons in the valley below. At Fort Laramie, they said the Fetterman Massacre might cut down the traffic up the Powder River Valley, but the army expected more pioneers than ever this summer on the trails to Utah, Oregon, and California. Nor was the Powder River Valley the only road to Montana. *They'll find a way.*

On the far western horizon, Bridger could see a lone mountain— Laramie Peak, another place named for some man who got himself killed. The peak wasn't visible from the valley, and it occurred suddenly to Bridger that this would be his last view of the Rockies for a while, and he tried not to take things for granted. While he intended to come back, the truth was that there was some possibility that he might not, or might not be able. For a moment it felt as his breath was cut off, and he realized that he had never been to the top of Laramie Peak. He questioned suddenly if he was making a mistake. Jim Bridger, trailblazer and scout, headed in the wrong direction.

The mare snorted, and through instinct Bridger scanned the horizons for any danger. There was nothing, though. The old girl just wanted some attention. Bridger laughed and reached into his saddlebag to produce a lump of sugar, procured from the sutler at Fort Laramie. He offered it to the mare on an open palm, and she accepted it with a smack of her big tongue. Bridger laughed again, laughed at the mare and how silly it had been to spend so much money on sugar for a horse. He took a final glance, and then he turned away from Laramie Peak and the setting sun and the West and looked east, where the Platte flowed onward downstream. He knew a campsite where a creek flowed into the muddy river with clear spring water. It was a few miles farther than he had intended to ride that day, but surely the old mare deserved clear, cold water after a hard day's ride.

APRIL 20, 1867

The embers of a low fire cast the only light in Moon's tent when Crazy Horse entered. The first sensations weren't visual, in any event, but, rather, a muddle of scents. Sweetgrass was the strongest, which Crazy Horse had always associated with his friend. But there was another strong scent, strange for so early in spring—roses. Crazy Horse saw the source—a crude wooden basin filled with dried flowers, including the crimson buds, floating in water.

As his eyes adjusted, Crazy Horse saw the curious collection of objects with which Moon surrounded himself. There were skulls of every variety, from tiny birds to an enormous bull buffalo. One skull was human, with an old stone arrowhead embedded in its forehead. There was a deerskin laid out flat with a collection of dozens of pieces of knotted wood, the branches twisted like an old person's hands. Another deerskin displayed an array of feathers, arranged from the largest to the smallest, some common but others in colors so rare that Crazy Horse had seen them only a time or two in his life, and a few not at all.

Crazy Horse did not visit Moon often, yet he knew he was always welcome. He came to see Moon when he had wrestled with a question for a long time without finding an answer. He knew only a handful of other men to whom he could turn for advice, usually older men like High Backbone or his father. Today, though, he sensed that Moon might be the only person in the tribe with whom he could share the thoughts that so vexed him.

"Sit and smoke, my friend," said Moon.

Crazy Horse sat down on a thick robe beside the glowing coals, appreciative of the waves of heat that seeped off them. The season offered the hope of warmth to come, but they were still far from summer. He watched as Moon packed his long pipe with tobacco, then lit it with a burning branch from the fire. He puffed a few times to make sure the spark was sustained before handing the pipe to Crazy Horse. For a long time they sat in silence, passing the pipe back and forth, the rich smell of the tobacco adding another layer to the mix of sensations. Something about the pipe seemed to lend itself to contemplation, and yet even here—in a space built by Moon to facilitate thinking and insight—Crazy Horse could not break through the fog that clouded his thoughts.

"You came here to ask about the future." Moon said it not as a question, but as a statement.

Crazy Horse nodded. "I've contemplated and fasted and prayed with all my might—but I can't see it."

"You helped our people to win a great victory over the whites," said Moon. "Doesn't that encourage you?"

"I'm happy for what we did—but I'm afraid of what I can't see."

Moon was quiet for a long time, so much so that Crazy Horse began to wonder if he would speak anymore at all that day. Moon had a different way of managing his conversations. He didn't always conclude his interactions with the normal good-byes. If a conversation took place outside his lodge, sometimes he would simply walk away. Inside his lodge, he might turn at some point to another task or even lie down and sleep. If other people did this, it might be rude, but with Moon, it was just his way.

Moon took a willow stick and stirred the fire, poking at the white-silver edge of a cottonwood log so that a chunk crumbled away and flames jumped up to consume the freshly revealed fuel. The flame illuminated Moon's face so that Crazy Horse could see him clearly, and he was certain that he had never seen his friend look so despondent.

"I've been having a dream," said Moon. "And I've been struggling to understand it."

Crazy Horse said nothing, but stared expectantly. When finally

Moon spoke again, he said, "I've been having a dream about the melting snow on the mountaintops."

Again Moon was quiet for a long time, until finally Crazy Horse asked, "In the spring?"

"Yes," said Moon. "And at first I thought it was a good vision—winter giving way to fresh life."

Part of Crazy Horse sensed that he did not want to hear Moon's vision, and so he stopped encouraging his friend, but Moon continued. "You know how the snow in winter is packed on the peaks of the Shining Mountains, higher than a man's head? In the spring, we know the snow will melt, and the water will gather volume and force as it flows down from the highest peaks . . .

"There'll be moments when the water finds a depression, pauses, pools up for a time, but as more water keeps coming, eventually it'll be pushed down the hill again. The farther it flows down the mountain, the more waters are gathered, tiny draws flooding into bigger ones. Until it courses into the valley."

Crazy Horse listened closely. He respected Moon, of course—it's why he came. But he sensed where this was going and felt compelled to push back. "The floods come each spring," he said. "The waters rise and then after a few weeks they begin to fall."

Moon shook his head. "In this dream, it's different. The waters I've seen come crashing into the valley. They overflow the banks and there's so much that even the broad plain can't contain them." He looked hard at Crazy Horse. "And so they wash over everything . . . wash everything away."

Moon looked Crazy Horse directly in the eye. "Perhaps someone who knew the flood was coming could go away. He could take his family and a few friends to high ground where even these waters couldn't reach."

Now it was Crazy Horse's turn to be silent. He reached for the pipe and drew deeply from its bowl, watching the embers turn crimson as he breathed through them, feeling the smoke fill his lungs. The smoke was supposed to cleanse—though Crazy Horse felt no such sensation today as he exhaled, pushing the breath from his body.

"Our people live together in the valley," said Crazy Horse after a while. "And that's where we've always lived."

Moon nodded.

Outside, the wind blew fiercely, causing the smoke that hung around the two men to draw rapidly upward before passing through the opening at the top of the lodge, then disappearing into the dark night as if it had never been.

HISTORICAL NOTES AND FURTHER READING

Ridgeline is a work of historical fiction. It is based on true events and real people, but I have imagined the many things that history leaves unclear, particularly the characters' inner thoughts, conversations, and details of events like the final battle, where the various historical accounts are incomplete and conflicting. I have worked to stay true to important facts so that readers are not left with a misimpression of historical events. (I took some liberties with more minor points of chronology. For example, I portray most of the major characters arriving at the site for Fort Phil Kearny at the same time, when in fact many arrived at different times over the course of the fall of 1866.)

When I read historical fiction or watch films with historical settings, I'm always curious about the line between fact and fiction, so below I call out a few places where I took more significant liberties and suggest further nonfiction sources for readers who want to learn more.

THE FETTERMAN FIGHT AND RED CLOUD'S WAR

The Fetterman Fight (known popularly as the Fetterman Massacre and known to the Lakota as the Battle of the Hundred in the Hand for the *winkte's* prophecy) and the broader Red Cloud's War of 1866–68 represent, in many ways, the zenith of Native American efforts to resist the white invasion of their lands in the American West. Shocked by the tribes' dramatic victory over Fetterman and still weary of conflict in the aftermath of the Civil War, the US government effectively surrendered to Red Cloud and the allied tribes, although the tribes' victory required more than a year of further fighting. In a treaty agreed to by US negotiators in the summer of 1868 at Fort Laramie, the United States effectively re-recognized the tribes' dominion of the Powder River Valley and a vast track of land including the Black Hills and much of modern-day South Dakota. The US also agreed to abandon the Montana Road (often called the Bozeman Trail) along with Fort Phil Kearny and two other forts built to defend the road.

When the US Army abandoned Fort Phil Kearny in August 1868, the Lakota or the Cheyenne (accounts vary) promptly burned it to the ground. For a few years, the Lakota, Cheyenne, and Arapaho tribes lived with less conflict in the Powder River Valley and nearby Black Hills—at least by comparison to the events soon to transpire.

In a tragically consistent pattern, the United States betrayed its obligations under the Treaty of 1868 in favor of gold. On July 2, 1874, the US Army dispatched a large expedition to explore the Black Hills. The primary purpose of the expedition was to find the site for a new fort. The commander of the expedition of more than one thousand men, Colonel George Armstrong Custer, had an additional priority. There had been rumors of gold in the Black Hills for many years, and Custer intended to find out if they were true. He personally made sure that his expedition included civilians with knowledge of mining. The Black Hills Expedition of 1874 did indeed find gold, and Custer dispatched a trusted scout to convey the news to Fort Laramie.

The gold rush to the Black Hills began immediately, setting in motion the events that would lead quickly to the tragic end of the Indian Wars on the northern plains. When a delegation of Indian leaders including Red Cloud refused to sell the Black Hills for $6 million, the US Army simply issued an order that the tribes must report to new, smaller reservations—or be considered hostile. Rather than accept reservation life, many Lakota and Cheyenne, including bands led by Sitting Bull and Crazy Horse, retreated to the plains of eastern Montana.

In May 1876, Colonel Custer led a regiment of cavalry with orders to force the Lakota and Cheyenne onto reservations. On June 25, 1876, less than a hundred miles north of the burned remnants of Fort Phil Kearny, Custer and more than two hundred of his men were killed after attacking an enormous village of Lakota and Cheyenne along the Little Bighorn River, known to natives as the Greasy Grass.

In the aftermath of the 1866 Fetterman Fight, the politics of the nation had recoiled from violent conflict on the distant frontier. By 1876, however, the nation's mood had changed. The manifest destiny of the United States was to be a continental nation, and no longer was there a place for migratory peoples who for centuries had made their lives on vast plains, following the buffalo. Once the US government brought the full force of "total war" against Native Americans on the northern plains, their destiny, too, was manifest. Within two years, the last of the tribes either had been forced onto reservations or fled into Canadian exile.

For readers interested in nonfiction books on the Fetterman Fight and Red Cloud's War, the classic account is Dee Brown's *The Fetterman Massacre*, published in 1962. Brown, also author of the influential *Bury My Heart at Wounded Knee*, is an evocative writer, but he presents the traditional explanation of the Fetterman Fight—placing much of the blame on Fetterman. This traditional history is based largely on Colonel Carrington's long effort—together with his two wives—to shift blame away from himself. The central pillar of this narrative was to place the blame on Captain Fetterman, both as the ranking officer on the battlefield and as having violated Carrington's orders not to cross Lodge Trail Ridge. This narrative was conveyed through a popular book written by Carrington's first wife, Margaret Carrington (see below). The same narrative was conveyed in a book written by Carrington's second wife, Frances Grummond (more about Frances below). Another entertaining nonfiction account of Red Cloud's War is *The Heart of Everything That Is* by Bob Drury and Tom Clavin.

In my view, the best scholarship on the Fetterman Fight, and the books that I believe provide the most persuasive historical explanation of the battle, are John H. Monnett's *Where a Hundred Soldiers Were Killed* and Shannon D. Smith's *Give Me Eighty Men: Women and the Myth of the Fetterman Fight*. Monnett and Smith both conclude that, while there was plenty of blame to share, it is far more likely that Lieutenant George Washington Grummond was the brash, arrogant officer who deliberately defied orders and fatefully led his fellow soldiers over Lodge Trail Ridge, with Fetterman left to trail after him.

One controversial detail of the battle is whether Fetterman and another soldier committed mutual suicide as the battle came to its climax. Dee Brown embraces this idea in his book, but there is also evidence to the contrary. The post surgeon, who examined the soldiers' bodies when they were brought back to the fort, claimed that there was no gunshot wound on Fetterman's head. (It is worth remembering that Fetterman's body, like most of the others, had been mutilated.) Another important piece of evidence is a credible claim by American Horse, an Oglala warrior, that he killed Fetterman.

Broader histories of the American West include *The Legacy of Conquest* by Patricia Nelson Limerick and *The Heartbeat of Wounded Knee* by David Treuer. Treuer's book focuses on the important history of Native Americans after 1890. A useful online resource for Native historical perspectives is *Reclaiming Native Truth* at rnt.firstnations.org.

The sites of Fort Phil Kearny and the nearby Fetterman Fight battlefield are preserved today as Wyoming State historic sites. The landscape of the Powder River Valley has changed in some ways over the past one hundred and fifty years, but it is not hard to imagine what it looked like in 1866. The sprawling perimeter of the old fort is preserved. There is an outstanding visitor center with a knowledgeable and friendly staff. Most evocative is the Fetterman Fight battlefield itself, with interpretive signage that provides insight into both US Army and Native American perspectives on the battle. Many days, visitors can experience the battlefield with few other people present. We all owe a debt of gratitude to the people, past and present, who have helped to preserve and interpret these historical sites, including Sonny Reisch, Robert Wilson, Misty Stoll, and the fantastic Starr Zabel. The nearby towns of Story, Sheridan, and Buffalo (don't miss the vintage Occidental Hotel, with a great bar and restaurant) all are well worth visiting. Visitors to Fort Phil Kearny can continue northwest near the path of the old Montana Road, stopping off to visit the site of the Battle of the Little Bighorn on their way to the mountains of Montana.

Visitors to Wyoming with an interest in history should not miss Fort Laramie National Historic Site, a font of Western American history, including the fur trade era, the Oregon Trail, and the Indian Wars. A significant part of my interest in history was born during my high school and college summers, when I wore an 1876 cavalry uniform and worked at Fort Laramie as a National Park Service "living history interpreter." Sadly, there is less funding for such programs today, but Fort Laramie and the North Platte Valley remain wonderful places to visit, authentic in an era of homogenized travel and culture.

RED CLOUD

While the Fetterman Fight was the decisive moment in Red Cloud's War, it was not until April 1868 that the US government's peace commission arrived at Fort Laramie to negotiate the treaty. Red Cloud refused to attend, insisting that the United States abandon the Montana Road and the three forts defending it *before* he would sign anything. Such was the impact of Red Cloud's Lakota alliance victory that the United States met his demands. Red Cloud ultimately signed in November 1868. The forty-seven-year-old chief rode into Fort Laramie in triumph, but also no doubt weary from a lifetime spent battling to protect his people and their culture against the tide of white settlement.

Red Cloud would not take up arms again, though he would fight bureaucratic and diplomatic wars—including among his own people— for the rest of his life. Red Cloud died in 1909 at the age of eighty-seven. As an old man, he said the following about his experiences in dealing with the United States government: "They made us many promises, more than I can remember. But they kept but one. They promised to take our land . . . and they took it."

CRAZY HORSE

Perhaps fitting for someone known for his humility, Crazy Horse, though much admired and much studied, retains an aura of mystery. For example, he never allowed himself to be photographed.

After the events in this book, Crazy Horse would spend the rest of his too-short life defending his people and their traditional way of life. His greatest fame would come for his bravery and skill in leading his people as the Indian Wars on the Northern Plains reached their tragic climax. On June 25, 1876, Crazy Horse was one of the Lakota and Cheyenne leaders who decimated Colonel George Armstrong Custer at the Battle of the Little Bighorn, known to Lakota as the Battle of the Greasy Grass.

The great victory on the Greasy Grass was short-lived. News of Custer's defeat didn't arrive in Washington, DC, until the Fourth of July—literally in the midst of the nation's centennial celebration. In contrast to the aftermath of the Fetterman Fight, the political call for defeat of the plains Indians was swift and resounding. And once fully mobilized in all its "vindictive earnestness" (to quote General William Tecumseh Sherman), the outcome was assured. In the fall of 1876, Crazy Horse led a band of his people, who retreated into the Shining (Bighorn) Mountains.

One aspect of the newfound resolve to crush Indian resistance was the strategy of fighting them in winter, when weather severely restricted the Lakota's mobility. On January 8, 1877, in a battle at the Crazy Horse band's Tongue River encampment, they managed to fight off attack from the relentless General Nelson Miles. Harried and hungry throughout the winter, though, by spring it became clear that the days of the Lakota as nomadic hunters were over. On May 6, 1877, Crazy Horse led eleven hundred of his people to surrender at the Red Cloud reservation near Fort Robinson in modern-day Nebraska.

The history of Crazy Horse's few months on the reservation is convoluted and tragic, including bitter rivalries among different bands of the Lakota. In September 1877, Crazy Horse fled the Red Cloud reservation for the Spotted Tail reservation, in part, he hoped, to place his ailing wife in the protection of members of her family.

The US Army sent their own forces along with Oglala allies to take Crazy Horse back to Fort Robinson, by force if necessary. Upon his return to Fort Robinson, there were orders to transport Crazy Horse to be imprisoned in Fort Marion, Florida. When he arrived at Fort Robinson under heavy guard, Crazy Horse realized that he was to be placed behind bars at the guardhouse. When he resisted, he was grabbed from behind by some of his own people, including Little Big Man, and a US soldier delivered two fatal thrusts with a bayonet. Crazy Horse died later that evening, on September 5, 1877, in the company of Worm, his father.

Of the many books on Crazy Horse, Kingsley M. Bray's *Crazy Horse* is the most comprehensive. I found Joseph M. Marshall III's *The Journey of Crazy Horse* to be particularly insightful, and especially important in understanding the Lakota perspective and the oral history of Crazy Horse's life.

LITTLE HAWK

While it is almost certainly true that Crazy Horse was a teacher and mentor to his younger half brother, Little Hawk, the difference in their ages was probably less than I've portrayed and may have been only a couple years. Little Hawk died in battle against the US Army along the Platte River in 1871.

MOON

I invented the name Moon for the character of the *winkte* prophet. Though the real person's name is not known, there is significant historical evidence that a transgender Lakota played a prominent role in the battle, consistent with my portrayal in *Ridgeline*. I relied most heavily on details published by ethnologist and conservationist George Bird Grinnell. Grinnell conducted extensive research of the Fetterman Fight at the turn of the twentieth century, including personal research on the battlefield in the company of White Elk, a Cheyenne who participated in the battle as a young man. Grinnell's 1915 book, *The Fighting Cheyenne*, relates White Elk's detailed account of "a person, half man, half woman," who prophesized the Indian victory over Fetterman and his men.

COLONEL HENRY CARRINGTON

Carrington's bad luck continued in the aftermath of the Fetterman Fight. Having been relieved of command of his beloved Fort Phil Kearny, he traveled via army wagon train to Fort Laramie through a frigid Powder River February. During the trip, he accidently shot himself in the thigh with his pistol and spent several weeks recovering.

Aided, eventually, by two wives, Carrington would spend the rest of his life seeking to avoid blame for the Fetterman Massacre, largely by creating a false narrative about Captain Fetterman that predominated for more than a hundred years: that an arrogant and reckless Captain Fetterman led his men to their deaths after ignoring Colonel Carrington's order not to cross Lodge Trail Ridge.

ADOLPH METZGER

Bugler Adolph Metzger fought in the Fetterman Fight, and there are historical accounts that he was found on the battlefield, covered with a buffalo robe, his body the only one among the soldiers not desecrated. (His crumpled bugle is displayed in the fantastic collection of the Jim Gatchell Memorial Museum in Buffalo, Wyoming.) The attack on the wood crew of November 9 and related events in the aftermath took place along the general lines as I've described them; however, I invented Metzger's role in this fight.

CAPTAIN TENADOR TEN EYCK

Though Captain Ten Eyck was not among the soldiers to cross Lodge Trail Ridge to their deaths on December 21, 1866, his role in the battle became controversial and contributed to a downward spiral of his life into sadness and tragedy. As part of Colonel Carrington's concerted and relentless effort to shift responsibility away from himself, he blamed Ten Eyck for being too slow with his relief force. There is evidence that Ten Eyck's relief force did move slowly, including that Ten Eyck allowed his infantrymen to stop and remove their shoes before crossing Big Piney Creek. However, it appears highly unlikely that Ten Eyck could have arrived in time to save the Fetterman force in any event. The trap had been sprung, and the size of Ten Eyck's relief force (around forty soldiers and an additional forty civilians pressed into emergency service, with no cavalry and no artillery) was pathetically small compared to the gathered forces of Lakota, Cheyenne, and Arapaho. If Ten Eyck had attempted to engage the Native alliance, there is little doubt that he and his men would have been killed as well.

The effect of Carrington's negative testimony about Ten Eyck, however, was to create whispers and ultimately a stigma of cowardice. Ten Eyck's drinking problem grew worse. In the years after the Fetterman Fight, he was twice arrested for drunkenness and court-martialed. The court-martial was later overturned, but Ten Eyck left the military in 1871. Unlike Colonel Carrington, who essentially devoted the remainder of his life to defending his own role in the Fetterman Fight, Ten Eyck withdrew from public life. He lived until 1905, dying in Chicago.

Fortunately for Captain Ten Eyck, his daughter, Frances, was a tireless defender of her father's reputation. She spent years lobbying historians, politicians, and military officers to remove the stain from Captain Ten Eyck's name. Ultimately, she converted Colonel Carrington to the cause. In a commemorative speech at the site of the Fetterman Fight memorial in 1908, the eighty-five-year-old Colonel Carrington included, in a lengthy speech defending once again his own role, the following line: "In justice to a gallant officer now dead . . . I wish to and do refute the aspersion upon the bravery of Captain Ten Eyck who hurried with his meagre command to the rescue of these men who fell here. I wish to say that Captain Ten Eyck did all that mortal man could do and did it nobly and well."

MARGARET CARRINGTON

Margaret Carrington died of "consumption" (likely tuberculosis) in 1870. There is speculation that Colonel Carrington was a latent carrier of the disease, as all of his six children and his second wife also likely died of TB. Before Margaret's death, she wrote a book about her time on the frontier, *Absaraka, Home of the Crows*. She devotes much of the book to defending her husband's role in the Fetterman Fight, and she helped to create the myth of the Fetterman Massacre that predominated for more than a century.

FRANCES GRUMMOND

I invented both of Frances's journals, though journal writing in that era was common. It is also true that no less than General William T. Sherman encouraged Second Battalion officers' wives to keep a written record of the history they were living.

According to historical accounts, Frances did not learn of Lieutenant Grummond's polygamy until she applied for his army death benefit—and discovered that his other wife also had filed a claim. (The army ultimately payed a pension to both of Grummond's wives.) Certainly Grummond's poor record as a human being makes it plausible that Frances had begun to discover his true character far earlier in their relationship.

In February 1867, Frances returned to Tennessee with her husband's body and saw him buried. A few weeks after arriving back in Tennessee, she gave birth to their son, William. When Frances learned of Margaret Carrington's death in 1870, she sent a message of condolence to Colonel Carrington. The two struck up a correspondence and in 1871 were married. Carrington adopted William, and Frances also gave birth to three children with Carrington in the space of four years.

Like Margaret Carrington, Frances embraced defending the colonel's role in the Fetterman Fight. In 1910, she even published her own book, *My Army Life and Fort Phil Kearny Massacre*, strikingly similar to Margaret's in the substance of its description of the battle, including the propagation of the myth concerning Fetterman's role. In her writing, she gives no hint of anger at Grummond—perhaps not wanting to harm the reputation of the father of her son.

Frances died on October 17, 1911, in Hyde Park, Massachusetts, and is buried in Boston.

In addition to Margaret's and Frances's own books, Shannon D. Smith's *Give Me Eighty Men: Women and the Myth of the Fetterman Fight* is an interesting nonfiction treatment of the lives of both Frances Grummond and Margaret Carrington. Smith also provides a detailed account of Frances Ten Eyck's long fight to defend her father's honor.

NELSON STORY

Nelson Story is an epic figure in Montana and Western history. (Story reportedly was one of the inspirations for Larry McMurtry's *Lonesome Dove*.) As I have portrayed in *Ridgeline*, Story and his herd of Texas longhorns did indeed roll up the Powder River Valley in the midst of Red Cloud's War. Story ignored Colonel Carrington's orders and proceeded to drive his herd northward, the first ever to do so from Texas to Montana gold country.

Story's story continued to grow with the Montana territory. (Montana didn't become a state until 1889.) He established a ranch in what is now Paradise Valley, north of Livingston, and he may have been responsible for naming the famous valley. He used the profits from his cattle venture to enter a number of other successful business ventures, and was Montana's first millionaire, a member of the notorious Montana vigilantes, and a founding father of Bozeman. He later would make an additional fortune selling Los Angeles real estate. An informative book about Story's life is *Treasure State Tycoon: Nelson Story and the Making of Montana* by John C. Russell.

JAMES BECKWOURTH

In doing the research for *Ridgeline*, I was amazed to learn that two giants of Western history—James Beckwourth and Jim Bridger—both were hired to scout for the US Army in the fall of 1866. I was even more excited when I learned that Colonel Carrington dispatched them to scout together north of Fort Phil Kearny to learn more about the position of the Lakota and Cheyenne. Imagining the conversations that Beckwourth and Bridger must have had—two epic characters riding through dangerous country at the end of their careers—struck me as the perfect domain for historical fiction.

Sadly, James Beckwourth's long and remarkable life probably ended shortly after he and Bridger parted ways. Befitting his character, there are some wild stories attached to his death, including that he was poisoned. More likely, however, is that he fell ill while with the Crow and died in the care of a tribe he loved. An army officer at Fort C. F. Smith, in Crow land along the Bighorn River in present-day Montana, wrote in his journal on October 30, 1866, that a Crow delegation had come to the fort for the purpose of reporting Beckwourth's recent death. In February 1867, Colorado newspapers were reporting that Beckwourth had died.

For further reading, I recommend Elinor Wilson's *Jim Beckwourth: Black Mountain Man and War Chief of the Crows*. Among other nuggets, Wilson's book includes Beckwourth's account of the death of Hugh Glass at the hand of the Arikara.

JIM BRIDGER

Perhaps ironically, Bridger's last scouting missions for the US Army were in the spring of 1868, when he accompanied a number of freight trains that hauled equipment from the three forts abandoned by the army after losing Red Cloud's War—including Fort Phil Kearny. Eighteen sixty-eight was also the year that Bridger left the Rockies and the high plains for good, returning to Westport, Missouri, near Kansas City.

By 1870, Bridger was in declining health and by 1875 was totally blind. He lived the rest of his life on a small farm with his daughter Virginia and her family. Understanding his restless nature, Virginia gave him a reliable old horse, named Ruff by Bridger, that knew the farm and could wander the property with Bridger in the saddle. A loyal dog, Sultan, also accompanied Bridger on his rides around the farm and, according to Virginia, would return to the farmhouse seeking help if Bridger and Ruff wandered too far.

Bridger died peacefully on July 17, 1881. He was buried on the farm but later reinterred in Independence, Missouri. The greatest monuments to him today are the wild mountain ranges in Wyoming and Montana that bear his name.

Two entertaining but dated biographies of Bridger are *Jim Bridger* by J. Cecil Alter (1923) and *Jim Bridger: Mountain Man* by Stanley Vestal (1946). *Jim Bridger: "The Grand Old Man of the Rockies"* by Grace Raymond Hebard and E. A. Brininstool compiles a number of interesting first-person accounts from people who knew Bridger.

ACKNOWLEDGMENTS

There are many thank-yous to distribute at the end of the long haul of writing a book.

I continue to be thankful for smart family and friends who offered encouragement and advice along the way. Thanks to Max Baucus, Josh Bayliss, Sean Darragh, Ken Doroshow, Liz Olfe Feldman, John Feldman, Cheryl Garrett, Brent Garrett, Mickey Kantor, Jennifer Kaplan, Carol Kinney, Ted Kinney, Samuel Kleiner, David Kurapka, Amy McManamen, Mike McManamen, Norma McManamen, David Marchick, Randy Miller, Sharon Peterson, Marilyn Punke, Butch Punke, Lori Otto Punke, Robin Olsen-Franklin, Shelley Reisig, Kitte Robins, Maria Saab, JoMay Salonen, Monte Silk, Amy Silk, Mark L. Smith, Barb Templeton, Jennifer Thibodeau, Pat Williams, Lynne Willstein, and Gary Willstein.

Thank you to Sharon Daniel at Hair Headquarters in Missoula. She is an excellent barber, but more important, knows a lot about cattle and horses—and patiently answered my questions haircut after haircut.

A big thanks to Mike Clayville, Peter Stark, and the members of the Mountain Man Book Club. Mike and Peter accompanied me on a memorable visit to Fort Phil Kearny and the site of the Fetterman Fight. We swarmed all over it for two days, imagining scenarios and considering mysteries like, *How do you hide two thousand horses—and keep them all quiet?*

Attempting to write about a culture that is not your own is daunting and humbling. I received advice about Native American history and culture from a group including old friends and new acquaintances who were kind enough to share their time and insights. I alone am responsible for the imperfections in this book, but the following people helped me to make it better: Keith Harper, Denise Juneau, Debra Magpie Earling, Deborah His Horse Is Thunder, Ron His Horse Is Thunder, Jodi Archambault, Richard Williams, Shane Doyle, and Donovin Arleigh Sprague, the great-great-great-grandson of High Backbone.

I have been lucky to have guidance from three great editors at different phases of this project. In the beginning, Stephen Morrison helped me to see the full potential of the Fetterman Fight as the topic for a novel. In the long slog through the middle, Jonathan Cox worked through multiple drafts and challenged me to be a better writer with his keen eye for the elements of story. And nearer the end, Caroline Zancan generously adopted this project and added countless refinements. Thanks also to other key members of the team at Henry Holt: Caitlin O'Shaughnessy, Kenn Russell, and Kerry Cullen.

I don't know what to say about Tina Bennett that her legions of admirers have not said over the years. She is a true thought leader and has shaped our culture in dozens of ways through her work, often unseen. She is a trusted advisor and friend and has been for many years. From the bottom of my heart, thank you, Tina.

My friend Keith Redmon at Anonymous Content also has been there over a time span now measurable in decades, something I value more and more as years pass. I'm also appreciative for advice from Dorian Karchmar, Elizabeth Wachtel, and Laura Bonner at Endeavor, Ryan Schwartz at Anonymous, and to Andy Galker.

Thanks to Phil Gardner, Peter Lambros, Larry Simkins, and Mark Porter—kindred spirits on scores of adventures where, along the way, we chew on questions from the ridiculous to the sublime.

Thanks to my brother, Tim, my coconspirator in life.

Thanks to my dog, Rocco, loyal friend and companion—and basis for the character of Jim Bridger's horse.

Thank you to my son, Bo, for helping me to appreciate and to describe the smell of spring rain and the many shades of green on Western landscapes.

Thank you to my daughter, Sophie, who joined me on my first trip to Fort Phil Kearny many years ago in the middle of a long haul from Denver to Missoula. Thanks also for your help with research, including especially on Frances Grummond.

And finally, thanks to my wife, Traci, there through all the adventures, always.